MW01118120

SECRET ILLUSIONS

BY

LAURA JAMES

Lorree,
I hope you enjoy
reading Secret Illusions
so much as I enjoyed writing
it. Michele will keep you informed—
but book 2 is almost finished! If
you like it—Book 2 is even steamier.
Best Wishes
Laura James

PublishAmerica
Baltimore

© 2003 by Laura J. Haupt.

All rights reserved. No part of this book may be reproduced, stored in a retrieval system or transmitted in any form or by any means without the prior written permission of the publishers, except by a reviewer who may quote brief passages in a review to be printed in a newspaper, magazine or journal.

First printing

ISBN: 1-59286-414-7
PUBLISHED BY PUBLISHAMERICA, LLLP
www.publishamerica.com
Baltimore

Printed in the United States of America

I would most like to thank my husband for his unending patience, generous love and continued support. He is *my* hero and truly the nicest person I know.

I would also like to thank my children for providing me a cause to champion and a lifetime of love. They have grown into self-sufficient young adults of which I'm very proud.

In addition I would like to thank:

My sisters, for making me feel as though they look up to me: and allowing me to believe it. I appreciate being able to bounce ideas off them and value their suggestions and opinions.

My mother, whose choices provided unwitting opportunities and gave me the ability to do things differently.

My friends, for letting me vent and providing me with honest answers, their companionship provides comfort.

My co-workers, who listened to my constant chatter and gave encouragement anyway.

My brothers-in-law, for not running fast enough! Their continued support adds balance to our unique family.

This book is a historical romance, taking place in 1776. Scattered throughout the book are real people like Joseph Fry, William the Elder, and William the Younger. They really did live and change history for the people of the UK. I took the liberty of using artistic licensing when I placed Gabrielle as William the Elder's ward. Most of their family drama I simply made up to fit the story and make it more interesting. I tried to follow the time line using correct terminology, dates and names of towns in England so it would appear my characters were real. All names, titles, and places are totally fictitious. Anything resembling real people or places is totally coincidental and should not be construed as intentional.

Chapter 1

Following a path through the woods, she hoped to elude the danger still pursuing her. They had followed her tracks for many days and still her hope that they would give up remained. Yesterday she got lucky and found a few moments' sleep in an old barn, today she had been less fortunate. Unless luck intervened soon, they would probably catch her. With no time for thought, she ran from the only home she had ever known. By staying off the main roads, she had been able to travel a great distance. Eventually a light appeared beyond the trees and she instinctively changed directions to run towards it.

It was a castle! There were lights blazing in every window. Even quite a distance away, she could tell it was not your average castle. Quickening her pace, her only thought was to safely sneak inside. As she got closer the lights were brighter and now she could hear music. Because the castle was the size of a small town, she felt certain she could blend in. Her heart raced from both exhaustion and fear. Stumbling past a small pond, she ran through a large field, then up a hill, stopping close to the edge of the road. She had covered the distance quickly. Standing behind a tree, she waited to slow her labored breathing.

Although it was almost sunset she could still see clearly enough to take notice of the unique character of the castle. The building was constructed of pink sandstone with four rounded towers and conical roofs. This enchanting castle seemed to be right out of a storybook. The two front towers had a gatehouse between them. Under the gatehouse was the arched entrance into the castle courtyard.

In order to gain access, she would have to cross the drawbridge without the guard seeing her. She stood there for what seemed like an eternity, trying to decide what to do. It looked as though this was the only way in. At first glance what had appeared to be a stream was in actuality a moat. Luck was finally on her side, for while she watched the gate, the guard moved away from his post. Fate had turned in her favor as he ducked into the trees to relieve himself. That was all she needed! She inched up to the clearing, and then made a mad dash for the entry. Running past the guard post, through the arched entrance, she suddenly came to a complete halt. Two courtyards loomed in front of her. The cobblestone courtyard on the right appeared empty. The left, far less fancy, was full of people, concentrating on their own chores. Quickly making her decision, she moved to the left, hoping to join the activities of the smaller courtyard. She couldn't help but admire the unique fountain, separating the courtyards. Swiftly moving towards the rear of the building, she followed the well-defined path. Waiting only a moment before entering what she believed was the servants' entrance, she pushed the door open.

As she entered, a sudden rush of warm air hit her and for the first time in days her body stopped shaking as the heat engulfed her. She found herself in the kitchens and began to rack her brain to think of a reason for entering. Without warning a large tray was thrust into her hands. "Hurry and get this tray out to the dining room and do not dawdle. I want you to carry another as soon as you get back," said a lady she assumed was the cook. Trying not to drop a tray that was larger than most people she knew, she tried to keep her balance. Again events were beyond her control as she took the tray being shoved at her and hurried towards the door. "Not that door, you ninny! The door on the end," the cook hollered. "Where do they get these extra helpers?" she muttered to herself as she turned to stir the sauce.

Without explanation it seemed they had accepted her as a servant, so she began to breathe easier. As she progressed from the kitchen, through the long passageway, she heard music. The farther she was from the kitchen the louder the music. She was both afraid and curious to see what lay beyond. Reaching the door at the end of the corridor, she took a deep breath as her trembling hand pushed it open. Finding herself in the largest most beautiful dining room she had ever seen, she couldn't stop herself from gawking. The soft glow of candlelight bounced off the small stain glass windows, causing everything to sparkle. It created an atmosphere of elegance. The buttery was to her immediate left with two serving girls in the process of filling goblets with wine. The elaborate screen they stood behind was made of a deep mahogany with hand-carved designs laced within. The same design flowed around the room upon the paneled dining room walls and the huge table and chairs. Although she wasn't close enough to clearly distinguish the pattern entwined throughout the dark furniture, she could tell the furniture was beautiful and unique. Even the mantel above the fireplace had the same pattern carved within, blending artistically into the very walls surrounding them.

Glancing at the food-laden table, she admired the six huge centerpieces, placed evenly along the length of the dining room table. Functional works of art, these graceful arcs of wrought iron held five tapers. Scattered among the buffet, the lit candlesticks not only provided light but also created a serene atmosphere. As the candles burned they added the blended aroma of berries and spice to the room. The eye-catching floor sconces, of various sizes, were made of forged metal and scattered in the corners, illuminating the darkened areas and entryways.

"Over here!" someone shouted. As she turned her head in the direction of the shout, she saw a large woman wearing an apron, waving her arms, pointing to an available spot on the table. As she glanced beyond the lady she could see into a ballroom. Catching only a glimpse of the twirling women in large skirts and finely dressed men, dancing to the music. Giving her attention back to the lady, she approached her with the tray. It appeared the table already had an abundance of food, but the woman still found additional room without problem. She emptied the tray and afterwards tried to escape back to the safety of the kitchen. Before she knew what was happening, a large hand grabbed on to her arm. "Wait," she said, "I am sure you are in the wrong area, where are you supposed to be?"

She panicked and without warning … everything suddenly went black! Later, opening her eyes, she didn't recognize anything. As she sat up, everything came rushing back to her. A little old lady sitting in the corner said very softly, "You are safe, and the doctor said you are well. You simply fainted. How long has it been since you have eaten? I can tell by your appearance that you must have been traveling for a bit." Not sure of what to say or what explanation to give, she simply stared at the woman. Again the old woman tried to start a conversation. "You had the castle in an uproar, fainting like that. Martha thought it was something you ate, but everything has settled down now. It seems you are a stranger among us, can you tell me who you are, and why you are here?"

Fearing for her own safety and not knowing whom to trust, she just didn't know how much to tell the stranger. With tears falling silently down her cheeks, she answered, "I am here because I had nowhere else to go. My name is Gabrielle. I am sorry for any inconvenience I may have caused, if you will forgive me I will be on my way."

The little old lady replied, "My name is Maude. I too have known great sorrow and great fear. Please trust me when I tell you this is a safe haven, so have no fear. This place will be safe for you as long as you wish to stay. By your demeanor, I assume you have been traveling quite a while. We'll get you some clean clothes, and then you can bathe. If you'd like to freshen up now there is water, over there," she said, pointing to the stand in the corner. "Then you can rest and I will have someone bring you a tray. Now I must inform my mistress of current events. I will be back soon." With a large smile she turned and departed.

After Maude left the room, she had a long walk through the hallways, up the stairs, then on to another wing of the castle. She finally found herself in front of her mistress' door.

She knocked and waited for an answer. "Enter," was finally heard from within and she pushed the double oak door open. Maude walked through the outer chamber into the large suite of rooms, occupied by Helena. The room was decorated in rich detail, all things complimenting the resident's taste. The unique tapestry on the far wall contained a picture of a castle, completely made from spun gold thread. The needlework was precise and well crafted. Ironically Helena's castle resembled the castle depicted in the weave. A friend, having traveled the continent, claimed the origins of the tapestry were unknown. Upon his arrival the Earl had been unprepared for the similarity between fact and fiction. Helena had been completely astonished when the Earl of Hereford had presented it to her. Originally the hanging work of art had been intended as a gift for the queen. Learning this, Helena decided it was quite a feather in her cap. Though she was quite sure it had been all the special attention received during his visit, which had prompted him to act in such a hasty manner. In truth, whatever the reason, she smugly enjoyed receiving the gift of his appreciation.

Finally through the outer sanctum, Maude entered Helena's bedchamber. On a pedestal in the center of the room sat Helena's large bed. Drapes of opaque silk hung from the canopy, used to shroud the occupant, they were currently tied to each post and held open by tasseled cords. The bedcovers, the chaise, and the surrounding chairs were all covered in cream-colored satin with gold embroidery.

Thick fur rugs covered the divan in front of the fireplace, creating an atmosphere so inviting it demanded attention. Several admirers had gifted Helena with a painting by Michelangelo and a few by Rembrandt. Though no amusing story accompanied the art, these too, covered her walls. Helena's favorite painting was a piece of art known as Creation, yet she had only been able to obtain an etching as so far.

The small portrait on her night table provided both comfort and sadness. The gorgeous couple in the center simply radiated love. Both fashionably dressed, each wore magnificent matching rings. Her father's irresistible smile dominated his features. Even dripping in jewels, her mother's twinkling gaze shone through. Standing on the steps, in front of the couple, were two precious children. Helena's attractive brother, though only eight at the time, was the image of her father. The young Helena was already stunning even at the age of seven. The entire family gathered closely together, sharing not only love and happiness but physical attributes as well. All were blond and blue-eyed, the children having both inherited their father's luminous cobalt eyes. Standing in front of their ancestral home, it was their last portrait together.

The room itself was spacious and classically decorated. Large white marble columns ran the entire length of her chamber and surrounded her private bath. An arched doorway in the center of the far wall opened onto a balcony with a fabulous view. Everything in the room had a style of elegance that simply fit Helena. Items were always kept in proper placement, completing the ambiance Helena desired.

The dressing table in the corner was the only exception. It was entirely covered with clutter! Sitting on top were several large, solid, brass boxes. These were covered in hand-painted, mosaic tones. Helena kept jewels in these containers. This did not include the vast array of treasures closeted away, nor the gems spilling out onto the top of the vanity. All available tabletop space had been filled with boxes, jewelry, hairbrushes, ribbons, creams, and lotions. Helena knew where everything was and enjoyed this bit of artistic freedom, though in unsightly disarray. Positioned on each side of the large mirror in the center sat two sparkling crystal globes. The hand-blown, gold-edged, oil-burning lamps were not only sophisticated but also practical. For in the evening while preparing her ensemble, they provided the luminance necessary to observe one's reflection.

It was here, sitting at her vanity, that Maude found Helena.

"Mistress, I have news." She spotted her mistress and had to grin. Helena was tugging a new wig on her head, dramatically changing her appearance. "I'm not sure I like the color," said Maude.

"You are rude! You are always supposed to tell me how beautiful I look!" muttered Helena. "There now, it's in place, is that better?" Although the only answer she received was a smile. "Maude, how am I ever to maintain my authority over all these girls if you are forever taunting me?" asked Helena.

The smile remained as Maude answered, "I am sorry you do not appreciate the humor, mistress, though your authority is never in question. I am always surprised at how different you look with each costume."

"Not only does it add variety, it also creates more of an illusion and after all, isn't that what we are all about?"

Maude merely raised her eyebrows in question.

"Also, Derek's ship has docked and he will be up shortly. You usually know all, why is it you didn't know he had entered the bay?" a curious Helena inquired.

Maude stated, "My answer to your question is also the reason I wanted to see you. Earlier this evening a young girl passed out in the dining room. Martha was trying to find out what part of the castle she should have been working in, as she was unfamiliar. Before she received any reply from the girl, she fainted. She was brought to the north wing and put to rest in the servants' quarters. I was immediately sent for and sat with her until the doctor finished his exam. She is fine, except she probably has not eaten in days. At least, that is what the doctor suspects was the reason for her faint."

"That and fear, I would suppose," guessed Helena.

Continuing, "I waited until she woke up and was rewarded with her name, but not much in the way of a story. You are right, she seems afraid. My guess is she's in some sort of trouble."

Helena listened thoughtfully. "Is she with child?"

Maude replied, "My instincts told me no, but as the doctor was examining her anyway, I asked him to check to be sure. The doctor confirmed that she is not with child, still being a virgin. She is young; my guess would be about fifteen. However, this I will also validate."

Helena interrupted, "What does she look like?"

Maude replied, "She is now one of the most beautiful young ladies I have ever seen, as she matures she will be simply dazzling."

"What?" screeched Helena. "Even more beautiful than me?"

Maude answered, "At the moment, she is a bit scruffy-looking, I suspect she has been on the road many days. However, she will clean up very nicely." With the experience and wisdom of her age, Maude repeated, "How can you wonder at your own beauty? Your skin is flawless, your beauty unsurpassed. Men see you and their jaws drop open. You are simply stunning. Helena, your beauty, grace and intelligence make you perfect in every way." Maude sighed before continuing. "However, Gabrielle – that is her name, by the way – Gabrielle reminds me of a small, frightened doe with the largest, most beautiful chocolate brown eyes I've ever seen. Her hair, black as midnight, is soft and straight and reaches to her hips. The girl has young firm breasts and is delicate in both stature and character. Her face is heart-shaped with high cheekbones, full pouty lips, and honey-colored skin tone. Again I say, she is beautiful, but when she matures she will be ravishing. She is polite, has a beautiful smile and–"

"Enough, enough already!" Helena interrupted. "You have surely sized her up very thoroughly in just a short time."

This time Maude interrupted, "But mistress, that is my job, you would be disappointed if I could not."

Helena replied, "Yes, yes, that is your job and I would be disappointed.

However, do you have to tell me she is so beautiful? You know with my birthday coming up, I am feeling very vulnerable."

Maude began to laugh, "Mistress, you are so funny, you are a creature of great loveliness. Every day you are surrounded by everything beautiful. You have heard from hundreds of attractive women that they wish they had your looks. More important, men always sing of your beauty and tell you how much they desire you. Surely it cannot upset you to hear about a young girl. This is something we talk of every day."

Suddenly Helena began to laugh too, "You are right, Maude, I think today I am a bit melancholy about both my age and my life. Stuart just left me; he had an incident with some men at the front gate. They were looking for a young runaway servant. They told Stuart she had stolen from their master. He has already denied anyone access, raised the drawbridge and sent them packing. However, I'm sure the event is related to your new arrival. You may want to inquire and see if she knows if she is being pursued." Heaving a sigh, she continued, "Do you think she wants to stay? Could she make a perfect addition to the west wing then?"

Maude thought for a while. "Let me find out the situation and if she will want to stay. If she does stay I am not sure where I will place her. Gabrielle seems to have a very sweet disposition. I'm sure she doesn't know anything about our home. I will report to you soon."

Helena smiled. "Derek's ship docked a short time ago, but by the time they unload the cargo it should be quite late. We will have dinner and share each other's company before he seeks other entertainment. Don't bother checking in with me until tomorrow. " She smiled at the elderly woman. Then continued, "When you leave, take a look in the east wing and make sure everything is in order. The west wing seems to run itself but the east wing is forever in chaos. You may see to that now." With a slight wave of her hand, Helena dismissed her and Maude quietly left.

Captain Derek Anderson and Helena had been friends since their youth and had remained very close. He had come to her rescue many times, forming a unique bond, and they trusted each other unconditionally. His obligations at the castle had declined and now he sailed the seven seas and his visits had become more sporadic. So whenever he arrived they closeted themselves away to share personal experiences.

They had been successful in several joint ventures and Helena was well aware of her good fortune when Derek agreed to handle the guards. Until the pact with Captain Anderson, Helena had struggled to find men willing to guard the castle. It seemed men deemed it a lowly position to guard a house full of women, let alone take orders from one.

Helena had had to make this allowance to safely operate her business. He alone had become responsible for choosing and training her guards. As captain of his own ship, Derek routinely transported indentured servants to the American colonies, and later to the Australian continent. Captain Anderson weeded out the dangerous criminals from the men who had simply made errors in judgment. He presented the certain individuals with a wonderful opportunity. Derek shortened their time of indenture if they worked for Helena instead. Helena needed reliable, efficient, close-mouthed men; and Captain Anderson could provide them. Of the chosen few he picked, none refused his offer. Not only would they diminish years of servitude, they would leave as free men with money in their pockets. When worthy men were found Captain brought them to Helena's.

Through it all, Derek continued to be her shoulder to lean on. He supported her decision to become a businesswoman and Helena persevered with little more than a lot of luck. A few years later, Stuart had taken over both the guards and the security of the castle. Though he reported to both Helena and Derek any decisions or problems that arose, he personally carried out both the punishments and rewards. With Stuart in charge, both Helena and Derek were allowed to tend to other duties. With more and more free time Derek traveled far and wide.

Patrick O'Keefe and Conor Carr were Derek's personal friends and shipmates. As Patrick was good with figures, he also kept the records. Conor was first mate and second in command when Derek was not aboard. These two dependable men were very close friends and had saved his hide more times than he could count.

On each of Derek's voyages, he would stop at Helena's. Her castle was located in a secluded bay, past the Bristol Channel near the Taff River. Mother Nature cleverly concealed the bay's entrance. The huge cliffs on the shoreline gave an illusion of being a wall of solid rock. If you entered the break in the wall, it seemed like you were headed directly into the cliffs, yet by veering quickly to the right one gained entrance to the unusual maze. The twisting and turning waterway eventually brought you into the isolated cove. The ship would set anchor, then drop small boats to go ashore. Once reaching land, a stranger would not be wise to the location of Helena's by merely landing on the beach. Only Derek and a few others knew of the secret entrance located behind the rocks jutting out into the water. Rather than go directly to shore, Derek would row around the rocks to reach the opening of a hidden cave. After docking the boat he would climb the lengthy stairway up the inside of the cliff, reaching the inner castle.

Helena's castle was located on the top of the cliff, in the center of a large peninsula. Only two means of entrance were available: a road leading to a drawbridge at the front of the castle and the narrow stairs leading from the hidden cave.

The castle had the usual assortment of men: guards, stable hands, farmers, carpenters, masons, blacksmiths, brewers, laborers and such. Most of the men continued to live at Helena's even after their indenture was up. One of these men was named Stuart Kendal. He did not leave and was now a trusted and valued servant in charge of the guards. Stuart stood nearly seven feet tall and could easily intimidate others. Although he was more of a "gentle giant" the men under him never disputed his authority. Stuart was a handsome, muscular man with sandy brown hair and hazel eyes. He always had a warm expression and a smile on his face. Stuart was very strong and had the reputation of being one of the best wrestlers in Cornwall; for all his size and strength he was very agile. Any that thought him big and stupid were soon surprised. Stuart was totally devoted to Helena and the running of her establishment. He enjoyed making improvements and tinkering with different modernizations. Stuart kept the guards in line and provided a shoulder for Helena to lean on. Stuart had become a trusted friend.

Another man who had stayed on was Jim Humphrey; he too had little reason to leave. With his sandy blonde hair, big green eyes and fair complexion, he was a favorite among the girls. Jim was lean and tall, but very handsome. He was a talented artist, and experienced mason. Working as a mason added the tone to his physique that painting never could. Jim looked up to Stuart as the father he never had. Jim arrived at Helena's brokenhearted after his fiancée terminated their engagement. Helena had befriended him and given him the opportunity to heal his body and his soul within the arms of her loving girls. Jim enjoyed the attention and rather than pick one woman for a lifetime, he decided to stay at Helena's and love them all. Jim used his talents as an artist to paint the miniatures of all the girls for the *Book of Illusions*. He created great murals throughout the castle and painted portraits for fantasies and gifts. Jim was a valuable asset and friend.

Maude walked to the lower levels of the castle, arriving in the east wing. With everyone running to and fro, here was the chaos Helena had described. "Where's Molly?" Maude demanded of the first girl to cross her path.

The young woman replied, "She is downstairs taking care of a problem. She said she would be right back. Oh, there she is," pointing to a doorway.

Maude hurried over to her, "Molly why is the east wing always so disorganized?"

Molly simply smiled and replied, " Everything is ready, it just seems like there are always those last-minute surprises. This time it was Anne and Mary arguing about whose turn it was to wear the same green outfit. A trivial matter really, hardly something to cause such jealous and catty behavior. With a bit of compromise we have worked out an agreement. Are you staying down here tonight?"

Maude thought about the evening in store and she grinned, "No, I can't stay. I have a problem of my own to take care of." Shaking her head, she finished, "I just don't seem to have the time or the energy I used to, for indulging in my own pastimes.

Molly shook her head in agreement. "Don't I know that story!"

Maude said, "Please make sure everything runs smoothly, and if you need any assistance, remember there are extra helpers on the third floor. Or maybe you could get your sister to help keep those girls in line?"

Molly's twin sister's name was Polly. Although they looked identical, their personalities always gave them away. Molly laughed and smiled more, but Polly was quieter and sterner. They both had beautiful, coal black, curly, hair. With bright, turquoise eyes. Usually they wore a different ribbon in their hair, or different hairstyle. Yet, even at there age, they usually wore matching dresses. They were funny that way. Of course, they said they had their reasons and who would argue? They had ample bosom, but as the years passed, they also had ample everything else. Yet if you didn't know there were two, or if you didn't have much conversation with them, it was impossible to tell which was which. They were twins down to the birthmark on their bums. Those twins had played many a trick on many a man. The best being the wagers they would make, for lasting longer than a man in bed. Little did the men know that they were actually taking turns with two girls. The losers, never learning the truth, thought they had been bested by only the one woman. It had earned them enough to provide a nice little nest egg. The two sisters were very valuable to the running of the household. Helena and Maude trusted and valued their opinions. But for now, Molly laughed at the idea of finding Polly. "My sister would have my head if I told her she had to work tonight, after just getting back from her trip. Trust me, it's better for us all if she sleeps now and relieves me in the morning."

Turning to leave, Maude commented, "If you do need anything I will be in the north wing, tending the new girl we found."

"Heard about that one, what's her story?" remarked Molly.

Maude sighed, "I figured you had. Don't really have any answers yet, I'll recount the tale tomorrow." Shuffling towards the door, she said to Molly, "I realize how crazy it gets sometimes. You really do handle it all in stride, doing a fine job of it too. Good luck!"

Molly answered, "Thank you for your faith in me and you're right, you know, sometimes it gets downright nuts! But I wouldn't have it any other way, it keeps me young!!!"

Then they parted, both on separate missions, both connected to the smooth running of the household.

Maude quietly rapped on the door and waited. Finally, as there was no answer, she entered. The young Gabrielle had fallen asleep. Taking a moment to notice that every scrap of food had been eaten and all drink consumed, Maude extinguished the candle on the nightstand. Then grabbed an extra blanket and made herself comfortable on the foot of the bed.

Chapter 2

Morning brought sunlight streaming through the window. Gabrielle was awake and stretching when she spotted Maude. Remembering the older woman's name, she said, "Good morning, Maude."

They exchanged pleasantries for a few moments after which Maude inquired about Gabrielle's condition. Gabrielle said she felt much better. Maude explained, "I stayed close by in case you awoke during the night and were frightened. Yet I need not have worried, you slept quite soundly." Getting up, Maude crossed the room to the door. "I'm going to have a bath and I'll have one sent up for you. By the time you finish, I will be ready too. Then I'll join you for breakfast." Before Gabrielle could reply the door had shut and Maude was gone.

Answering the knock at the door, Gabrielle opened it to find a troupe of young boys carrying a metal tub and buckets of water. She quickly moved out of the way and within a few moments the tub was filled and they were gone. She felt slightly confused, but the tub looked so inviting she decided to figure out more about her whereabouts later. She was unable to slip off her dress and her shift, as it buttoned down the back. Realizing her dilemma, she knew it was impossible to finish alone and that she would need assistance. While pondering what course of action to take, a knock brought a young girl with towels and clothes. "My name is Daisy and I am here to assist you." Gabrielle could not have been happier. Daisy turned and unfastened her dress. She helped to remove her garments. When Daisy released her from the restraint of the corset, Gabrielle could not contain the huge sigh of relief. She quickly finished undressing and climbed into the large brass tub. The warmth seemed to seep right through to her bones, so she simply relaxed. A long while later Daisy washed her hair and helped to towel her dry. She sat in front of the fire as Daisy brushed her hair. It wasn't until after Daisy had helped her dress that Gabrielle felt comfortable enough to ask some questions. "Can you tell me what town we are closest to? Who owns this castle? How long will I be able to stay?"

Daisy raised her hand to silence her. "Shush, shush, shush. You don't even give a body a chance to answer. I don't have any idea where the mistress is going to place you. I don't know the answer to any of your questions, so you'll just have to wait. However, I will tell you that the water closet is the last door on the left, right before the stairs. You may prefer that." With that, Daisy left the room.

Gabrielle tried to wait patiently, yet she soon became restless. She opened the door and took a peek. At first glance, looking down the wide hallway, both the right and left choices seemed exactly the same. The same amount of doors on either side lining the corridor, the same amount of torch holders and the same distance to each end of the hallway. Looking left or right, both appeared to lead to yet another hallway, nothing at all to give any indication of which way to go. The walls were stone, the floor the same. Each door on this floor was a soft white ash, as was the bedroom furniture. The simple decor led her to believe she was probably in the servants living quarters. The furnishings were of good quality, but the lack of abundance and spaciousness seemed to confirm her thoughts. Light streamed through the window and though there should have been some sort of activity, there was none. Not wanting to just sit there, she thought about looking for Maude. After a few moments of indecision, she walked out and turned to the right, praying that way would lead to the kitchens. Somehow she must have made a wrong turn, because it seemed like she had been walking a long time, down hallways that led only to other hallways. Now she could not even find her way back to her own room! Finally at long last, a young serving maid came across her path. Gabrielle asked for her assistance in finding Maude. It was actually very funny, because when the young girl opened the door to where Maude was, Gabrielle realized they were all standing in the very room she had left a short time ago. She burst out laughing! Before long, all three of them were laughing. The young serving girl couldn't even explain what was funny, yet she continued to laugh. Maude knew exactly why she was laughing. As soon as she had entered and found Gabrielle gone, Maude had reasoned Gabrielle had gone exploring. Maude also knew with a certainty that the lost Gabrielle would be returned shortly. Maude had been rewarded with such a baffled expression upon Gabrielle's face that she had also broken out in laughter. After the serving maid left to resume her duties, Gabrielle noticed a table had been set. "Oh, I'm so sorry, Maude, when you didn't come back here I thought I had misunderstood your instructions. So I went to find you, about breakfast."

Maude, with a twinkle in her eye and a grin on her lips, replied, "I didn't want you to get lost. I thought we could eat here, where it's quiet and we can get to know one another. I'll pour the tea, do you like lemon or sugar in yours?"

Gabrielle hurried over to the table to sit down. "Both would be fine." As Maude sat down, Gabrielle bowed her head in prayer.

"Hum," Maude muttered, thinking to herself perhaps Gabrielle might not have an easy time fitting in here.

They ate in silence for a few moments and then Gabrielle said, "I can't thank you enough for letting me stay here. I was so tired and hungry that I wasn't sure how much longer I could go on." Her head slumped forward looking down into her lap, her shoulders sagged, and she was on the verge of tears again.

Maude again explained, "This has been a place of safety for many people. Most have had terrible circumstances to overcome. Some have run away from masters, some escaped evil spouses and some dodged death. Yet those that live here are happy and safe. Everyone that lives here is here because they want to live here. You can stay as long as you want, or leave as soon as you want. The choice is yours. Know that if you desire to stay, you are among friends. Do you have a next of kin, would anyone be sending inquires this way?"

Gabrielle was lost in thought.... How much should she tell? Would the information put others at risk? Could she confide in Maude and still be safe?

Maude repeated, "Do you have any kin or anyone that may inquire in your whereabouts?"

Gabrielle's head jerked up, her eyes wide and terrified. She couldn't seem to get any answers out.

This time Maude tried a different approach. "There are as many stories here as people to go with them. I need to know your story, dear, so I can protect you. Sooner or later, will someone come to inquire of a Miss Gabrielle?"

Gabrielle reflected a moment. The truth was, she had been followed. Who, how many, even why, were answers she just couldn't give. "I can only tell you that as far as I know, it won't be a relative interested in my well-being that will look for me. I will also tell you I have been chased from my home and I do not feel safe. I can't tell you how many, but I was being followed!" This short statement seemed to have exhausted her.

"I understand you're not feeling safe, but again I assure you that here, you will be. Thank you for telling me the pertinent information. When you feel more comfortable with your new home, you can tell me the rest of your story. However, for the first few days, I would like you only to eat and rest. If we receive any inquires about you, we will send them packing." She decided to keep silent about the strangers and their recent visit. Maude figured there was no need to worry the girl unnecessarily so she simply reassured Gabrielle again. "No one will know that you have landed here."

Gabrielle sighed with relief. She would get some rest and then try to figure out her situation. Yet for now she could breathe easy. "Thank you so much for your concern, a few days of rest and I should be good as new. I can't thank you enough for helping me. After relaxing for a few days, I would then appreciate the opportunity to pay you back by helping in your home."

Smiling Maude responded, "You do not have to pay for a simple kindness, however, if you remain here you will have to earn your keep. What is your age, girl? Do you have any special talents?"

Feeling a bit anxious, Gabrielle answered, "Being sixteen and an only child, Father didn't expect me to do much to earn my keep. Though I am a fast learner and I will work hard not to disappoint you. I ride horses, I love animals and I have helped our cook Anna with pies. I helped old Joe tend the garden a bit and I dance fairly well. I do an appropriate job playing the harp, my sewing is adequate and I plan a decent menu. I am very willing to be helpful, just point me in the right direction and I'm sure I can assist you just about anywhere in your home."

After listening to her list of talents, Maude snorted. Maude knew Gabrielle would not be able to help just anywhere, but she was hoping she could find something suitable for Gabrielle to do. Maude could recognize the list of accomplishments from someone of genteel society and thought for a second time that Gabrielle might not fit in here. Walking towards the door, she explained, "I want you to stay here and rest. Before I can find a position for you to fill, I have to keep the rest of the household from falling apart. Everyone here has a job to do, mine is making sure everyone else does theirs. Cecilia is in charge of wardrobe. She will stop by shortly to assess your size and take your measurements, but that is the only time I want you out of bed. Your meals will be brought to you, so just lie back and relax. Do not leave this room at all until I return. I have work to do and if you want to pay me back, you will not make me worry about you." No sooner said, than she was gone again.

Gabrielle could have felt Maude was a little bossy, but instead she felt relieved, content in the fact that Maude would take care of everything and Gabrielle really could unwind. She must have dozed off, for the next thing she knew, a lady with long chestnut-colored hair was shaking her awake. Finally alert Gabrielle yawned, "You must be Cecilia. I am Gabrielle. I'm sorry I fell asleep. Have you been here long?" Cecilia simply smiled and shook her head no. Then she motioned for Gabrielle to get off the bed and stand up. Following her instructions, Cecilia took her measurements. She wrote everything down in a small book, when she finished she picked up her measuring tape and put both items in her basket. She smiled, waved good-bye and walked out the door. It wasn't until after Cecilia had left that Gabrielle realized that Cecilia had not uttered a word. Gabrielle knew she must have a bewildered look on her face because that was exactly how she felt. She began pacing back and forth and thinking out loud. "With such a large staff the owner of this castle must be very wealthy indeed." She thought again of the list of talents she had given Maude. *My talents must seem very lacking indeed. I wonder what I could possibly do for them that would convince them that I could be an asset so they would let me stay.*

While she was trying to come up with some answers, Maude was on another floor doing the same. Pacing back and forth, Maude was not really sure what answer to give Cecilia. Uncertain of Gabrielle's fate, the type of clothing to provide her was a bit perplexing. Cecilia stood by patiently, waiting for Maude to make her decision. Speaking out loud, Maude began, "If we put her in a simple servant's tunic, she may believe this is now her chosen position. Putting her in something provocative might make her believe we want more of her than she would have chosen on her own. She really must decide her future without influence. If handed a dress and apron, she may be content to clean and scrub all day. Though she may be helpful in the kitchens."

Snapping her fingers, as an idea came to her, she cried out. "All right, Cecilia, this is what we are going to do. Replace her undergarments. No thick, coarse, scratchy leggings. No tight bindings, no ribbons and no heavy fabrics. Every piece of material next to her skin will be thin, light, soft silk. These garments will constantly remind her of her femininity. From her hose to her camisole, her drawers will provide sensations of delight. Teaching her to become accustomed to the finer things without even realizing it. Thank heavens, some of the newer styles offer the simplicity we are trying to achieve. Those darn dresses with the wide skirts are too formal and confining. Her manner of dress will be the image of a modest, young girl. So even though the rounded neckline is fashionable, do not make it too low. I don't want more than a slight glimpse offered for view. Understand that I want the material for her outer clothing to be serviceable and practical. Do not use any whites or creams, though her coloring would be marvelous with them, they dirty to easily. There is no reason to add lace or ribbon, soon enough she will make her decision. A few outfits will be enough for present."

The modiste nodded in confirmation as Maude continued. "Underneath, she will wear the lingerie of a stylish, captivating woman. She seems bashful; I would have her be more confident. Later we will work on her sensitivity and confidence. First we dress them, and then we shape them. Eh? Cecilia?" Maude cackled.

With Cecilia taking notes, Maude pressed on. "Eventually she will have to have boots added to her meager possessions, but until then just replace her shoes. Until I decide where she will work, a pair of plain serviceable slippers should do. Also make sure when you see Juliana, inform her that Gabrielle does not need an abundance of cosmetics. She will spend most of her time recuperating and relaxing. If she feels the need to pamper Gabrielle, tell her to give her a simple egg white and honey mask. You know how Juliana has a tendency to go a bit heavy with the powder and rouge." With a heavy sigh Maude muttered, "In the end, Gabrielle may even choose the kitchens. Yet I think this girl is special. I would give her the opportunity to explore being a woman for a time before she makes any decisions." As Cecilia turned to leave, Maude continued. "And no corsets! I want her to feel free and comfortable." Cecilia shook her head in agreement, and then scurried down the hall.

Helena sent for Maude shortly before the dinner hour. After handling an argument between the cook and a peddler, she met Helena in her apartments. "Maude, what was the problem with the cook?"

Maude smiled, no secrets here. "Cook was trying to tear off the ear of Tom the peddler. She had planned the menu for squab, with a special wine and mushroom sauce. He guaranteed that he would provide the mushrooms. Unfortunately the mushrooms he had promised were not delivered. I think he's sweet on her and thought to appease her temper the last time, by promising her something only he could provide. Seems he knows of a place where they grow in abundance. Yet his promise to ease her temper last time, then letting her down again this time, seems to have him in more hot water than it was worth. Seems he simply forgot to go pick the mushrooms. Right when he got here she confronted him for being late, as she needed the mushrooms. He tried to beg her forgiveness. It didn't seem to be working. So, lovers' quarrel or not, tonight we will have no mushrooms for the sauce. Cook feels the slight personally and is tired of his screw-ups. I felt she was right and let her have a go at him, and last I saw he was running down the road with her not far behind."

"I too had my share of arguments today. Emma and Isabelle were at war over the Gilbert brothers again." Pouring herself a glass of wine, she sighed and said, "That story is really too long and tiring to go into now."

A tired Maude agreed with the nod of her head as Helena continued.

"What did you do about our new guest?" asked Helena, changing the subject.

"I suggested she spend the next couple of days in bed, as she is simply exhausted. After that she can help clean the bedchambers or help in the kitchens. I'm keeping an eye on her to gauge both her aptitude and ability toward housekeeping. She said she likes animals; maybe she'll end up helping in the stable. If she proves to be talented at sewing she can work in the sewing room. She has been properly educated, so maybe she can teach. I am hoping after food, rest, and safety have been furnished, she will be more willing to share her life's story. Anyway, right now she will be resting and I have no intention of making a decision about her for a few days."

"That sounds fine with me. Let's just relax and enjoy our dinner. We'll try to forget about our house of mayhem for a while. Oh, but before I forget. When you go down, you should check the baths and see how Kathleen is doing. She has had her heart broken and has been crying for two straight days."

"I guess it's a good thing she is working in the baths. What's a little extra water?" giggled Maude.

"I would never have guessed she was so serious about that man. After he had proven he was a free man and provided the coin to pay his debt, I should have sent him packing. Instead I tried to ease his suffering by providing him with a week of wicked splendor."

"It was a right nice thing you did for the fellow." Stated Maude.

"Ha! I plead stupidity. Kathleen's feelings would never have been hurt if I hadn't thrown them together." Insisted Helena.

"You can never know what would have happened. He could have chosen to stay without your invitation at all. It could have been Millicent that had been first available. He still may have found Kathleen on his own, as it was he stayed longer than the free time you provided."

"Kathleen insists it was because they fell in love." Here Helena frowned. "I thought she knew better than to believe a customer's lines."

"I know you have never experienced Cupid's arrows, but believe me when I say, seldom is there a choice. She is a right smart girl. She does know better than to believe any bloke. Happens to all of us at one time or another. She'll get over him. Just give her time."

"I've already talked to her, you may want give it a try. Meanwhile, I will check on the children. If I find the classroom too crowded we will simply have to get Mrs. Curry some help. Who knows, maybe that's where your young friend will end up?" As the young serving girl entered with the last of the dishes and finished setting the table, Helena continued. "Now let's forget work for a bit, and mushrooms or no mushrooms, I intend to savor our food."

Meanwhile Gabrielle slept. She ate a quiet supper left on a tray next to her bed, then slept again. It had to have been almost sunrise when she woke to hear someone sobbing. She hustled out of bed, throwing on her wrap as she went. The crying continued, it sounded as though someone were in great pain. She opened her door very slowly, her eyes trying to focus on the surroundings. Everything was very dim with only one torch left burning. The wailing continued, she could not stand there and do nothing. She hurried out the door, following the noise. She had gone down the staircase to the left of her room and past several doors, after turning down countless dimly lit corridors, she finally stopped in front of a doorway. If the sobbing had diminished she may have turned back, but someone still seemed in great turmoil. She slowly turned the handle; after all she had no idea what lay beyond. And it wasn't as if she were brave. Yet she simply had to help whom ever was crying so loudly.

Slowly she entered, walking carefully through a short hallway. The first thing she noticed was the heavy smell of marjoram. She poked her head around the corner, yet she could hardly believe her own eyes. The most beautiful white marble room lay within. There were huge supporting pillars and long, polished benches. Each circling the big sculptured pool, with a fast-flowing fountain in the center. In the water, near the edge of the large pool, sat a beautiful young woman. She was crying as if her heart were breaking. Feeling unsure of what to do, Gabrielle hesitated. The young woman in the water was all alone. No one seemed to be nearby inflicting any pain. From what she could see, she didn't seem to be hurt. Could she really be making all that racket if she were not in pain? She was undecided about her next course of action. The gentle glow from the hanging oil lamps caused a luminescent effect upon the water. Finally Gabrielle couldn't stand the racket any longer. So she marched straight over to the edge of the water and inquired, "Is there anything I can do for you, miss?" At the sound of another person's voice, heard in between sobs, the young woman's head instantly jerked up and she stopped crying.

"Oh, you frightened me!" said the young woman. "What do you want? Leave me alone! Can't you see I want to be left alone?" she exclaimed in one quick sentence.

"Please do not become alarmed, I was frightened for you. I thought someone's safety was a stake. I am sorry I bothered you." Gabrielle turned to leave.

"No, no, don't go, I'm sorry I was so rude. Did you really hear me crying all the way down the hall?" inquired the girl.

"Through the doorway, down some halls and up two floors. I thought someone was being beaten or worse," replied Gabrielle.

"Oh, bother! I hope no one complains, last time I kept someone from their sleep I had to empty slop jars for a week!" She took a deep breath and tried to dry her eyes, "I'm such a baby, and I just can't keep my unhappiness under wraps. I'm sorry I woke you. I'll try to be quieter. Who are you anyway?"

"My name is Gabrielle. I have just arrived."

"I thought you were new, I know most everyone. My name is Kathleen. I know I should be glad and feel better off. But that lying Scottish savage, Kevin MacDonald, broke my heart. He promised to make me his wife and take me to Scotland with him."

Kathleen just looked at Gabrielle, waiting for her to make the agreement that all men were scum and certainly Kevin MacDonald. Yet after a few moments, silence was still the only thing Kathleen heard. Kathleen just stared at Gabrielle.

"I hope you're not looking to me for any advise, as I have none to give," stated Gabrielle.

"Surely you can agree with me, that is not so much to expect."

"I am not trying to be rude, but I must point out that I don't know you, I don't know Kevin and I don't know anything about the situation in which you find yourself. You can't possibly think I would just agree!"

Kathleen unexpectedly began to smile, and then she began to laugh. Great belly laughs came rolling out of her mouth where only moments before were sobs. After what seemed an eternity, her laughter began to subside. Finally she stopped completely and said, "I like you and I think we are going to be great friends."

"First you wake me in the middle of the night. You cry and scream like a banshee, scaring the wits out of me. Then you can't believe I won't agree with everything you say. You laugh at me and after all this you think we will be good friends? I have never heard anything so lunatic," Gabrielle snorted.

"Not just good friends, great friends. I really like you. Not very many people are honest enough to tell me they don't agree with me. And as you can see," turning her head from right to left "you're the only one who has come to check on me. My heart was broken and I needed to release the pain. I've been a big pain in the neck and I suppose I owe everyone an apology. That can wait until tomorrow though. For now, I simply want to say I'm sorry. Will you take the time to be my friend?"

Gabrielle was dumbfounded. She originally started out to save someone else and yet here was someone helping her. Not only wanting to be her friend but honestly liking her. She could not help but smile, and her smile was radiant. "I would like that."

"Good!" As Kathleen answered she stood up and reached for a towel. "I can be dressed in just a few moments, then we can go down for breakfast." Watching Kathleen stand naked in the water made Gabrielle feel just a little self-conscious. Unable to stop looking, she realized that Kathleen was stunning! She seemed about a head taller than Gabrielle, with long, thick, auburn red hair. She had just a few freckles sprinkled across the bridge of her nose and her skin looked soft and creamy. Besides having a huge bosom she also had big green eyes! They were so green they reminded her of the green moss growing on the side of the stable at home. Although she didn't think Kathleen was much older than herself, Kathleen's body seemed much more developed. Gabrielle had seen few female bodies up until this time. So she hardly had a basis of comparison. Yet instead of thinking others too small, she decided Kathleen's bosom must be unusually large.

Kathleen's nipples were puckered from the chill in the air, after the warmth of the water. Her long, beautiful hair reached her very tiny waist. Looking down, she caught a glimpse of hair between her legs. That patch of hair was the same auburn color as the hair on her head. A glistening droplet of water slid down her throat, down her chest, directly to the firmly erected nipple, and fell into the water at her thighs.

Suddenly Gabrielle turned around so it wouldn't seem as though she were staring. Even though she had been. Gabrielle took the opportunity to look around. Large ferns and plants were everywhere, giving the area a very tropical effect. There were different alcoves all around the room with large worktables in each area. Thin green mats covered the surfaces and sheer curtains covered the arched doorways of all the alcoves. Scattered around the room were several statues of naked men and women. Burning oil lamps and candles held in sconces on the wall created the perfect effect. Gabrielle continued to inhale the light fragrance of musk. The steam, the aromas and the tropical atmosphere resulted in producing a warm, comfortable feeling.

She inhaled deeply, "I have never seen a bathing area so grand. This pool of water is larger than the pond we have at home. What is that area for?" Gabrielle pointed.

If possible, Kathleen's emerald green eyes grew even larger, as she asked, "Have you not been given the tour yet?"

Gabrielle looked at her feet, realizing at this moment that they were bare, and answered. "No, no tour. I haven't even been allowed out of my room. I'm to rest for another two days. Then Maude will decide where to place me."

Kathleen started pacing back and forth. "Oh no, oh no, I'll be emptying slop jars for months! Hurry up and get out of here! You must go back to your room. Oh no! My crying is really going to get me in trouble this time! Hurry up, get out of here!" She was truly in a panic.

"What's the matter?

"Just get moving, we don't have much time. You should not be here!" screeched Kathleen. "Later, after you have gotten to your room, I'll find you and explain. But you have to get out of here and fast!"

"Okay, okay," Gabrielle muttered, "I'm just not exactly sure where my room is."

"Well, we are going to have to find it and fast because at first light this room will be packed and my name will be slop!" She threw on a frilly, lacy lemon-colored wrap and grabbed Gabrielle by the arm. Turning her around and telling her to follow, she immediately ran out the door. Gabrielle had no choice but to follow or be lost. They ran down the corridor and to the landing, Kathleen trying to decide which way to go. Gabrielle pointed to the staircase. They ran up the stairs and through a passageway, and then Kathleen turned around to signal "quiet" by placing her finger in front of her mouth. She reached her arm in front of Gabrielle to hold her from continuing, and after making sure no one was in the hallway, Kathleen whispered, "Any idea which room is yours?"

"I think I left my door open. Will that help?"

They darted out of the dark corner and down the hall. The only door open was third from the end; they quickly headed in that direction. Kathleen ran inside, Gabrielle followed. The door was quickly shut. Knowing all the rooms in this wing were all very similar she asked, "Is this the right room?" Gabrielle looked about and spotted her shoes on the floor near the bed and nodded. "All right, now listen up. You never got out of bed all night. You may or may not have heard someone crying, that doesn't matter. You, however, were so tired you stayed in bed and drifted back to sleep. I will explain everything when I can, but please act like you have never met me before if we are not alone. I truly want to be your friend but our chat will have to wait. I have to get back to the baths. I'll be back when I can, now get in bed and stay there!" With that she pushed Gabrielle out of the way and flew down the hall.

Gabrielle really didn't know what to make of the whole thing. She tried to figure out what went wrong while she undressed. After climbing into bed she did not have to pretend to be asleep, because a few moments later, she really was.

Chapter 3

The sun was high in the sky the next time she awoke. She stretched and looked about the room. There were garments hung over the side of the chair in the corner. Someone had replaced her old tray with a new tray and also brought clothes. *I wonder how many people have been in my room,* Gabrielle thought to herself. *I slept like the dead, for I never heard a sound!* She reached over and grabbed the bowl of porridge, finding it cold she replaced the bowl on the tray. Settling for the fruit, it quickly disappeared. She was about to throw the covers back when Daisy appeared. "I thought you were going to sleep the day away! I'm glad to see you up, how about a bath?"

"That sounds wonderful!" sighed Gabrielle. She thought to herself, maybe she would run into Kathleen in the baths and then get some answers. At the same time Daisy opened the door for two young men carrying a large brass tub. Well, any idea of going to the baths was certainly curtailed by the fact that the tub was in her room. She couldn't ask Daisy any questions about the baths, because she wasn't supposed to know about them. After the boys had filled the tub, Daisy helped her disrobe and into the tub. For some reason baths had never felt this relaxing before. Of course, life had never been this hectic before. Daisy hummed as she washed Gabrielle's hair, this helped relieve the tension and kept conversation to a minimum. Daisy had learned long ago ways to divert conversation. And a conversation was exactly what she didn't want. She knew Gabrielle had a million questions. She also knew she was not the one to answer them. So Daisy washed Gabrielle, dressed her, and fixed her hair all the while humming a little ditty. The shift Daisy handed her was not her own, it was lighter and softer. Standing there as Daisy buttoned up the back, Gabrielle wished the dress could have been a lighter hue, rather than dark blue. She favored creams and yellows; she believed they made her look prettier. However, as Daisy had not put a corset on her, Gabrielle decided not to voice any complaints. She was just too comfortable! The tub had already been emptied and carted out by the time Maude got there.

"Good morning, Gabrielle, I trust you slept well. Are you ready for breakfast?"

Gabrielle looked at Maude and replied, " I slept like one of the dead. I feel very rested this morning. I must say that Daisy is wonderful! My hair has never looked so stylish! I am starving."

"I have taken the liberty of ordering breakfast. After breakfast we can see to the rest of your wardrobe. By tomorrow you should be up to a short walk in the gardens. I thought perhaps you would like a little fresh air, so I asked Lizzie to set our breakfast out on the terrace. Follow me," Maude commanded.

Gabrielle followed her down the hallway to the left, past rows and rows of doors, to the end of another corridor. On the left side of the hall were a set of double doors, both held wide open. The bright light from the sun's rays poured through the doorway. As they walked through the doors, the smell of the great outdoors overpowered her. The fresh air was irresistible, so she took a deep breath. The sky was clear, the trees and flowers were in bloom, and it was impossible not to react to her surroundings. Everything she looked at made her smile bigger and brighter! A short-bricked wall on the third floor of the castle enclosed them. On the right side was a door leading to the tower, which connected to the upper wall. The rest of the area had assorted benches, tables and chairs. Potted plants and flowers growing all over added to the beauty. The ivy growing on the castle walls truly added the final touch. They walked to the table farthest from them, located closest to the wall. It was set with a pretty yellow woven tablecloth and yellow and white napkins. Everything here was crystal or china. Gabrielle could not help but notice the difference of the tableware from previous meals. She knew expensive decorating when she saw it. She was uncertain where this breakfast was going to lead. As she gracefully slid into her chair she could not help but to stare at the water below, the sun, now high up, in the bluest, clearest sky. The effect was wonderful. She felt more relaxed and at peace than she had had since fleeing from her home. It seemed like only a moment that she sat there enjoying the panoramic view, soaking in the atmosphere. By the time she quit her daydreaming Maude was almost finished with her meal.

"So you're back, I was wondering how long it would take. It is a most pleasant view, isn't it? As I am almost finished, and you've yet to begin, How about I talk and you eat?"

Gabrielle merely nodded her head yes. She poured the pot closest to her into her cup. "Oh! Chocolate! I love chocolate. I haven't had a cup of chocolate in ever so long!" She sipped slowly, savoring the warm, sweet flavor. Then she began to investigate by lifting all the covered dishes. She passed on the fish and capers, but took some of the eggs and sauce. She also selected a tart and a small piece of ham.

As she started to eat Maude began, "First let me tell you how radiant you look this morning. You look healthy and well rested, the circles under your eyes seem only a memory."

"Thank you, Maude, I did sleep very well. I feel like my old self," replied Gabrielle.

"This area we are sitting in was the guards' storage and repair station in wartime. When we first opened those doors, the ground was littered with muskets, swords and barrels of gunpowder. Yet the moment my mistress first opened the door and saw the sights from here, she knew she would transform this area to a beautiful terrace. Now, after a lot of hard work and proper maintenance, we come to relax, enjoy the view and bask in the sunshine. Our home is a most secure fortress, so we need never worry.

"Although this castle has had improvements added from previous owners, we are quite proud of our own renovations. Combined works inside made by Helena's ancestors and by Helena herself have given the castle the fanciful feeling of today. Even the exterior of the castle has had reconstruction, for Helen enjoys innovations. Trying to create a less dreary look, an earlier architect dreamed up a more mystical design. If you look up you can see some of the fascinating features the masons created," Maude said, pointing to several different areas.

"Except for the bedrooms and servants' quarters, most rooms have huge vaulted ceilings. You will only appreciate their splendor if you don't have to clean them." Gabrielle laughed, as Maude continued, "We have everything we need inside the castle walls. Though Helena owns several thousand acres, beyond the castle, some of that land is let out to tenants.

"You would hardly have believed it possible if you had seen this mess in the beginning. She inherited the castle shortly after a siege had destroyed nearly half and the rest was in sorry shape. Now it is beautiful and unique." Maude hesitated and just as she was about to continue, Helena walked through the doorway.

"Good morning, Maude. And who is the young friend you have with you?" questioned Helena as she crossed the terrace and sat down at the table. She even had a cup of tea poured before Maude responded.

"Good morning, mistress. This is my friend Gabrielle. She would like to stay with us for a while. I'm so glad you had the opportunity to stop by for a chat."

"That may be all I have time for, I am currently organizing a concert and a dinner party. I will have to be downstairs when the set designer is ready."

Gabrielle could not help herself; she swallowed her food, took a deep breath and said, "How wonderful to meet you. Should I refer to you as mistress also?"

"Yes, that would be fine. How do you like it here?"

Gabrielle smiled. "I love it here! The people are kind, the castle is safe and I am afraid I have never eaten better!" Laughing, she also added, "I am a miracle worker with dinner parties, my aunt often had me helping her. I would like to volunteer, if you don't think I would get in the way."

Fortunately Gabrielle missed the look exchanged by Maude and Helena. "Thank you for offering. It will not be necessary today, as everyone already has his or her assignments. I will remember you for future engagements though." Helena smiled warmly at Gabrielle. "Maude insists you need to rest a bit longer. Why don't you take one more day? Tomorrow you and Maude can discuss what position in the household you would like to be assigned too. Have you any favorite chores?"

Gabrielle stated, "I must be honest, my maid did most things for me at home. I'm not really sure how much help I will be in any area. I only know I would like to try."

"Surely a genteel young lady such as yourself has had lessons. I can't imagine any family not seeing to your future. You seem a very accomplished young woman," Helena commented.

"Yes, I have had lessons of all kinds, but that hardly included the more practical experiences. I can't cook or clean, but I can follow directions. I can't even make the covers on my bed fit right! I am hoping I can learn and be an asset to you."

"Darling, I'm sure you sew very well. You probably know several languages. Most mothers make sure their daughters can dance, entertain and dress correctly. Those are things that are very valuable here. You will not have to learn to clean unless that is what you choose to do. Here you have the freedom to be anything you want." She turned to Maude. "Gabrielle may need a bit more time than first anticipated. She is very young and naïve. I think she should spend time with the students. If this is agreeable to you, I will tell Mrs. Curry that she has some help on the way. In no way does this have to be permanent, as I would like to see her make a different choice. She is too beautiful to be kept with an old woman and young children. Yet she needs time to blossom and a place to be sheltered. What is your opinion?"

Maude smiled. "An excellent idea! I was thinking the sewing room or garden area, but that is by far the best idea." Maude turned to Gabrielle and said, "You really should have another day for just yourself. I want you to rest and pamper yourself. And in a fortnight you can learn to help in the schoolroom. Would that be acceptable to you?"

Listening to them talk about her as though she was not even present, she concluded that they didn't even realize what they were doing, so she did not take offense. "I like children and I'm very good with my studies. I didn't realize there were children here, but I would be happy to be placed where I can be of help."

Helena stood and took a deep breath, "I never get tired of this view and I look across the way and say to myself, 'How lucky I am!' Sometimes I sit for hours just gazing out at the water. This is a place of solace. You are welcome to come here anytime."

As she turned to leave she hesitated near Gabrielle. "I just want you to know that you are not the only one who has had trouble. Almost everyone here came seeking safety at one time or another. There are as many occupations here as in a large city. The difference is that the many people that live here are happy and safe. So no one wants to leave. Remember everyone chooses his or her position, just as you will. It is not for you to judge anyone or even the choices they have made. The same as no one will question your choice. Everyone has a story, we all have jobs to do and we do them. After Maude explains more about our lifestyle, you will have many questions. Ask them. I hope you stay. I hope you will be happy, I know you will always be safe here. However, if for any reason you do not think you will be happy, or be able to adapt to our rules, you need only to ask to leave and I will have someone escort you to the next town." She reached down and gave Gabrielle a swift hug. Then she glided down to the end of the table and gave Maude a very long hug. Helena whispered, "Goodness, she's gorgeous! I sure hope she stays. Good luck!" Like a soft, gentle breeze, she floated out of their presence.

"Wow," sighed Gabrielle. "She is fabulous! Smart, witty, and compassionate. She is the most beautiful woman I have ever seen. Her hair is the color of sunshine! Surely she is too young to be in charge of this whole castle? Why isn't she married to some handsome duke? Or prince? I can't believe she would think I would ever leave here!"

Maude softly whispered, " She has also had her share of distress. Helena would never burden anyone with the unhappiness of her youth. Yet like you, everyone must make peace with their past and look to the future."

"What do you mean, like me?"

Maude gently explained, "It is time for you to be truthful about all things. I need to know your past so I can prepare. You need to talk about your past so you can heal. Let's move over to the seating area." Maude marched across the terrace and sat on the chaise, waiting. Maude decided to give Gabrielle the opportunity to gather her thoughts, so she began reciting information about their home. "Our home is a fairy-tale construction of wood and stone.

An eccentric architect using red sandstone created it. The stone's coloring seems so appropriate now that a woman owns it. It seems so feminine. We have an operational drawbridge and guards at all times. Besides the moat dividing the front gate from intruders, the castle is also surrounded on the other three sides by an inlet connecting to the river. However, this is for our safety, not for our restriction. It is a very commanding view, nestled in the cliffs as we are. Being so close to the Bristol Channel, we are fortunate the walls are over ten inches thick, allowing very little draft in. As we are a household of many women it is fortunate our home is well hidden. The thick forests conceal us, until you come to our road. Even then you must gain access to our drawbridge to get inside. If the drawbridge were up, the moat keeps the unwanted element at bay. However, being isolated on a peninsula, high above the coastline, helps to keep our location secret. We have a double courtyard, not a very common feature for most castles. Guests immediately go to the right of the fountain and they never see the activities of the other courtyard. It would not be good for business if the gentry had to wait until a wagon with supplies was unloaded before entering."

Maude's rambling on and on about Helena's had not loosened Gabrielle's tongue, so Maude changed her tactics and said, "I'll just sit here quietly then, till you're ready." And she did.

Gabrielle thought about what she had said. She just couldn't find the words to begin. Looking over at Maude, her eyes flooded with tears. Without even realizing how she got there, the next thing she knew was she was in Maude's arms and crying a great river of tears. After a while, when the crying subsided, she thought perhaps she had even put Kathleen to shame. This brought about a small smile.

"There, I knew you would finally run out. I hope you feel better now."

Gabrielle stated, "Not really."

"Do you hesitate because you do not yet feel safe?" questioned Maude.

"No, I feel very safe, and I have you to thank for that. No," she repeated, "it's that I'm not sure where to begin."

Maude just waited. And waited. And waited.

Finally, after what seemed ages, Gabrielle pulled herself away from the breath-taking view and began, "My name is Gabrielle Cartwright. My father is Lord Richard Cartwright. Maybe you have heard of him?"

Maude shook her head no as Gabrielle continued.

"Several months ago, after receiving a message, he left to take a voyage. As Father and I are very close, he explained that although he was changing his plans, it was a journey that was necessary.

"A few weeks ago I was asleep in my *own* room, in my *own* bed, in my *own* home. I was feeling a bit restless. While my father was out of town, my aunt had begun pushing a union with Viscount Herrington. Numerous times she implied that even my father agreed it was a good match.

"My home is in Northumberland. We own a manor and lands, near Teesdale. Our property borders the castle and lands he owns, in nearby Durham. With our money and his lands, it was to be the wedding of the century! At least that is what my aunt kept saying."

Tears trickled down Gabrielle's cheeks as her gaze met Maude's. "Oh, I wish you could see him. He is old, fat and balding. He has chubby hands and thick ankles. He wears many rings and bright-colored outfits. He struts when he walks and believes everyone beneath him. He inhales snuff so frequently he seems to be sneezing all the time. Needless to say between his personality and his nasal voice, it's a toss-up as to which irritates me more.

"My aunt has lived with us since my mother died, when I was eight. Up until this time I would have trusted her with my life. Now it's my life she wants. Anyway, I was wound up and having trouble sleeping. I had finally drifted off when there was a loud pounding at my door. I hurried to answer and there at the door stood Viscount Herrington. As I had only a thin gown on and knew it improper, I tried to slam the door shut. With very little difficulty he threw the door open. He was leering at me. He grabbed my arm and forced me down the stairs. I asked to grab my wrapper, but he said he would see it all soon enough. I still was unsure what was happening, but I could tell this was not good. He dragged me down to the library where my aunt was seated at my father's desk. Things seemed to have been scattered about and the desk was a mess. I asked what they were doing among my father's personal papers and my aunt seemed annoyed. But then she turned to me and her face seemed to change from anger to sadness right before my very eyes. She said, 'Your father's ship has sunk, my pet, and there are no survivors. I am in charge now.' I believe I fainted, because when I came to, I was seated in the large leather chair by the fireplace. My aunt had gotten a cloth for my head and a small glass of sherry. She explained that she knew it was a shock for me, as it was a shock for her also. Now that she was in charge I was to marry the viscount as soon as possible, then he would take care of us all. I tried to explain that my father couldn't be dead. After all he had been a naval officer, he would certainly be able to save himself.

"I couldn't tell them at the time that he often changed his schedule and destination. He informed me of this one time, when I had panicked at his late arrival. He explained that he continuously missed a connection or two, attributing it to weather or the dependability of conveyance. He always made me promise that I would not give up hope for a full year, that in that time he would appear. He also confided in me the location of important documents if that year came up and he did not arrive. So you see? I could not accept what they said. Neither could I explain why.

"I kept insisting that they were wrong. I argued and persuaded; yet they wouldn't believe me. Finally I started to explain that I had a legal guardian that would step in and handle everything. I thought they would be delighted not to be burdened. Instead it made them more upset. In the end they just wouldn't listen to anything I had to say. My Aunt Penelope kept looking at Viscount Herrington, smiling. She kept shushing me. Finally she instructed me to go to bed. That everything would be better tomorrow. Explaining that the following day the viscount would get a special license to marry me. That as my father was not there to take care of us, my new husband would. I screamed, I cried, I hollered and I begged. Nothing did any good. I became insolent. I stated if he wanted to marry someone he could just marry her. It wasn't until he said, 'As you are just a child I'd be happy to marry your aunt, but she's not the gel with the money.' That's when I broke out in a true sweat. This never had anything to do with me; he just wanted my father's fortune. At that time I could not tell if my aunt was really worried about our future, or if she had been completely fooled by him. As I stood in front of the fireplace with the roaring fire, still wearing only the thin cotton gown, I looked at the viscount as if he were crazy. He stood licking his lips, his large eyes staring at me. I could do nothing but shudder.

"So finally I pretended to agree to their demands, when just as quickly my aunt hurried me from the room. She mentioned to me that if I did not want his attentions even a little, why had I stood where he could see through my gown, enticing him in a suggestive manner? I could not believe what I was hearing. I was wary of her company until we reached my room. Where she seemingly became the aunt of old, tucking me in and kissing me good night. She gave me a hug and told me everything would be all right. I took the opportunity and said he was old and ugly and I didn't see why I had to marry him. At that time she went on to explain that I wouldn't have to bed him, that he had other women for that. And that he probably wouldn't want an heir right away anyway. She said all girls have to marry eventually and most marriages were arranged. I would grow to love him and we could all continue to live there and be happy. I still couldn't figure out if she was fooled by him or if this crazy idea was hers. After she left I began pacing, I just couldn't believe my father was dead. I especially couldn't believe she thought our only answer was my marrying that old sod! I quietly opened my bedroom door to go to my father's room. I needed the information about my guardian. I was very young when I last saw him. I remember my father saying he spends a great deal of time in London. His name is Uncle William, but as far as rank or title, I just don't know. I need the information in my father's papers. Anyway, Father had always said in an emergency to get a hold of my guardian. I knew where the papers were secretly stored and I was on my way to father's room, when I heard noises coming from downstairs. I didn't recognize the sounds and went to explore. The library door was ajar so I peeked inside. There was Viscount Herrington standing buck naked behind the desk. I thought he was ugly with clothes on, but without his drawers he is downright scary-looking. There, sitting atop the desk facing him, was my Aunt Penelope. You can't imagine my surprise! My maidenly, gray-haired, full-figured aunt. She who constantly preached about proper dress and behavior, there she was, cavorting with the viscount. Not only was her hair out of its usually severe bun, but it also was completely in disarray. He was holding her and asking if the arrangement was really going to work. Every time he moved, his body jiggled and wiggled, with folds of fat, gray, wrinkly skin. My aunt didn't seem to notice, she just went on and on. She said everyone got what he or she wanted. He would get a young virgin wife, a mistress, and a lot of money to boot. She would get him as a lover, money and freedom to come and go as she pleased. My Aunt Penelope even had the gall to say that I was just too young to make decisions and that I would come to realize this was what was best for me. But then the viscount started to get rude, saying stuff about after I was no longer a virgin, could we all sleep together? My aunt laughed and said that she should be his secret as he may not even like virgins and prefer her every night. He made a 'humph' sort of sound like he didn't like her answer, so she quickly changed her answer and the next thing I knew she was telling him that anything he wanted was possible. After caressing her shoulder a bit, he then grabbed the front of her dress and ripped it wide open. I thought she would scream. I know I wanted to scream. I was simply frozen in place. Then he pulled her camisole over her head. After he had removed her corset he had her bosom in his hands. It was when he leaned down and put her nipple in his mouth that I could watch no longer. I heard groans as I backed away, but they were not the noises of pain. Then I heard laughter as the viscount roared about putting one over on everyone. I'm sure he hopes to combine our lands and make it one of the largest estates around. This was not acceptable to me. I hurried up the stairs as fast as possible. I had to awaken my maid to finish tying both my corset and the back of my dress. She also provided a bit of food while I grabbed my meager allowance. After quietly dressing and sending her back to bed, I attempted to go to my father's room. I thought I heard someone coming up the stairs, so I abandoned that idea. Without any real forethought, I walked over to my window, opened it and climbed out. I guess I wasn't thinking straight, I just knew I had to get out of there. I was not going to be there to marry that old lecher when he got that license! When I was almost at the bottom I lost my footing and fell. That set the dog to barking and the viscount's driver to come looking. I ran as fast as I could. I made it to the barn. Just my luck, the horses were in the pasture. I hopped on Fred, the mule, and took off. However, before I ventured very far, I got off the mule for a moment to take care of necessities, when Fred took off for home. It was at that time I realized I was already being followed! To me it was both unknown and unimportant who sent the men, my aunt or the viscount. Either way I had to keep running." Taking a large breath, she pleaded with Maude, "You must understand! One, I must find out what happened to my father. Two, I now realize that my aunt was working with the viscount. Three, my freedom is at stake. And four, after I am sure my aunt gives up on finding me, I must find my guardian." Finishing her story, her shoulders sagged, and she began to cry again.

Several moments had passed when Maude hugged her and said. "I simply cannot believe how far you traveled. Do you realize how far south you have come? But now that you have gotten that out you will feel better. I see hope in your story. Your guardian will be able to set everything to rights. But if worse comes to worse, you can always stay here."

"Thank you, I appreciate your offer. However, I really do not feel better having told you my plight, I feel as though I have been run over by a horse."

"You will feel better in no time. You surprise me, I first thought you young and naïve. After listening to you I have learned that you are very intelligent. You are a quick thinker. You do what needs to be done. And you can take care of yourself. You may have been duped and your freedom forfeit. Yet you clearly saw your way out and have given yourself time to change your future"

"I hope I have not offended you, I really do come from a good home. I really will be an asset to your household until I know what to do about my future." Gabrielle hesitated, then went on "I just want you to know, up until the end my aunt treated me nicely. If I hadn't spied on her I wouldn't know of her involvement with the viscount. We didn't talk about those kinds of things! I saw more that night than I had ever heard even the servants gossiping about."

Maude gave her a hug and said, "Now that I am aware of your knowledge of men and women, it will make it easier to explain many things."

Gabrielle gave her a confused look.

Maude continued, "There are so many different things for a woman to do.

There are many different paths to follow. Most follow the road shown to them by their mother. They get married and become mothers themselves. Others are impressed by examples, like teachers or nuns. So some women choose to follow these professions. Sometimes we don't get to pick, sometimes circumstances beyond our control become our destiny. For instance, if a young girl becomes with child, she is married before you know it. What if she is left alone to fend for herself? Or if she is sold as a servant, she has little choice but to do as her master bids. Or like you, a situation becomes unbearable and they run. Many situations create our destiny. Sometimes we get to pick the path to follow; sometimes we are pushed in a certain direction. Regardless of how we get there, for whatever reason, we all follow a different path. Some are good, some are bad. Some are safe, some are not. The thing to remember is that what is right for one person may not be right for someone else. What is comfortable for someone else may not be comfortable for the other person. Here, everyone can choose what they enjoy most and do that to earn a living. No matter if anyone else understands their choice, it is theirs to make."

Gabrielle interrupted, "I don't understand."

"Give me a chance, child." Maude explained, "Our home is called 'Helena's'. Short for 'Helena's House of Pleasure'." Maude watched the expression on Gabrielle's face. It didn't seem to register. "Gabrielle, this is where men come to seek their pleasure with women. Pretty much like your aunt and her lover." Finally Gabrielle seemed to understand. Maude thought to herself, *Well, at least she didn't run from the room screaming.* Maude continued, "Helena's started years ago, when she needed to find a way to pay back taxes. It was at that time a small house of entertainment in another town had caught fire and the man that ran it died. The girls had nowhere to live and no way to earn a living. It was almost by accident they came here and the mistress offered them a place to stay. At that time my mistress was little older than you and just about as educated in that department. After a heated debate about careers, they finally agreed to terms. My mistress would let them use a few rooms on the first floor and continue their business, in exchange for rent. However, it wasn't long before the word was out and many of their friends showed up. With more and more girls living here, more and more clients showed up. There were drunken men, fights and noise everywhere. Then my mistress got fed up and decided to run her home and business instead of it running her. So she cleared out the rabble and held a meeting. She would hire protection, run the operation, and charge a fee. My mistress spent the next few years perfecting an illusion. Now Helena's only caters to the wealthy. For every coin there is a fantasy for the person paying.

We have women that do everything and anything a man desires. For this they pay a heavy price. Here we have guards to protect both the women and the clients. No one ever has to worry about safety. Our home is located in a remote area so no one really knows who's coming or going. The peers of the realm like it here, they can be as wicked as they please and it will have little effect on their personal lives. Sometimes privacy is preferred, unlike going to a house of ill repute in the city, where everyone has knowledge of your business. Our home provides protection and satisfaction and we charge a huge amount of money for that convenience. I will not be able to explain it all to your satisfaction, but I will give you the tour tomorrow."

"The tour," Gabrielle repeated. She knew that meant something because Kathleen had gotten crazy over it. "The tour is what exactly?"

"We have different festivities going on all the time. Providing different costumes, countries and seasons for each fantasy. We have parties, concerts, and balls. We create scenery, drama and illusions. We have girls that dress in these costumes and entertain men. But in order to invent these images we have many, many, more people behind the scenes. We have tailors and seamstresses. They create and sew not only the special outfits but also the everyday wear of our staff. Everyone must have clothes. The sewing room and the laundry are the busiest rooms we have. Cooks and bakers are always trying to keep up. The kitchens must always have a full staff. Everyone here eats, including the customers. The cobbler is also a busy person; he has several young men under his apprentice, all occupied. The counting room takes care of all the money, both coming in and going out. Many things must be done every day, so as not to fall behind. There are girls that string jewelry and mend torn costumes. Several women that spin wool run looms and dye cloth. Candle and soap makers are a necessity. Even in these modern times with oil available for lighting. We have found it easier and cheaper to continue with candles, though Stuart has started adding some new lamps in the upper chambers. Besides the servants that keep our home clean, we have boys that work in the stables, haul water and run errands. On staff we have painters, carpenters, masons, artisans, farmers, guards and teachers. For every employee you see, there are several you don't see. Added to that, there is someone coordinating all his or her activities. We have a huge office filled with charts cataloging who is working, where and when. For as busy as we are, a guest will never see our preparations. They will never be aware how hard or long we all worked to pull off his fantasy. For by doing our jobs quickly we maintain order. By doing our jobs efficiently we guarantee business." Observing the blank expression upon Gabrielle's face, Maude could see she had overwhelmed her young friend. "Tomorrow on the tour, I will show you what and where we do things. Now, I'll take you back so you can rest, tomorrow will be an active day."

Much later, as Gabrielle lay in her bed, she heard her door open. "Who's there?" she questioned.

The intruder standing in the shadows finally walked across the room and was unmasked by the shaft of moonlight coming through the windows. It was Kathleen! "Shush! You are about as quiet as a heard of cows. I had to make sure you were alone."

"Where have you been? I have been so worried about you. Are you all right? Have you heard from your beau? I haven't heard you crying so I assumed you were better, why didn't you come and see me?"

"Are you going to give me a chance to talk?" Inquired Kathleen. Gabrielle nodded. "You have been under Maude's watchful eye, and I didn't want anyone to know how we had met, so I had to be careful. I heard they are making you work in the schoolroom. Is that true?"

"They did ask if I would like to try that, as I am not mature enough for much. Do you think I should ask for something else?

"I could not really say what you are capable of doing. Are you staying in the servants' quarters?"

Gabrielle replied, "Maude never really explained where I would be staying. But I am having the tour tomorrow." She added this information hoping to make Kathleen happy. Instead, her news seemed to make her friend anxious. "Is that all right?"

"I work in the baths tomorrow, you must not act as if you know me. It is very important. Will you remember?"

Gabrielle nodded. "I would never get you in trouble, you have been so kind to me."

"Sometimes people don't mean to get others in trouble, yet you might be surprised by my actions and say or do something."

"Oh!" Gabrielle suddenly realized "You're one of the women that provide favors to men, aren't you? You are worried that on the tour tomorrow I will see you doing something and be shocked!"

"So Maude already started to explain everything to you. I didn't know. And yes, I thought you might scream or something."

"No," said Gabrielle, laughing, "you're the screamer!"

"Now that you know what I do, will you still be my friend?"

"Kathleen, I thought things were different here, that everyone likes each other? Why would you think I would have a bad opinion of you?"

Kathleen nodded her head. "Yes, but you're not from here."

"Well, you weren't always either. I would hardly judge you for the choices you made, I've yet to make any myself." Just as she finished her sentence, both Maude and Helena's earlier conversations became clearer. "Do you like what you do? Are you happy?"

Kathleen sighed, "Some women do not enjoy the act of bedding a man. I cannot understand them, myself. I enjoy everything about it. Men have said my body was made to delight them, little do they know how right they are. I have been mating since I was thirteen, when a stable hand showed me the ways of being a woman. My mother must have been very much like me, because I am one of eleven children. After Pa died and my ma had to find a husband, the oldest five had to go with relatives. My choices were live with some bible-thumbing relatives, get married to the pimple-faced boy next door, or run away. So I left! I said good-bye to my brothers and sisters, kissed my ma good-bye and started walking. I went from one man to another and somehow just ended up here. And here is where I'm staying. I'm safe, I'm fed and I get to couple with dozens of men without worrying about my reputation. It's really quite fun. You get to dress in beautiful outfits and pretend you're a queen or gypsy or wife. Whatever their fantasy is. Or like tomorrow, I wear nothing and work the baths. That is where they are supposed to be bathed and massaged. However, I have never been able to get them clean without getting dirty, if you know what I mean," giggled Kathleen.

"I don't know exactly what you mean, but I have an idea. Do you think I will be sleeping with men?"

"Are you still a virgin?"

"Yes, and don't say that with such surprise. I was saving myself for my husband. Although I didn't have to do much saving as there were not too many men around to try to talk me out of my virtue."

Kathleen was now laughing. "I can see that you were probably well guarded. You still can remain a virgin. No one here will make you do anything you don't want to do. The choices really are yours to make. Will you be happy working with the children?

Gabrielle grinned, "We will have to see, there were not many youngsters near my home. Tell me, why is this place such a secret? I had never heard of such a place before I landed on their doorstep."

"I guess it's as hard to understand as it is to explain. Men always like women they can sleep with. They enjoy the relaxation, the entertainment and the pleasure associated with it. They treat us very special to our faces. However, these same women they enjoy are not the women they choose to marry. We are seldom picked to share their life or bear their children. They feel because we enjoy our lifestyle without benefit of marriage, we cannot be trusted. They feel our loose morals will be passed on to our children. So in our company they treat us like princesses, in public they shun us or call us names."

Gabrielle just cringed. "How can you live like that? I don't think I would like it."

"In many places it is not safe for women like myself. But here we are safe. Here only the wealthy are allowed. No one comes without proper introduction. There are no jealous wives, no innocent daughters to influence, no priests to judge. Here we are happy to service the upper class and enjoy what we do. Not to mention the fun, we also make a lot of money. When my body is old and no one wants me I will have the money I have saved and buy a small house by the ocean. I love bed sport and I love living here. And it really is only a secret to peasants, women and strangers. All the male aristocrats know of this place, even the king himself has visited here. We have even catered to some upper-society matrons. So you see, the only people who do not know of this place are the people who should not. I guess if we had a motto, ours would be, 'If you don't know about us, we don't want you to.'" Then Kathleen burst out laughing. " After all this, will you still let me be your friend?"

"Of course you are my friend, you think so little of me that you would ask? Besides, I haven't even decided if I will become one of the girls like you or if I will be a servant."

"Have you any desires yet?"

Gabrielle's face turned red, "I simply cannot believe we are having this conversation, do you know up until last week, I was still pretty naïve. Now this week I am trying to decide if I should give up my virginity as an occupation!"

"If I had met my Kevin, I would never have started in the life. I have never had a man that made me feel so special." Tears fell from her eyes as she continued. "I know in my head he is not coming back, but my heart just won't seem to give up."

"Maybe...." Gabrielle offered.

"No, no.... It's all right. Let's chat of something else, shall we?"

As the night wore on the girls talked and talked. Sharing deep secrets yet laughing at silly things. By early morning Kathleen had pretty much informed her – as much as Gabrielle could understand, anyway – about men and love. Kathleen had shared her childhood and her hopes for the future. In turn, Gabrielle had shared her childhood, her memories of her father and her adamant insistence that he was still alive. She also shared her dreams, because until reaching Helena's she had not planned a future, she had dreamed a future. Now she was at the planning stages. She would someday soon have to choose an occupation, and she really had no idea at all! They talked till the rooster crowed and then Kathleen had to slip out unnoticed. She had also explained that soon she would be introduced to her and then they could be friends openly. Until then they couldn't be friends without both being in serious trouble. Kathleen for disturbing the household AGAIN! Gabrielle too, would be in trouble. Both offenses earning positions of non-trusted personnel. These jobs Kathleen didn't ever want again and Gabrielle not at all. So after Kathleen had silently gone back to her room, Gabrielle had no trouble falling asleep.

Chapter 4

Daisy arrived early, followed by the boys with the tub. It took her even longer than usual to rouse Gabrielle. She had no way of knowing Gabrielle had been up all night. Finally after her bath was finished, her hair braided, her body dressed, and her breakfast eaten, she was escorted to Maude. They walked down so many corridors and past so many doors and down so many steps that Gabrielle knew she would need a guide for a very long time. Daisy led her to the kitchens, where Maude stood tasting Cook's Sienese Tarts. As Maude was occupied and Daisy had made a hasty retreat, Gabrielle took a moment to look about. The room they were in was huge, all brick and smelling of fresh bread. On the far right side, two women were kneading dough. They were located in front of a long table, with mounds and mounds of dough in front of them. Next to them was a counter with rows and rows of bread tins. The bakery had four huge fireplaces. Two women stood in front of each hearth, one loading food in, the other taking the baked goods out. Glancing to the left, two women were rolling out dough for pies. Near that table was a woman stirring a large vat. That was where Maude was standing, sampling the tarts.

"I believe these are the best tasting tarts you have ever made!" Gabrielle heard Maude exclaim. Shortly after her discussion with the cook, Maude crossed the kitchen to greet Gabrielle. "Gabrielle, you look lovely this morning. How long have you been standing there?"

"I did not want to interrupt you, but this is where Daisy left me, so I was waiting until you finished with the cook," answered Gabrielle.

Maude looked over her shoulder to make sure none had heard Gabrielle's comment as she leaned in closer and said. "That is our head baker, Agnes. Don't let her hear you call her a cook, she will not give you treats for weeks!" laughed Maude. "She is not only our most talented baker, she is totally in charge of all our baked goods. She gets a bit haughty sometimes, yet her food is simply to die for. So we tolerate her ego."

Maude took the time to introduce Gabrielle all around, and then led her through several passages to connecting kitchens. Following Maude through the larder, the spicery, the scullery, the bakery, the laundry, the cellar, the boiling house, the pastry, the pantry, the poultry, the main kitchen, the brew house and the chaundry. Every division of the kitchens had a supervisor, with assistants under them. Gabrielle wondered if she would ever remember them all! After all the introductions and viewing the kitchens, Maude directed her towards breakfast. They walked into a clean white room, with rows and rows of tables with benches. The food and beverages were located on the sideboard. Gabrielle simply followed Maude through the line, taking a couple of muffins and a cup of tea. Maude explained that Gabrielle would have her meals here from now on, as she was now one of the workers. It would not be fair to have servants waiting on her any longer. She would come here before school and after. At lunchtime, she was to eat with the schoolmistress. She would have a lot of learning to do, so she was to learn from all those around her. Maude explained that Gabrielle would have to ask questions when she needed to and learn by watching and listening to others. She went on to inform that the rest of her tour would not be until this afternoon, as pressing business had come up. Maude also explained that she would not be with her all the time, but she would be informed of Gabrielle's progress. Maude was very serious when she added that if for any reason she needed her, to ask anyone to take her directly to Maude. Then they would lead her to Maude posthaste. It did seem like Maude was giving her a pep talk, but Gabrielle just couldn't concentrate. After they had gathered their dishes, she was led to the classroom.

The classroom was out the kitchen door and down the hill. It was still inside the castle walls, but a good deal distance from it. The path led to a small cottage, near a small apple orchard. On the large oak tree standing near the front of the cottage hung a swing. They had just about reached the cottage, when a maidenly older woman came to the door. She had a warm smile and shining eyes. "This must be my helper!" exclaimed Mrs. Curry, clapping her hands together. "Maude, it's so good to see you and I'm so happy you could find help for the children. Please introduce me."

"Gabrielle, Mrs. Curry. Mrs. Curry, Gabrielle," said Maude, pointing from one to the other. I am glad I could be of help and you are right, this is your new assistant. Her name is Gabrielle. She will be helping for a while; we still are looking for someone permanent. Gabrielle has not made her life choice commitment yet. However, until we find someone else or she chooses to change positions, she is all yours."

"Splendid!" said Mrs. Curry

"Then I will leave her to you." As she turned to leave, Maude said to Gabrielle, "Good luck, I'm sure you will do fine. I will return at lunchtime today and give you the tour. Tomorrow you can start your first full day."

Maude gave her a little hug and left. Both Mrs. Curry and Gabrielle watched her amble up the hill before Mrs. Curry turned to her and said, "I'm sure we will get along just fine. We can chat a while until school begins. How does that sound?" Gabrielle merely nodded her head yes. So Mrs. Curry continued, "After lessons are over the children visit their mothers. Before dinner they do their chores, and after dinner, their studies. You are only required to help in the schoolroom, as there are others to assist with the rest. Tell me, how did you come to pick the classroom helper position?'

Gabrielle smiled. "I was undecided as to what to do and they said I could do this until I decided. However, no one has explained to you that I have no experience with children. This I think you should know."

Mrs. Curry smiled. "You can read?"

"I can read and write in English, Latin, and French. I am not quite as strong in Latin as French. I know absolutely nothing about small children though."

"You know more than most of my other helpers have known in the past. You will do fine. The children will love you."

Gabrielle gave a little smile. "I will try."

Mrs. Curry turned around and walked back into the small cottage, Gabrielle followed. Inside were rows of benches and tables. The large table in front was for the teacher; the smaller one down to the side was for Gabrielle. There were small chalkboards at each spot, along with several books. The next moments were a little hectic, but only to a stranger of children.

All of a sudden, the sound of running footsteps and loud shrieks could be heard outside. Mrs. Curry smiled and said, "Forgive the interruption, my dear, but the children are here." With that she stood up and waited. The next moments were a little hectic, but only to a stranger of children. They ran in, found their seats, and sat down. Mrs. Curry began, "Children, how happy I am to see you. Today we have a surprise." She waved her arm over towards Gabrielle. "A new tutor to assist us with our lessons. Please give a warm welcome to Gabrielle."

"Good morning, Gabrielle," they all sang in unison.

Gabrielle did not know if she should be frightened or flattered when she replied, "Good morning." There were only fourteen children, far fewer than anticipated.

Mrs. Curry continued, "I hope everyone studied. Gabrielle will leave at lunch today, but tomorrow she can stay all day. Now everyone settle down to work."

Gabrielle could not believe it was time to go when Maude tapped her on the shoulder. She had been helping little Elmer with his mathematics as he had been having so much trouble. She gave him a smile and a pat on the back and told him to keep trying. She excused herself with Mrs. Curry and then out the door they went.

"How did it go today? Do you think you will like it?" asked Maude.

"I really enjoyed myself, I felt like I was really helping."

As they walked up the hill, Gabrielle filled Maude in on her day. She had been surprised when little Tommy had spiders in his pocket and Elmer had a frog. She had been excited when Angela could recite her numbers. She had even been a little nervous when Mary pulled out a tooth. But all in all it had been a good day. Maude listened to her rattle on and on about simple everyday events, as though no one had seen or done them before. Maude reaffirmed her hunch that Gabrielle had been quite sheltered and probably was not a candidate for seducing men.

Maude stopped by a bench and motioned for Gabrielle to sit down, and then she spoke. "Mrs. Curry told you about the children's daily routine?" Gabrielle nodded. "Mentioning the children visit their mothers every day?"

"Yes, I remember," she said.

"Yet, you're not curious about the fathers visiting them?"

"I had not thought much about it, but wouldn't it be at the same time?"

"No. Most children do not know their fathers, and even if they do, few are acknowledged."

Gabrielle seemed perplexed, but nodded in agreement.

"Careful as they are, some of the girls end up with child." Watching Gabrielle's eyes grow wider, Maude continued, "Here everyone is provided for. It is a very unusual arrangement. We do try to find homes for some, because most mothers want what is best for their children. The homes we find are nice and we try very hard to express that to the mothers. Yet some of the mothers choose not to be separated. Here we pride ourselves in providing for all residents and that includes the children. Some children help the deliverymen; some work in the kitchens, most work the fields with the tenant farmers. However, the mistress is of a mind that the child is not to blame for its conception. So, as we provide safety for adults, we also take care of the children. It is impossible to find another place like this. Most are thrown in the streets. I'm not sure if it's because a woman runs our home or if it's just compassion and common sense. But everyone has proved to be a far better employee if his or her children are taken care of. As far-fetched as it is, it seems to be working. If a girl is unable to do her job, providing for the men, she is moved to another area. So maybe while her time of confinement grows near, she may work in the sewing room or the classroom. She can work wherever she can be useful. Many of the girls work in the nursery, learning how to care for the babies. Here we never condemn people for mistakes. We simply raise them and teach them and provide a home for them. Then after they are grown they can decide what they would like to do. So do you understand that most of the children in our classroom do not have fathers and we very rarely bring up the subject?"

"I had not thought of the consequences they encounter, how could they stand to be separated from their children?"

Before she answered she stood, waiting for Gabrielle to do the same. Then she began to walk as she talked. "Most places, the women are dismissed if they become with child. They fall on hard times, even miscarry. They sometimes try to get other positions and keep their children. Some end up giving their children away. Here everyone is safe and accepted. We take every precaution to prevent conception. When that is no longer an alternative we take care of the mothers and the children. The mothers have complete access to their children at any time. No one has to endure slander or shame. Here it is just the way of things. If a girl misses her cycle she is watched. If she misses two, the doctor comes in to examine. By the time she misses three she has been removed from her activities. She will work in another position, until her confinement draws near. After the birthing she will work in the nursery, three days a week for the next year. This keeps her with her child and a light load from other duties. After her child is one, she only has to work in the nursery one day a week. This does not mean she cannot go there more, only that she is required just one day. Many days there are too many women there. The children stay in the nursery until they are five. By the time they reach five, they come to my schoolroom. From ages five to ten we do what we can to educate them and just let them be children. However, after they are ten they are able to understand the way of the world, and that they must contribute. The boys often apprentice with the blacksmith or cobbler. Most choose the stables and training of horses. Some believe they will one day grow up to be a great soldier and who knows? The girls usually choose sewing or art rooms. The ones with little talent are moved to the kitchens. Some are lucky and raised by childless people and they go on to lead normal lives."

Reaching the landing they stood in front of the very large, double doors. Both women stopped to examine the opulent entrance of the castle.

"Well, what do you think?" said Maude.

Gabrielle wasn't sure what to say; her first response was, "It's very impressive, isn't it?"

"Indeed it is!" said Maude. Once again, Maude began to explain how they operated. "If you were a guest, you would ride into this courtyard. The stable hand would take your horse, or carriage, at the same time directing your coachmen or driver to the rooms located over there," she said, pointing across the courtyard and near the stables. "Located where we are, it is very rare that a customer stay only one evening. The servants remain housed there until their master is ready to go. We cater to the ton's elite, so of course, their help is never allowed inside." At Gabrielle's expression Maude said "Do not fret, those simple rooms for staff are better than most of their currant residences." Gabrielle smiled. Maude began again. "Now your horses and men are taken care of, so you continue through this entrance." As Maude moved she pointed out interesting things to Gabrielle. "As we make our way through the entrance, a servant opens the door. Today it is young Tim. Good morning, Tim," she said to him as they passed. He was a striking boy of about twelve with freckles and red hair, who smiled in response. "He is working the door today because we are not very busy. The younger staff is not allowed to work the doors for large gatherings. A more menacing presence is required." Maude turned to Tim and said, "When your shift is over you may want to go to the kitchen."

"I usually do," replied Tim with a grin.

"Yes, but Agnes made Sienese tarts and I know they are your favorite. I also know that Henry is here today and they are his favorite too!"

"Sienese tarts?"

"I knew that would get your attention. And if Sienese tarts are around, that is where I'm sure you will find Henry. Don't stay up all night, trading stories. I think he will be here for a while," said Maude as she continued on.

"I appreciate you letting me know about both the tarts and Henry. Thanks, Maude," shouted Tim. Then he returned to his post near the door.

Walking with Gabrielle, Maude mentioned "Henry is also a young man who has been raised here, at the castle. His mother is Rachel; she works in the spinning room now. Henry is a fine gentleman; both he and his mother are well liked by all. Recently Henry has become apprenticed to Joseph Fry. Mr. Fry has employed several of our children. He is practically like family. Mr. Fry owns and operates a factory in nearby Bristol. Mr. Fry is a favorite visitor among the staff. Although he is charming and distinguished, it isn't his personality that they favor. It is his presents! Because the factory he runs manufactures chocolate! And Mr. Fry never comes to visit without bringing lots of sweets for Helena and her girls."

Although Mr. Fry was already forty-nine years old, he and Helena were the best of friends. It had all started when Helena had first taken possession of the castle. Shortly before she started running her business, one of the servants had become ill. Helena had gone into town to find a doctor or a midwife. She stumbled onto Joseph Fry by accident and he volunteered to come and see the young girl. It appeared Joseph had been educated as a doctor. Earlier in his career he had even set up a business as an apothecary. Later on, it was he who had taken the responsibility of setting up and choosing, the rooms and apothecary for Helena's.

Although he no longer remained in practice, he felt he could be of assistance. He sat up with Helena and the young girl for two nights and finally she recovered. During those long two nights, they had shared many stories. Both had grown up as children of well-off parents. After leaving home, he continued on his adventure as entrepreneur. She, however, was just on the brink. He made many suggestions that would help a woman alone in business. Including using his name, as a front, for many of her investments. Men would simply not allow her access to business. Helena touched his heart as no one ever had. She had simply delighted Joseph. Long after the sick girl brought them together, Helena still looked to him for advice.

Joseph Fry was very successful in business. Not only was Joseph a good friend, but a huge asset in placing children in apprentice positions. For besides chocolate, his other business ventures included the manufacturing of china, soap and books. He was a dedicated family man, keeping both his friendship with Helena and his infrequent liaisons discreet. Helena's was the soul of discretion. Though he had not needed the extra capital, he had allowed Helena to buy a percentage of his endeavors.

With so many businesses to choose from, Henry had a unique opportunity to learn several trades. Of course being the young, healthy boy that he was, he favored the making of chocolate and chose to apprentice at the chocolate factory.

Maude turned to Gabrielle, "Henry left us only recently. He was allowed to accompany his employer for our latest delivery. Normally neither brings the supplies, however, Joseph Fry is in need of a little rest and relaxation. As he knew he would be spending a few days, he allowed Henry to come and visit. So while we pamper Mr. Fry, we will also have the opportunity to visit with Henry. We have all missed him terribly, but most of all Tim. He and Henry are very close. I suspect when Tim is older, he will leave to live with Henry. Henry is like the brother he never had." They continued on their tour. Returning to the earlier conversation about the front entrance, Maude said, "On his watch, if no one is expected, he must wait for confirmation from his superior before letting anyone enter. Because of our choice of business and the many women within, we can never be too careful. The staff uses those loopholes in the wall to see outside," pointing to the small rectangle slits in the wall of the castle that were used to view the outer area. "What was built into the castle for defense, in earlier times, still comes in very handy. Though someone would have to get past the guards, through the gate and up into the courtyard, before getting to these doors, we always check and double-check, and because we have been so cautious, we have never had invaders."

"Tim seems like a nice young man," mentioned Gabrielle.

"He is both nice and consciencious. I like and respect him. He works very hard. He trains with the guards, studies hard with his tutor, and works his post during the day. And Tim is very happy to have secured this position, because it is one of the easier tasks. He gets a small room to himself, behind the large entryway, which allows him some privacy. Soon he will be allowed to apprentice for an occupation."

Gabrielle whispered, "Seems like you know about everyone here, or does everyone know about everyone else?"

"Oh Gabrielle, not many things happen here, that everyone else doesn't know about. With so many women, gossip and rumors are just part of the everyday activities." She sighed. "Now, let's get back to the tour. After we come through this doorway we enter the hall. Once reaching this point, the maidservants come out and take your wrap. They clean your boots or shoes, give you something to drink and make you feel comfortable." Maude turned and grinned at Gabrielle. "The patrons feel from the moment they walk in the door as if we exist only to pamper them. And of course they are right. But we learned the hard way not to let any callers in with dirty boots or the cleanup was twice as bad. So better to think it's all part of the pampering, rather than making our work easier. The customer is greeted and cleaned up, then he may relieve himself down the hall over there." Maude pointed to the privy at the end of the hall. "Most of the rooms still have chamber pots, however, ever the front runner in new inventions, Stuart had constructed several water closets within the castle." Going back to the original topic, she continued, "After he has finished and is ready to continue, he steps up to the desk over here." They walked up to the front desk; behind the desk were three very beautiful girls. All three had long blonde hair, and warm expressions. They were dressed in very elegant but very tight, revealing dresses.

Gabrielle took a moment to look around. The woodwork in this room was superb! It was a dark mahogany, shined to a high gloss. The hall was simply enormous. With a smooth stone floor and matching support pillars, the room should have seemed ordinary. However, the mood was enhanced with the artistically placed furnishings. The large sconces on the wall matched the tall, rod iron candleholders scattered throughout the room. To the left was a wide, magnificent stairway, leading to the gallery overhead. The lower walls were covered with rich tapestries. The walls above the landing were full of portraits.

In the center of the hall stood the large stone fireplace. A fireplace so large one could stand inside. The comfortable chairs nestled around the hearth, just inviting one to relax by their simple arrangement. The last ingredient necessary for creating the perfect atmosphere was the warmth of the fire.

She glanced back to the women behind the desk. Each was showing far more cleavage than was fashionable. The dresses seemed about two sizes too small, definitely too snug. While Maude conversed with the girls, Gabrielle stood and gazed about the room. They all seemed genuinely happy, and very personable. After a short time, Maude turned to introduce Gabrielle. Finally they concluded their chat and Maude began the tour again.

"If you are a regular customer, you need only to sign in. Your tastes and preferences have already been recorded. However, if you are a regular who wishes to change your standing reservation, or a new customer, you will have to decide what you would like. Sometimes you can just think up fantasies, other times they look at the *Book of Illusions.*" Maude directed Gabrielle's attention to a large podium in the corner. It was also a dark mahogany, beautifully hand-carved with different designs. Upon the surface of the podium was a huge hard-covered red book. The gold letters embossed upon the cover simply said *Illusions.* "You may look at it another time, as there are many pages to go through. After they decide which they would prefer, one of these girls take them into the pub." Maude looked at Gabrielle. "Are you still following, or am I going to fast?"

"No, you're doing a fine job, I'm just in awe."

Maude nodded and continued, "When a girl must leave her post at the front desk, she rings the bell. Then another girl comes from that doorway and takes her place. Never is any area ever unattended." As she guided Gabrielle by the arm, she explained, "While the men wait, they can relax and have a drink. The barkeep and girls keep the ale flowing and the customers entertained. After leaving the client in the care of the staff, the girl working the desk needs to inform her superior of their choice. Either the superior in the west wing or the superior in the east wing would then be in charge of setting up the man's fantasy. If the customer was a regular or if he had a reservation, it goes much faster. Extra time is required if the customer is new or the fantasy unique. That is why it is necessary for the client to be entertained during the 'setup time'. As soon as the room, the fantasy, and the woman or women are complete, the girl from the front desk will be sent to find the client and bring him to his destination. A man wanting a nice, tame fantasy goes to the west wing. If he wants an unusual or naughty fantasy, he is taken to the east wing. For now we will go up the west staircase." As they walked up the stairs, Gabrielle soaked in the ambiance. She viewed the portraits, most not too risqué at all. They reached the first landing and heard pleasant violin music. They continued down the hall to a doorway on the left. Maude opened the door and as she did, steam met them as they entered. The walls were mostly white tile with royal blue mosaic tiles sprinkled within. Hanging from the ceiling were huge, bronze oil burning lamps. Statues of well-endowed naked women circled the room. Along the far wall, the carved arches created small alcoves, which had sheer curtains hanging across each doorway. Ferns and tropical plants were sprinkled among the potted palms. Everywhere fragrant flowers and beautiful plants enhanced the decor.

Water cascaded down from a reservoir basin over the pool area. The baths contained an extremely advanced system of drainage, ensuring that all moisture was led off into large sewers of stone. The sound of running water not only had a pleasant, soothing sound. It served a purpose.

Maude began to explain, "In those first alcoves the men are divested of their clothing. They are soaped, lathered and rinsed. Then they are soaped, lathered and rinsed again. This ritual is not only practical but also essential, for many of our clients do not bathe nearly enough. The alcoves lining the wall are approximately fifteen feet square. The first four rooms all have a fountain for washing and a drain in the floor for rinsing. The floors of these rooms were overlaid with powdered limestone. They slope to the center of the room, where the water drains off in small runnels by earthenware tiles. Large cisterns are located on the roofs to collect the rainwater. The terra cotta pipes running from the top form a labyrinth within the castle, transporting water to all the bathing chambers. We are also fortunate enough to have hot water in ready supply. The water is heated by kettles over an open fire and carried to large tanks located next to each bathing chamber. If the water runs low in the fountains the servant in charge simply pumps in more. Remind me to take you to the bathing chamber over the kitchens. It is more moderately decorated, yet is the girls' favorite. The heat from the kitchens located underneath warms the bricks of the floor, creating not only warm water, but warm air, of consistent temperature, year-round."

As Maude rambled on she observed Gabrielle, then she said, "You probably are not even interested in the plumbing or the heating. Some often wonder, so I simply include the information. Helena's architect friend helped us remodel. He is Persian and fully responsible for the layout of all the baths. He also designed the eastern theme rooms, which are said to be exact replicas of palace harems. As Helena had not traveled much, she relied on both his artistic and his masculine attributes. All in all, the exotic setup of the baths makes it most convenient for cleaning and relaxing.

"After the men are cleaned, they are brought to the steam area. There they sweat and are rinsed, yet again. Then they are led to the pool. They can be scrubbed, or they can be played with or both. It is all up to the customer. I'm sure you realize their preference," she said, wiggling her eyebrows. "After they finish with their bath, they go to one of the massage areas." She pointed to the remaining alcoves off to the side. "There they are massaged, oiled and massaged again. There are different ways to apply scents to the body. Solid unguents, scented oils and perfumed powders. Most favor the oils, but the solid ointments provide a more therapeutic massage. The men favor the use of musks over perfumes." She pointed to an area over near the alcoves. "On those shelves you will find an assortment of scented ointments: marjoram, thyme, wormwood, chamomile. There are also bottles and bottles of jasmine, coriander, cardamom, pine, saffron and clove-scented sesame oils. We even have the imported aromatic salves and oils: sandalwood, Tibetan cedar, myrrh, cinnamon, sassafras and vanilla. When massaged, the girls can work wonders on sore bodies. When they are finished you feel completely relaxed. The customer can again have sex or be led to another room to enjoy a fantasy. Again, the option is only up to the client. This room provides enjoyment for the customer and assures cleanliness for all. Even if a customer does not request a bath with his fantasy, all are led here anyway. His clothes are laundered if necessary while he engages in bedding the woman of choice. All are returned to him when he pays and leaves. It leaves very little arguing room," snickered Maude.

Gabrielle said, "This is a very beautiful bathing room."

"The mistress had the tile imported from Istanbul. She also has seventeen eastern women that were sold at auction. They are our most popular bathers. Helena bought their papers from a merchant, who had bought them from a pirate. They had been abducted from a caravan moving from the desert to the palace. After paying for them, Helena then explained to them that they were free. This they would not even consider. They were grateful to Helena by then. So she brought them home with her and after they had been to our home, they wanted to stay. They felt as comfortable as being in the harem from their country. They did not want to risk travel overseas again, having found happiness here. In their country they were known as ickbals or concubines. Many women had to share only one man. Their master rarely had time for them; they were many women for one man. Here they are few women for many men. This pleases them. You will meet them soon. You will like them, they are very nice." After looking over the whole bathing area,

Maude finally turned to leave and motioned Gabrielle to follow.

They walked past a few more doorways, and then entered what appeared to be a throne room. At the upper end of the room was a raised platform, upon which a large, throne-like chair sat. In addition to the large fireplace, located at the end of the hall, a large hearth was located near the dais. Though off to the side, it was needed in a hall this size, for additional warmth. Above the dais was a multicolored covered canopy. It helped to create the illusion of a real throne room. It was also used as additional protection for those on the dais. Oftentimes with a room this large, containing an open hearth, soot sprinkled down on them.

Windows lined the far wall, allowing sunlight to stream through. For evening events, giant candelabras hung from the large, rectangular beams overhead. With the sconces distributed resourcefully, throughout the room, enough light was created for any affair. The vaulted ceiling made the large room seem enormous. "This room is for the man that wants to be king," Maude laughed. "Funny, this room is always booked."

"So a man rents the room, rents the woman, then goes about the business of pretending he's the king?" asked Gabrielle.

"That's just about it, different situations depending on the client. Like tonight the room is to be full of people, for a coronation. Everyone will be in costume. He sits up on that marble platform and lets the participants parade past him. When he wants to pick a queen, the dancing will stop and he will signal the coronation to begin. They will start off in a fabulous costume, like that of a queen. Everyone attending will be dressed to the hilt. Hoop dresses and large heavy wigs adorn the women. Yet under each full skirt, they wear nothing! Each woman flirts outrageously with the man pretending to be king. At one time or another, all will lift their large hoop skirts, trying to bribe the man sitting on the throne with their unique attributes. By the end of the night, he will have chosen his queen. The music will stop and the coronation will begin. Afterwards, the customer in this fantasy will take his queen and retire. He has picked the red room to spend his evening with her. It should be quite an event."

"Oh!" replied Gabrielle.

Maude led her out, and down to another door.

"Maude, you just open the door and walk right in, how do you know you will not disturb someone?"

"That is a very good question and something you must take note of as well. See the sconces on the wall, next to each and every door? If the candles are burning, there are customers within. It is a signal that that room is occupied. Then you may not enter, unless you are part of the fantasy. You may go to a viewing chamber, or continue on to another room."

Gabrielle smiled, "It was a very good question, wasn't it? I sure don't want to walk in the wrong door. But what is a viewing chamber?"

"Here, let's go back to the room we just left, see the sconce on the wall? The candle is not burning now, but suppose it were. Then we couldn't go inside because a fantasy is in progress. However, the candle is not burning in the sconce next to the following door. So we can go into the viewing chamber of the throne room. Maybe the client simply enjoys watching others participating. So we charge him for watching instead." She led Gabrielle through the door and up a narrow stairway. Into an unlit chamber, lighting the candle inside the doorway. The room was furnished with a large dark brown chaise longue. The rugs were thick and ran the length of the room. There were dark curtains hanging along a wall with a row of straight-backed chairs in front of it. Maude reached over and untied the curtains. Pulling the curtains to the side enabled them to see the lattice-covered, rectangle-shaped opening. The latch in the center allowed the watchers to unlock the criss-cross covering, giving them an unobstructed view. Some customers liked to feel they were peeking and leave the covering in place. Most opened the covering for unhampered gazing.

"This chamber is located on the far wall in the throne room. Some clients just want to view the activities of the people in the room below, hence the term 'Viewing Chamber'. Many people are voyeurs, meaning they like to watch others. Sometimes they come in alone, sometimes they bring in a girl to soothe them as they watch. If you were in the throne room, it is very unlikely you would notice anyone up here. Even if you did, no one would say anything. After you are comfortable here, you are welcome to watch anytime. Just check the schedule and make sure no one is going to use this room and remember to check the sconce next to the door." She blew out the candle and both Maude and Gabrielle walked back down the tiny hallway steps and out of the door.

For the rest of the day, Maude guided her through every nook and cranny of the castle. She saw the rooms, the costumes, and the sets. She briefly saw two fantasies in progress. Of all the rooms in the castle, her favorite was the apocathary's chamber. It was fascinating! She also decided the wardrobe room was interesting. All the costumes were so beautiful and unique. She had even been to the office and read the charts. She was amazed when she found her own name, located under schoolroom helper. She was excited to visit the gem room; she had never seen such riches. She volunteered to help in the sewing room when she was told that they could never seem to catch up. The head seamstress said she was always welcome. The least exciting rooms were

LAURA JAMES

the laundry, kitchens, spinning and candle making rooms. These mundane, dreary, routine jobs were vital to the smooth operation of the castle but boring nonetheless. Gabrielle sincerely hoped she did not get sent there. Gabrielle thought the counting room very interesting, yet very busy. Maude had even led her through the stables and kennels. Finally the tour was over. Gabrielle had seen so much. She had listened, observed and tried to pay careful attention. Still she knew it would take forever to remember her way through the castle. She felt completely overwhelmed. After a quick bite to eat, Maude guided Gabrielle to her room, where she quickly fell into a deep sleep.

Chapter 5

Almost a year had gone by, passing pretty uneventfully. Gabrielle had successfully learned her way around, remembering the names of the servants, the guards and the rest of the members of the household. She was finally beginning to become accustomed to the chattering, whining, laughing, women that filled the castle. Most were cheerful, friendly and helpful. However, some were jealous, mean and spiteful. Gabrielle kept very busy, usually helping in the schoolroom. When she was not needed there, she could be found doing some odd job or another. She seemed to help in almost all areas of the castle. Gabrielle was artistic with the set designs. She was clever with colors in the sewing room. She had helped serve at several parties. Gabrielle often spent time cleaning, repairing and polishing silverware and jewelry. Though others laughed, she was fascinated by the enormous array of both. She had washed, dried and folded items in the laundry. One day, while helping the brewer, she had even gotten a bit tipsy. The day she was sent to help in the wig room, she spent more time trying them on than brushing and decorating. Gabrielle had even offered her services in the counting room. Now that was a tedious, unappreciated job. For in those offices, ten clerks kept track of employees, deliveries, shipments, investments, payments and acquisitions. No matter where she was needed, Gabrielle was always eager to help and show her appreciation for being given a place of safety.

After long hard days, Gabrielle sometimes ventured into the gardens to relax. She loved the gardens. Growing in age, wisdom and beauty, Gabrielle began to feel more and more at home. She was beginning to feel less inhibited and more confident. She even learned not to be so shy about her body and was now enjoying the daily baths and massages. She was less embarrassed and now even asking for different creams and scents. However, she had not yet worked up the courage to attend any of the classes taught by the more experienced women. So she was still bashful and uneducated in the more erotic arts. What she did know, she had learned solely upon observation. However, she was blossoming into a stunning beauty. But as she matured, both her mind and her body began to crave affection.

Both Gabrielle and Kathleen worked hard; each girl's schedule kept them both very busy. Whenever they coordinated free time, they used their time to instigate trouble and create fun. Gabrielle knew she had never laughed or danced or smiled as often as she had this past year. She also realized what a wonderful friend Kathleen was. They traded stories, shared secrets and argued about everything. Kathleen was still trying to mend her broken heart, but Gabrielle was feeling content. It was only when she thought of her father she became a bit melancholy.

The next day brought the arrival of the King of England, King George III. Now this was very unusual, for whenever the king was in the area, he stayed at his hunting box in Kingswood. Ordinarily, the king sent a messenger with a list of items to be stocked for his visit. Helena would have the lovely ladies waiting for him and his followers in advance. Stuart would drive the wagonload over and the event would unfold without any hitches. The only disadvantage to supplying ladies to the king was the lack of payment received. One always knew when dealing with the king it was suppose to be an honor simply to serve him, with no reward ever gained from this privilege. Usually the king promised the placement of a relative within his household, to repay a host. Yet Helena never required anything. She had long ago realized it was better to be friend than foe to the king. One simply had to applaud the audacity of royalty and with no recourse, allow this as tribute to him.

However, this time, by showing up unannounced it sent the entire household into an uproar. This was because the king traveled with such a huge entourage. Suddenly the atmosphere in the castle became hectic. The efficient staff quickly banded together, finding a spot for them all. Stuart was in charge of the groomsmen and soldiers. He had everything under control in the stable and barracks. Every stable keep was busy, rushing about with all the extra horses. As usual, the king's friends all demanded immediate attention. Finally the chaos had settled and every guest situated. Both Helena and Maude knew they could not let down their guard for a moment with the king in residence. They reminisced about the last time he had stayed with them. He had simply wreaked great havoc the entire time he had been here. Several fantasies had been interrupted when he had walked in to watch, informing the guest whose fantasy he had invaded and Helena that it was a privilege to share their bed with the king. So basically he had run amok for several days. Helena was desperately hoping he had changed since then.

The next morning, after his bath and before a new fantasy started, Helena went to visit King George III. As he had just come from the baths, he was thoroughly complacent. He was lounging on the settee when she was allowed to enter. His room was designed with royalty in mind. All of the furnishings were gilded. There were thick rugs on the floor by the fireplace. The king required four beautiful handmaidens to surround and serve him at all times. The lap robe and bedspread were both made from the softest, thickest furs. The bed had been built longer and wider than most and sat upon a dais in the center of the room. The curtains surrounding the bed were tied open at the moment. Helena personally thought this room a bit garish and ostentatious. As were several others that she supplied the royals, however the ton was partial to them.

King George III went through the women like other men go through gunpowder, loud and quick. He never picked any German women or German fantasies. Helena knew this request was because his wife Queen Charlotte was from Germany. King George was very discreet about his liaisons, for he was totally devoted to his wife. As king, his only true obligation was to supply the royal heir, however he had grown to love his wife and had provided fourteen other children as well. Because he had genuine affection for his wife, he went to great lengths to keep any indiscretions from reaching the ears of either the general populace or his wife.

Helena had been apprehensive dealing with him at first, thinking he may know her past circumstances. Proven unaware, he did not associate the frightened young girl of the past with the ravishing woman of today. He never said and she never asked. Still, being unable to clear her family's good name was a sore spot with her. After all, her vicious uncle and his associates had done a thorough job of framing her family as traitors. Believing her family had all been involved in the treasonous acts, they had been stripped their dignity and heritage. Parliament had been unwilling to believe her family. They were even more suspicious after seizing the family's assets and finding much of the wealth missing. In the end, she was lucky not to have been thrown in the goal.

It was while in pursuit of the guilty parties that her family had met with a tragic accident. Having been ill at the time, she had been left behind. The rest of her family had perished following a lead. Her parents' bodies crushed on the rocks below after the carriage failed to make a hairpin turn. Her brother's body, never found, was believed to have been washed out to sea.

Yet after Helena's brother and parents had died, she had been given a reprieve, by being awarded to her grandmother's custody. This allowed Helena to remain in seclusion and provide companionship to her invalid grandmother. Time passed, permitting her heart to heal, gossip to fade, and people to forget all about her. Later, after the death of her grandmother, she had been permitted to accept the inheritance left from her mother's family.

After Helena's had opened she had made the king's acquaintance. He appeared to have no previous association with her. That worked for Helena just fine.

However, he was very familiar with her current persona. He very much liked Helena, her ambition and her establishment. The king appreciated two things at Helena's. Discretion and as many of her girls as possible! Not necessarily in that order.

Occasionally it appeared as though his memory was not as sharp as before. Maybe what the people were saying was true, maybe he really was experiencing mental breakdowns from time to time. However, at the moment he seemed fine, so she was skeptical of the rumors. It was at this time the king informed her that he would only be there one more day, as the queen was due to arrive in Bath. The king went on to say that his original destination had been to Lord Brute's castle, but that those plans had been changed en route. Queen Charlotte had decided to stop in Salisbury to visit a friend after childbirth, while he refused to add the visit to his agenda. Whereupon the king insisted the majority of the guards stay behind with all the females and the remaining men accompany him. That explained his sudden appearance at Helena's with no word of warning.

Helena and the king enjoyed each other's company a while longer before she guided him to the Turkish Fantasy. There he selected several women, one young girl that he said reminded him of Sarah Lennox, the girl he had fallen in love with during his youth. They entered into the dimly lit room. Lushly decorated with Turkish designs and tapestries. The soft blue drapes were held open by large golden ropes. The smell of burning jasmine was thick in the air. And there among the large throw pillows scattered about the thick carpets lay the young, nubile women. The king ushered Helena out the door. As the door shut she heard him say he could handle the rest on his own. Helena giggled and left.

She immediately went to inform Stuart and Maude that the lot of them would be leaving in a day. Stuart would be glad, as he and his guards could not rest with so many strangers within the walls. Maude would be happy, as she and the rest of the staff had to bow and scrape to a bunch of pansy, ugly-faced, mealy-mouthed lechers. These being the same men the king referred to as retainers, followers, and friends. The rest of England referred to them as shiftless, lazy, and cheap! In a business like Helena's, where the aristocrats gathered en masse, these qualities were not uncommon. It was the abuse of hospitality, accompanied by the absence of payment. That made the entire household elated to see them leave.

Things became routine again and time flew. Two months later, Gabrielle was feeling a bit lonely, so she went to look for Maude. She found Maude in a heated discussion with Helena and decided to wait in the corridor until the conversation was over.

"How long before he is coming?" asked Maude.

"He will be here in three days. I knew this would get out of hand. But short of killing him, what was I to do?" shouted Helena.

"First of all, we have very little choice. We will simply wine him and dine him as usual," Maude firmly said.

"Yes, we will wine him and dine him. You just do not realize what a foul taste this leaves me with. If he didn't have the ability to create such problems, I would simply castrate him." Taking a deep breath, finally Helena smiled. "I am better now, sorry I screamed. It was just the tone of his letter. Demanding his usual reservation with the two eastern girls, Isthmus and Isis. And of course at the usual fee, FREE!!!"

"He will not hold the office forever," stated Maude. "Maybe then he can simply disappear."

"Oh Maude, if only that were true. Unfortunately, whether Deputy-Constable Muden is in office or not, he will continue to cause trouble!"

Maude replied, "We will find the evidence one day."

"That I will never receive the revenge I so richly deserve for myself is one thing. But I cannot give up until I find the proof I need that he was one of the traitors to the crown. I know in my heart he was one of those in league against my father."

Maude said, "Someday we may have the opportunity. For now, what are your instructions?"

Looking at his file she began naming things off. "Please make sure his room is ready for him. He will want Isthmus and Isis. Make sure there is plenty of gin in his room, we certainly don't want him roaming the hallways looking for more. He likes the color blue; please make sure he gets the blue room. Also he wants the girls dressed as roman slaves. No fresh fruit or flowers in his room, last time there was such a mess. He requests the honor of my presence, to dine with him, before his evening of pleasure." Helena rolled her eyes, "Can the cook arrange poison with the appetizers?"

Maude began to laugh. "Funny," she muttered. Helena stomped and hollered a little more, and then the conversation ended.

Maude came out of the doorway and was surprised to find Gabrielle. "What are you looking for, child?"

Gabrielle replied, "I was looking for you. I was feeling a little lonely and wanted company."

"Come, you can talk with me as I go," said Maude. So they continued their conversation as they walked along.

Later Gabrielle went up to her room, just as Kathleen was approaching her bedroom door. She invited Gabrielle to go to the baths and relax and chat. Of course after such a remarkable massage, they felt like limp dishrags. They didn't want to talk in front of anyone, so they ended up on the north terrace. Gabrielle loved the terrace and could be found there quite often. Just coming from the baths, they were in nightgowns and wrappers. Sitting under the stars, letting their hair dry, enjoying the gentle breeze and company of each other. Finally Kathleen broke the silence. "How are you adjusting?"

"I know my way around pretty well, though I still get lost about once a week. I really enjoy helping the children, but I don't find it fulfilling. I long to have a home, a household to run. I need to find answers to the questions filling my head."

"Are you still confused about men? Because I told you before, the easiest way to clear the rumors from the facts are to enter a viewing chamber. You can see for yourself what happens. It is actually easier than trying to explain to you again. I think Megan is in the harem tonight. That is a good one for viewing, do you want me to go with you?"

Gabrielle said, "As usual your thoughts are on men. I have plenty of questions about men, but I was talking about my father. I really don't have any idea what happened to him. I can't help but wonder if my aunt and her horrendous lover are still looking for me. I want to find my guardian and I am starting to get a little anxious. And you're right, living here, men are starting to be on my mind a lot and I'm still not sure I'm ready for it."

Kathleen smiled. "You will know when you are ready, because you won't ask, you will jump right in. You are also having these feelings not only because you are surrounded by all erotic things, but because as you grow these feelings are natural."

"Are you still missing Kevin?"

"He was the love of my life, but Helena has said that we all have one. I try not to think about him every minute anymore. I guess they are right when they say time will heal my heart. It's just that I truly believed he loved me and I do not usually fall for the lines men give. He seemed so sweet and genuine. He was a guard here. But he was really the son of a laird. Captured by enemies he was sold into bondage. He finally was able to convince Derek and afterwards was able to get proof and money to pay for his freedom." Here Kathleen sighed and lowered her voice. "I know it sounds funny, but I was his reward."

"You're right, it sounds funny. What do you mean?" asked Gabrielle

"Well, Helena felt so bad that she made him work until proof and payment arrived that she rewarded him with a week of fantasies. I just happened to be the recipient of his attention and at first I thought of him only as a customer. Then without warning he just sort of crept under my skin. Suddenly I couldn't get enough of the man. Even when his free time was up, he continued to pay for me, so we could be together."

"Kathleen, I hate to say it but if he was paying...."

"I know what you're thinking. I thought the same. I denied both the feelings I was having and his sincerity. He argued, cajoled, seduced, and demanded, until he had me believing we both really felt something. He is from Scotland and he had to travel to his home and promised to return for me when it was possible. I am not one to believe tall tales, yet he wore down my defenses and then finally even I believed it possible to be his wife. He was going to come back, but he never did. I will never let down my guard again, for he had me believing his soft-spoken words." Suddenly she changed the subject. "Now, let's talk of something else. Do you want to go to a viewing chamber now?"

"I guess I will not get you to leave me alone until I do. Fine, let's go."

Kathleen sputtered, "Really?"

"Yes, on to the harem!" So wrapped in robes and slippers, they descended the stairs. Kathleen informed Gabrielle that it would be a bit of a walk as they were headed over to the east wing. The harem was located there. They would stay in the servants' area as long as possible, and then discretely cover the short distance in the customer area. Silently darting down the steps, they went off on their adventure.

Sitting in the lounge area, waiting for the pretty girl from the front desk to return, sat a large, strikingly handsome, dark-haired man. Lord James Armstrong, Marquee of Scarborough, sipped his drink and relaxed. James was tall and broad-shouldered and even with his narrow hips, the chair he was sitting in was getting uncomfortable. So in an attempt to relax he stretched out his long legs, crossing them at the ankles. Traveling by horseback, at a breakneck speed, he had finally arrived. His coat had been taken and his boots cleaned upon entering, immediately earning his favor. James never wore a wig and seldom bothered having his hair powdered. Now that fashions had changed, he was actually in style. Therefore, his thick, black shoulder-length hair was tied back with a ribbon. He wore no cravat, just a simple white lawn shirt, open at the neck. From both the damp weather and the bulging muscles, his tan breeches seemed molded to his thighs. He folded his hands across his waist and rested for a moment.

It had been a long ride and he was very tired. As far as anyone was concerned, he was simply here as a customer. Because his father was Donald

Armstrong, the Duke of York, his family was well known. In reality he was not here to assuage his baser instincts, instead his reasons were twofold. The first reason was to serve as escort for a friend. The second, a totally unrelated mission, he was trying to ferret out information on a Sheriff Muden.

Instead of being a wastrel, as so many of the children of the ton were prone to do, James had decided to buy a military commission. After several campaigns, with endless waiting, poor decisions and countless lives lost, he bid farewell to the military. Needing another outlet to feed his restlessness, James was soon dabbling in espionage. As heir to a dukedom, he was hardly in the position to be a government spy. However, he had the next best thing, a friend in the business.

Lucas Fenwick was already a spy for the government. They had met in the military with Lucas under James' command. James knew he was honest and dependable, someone he would trust with his life. But when Lucas first came up with the ridiculous idea of having James help him, he immediately shot it down. Coercion, bullying and bribery had all failed to sway James.

However, boredom soon set in. Attending balls, parties, clubs, hunts and women were all that filled his days. None of these amusements kept James interested, none challenged his mind. Grudgingly, James agreed to help on a case Lucas was working on. At the conclusion, Fenwick declared, James had been a huge asset. It was agreed to enlist James' sporadic aid. Though James was never able to receive any recognition when a case was solved, that was fine with him. He had never been after the adulation. He simply thrived on the risks and challenges accompanying every case. This unusual partnership provided James the opportunity for the adventure he craved and Lucas the support of the silent partner he needed. It was a win-win situation for them both. His superiors were amazed at how diligent Lucas was. Never giving up until the case was solved. They would never know James repeatedly helped with the legwork.

It was all very simple. James could go places Lucas would never have access to. James' cover was actually his real life. He put on airs when necessary, acted rude when it wasn't. He whored, drank and gambled with the ton's most elite. He was a rake and a scoundrel, yet his presence was always in demand. He was popular with both the men and women of society. The men appreciated his opinions and humor, the women his looks and title. Commoners respected him because of his rank, but liked him because of his fairness. No one ever suspected him of spying to uncover crimes.

Adding another unusual piece to the puzzle was the unique closeness of his family. His parents had been a love match and continued to remain entirely devoted. The relationship with his brothers was constant and inseparable. Sharing many escapades of their own, they remained fiercely loyal. Unlike most of his acquaintances, there was no bitterness or jealousy because he was the heir. The Armstrong wealth was vast and each man was financially secure in his own right. The Armstrong family tree was huge, with titles of nobility in abundance. Though the heir always inherited the family title, the ancestral home and the bulk of the fortune. There were plenty of titles to pass round, from generation to generation.

All the Armstrong men were healthy, virile and good-looking. All were similar in size, height, and coloring. In fact, the three brothers, Jared, Jake and James, were all known to turn the ladies' heads, especially when they accompanied each other. Jared's features were finely chiseled, James with the cleft in his chin and Jake's dimple gave them all something distinguishing. Yet they all had dark brooding looks that even dimples did not soften. However, it was when they smiled that their true characters emerged. Smiles made the Armstrong men look friendly and approachable.

James knew his escapades with his friend Lucas would only continue until he inherited the title. While he remained a carefree bachelor, he was available for any unplanned event. However, once he inherited the title, not only would it bring him the extra responsibilities of marriage and children. It would also include the added burden of overseeing all the properties under his domain. His father often complained of the huge undertaking it entailed. Therefore, before all the obligations of a dukedom fell in his lap, he intended to enjoy every minute. With luck on his side, his father would be around for many years, thus allowing him to continue disappearing on mysterious adventures and chasing women.

While sitting there, James suddenly saw something dart from one statue in the hallway to another. His mind must be playing tricks! No, there it went again. In an instant, he was alert. However, he remained in the same position, giving little indication on the outside that he was now poised and ready for action. Looking out the doorway and down the marble hallway, his vantage point was perfect. Hanging oil lamps lit the way, burning low, providing soft light and shadows. As the first person moved from their hiding place, he realized it was a well-endowed, red-headed woman. Still in the shadows, it was a moment later that the second person, also a woman, moved on to join the first. The second girl was much smaller than the first, with long sable hair. Sneaking from statue to statue, one behind the other, they silently advanced up the dimly lit hallway. When they came to the end of the corridor the girls were so close if he had stood up in the doorway he could have touched them. He smiled at the picture they formed. Their flimsy attire seemed molded to their bodies, while their untied wrappers flapped behind them as they ran. They looked dressed for some man's fantasy in such nightwear.

It was when they were about to reach the wide staircase at the end of the hall that the second girl turned and looked over her shoulder.

The beginning of the stairway was flooded with light, streaming from the lounge doorway, creating an inky black darkness beyond.

Stopping directly in the path of the light, he could see her clearly. At that same instant he was gazing at her, she was looking directly at him and their eyes met. They each seemed frozen in place for just a moment. Each of them intent on memorizing every detail of the other's face and form. She was a rare jewel. He had never been so quickly attracted to a woman before. His heart began to pound. He closed his eyes and shook his head. He opened his eyes a moment later, but no one was there.

He stood up and stretched, he must have been mistaken. Maybe he had dozed off. With no one around and no explanation, he paid little attention to the racing of his heart. He walked up to the bar and got another drink. Just as he turned, the girl who had admitted him approached. She motioned for him to follow her, so he did.

He was guided straight to Helena's office, where Helena was introduced to him. Helena was as beautiful as he had heard. She was a voluptuous, raven-haired, creamy-skinned woman. Though he knew it was fashionable, he smiled at her artistically styled hair, piled so high. Her sultry eyes were a cobalt blue and her voice melodious. She made him as comfortable as possible and offered him a drink. She went on to explain that they had run into a bit of a problem. The woman he had requested for the evening was already booked. As they had no notice he was coming and no advance request, there was little they could do. These things happened here. Three solutions were possible. One, pick someone else to share the evening with. Two, leave and come back tomorrow. Three, stay, have a message, and then spend the night in one of her guest chambers. While he decided which offer best suited him, they traded compliments and conversation for about thirty minutes. At which time he explained he was really too tired to ride out and back again. Nor did he feel he was up to nighttime activities, being as exhausted as he was. The massage and sleep sounded too good to be true. So Helena rang for a servant girl who first showed him to his room, then to the baths.

Meanwhile Kathleen and Gabrielle had made their way up the stairs and to the Harem Viewing Chamber. Thankfully the sconce on the wall was unlit, indicating it was empty. Kathleen held up her taper, using her candle to light the one upon the wall. Quickly and silently they entered. Pulling the curtain aside they stood near the windows watching a veil dance in progress. Below them exotic drapery, creating the allure of a Turkish tent, fell from ceiling to floor. The dimly lit room was filled with the smell of burning incense. There were piles and piles of huge cushions scattered about the room. In the corner, behind a large dressing screen, sat several musicians. Romantic lighting, soft music and heady aromas blended together to create the perfect exotic illusion for romance. There were many women, all assorted shapes and sizes. All dressed in colorful sheer outfits, wearing row upon row of beaded jewels and all barefoot. The sound of tinkling bells floated through the room. The customer was watching all the girls and trying to choose the ones he liked best. He walked among his own little harem of women, sometimes kissing or touching them, then discarding those he did not like. "I would never be able to get my body to move like that," whispered Gabrielle as her eyes remained glued to the belly dancer.

Kathleen whispered right back, "Megan can teach you."

"Do you know anything about this dance? Oh, gosh! He just ripped a scarf off her outfit."

Kathleen whispered again, "This is the Veil Dance. The customer has requested this. If he pulls a scarf out from a girl's outfit, she is a chosen woman for the evening. She will do the veil dance for him. Sometimes there is one dancer, sometimes more. It all depends on the customer and how many women he wishes. That is how the choice is made, if you have not been chosen, you do not do the dance and he will not sleep with you that evening. Sometimes men are greedy and pick several women, most usually pick two. Sometimes they only pick one woman. This customer has now narrowed the choices down to only one woman. Watch closely. As she dances he will pull out each and every scarf. Observe how she dances close, then darts away, then close again. She is teasing him."

As the girl continued to weave a spell of enchantment, the tempo changed. It seemed as though the music matched the rhythm of the dance. Slow, and then fast. Fast, then slow. It also seemed like Gabrielle was breathing to the same beat.

"She is only to touch him if he allows it. In this fantasy he alone is master. Hear that? She wears tiny bells around her ankle. Soon that is all she will be left wearing. He will take his time, taking off the veils. As she dances, she entices him. As he stalls, he prolongs the enjoyment. After all the veils have been removed, she is naked and he is hot. By the time she has him naked he is anxious to have his way with her. This goes on, reaching a fevered frenzy, until passion consumes them. Often he will take the woman again, if that is his wish. He may send her back and pick another from the harem, beginning yet again. There are many choices throughout the evening. Sometimes the men couple with the chosen one on the floor in front of the others. Occasionally he will want privacy and pull her off to the side upon the divan. Either way intimacy is guaranteed. The fantasy continues as long as the customer wishes. Later, those girls standing near the pillar, in the corner, will provide nourishment."

"Oh! He just took off the scarf that was across her bosom. She is smaller than I am!" whispered Gabrielle, grinning.

"I didn't know you were concerned. You have really developed since you have come here. As you get older, your body will change. You are at just the age that all these changes will occur. Besides, you are hardly small!"

"I am not big!"

"No, but you are not small."

"Yes, but you are huge."

"Yes, I am," laughed Kathleen. "You will soon stop complaining, though. As I know that the size of your new chemise is larger than your last. You are growing, as you should. Are you in a hurry for a man?"

"I think I am in a hurry for myself." As an afterthought she added, "What do you mean, you know my chemise is a larger size?"

"Not many secrets around here," she grinned.

Gabrielle gazed back down at the room in front of them. "What the heck does she have on her chest?"

"Those are gems that cover her nipples. There is a tiny, clear thread holding them in place. Of course, you can't see them. So it appears to simply cover the nipple. It hangs around her neck and is also secured around her bosom. Yet you can't see the threads and the illusion it creates is great! Look at her navel. That stone matches the ones on her nipples. You won't believe this, but her stomach muscles are so strong, they alone hold the stone in place. She once told me the stone is small as a young girl begins her lessons. As she practices and her muscles develop they begin adding larger stones. Finally a beautiful gem, the size of her navel is placed inside. It is hers to keep when she reaches maturity and no longer requires training. Watch how she dances, the lights, the fire, the music. Everything works together to get him excited." Pulling chairs closer to the window they sat down and quietly watched. The rhythm of the dancer's body, the music, the aroma from the burning candles, all creating a sensual atmosphere. Her hips swaying to the tempo, showing more and more skin as the veils are removed. At one point, the customer must have sent the other girls off someplace, because they ceased to be noticed. The music played faster and faster and Megan danced faster and faster. After the last veil came off, she stopped and bowed before him. He laughed and grabbed her in his arms and began kissing her. After he kissed her a bit, he carried her over to the cushioned area, near the terrace. He cradled the dancer in his arms and immediately began to cover her body with his own. A long groan was heard, over the music. Their gyrating bodies could be seen and the moans and squeals heard. However the distance was too far to be seen closely. When he had finished, he rolled over and began to snore. It was only then that Gabrielle realized she had been holding her breath. She felt unsatisfied and naïve. Even though she had watched the event unfold, this mating thing was still a mystery. She felt slightly angry and very confused. Still, being a voyeur had a certain erotic appeal, which appeased her somewhat. She turned to Kathleen and said, "We'd better get going, the morning comes quickly.

"Isn't that like a man, to have his pleasure and fall asleep!" laughed Kathleen. "You're right, we might as well go, not much is going to happen anymore. She will have to wait for him to wake up to continue any activities. What did you think?" she questioned as they put out the candle and exited the room.

"I'm not really sure. I feel a bit tingly and brazen. I know I've viewed something I shouldn't have and feel somewhat guilty. Although it was different than I imagined," said Gabrielle.

"It always is. Let's get back. You really should have her teach you, it is not as hard as it looks."

"Have you done it?"

"Yes, but for some reason I do not seem as graceful." Laughing, Kathleen said, "Let's hurry."

As they made their way back to their sleeping quarters, they almost ran straight into Helena and Polly. Suddenly, without warning, a hand was covering Gabrielle's mouth and an arm was pulling her inside the nearest doorway. "Any idea where she might be?" asked Helena.

"You saw as well as I, the chart said she is off duty tonight. It certainly didn't say anything about using any of the rooms or leaving the premises. She could be anywhere," was Polly's reply. "By the way, I don't like the black wig you're wearing today, black makes you seem sickly."

"I like the red one best and I do not look sick or pale, but creamy and white."

"Oh, and sure you do," Polly laughed.

"The man I saw earlier tonight said I looked beautiful."

"Sure and don't they all?"

Ignoring Polly's comment, Helena continued, "Let's look a while longer, she has to be someplace."

Standing inside the doorway both girls had their ears glued to the door. Their hearts were beating a mile a minute. They both looked at each other at the same time and whispered, "The chart!" After what they thought was enough time to be safe, they looked at each other.

"I do not want to empty those damn slop buckets!! Do you have any idea how many water closets and chamber pots we have here?" screeched Kathleen.

"It seems like the only way to get out of it, is for you to say you fell asleep in my room. But before you can explain anything, we have to somehow get back there, without getting caught," whispered Gabrielle. "Any ideas?"

"I guess the only thing to do is to move fast. I'll go first; do you remember your way back? Because I think it will be better to separate. I'll go first, in case they find me. After all, they aren't even looking for you."

Gabrielle smiled. "I'm pretty sure I can find my way back."

"Never mind, we'll just have to take our chances. Let's go."

"No, I'll be fine. I think you were right the first time. We should go separately. Will we really be in so much trouble for merely forgetting to put down where we were?" asked Gabrielle.

"I will be. You have not been here long enough to know better, so chances are for you it would just be a warning. Haven't you heard the speech often enough? Kathleen began to mimic Polly. "We simply do not have time to look for everyone, it is up to the individual to keep us apprised of their location at all times. The rules apply to everyone. Even Helena must have her whereabouts known as a problem could arise at any given moment. In order to run efficiently we must be in constant contact … blah, blah, blah."

"I'm sure they would understand, just this once. We simply forgot."

"Please believe me when I tell you I'm not overreacting. You will probably get something like kitchen duties. But I tell you, they always give me slop pots, because they know I hate it so. It's to try to rid me of my evil habits. Now we have to get out of here. I'll slip out this door, and get to your room. You wait at least ten minutes, and then follow. Try not to get lost, that would not be good for either of us. I'm going, be careful." And out the door she went, leaving Gabrielle all alone.

Chapter 6

It seemed like hours had already passed, but Gabrielle knew it hadn't yet been five minutes. Then without warning came a sound from behind her, "Mmmmmmmmmmmm." Gabrielle's hair on the back of her neck stood up. She could feel the goose bumps on her skin multiplying. She slowly turned her head in response but the room had very little lighting and it was hard to focus. She couldn't see anyone. Perhaps she was mistaken. Maybe it had been a noise from the other side of the door. She turned back to the door, lightly pressing her ear against it. The silence on the other side urged her forward. Just as she reached to open it and peek into the hallway, she was once again startled by a strange sound coming from behind her. "Mmmmmmmmmmm." Suddenly she couldn't seem to move or breathe. Her heart was racing and she began to shake with fear. She silently stood there trying to calm down. After what again seemed like ages, she turned and tried to look about the room. Her eyes had adjusted to the lack of light so she inched slowly forward. The sound of trickling water accompanied by a slight echo confirmed her location to be a bathing chamber. She didn't remember exactly which one. Walking deeper into the room she exercised great caution. The sconce on the far wall across the room was burning, emitting only a small circle of dim light. Still she didn't see anyone about so reaching the first alcove, she peeked within. A small candle burned on the table in the corner, providing a soft glow yet the room remained shadowed. A faint movement caught her eyes. There was someone lying on the massage table! She stood paralyzed wondering what to do, when he moaned again. "Mmmmmmm."

She realized with relief, it appeared the customer was fast asleep. She turned to leave, when the candle flickered brightly for a moment, causing her to notice his face. It was the handsome man she had seen earlier, while sneaking up to the viewing chamber. What was he doing here? Why was he alone? As she gazed at him, she instinctively moved closer. Passing through the sheer gauze curtain she inched forward. He was more than handsome, he was perfect. She stepped even closer. Standing next to the massage table, looking at him lying there in all his naked glory, she simply stared. His dark hair fell loosely, curling slightly at the base of his neck. His shoulders were firm and wide, his muscles rippled down his torso. His bum was firm, yet paler than the rest of him. His legs were thick and long, and also a lighter shade than his upper body. His back and arms were golden, his hair black and wet.

She couldn't have stopped herself if she had tried, without warning her hands began to touch him. Careful not to wake him, at first her hands felt as she felt: shy. Then as he continued to sleep, she felt a bit safer. It was as though her hands expressed her feelings becoming bolder, more curious. She touched, stroked and massaged. His skin was not soft like her own, but firm and muscular. He had little hairs on his legs and bum. She was simply mesmerized by the shape and contour of his body. She couldn't seem to get enough of just touching him. Silently his body seemed to dare her to recklessness. She ran her hands along the contours of every inch of him, trembling from the temptation. After trying to drag herself away from him for the second time, she finally stopped and turned to leave. As she turned, the man's hand grabbed her arm. "Don't leave without kissing me good-bye," his husky voice muttered. Gabrielle concluded he must think she was the same girl who had massaged him earlier. Still, no matter what he thought, she was not experienced enough to know what to do. She was still standing there trying to decide, when he yanked her forward. Pulling her closer and turning his body sideways at the same time, their lips met. At first it was a simple touching of their lips, then the tip of his tongue ran along her bottom lip. Suddenly he pushed his tongue inside her mouth and reached around her shoulder with his other arm. She froze at first and was not quite certain of what to do. Yet as his tongue probed and his lips crushed hers, she simply leaned in and melted against his hard chest. Later, all coherent thought was gone, as her tongue sparred with his and demanded as much from him as he demanded from her. Several moments later he slowed down and began to nibble her lips. Then with a tender kiss on the lips, he simply turned back over and seemed to go back to sleep. Gabrielle stood there in shock; convinced her inexperience had caused him to turn away. Then embarrassment set in. As she stood trying to get her emotions under control shame turned to excitement. She didn't understand her own churning feelings, she didn't even know if she had kissed him correctly. But this man had touched her as no other and she didn't even know his name. Anger mixed with her emotions before she knew what was happening. Was she upset that he kissed her or that he stopped? Her feelings were all a jumble as she backed out of the room. Finally pulling herself together, she made her way towards the door. If she didn't know who he was, then he didn't know who she was. Maybe that was for the better. Her heart was racing, her lips were tingling and her mind was confused. She was a mess and she still had to get back safely. She wasn't even sure she could think, let alone maneuver her way back. Yet she didn't have a choice, so after making sure the hallway was clear, she quietly escaped.

After the door closed, James looked up. He still couldn't believe the same beautiful woman he had seen earlier running through the corridors had simply appeared in his bath. When the two girls had first come in and huddled near the door, he realized they were hiding from someone. He had been in the process of putting on his robe and going back to his room when they had barged in. He had simply tossed his robe aside and lain back down on the table to watch the events unfold. After the first woman left, he couldn't help but to have a little fun with the second. It wasn't until she had come into the candlelight that he had recognized her. When that had happened he wanted her to come closer, lest he lose her in this large castle. So he made a few more noises. It drew her attention all right. Who knew she would so skillfully maneuver his desires. Who could have figured she would play his body like a violin. When she had finished massaging him, he just couldn't bear to have her walk out on him without kissing her. As she had begun to move away he had grabbed her and demanded a kiss. Again, who could have ever imagined the sheer perfection of that kiss? Though she had acted timid at first, she progressed quickly enough. Then those hesitant kisses had turned demanding. He would have her! James had thought to coerce her, but he suddenly remembered that was her job. So he pretended to fall asleep to irk her into outrageous behavior. Instead she had used the opportunity to flee. She was a delight and as he licked his lips he could still taste her. Slipping on his robe and walking down the hallway to his room, his mind was churning. Damn! He had forgotten to get her name. Oh well, it would add mystery to the adventure. After all, he was well trained, how hard would it be to find her?

Running all the way, Gabrielle's breath sounded ragged. Her heart was pounding so loud she thought everyone could hear. Up and down all those steps, through all those hallways, her bare feet slapping against the stone and marble floors as she ran. She was exhausted, lasting only on sheer will power. Almost there, she had made it on instinct alone because she was simply not capable of rational thought. Finally she reached her floor, found her door and slipped inside. Kathleen was pacing within. "I was just about to come find you!" whispered Kathleen, running to her and hugging her fiercely. She stood back a moment and looked at Gabrielle. "Something's wrong, what happened?"

"No, nothing is wrong, I'm fine." Trying to slow her heavy breathing she muttered, "I ran most of the way, I'm just out of breath."

"You're lying, it's not just the running. I can tell you're upset"

"I do need to talk to you about something, but I need to sleep first. Trust me when I tell you nothing is wrong. We can talk in the morning." Needing to keep her thoughts to herself a little longer, she moved over to the bed and turned down the covers.

"All right, sleep first, then we talk. You're sure you're fine?" she said as she hopped into bed.

Gabrielle smiled, "I have never been better, now move over." They both drifted off to sleep.

Unfortunately the next morning they did not get to have their talk, because they overslept. They were running down the hall and trying to get to the kitchens before they had to go their separate ways for the day. When Polly spotted them she demanded that Kathleen stay with her and Gabrielle continue on her way. So having little choice Gabrielle continued on. Polly asked, "Where were you last night, Kathleen?"

"I went to Gabrielle's room last night for a chat and ended up falling asleep there. Why, did you need me for something? I was off duty on the chart, wasn't I?" Kathleen asked in false alarm.

"Yes, you were marked off duty. However, something came up and I was looking for you and couldn't find you. I thought perhaps you had gone somewhere and not written it down. Anyway, a customer came in last night and requested you. As we couldn't find you, we had to come up with an alternative. Make sure you stay close at hand today, Helena may need you. I forgot to look, where will you be today?"

"I am working on the first floor today, in the sailor's fantasy. It's my turn to be the mermaid. If you need me, I should be done by dinner. Who was the customer that was looking for me?"

"Can't say as I know him, some gent named Armstrong."

"I'm not sure I recognize the name, maybe I'll recognize the body. I'm open tonight if he needs me."

Polly said, "I'll make sure Helena knows. I'm glad you weren't getting in trouble last night. Nothing I like less than hearing you scream about slop buckets!" She turned and walked left the room, her laughter following behind.

Kathleen hurried on to the kitchens. She found Gabrielle at a table and hurried to fill a plate and join her. "Well, our plan worked!"

"What do you mean?" asked Gabrielle

"Our plan to say I fell asleep in your room. I've been interrogated and she accepted my answers. Now on to you, what happened last night?"

Gabrielle took a moment, then rushed headlong into her story. "I was waiting for ten minutes to be up, when I heard a strange noise coming from inside the room I was in. I couldn't leave quite yet, and was afraid if I didn't check it out, I'd get caught. So I carefully walked about the room, did you know we were in one of the baths?"

"Yes, and that is one of the more opulent baths. Most of the ornaments are gold and the cushions on the massage tables are a cinnamon color. It is one of the few baths with heated floors and its own water closet. The cushions in that room match the marble. It is gorgeous!" stated Kathleen

"Never mind the description," interrupted Gabrielle. "I just wondered if you knew. Anyway, I went to investigate the noise, and you will never guess what I saw."

"People coupling?"

"No, a naked man. And not just any naked man, the most handsome man I have ever seen."

"Do you think because you have watched one sexual encounter and saw a naked man that you are able to judge that he is the most handsome? I have seen hundreds of naked men and my Kevin still puts all of them to shame," said Kathleen, completely off the subject.

"You can't keep calling him your Kevin. You have to get over him. How were you going to limit yourself to just one man? How were you going to make him believe that you could?"

"I could limit myself to one man because he is the only man I have ever given my heart to. I didn't have to convince him because he loved me also. Though I have a scandalized past, he too has led a philandering lifestyle. If we had been able to marry, we would have had a fine future together. I just can't believe he would leave me without some kind of explanation. Now see what you did? You got off the conversation about your pip-squeak of a man, and got me talking about my mountain of a man!" she said sadly.

"I didn't get off the subject, you did. You simply won't believe me when I tell you I have seen the most perfect specimen ever! Anyway, that's not all."

"You did more than look?"

"I can't explain it, suddenly I was touching him," squealed Gabrielle

"Oh, my gosh! I can't believe it. Shy Gabrielle was experimenting with some guy last night. I can't believe it!"

"That's not all!"

"There is more?"

"He kissed me."

"I can't believe it!"

"Then he fell asleep"

"Now that I can believe. All right, I need details. What happened?"

"I can't really understand it myself. One minute I'm simply looking at a handsome, naked man. The next, my body had a mind of its own and I'm massaging him. Oh, I could have done that forever, I never felt so connected to anyone. I don't know how long I stood there, just stroking him. Finally I tore myself away and turned to leave. He demanded a kiss, reached up, kissed me. To me it was perfect. I had a floating sort of feeling and wished it would last for hours. Then, before I knew what was happening, he turned over and went to sleep. Do you think I did something wrong?"

"No, I think he was probably exhausted. He probably had a few drinks, a leisurely massage and then fell asleep. He was probably hazy, thought you were the girl that massaged him and grabbed a kiss and fell asleep. That's a typical gent. Which by the way proves my point, your man may be fine but my man is perfect. He would never fall asleep!"

"No, your man doesn't fall asleep. He just doesn't come back for you. And he's not my man. I don't have men. We didn't even talk."

"Well, that may have been for the best. Maybe if you're starting to be interested in men, you should have Helena move you from the school room?"

"I'm not interested in men. I'm interested in one man. And Helena already decided to move me, I told you last week. Today I start work in the costume room. Why didn't you tell me men kiss with their tongues?"

"I did tell you. You probably were not listening at the time. Sometimes even having the correct information doesn't prepare you. Knowing or watching, is very different from participating. Once your senses are involved, everything has a magical effect. Just don't go falling for him, or you'll feel like I do when he leaves! Did he use his tongue for anything else?"

"I told you, we only kissed."

"I'm just checking. Are you going to try to find him again before he leaves?"

"I don't think so. It was just a wonderful fantasy. Oh, my gosh! I just realized! This is why I didn't understand when we were in the viewing chamber. I didn't understand the passion of the fantasy. Now I do!"

"Why didn't you tell me you were confused?"

"I was going to, but so much happened on the way back."

"Well, now you have had your first sensual experience. Let's see how long it is before you want another."

"Do you think I should tell the mistress I'm ready for a man?"

"Let's wait, you're still very new to all this. And as you said, you have only been attracted to one man. We can change things later."

"You know, maybe we can find him again, I sure wouldn't mind."

"What if he is with one of the other girls?"

"Well, it will be very hard not to be jealous. That he would be with someone else when I have such desperate feelings for him."

"Men are men and usually have other women," shrugged Kathleen.

"My father promised me a love match and I will not settle for a man that has a mistress. I want a man to love me for me. I guess I'm foolish to think I could fall for a man that comes to a brothel. I will control my feelings until I leave, then I will look for someone to love. I still think I would like to see him again. If only to say good-bye."

"Often you sound very mature, yet in this instance you sound very immature. You will not be able to control your feelings. Love is an arrow to the heart. Once it has been sent, it will hit. Once it hits, it consumes you with passion or pain."

Gabrielle grumbled, "Aren't you the psychological one today?"

"I am practical. Though you are right to try to control your curiosity about this man. Soon he will be gone and you will be glad to still be a virgin. After all, when you find your guardian, you will still be able to set a secure marriage. We'd better get going; I'll see you tonight. Unless the customer who was looking for me last night shows up, then I won't be around till tomorrow. Are you sure your going to be all right? You won't go looking for him without me, will you?"

"I'll be fine, and no, I won't look for my temptation."

"Good, I'll see you later. Unless I have to entertain that customer."

"Is that why they were looking for you?"

"Yes, and let me tell you, we are both very lucky not to have been caught. Polly could hardly stop laughing about the slop buckets that are always waiting for me."

"See you tonight then," Gabrielle answered as she cleared her place.

At that same time Helena was pacing her floor. "Maude, do you and Polly believe her?"

"Yes, it was a simple matter of a night off, spent with a friend," answered Polly.

"They are not prisoners," Maude muttered.

"I understand that, but there is nothing I hate more than looking incompetent. When you can't find a simple maid for a customer, I look foolish. This establishment is one of the most elite and organized businesses of its kind. I never want to look incapable to the customers."

"That is not what happened," said Maude

"Fine, you see it your way, I see it mine. Just make sure to remind the girls to mark the chart every time they go somewhere."

"What is on the agenda today?"

"The list of customers due to arrive this afternoon, is on the table over there," Helena said, pointing. I have a beautiful new gown for the costume ball tonight. Tomorrow I have to deal with the sheriff, but tonight I dance!" laughed Helena. They sat and discussed arrangements and fashions. They had breakfast and then both left to carry on different duties.

Meanwhile Lord Armstrong was sitting on his terrace, having breakfast. Neither the girl in the flimsy dress with an abundance of bosom they sent to dress him nor the young maid that brought the food had appealed to him. Both had offered to give him generous attention, but he just couldn't get his mind off the girl from last night. A knock at the door caused his thoughts to vanish. "Enter."

"I'm here to give you a message, sir," said the servant.

"Please come in."

"Mistress Helena says your gel will be ready after supper if you still want to see her. She also says to tell you that as last night was free, tonight is full price. She says if you need to see her, she is available any time. Or if you need someone else before tonight, to send for her and she will take care of it. Otherwise you are free to roam the gardens, the first floor and the lounge. You're to remember the rest of the castle is off limits, as other fantasies are in progress. Do you need anything else, sir?"

"No, that will be all, thank you." He returned to his thoughts. What a fabulous place this was! The girl from the previous evening had been thoroughly trained. He wondered what sort of schooling they had to have to be so perfect. Never had he ever lost his train of thought while with a woman. She had totally bewitched him. However, the only way to get a woman out of your head was to take her to bed. So maybe today while he was waiting for one woman he would spend the day with another. He should have brought his brothers with him for this little adventure. They would have loved it!

Now, how was he going to find this little doe of his? He finished his breakfast and put on his boots. Everything from his hat to his boots had been thoroughly cleaned while he had been in the bath last night. He had stayed at inns that didn't offer such accommodations. This was one hell of a place! So he dressed and went on a tour of the castle. As he walked through a few of the hallways, he thought it very similar to his ancestral home. With the amount of people he knew they must have throughout the castle, it seemed too calm and serene. After wandering the castle and not running into the girl in question, he ended up in the gardens. As he was sitting on a bench enjoying the view, a pretty young maid came up to him and asked if he would like something to drink. He laughed out loud and nearly frightened the poor girl to death. He ordered both a hard cider and a sweet Virginia cigar. "How ridiculous I was to have thought no one would notice my roaming about," he muttered. When the young girl came back, he asked her, "Why is it, with all the people in this castle, it seems so empty?"

"I don't know what you mean, sir."

"Where is everyone?"

"Everyone is doing their job, my lord."

"The place seems so quiet."

"Everyone is busy getting ready for the ball. The great costume ball Helena throws for her birthday every year. By tonight, we will be full to capacity. So if it's other people your wanting to see, the place will be very crowded. Are you staying?"

"Well, well. A costume ball you say, that would be great fun. But where do I get a costume?"

"You can go up to wardrobe. I'm sure they can fit you for a costume. Do you want to follow me? I can take you there."

Wanting the opportunity to observe and contemplate, he replied, "Let me sit here a while and enjoy the view. Why don't you come back in an hour?"

"Sure, my lord, an hour it is."

So James sat and sipped his cider, smoked his sweet cigar and admired the view. He wanted to go to the ball but he was to meet and give his message to the girl tonight. Maybe he could combine his activities and request that she attend the ball with him. In that manner, he could also look for the beautiful dark-haired woman that held him captivated.

"If you would just hold still a moment, I can finish this hem," muttered Gabrielle.

"I have to be in the bridal chamber in five minutes. My groom will be most upset if I'm late," screeched Wilimena.

"I am very sorry, but as you can see, everything here is chaos. I am doing the best I can." She finished her dress with just a few more strokes. When she had finished, Wilimena jumped off the stool and tore down the hall.

"I'm sorry your first day in here is so crazy. With the ball tonight and the usual amount of fantasies to provide for, we are just swamped. I can't tell you how much all your extra help means to me. But why don't you run down and grab a bite to eat? When you get back, we'll tackle that dragon costume," said Vivian, the head seamstress.

"You would think she was really getting married, the way she was

81

acting," muttered Gabrielle.

"I don't think she is as excited for the wedding as she is for the wedding night, if you understand my meaning," replied Viv.

"Yes, I guess I do. They get so excited about lying with a man, any man. How can that be fulfilling?"

"It is all they have. There is no prince coming to take them to a life of luxury. There is no man, no home, and no family. They are faced with a dose of reality early in life, knowing they can work in this profession only as long as their beauty and figure remains intact. When they can no longer attract customers, the flow of coins stops. With their chosen lifestyle, they are fortunate to live here. Within our home, other positions are provided for women as they grow older. I myself used to sleep with men." At Gabrielle's wide-eyed stare Vivian nodded before continuing, "I was young and agile, completely enjoying the rapture found in the arms of men. Yet as I grew older, the swelling in my joints caused me to refrain from my favorite pastime. The pain was excruciating. Several years ago, I was lucky to be traveling this way when our conveyance broke down. We had to impose upon Helena's hospitality. While awaiting repairs, Helena and I became aquatinted. She explained her vision to me and I shared my past with her. She talked me into staying on to help. Now I am part of a home and a business, both giving me the opportunity to pass on my knowledge, feel as though I am contributing and grow old gracefully. For I am not only a very competent seamstress, I also teach classes in the art of eroticism to the young girls. I can't tell you how fortunate I was to land here. For my destiny was bleak until I arrived here." She stopped short, coughed, continued, "We got off track a bit," she muttered.

"I think the reason the girls get so worked up, while participating in a fantasy, is because it is a wonderful way to forget reality, in the arms of a man. It is an opportunity to experience happiness, even if they have to pretend. It may last only for a little while, but the joy may stay with them much longer. And then, there is always tomorrow and a new fantasy to experience. Gabrielle, do not ponder upon it so. Most of us just take one day at a time, thinking no further than that. Not of our actions, nor their rewards or consequences. We simply get up and see what the day brings." Changing the conversation, she huffed, "Now go have lunch!"

"That would be wonderful, I'm so hungry. Thank you for your patience with me today, I feel as though I'm all thumbs. Thank you also for trying to help me understand life here." She wandered out the room and down to the kitchens for lunch. As she took her leave, Vivian wondered to herself, just how long such a sweet, innocent, would remain untarnished....

With unlucky timing, just as she was sitting downstairs eating in the kitchens, James appeared in the wardrobe room looking for a costume. He patiently waited while the three people ahead of him were serviced. The seamstress, kneeling on the floor, motioned for him to come nearer. Hollering, "Next!" she seemed a bit impatient as James explained to her, that not only would he need alterations, he also required a costume. Viv took the time to explain that with the ball being tonight, costumes were high in demand and low in stock. All that was left now for the male patrons were soldier uniforms or roman togas. Choosing the soldier uniform, Vivian ushered him into a corner to change as she continued with the others in line. Approximately eleven women were busy with alterations as Vivian belted out orders. Standing behind the screen he suddenly laughed at both the outfit and the circumstances. Having really been a soldier, he smirked at the idea of a man in battle wearing this uniform, admitting to himself that the outfit was simply for dancing and parading around in. He decided, rather than make a fuss, he could wear the costume, though it made him look like a toy soldier. Finding a lull in the line, he again waited for a fitting. Just as Vivian was adjusting the fit of his trousers, Gabrielle rounded the corner. With pins in her mouth and her eyes on her sewing Vivian did not see her enter. Likewise, the man she was fitting. Recognizing the man immediately, Gabrielle entered unseen. Hiding behind the nearby screen, she positioned herself to watch and listen.

"I am very grateful you had a costume left at all. I appreciate your taking the time to fit me," said James.

"Oh, it's my job. Besides, it's the only opportunity I'm given these days to handle such good-looking men such as yourself," replied Vivian, running her hand up his thick thigh.

Ignoring the blatant handling, he continued, "Will you be attending the ball tonight?"

"Oh no, sir, I'm much too old now to entice the men. Besides, I have too many last-minute things to handle here. We have been real shorthanded lately, so I have much to do. Have you picked out your date for the evening?"

"I have indeed," James assured her.

"You sound most excited."

"I am. I have not been drawn so to any woman in a long time." Thinking about the raven-haired beauty from the night before, he continued, "Usually after a night or two, I lose interest. But just recently I decided I've been too busy working, with not enough leisure time. So I'm going to stay a few days and see what happens." He smiled.

As he smiled, it warmed his whole face and Vivian drew in a sharp breath. From two different locations, both women could not help but admire his blatant sexuality, handsomeness and charm. Each was mesmerized and responded with a smile in return. After letting out his topcoat a bit, he was ready. She smoothed the top of his shoulders and ran her hand down his back. Everything lay flat and the cut of the jacket was perfect. She picked up her sewing basket as she stood up. "Have a wonderful time tonight."

"I intend to." Searching for information, he inquired, "Will everyone be at the ball tonight, excepting yourself of course?"

"Everyone that isn't already in someone else's fantasy. Of course the servants don't attend, they will be busy dealing with both the party and the fantasies. Everyone is always busy here. I guess most of the girls will be there and that's what you're really asking isn't it?" Though he didn't know her name, even her black tresses could not be forgotten. Yet it was her demure attitude and sultry laugh that truly piqued his interest. So thinking of her, with a dreamy tone he answered, "Yes, I am looking for someone very special. She is what my heart desires." Suddenly he realized he was sounding a bit sappy. So he quickly wished her a good day and joined the young maid still waiting outside the door to guide him.

Vivian sat down and began work on a bright beaded costume. While her eyes were busy, Gabrielle came out from her hiding place. Pretending she had just come in, she said "Thank you so much for letting me get lunch, I was so hungry I thought I was going to faint."

"You're most welcome, I'm not sure I did you a favor though. If you had stayed you would have met the most wonderful gentleman. He needed a costume. He had shoulders like this," she said, holding her arms out wide. "And thick, long, legs. He was also very nice. Not like some of the gents I measured this morning. He would have been good to take up with."

"Now Viv, you know I'm not one of the girls. He would not be interested in me at all," trying to hide her real emotions. Yet after realizing he would be at the ball looking for his heart's desire her heart began to race. Could it be possible he would be looking for her? No, he said he had her all picked out, who would it be? Now she knew she had to get there. The little green monster on her shoulder demanded she find out who he was looking for. "Is there a costume I could wear, if I decided to attend after all?" she asked, trying to seem casual.

"The sorceress costume is available. Or you could work the party, wearing a maid's outfit." She smiled, while attacking Gabrielle's vanity. "This one is beautiful!" holding up the cape to the outfit. "Or you could carry trays and refill drinks."

Gabrielle was not even sure that she was going, but she was sure if she saw him again, she damn well wouldn't be dressed as a servant. Looking at the dress along with the cape she really didn't take much time to inspect it. It seemed too elegant, too conspicuous. She thought maybe something less noticeable. "What about the dress you're sewing?"

"You'll notice if you look around, we are left with few choices. Besides that outfit, the Egyptian slave costume and the servant uniform, there really is no more. Those dresses left are for fantasies. And those over there," she pointed, "you still have to take to the correct rooms. That leaves nothing."

Gabrielle mumbled, "Thank you, if I go I'll wear it," trying to appear vague.

"Well, with that decision made, hurry and get those dresses to the right girls. I still have to finish this one," ordered Viv, trying to hide her smile because of Gabrielle's pouty answer.

Everything was in order. Maude had checked everything: the food, the lighting, and the music. Helena would not be wearing a wig tonight, on her birthday she always came as herself. Maude favored Helena's beautiful blonde hair. She would be wearing the beautiful blue dress she had helped her into only moments before. It matched her stunning dark blue eyes. Maude walked out of the ballroom as it began to fill with people. The music began. People were busy chatting and dancing, eating and laughing. Finally everyone had arrived, her friends and her customers. All of them loved her. Helena made a late entrance, she loved to be dramatic. She walked down the stairway with elegance. The music stopped as she entered the ballroom, a hush fell over the crowd. Her golden blonde hair was swept up in a layered coiffure and on her head was a brilliant diamond tiara. She wore large diamonds both on her ears and around her neck. Her royal blue dress was sprinkled with slivers of silver that shimmered as she walked. The bodice cut so low her ample bosom threatened to spill out. The mask she wore matched the dress and the shoes. She spread her arms wide and said, "Welcome everyone!"

After thundering applause the music began again. Most people resumed their conversations; others came forward to wish her well. Enhancing the romantic atmosphere and adding just the right amount of luminescence were thousands of burning candles in the opulent chandeliers overhead. Helena's face glowed as she thrived in this setting. She was a born aristocrat, a natural hostess and beautiful woman. As she danced, partner after partner showered her with compliments. For the rest of the evening Helena wore a radiant smile. Helena was almost able to forget, that this too, was only an illusion.

Gabrielle looked in the mirror again. "I simply cannot wear this." The dress was like a spider web. The material so light you could see through. The design was simple and clinging. As though a sheer web had been wrapped around her body. Wasn't it just yesterday she was saying she didn't have a bosom? Though her chest had grown to a generous size, this dress pushed her breasts together and up, creating a cleavage she surely didn't have. Everyone was downstairs by now and she didn't even have time to do her hair. She left it loose. She put the long dark purple, almost black, cape on. That wasn't bad. In fact, you couldn't see any of her body. She could go down, watch the fascinating man and then leave. No harm done. Maybe she should put something else on instead. No time, just leave the cape on. Adding the mask, even she didn't recognize herself.

Meanwhile, Kathleen had just finished playing the mermaid in a sailor's fantasy. After taking a luxurious bath, she changed into her lovely, forest green ball gown. The green of the gown complimented her green eyes. Her thick glossy auburn hair piled on top of her head. A beautiful set of emeralds surrounding her throat and wrist. She was to meet her customer at the entrance to the ball. She headed down there, not quite sure she wanted to go dancing. Also knowing she had no choice. When she got to the bottom of the steps, her heart squeezed. This man would be no hardship to spend the evening with. He was very good-looking! She introduced herself to him and he to her. Then they went inside to dance. He couldn't get over how pretty she was. Kathleen's manners appeared perfect and her style seemed easy-going. She was as nice as his friend Kevin had said. Yet he still couldn't believe his friend had proposed to a whore. Not that she wasn't everything he had claimed and more, it was just the idea that, after sleeping with other men, she would not be a proper wife. James just couldn't believe it didn't matter to his friend. It was just not heard of. Kevin was a Laird; after all, he could pick and choose half the lasses of Scotland. How he had saddled himself with a prostitute was beyond him. If he hadn't talked to Kevin himself, he would never have believed it possible. However, Kevin had made it very plain that it was Kathleen whom he loved and Kathleen he would have.

Seems Kevin had long ago gotten beyond Kathleen's past. It was James and his own personal beliefs that couldn't swallow such a bitter pill. Looking at Kathleen he thought, *She smiles at me so sincerely. Yet it is her job, just a rouse.* In fact, he could have her tonight; after all, he had paid for her. This was not how a woman acted if she was in love. How did Kevin feel, knowing he was not the first? That while he was detained he was not even the last?

James could not accept this for his friend, because he would never accept it for himself. Then and there he decided to marry some mousy woman that would never give him a moment's worry. These thoughts and many more were in his head as they circled the dance floor. Finally taking a break, they stopped and grabbed a drink and walked out onto the balcony to talk.

"You are a very good dancer," she said to him.

"You also. You are very pretty, Kathleen."

"Thank you."

"I have come to give you a message."

"What did you say, sir?"

"I have come to give you a message, from Kevin."

"You have a message from Kevin?" Kathleen asked, totally bewildered, and took a step backwards.

"Stay close to me," he said as the arm around her waist drew her near. "I do not want to be overheard."

"How is he? Where is he? Is he coming?"

"Hold on, hold on. One question at a time."

"I'm sorry, I'm just so excited. I guess I sounded just like Gabrielle, didn't I?" muttered Kathleen

"I don't know. Who is Gabrielle? What is she to Kevin?"

"Oh, I'm sorry. I'm getting you all confused. Gabrielle is my friend and nothing to Kevin. It's just that she usually gets excited and rambles on and on and I sounded just like her. Never mind. Tell me of Kevin."

"Kevin's been hurt."

"Oh, no!" She began to cry.

"I'm sorry, I'm not doing this very well." He pulled her even closer and let her put her head on his shoulder.

The party was a huge success. Gabrielle had never seen this many people in one spot before. It was defiantly a crush. She had enjoyed viewing the array of costumes. She had been groped several times and even asked to dance before she could make a getaway. She had scoured the room. She was having trouble picking out her soldier. He just didn't seem to be there. After looking throughout the whole ballroom, she went on to the dining room. She checked everywhere, and after hours of looking, she finally had to admit, she couldn't find her soldier anywhere. She was just taking a shortcut back to her room, when she nearly collided with an embracing couple on the balcony. She quickly darted into the shadows and hid. She immediately recognized Kathleen, but who was she with? Why was she crying? She decided to wait and see if Kathleen needed help. Then she saw him pulling her closer. Maybe she should go. Gabrielle knew she could never watch Kathleen participate in an illusion. But Kathleen was still crying. She decided to wait.

She tried to hear what they were saying, and then she heard Kathleen say, "Oh, my Kevin."

James took out his handkerchief and dried her eyes. Speaking very softly he continued, "Kevin was in a border skirmish. He was wounded in the shoulder. Fortunately for him, another good friend, Scott McTavish, saved his life. As the story goes, Scott threw Kevin over his shoulder. With one arm brandishing his sword, the other holding Kevin, Scott continued to fight. With a lot of effort and a little luck, Scott got him to the edge of the skirmish. Finally, after throwing him across his horse he was able to get him to safety."

"Kevin is not a small man, he stands over six feet. How was this Scott able to save him in such a manner?" Kathleen whispered in return.

"Let me just say this. Compared to Scott, Kevin is scrawny." James said this while shaking his head yes, to emphasis the point. "Anyway, Kevin is now safe, he will be fine. But much time had elapsed and he said you and he had an agreement to marry. If he were not back at a certain time, you would carry on with your own life. Is this right?"

"Yes, and I can tell you it was months ago that he was supposed to come and get me. He said he needed to clear up some things and if he didn't get back, to assume the worst and continue with my life here."

"So you assumed him dead and continued on. How brave," he muttered.

Trying to remain quiet, she hissed. "I assumed he jilted me, not that he was hurt. I don't expect you to understand, but it was very difficult for me to believe that Kevin really wanted me to be his wife in the first place. So when he didn't come back, I figured he had changed his mind."

"So without checking, you jumped back in the sack with other men?" he sneered. "Maybe you are not right for him after all."

"I don't appreciate your attitude and I don't expect your acceptance. What would you know of hardship? I had no way to confirm his whereabouts. I had no opportunity to locate him. I had no reason to doubt his word. He said he would be back to marry me and if he didn't come back, to assume he wouldn't. How hard is that to understand, Mr. Fancy Pants?"

"Calm down, Kathleen. I am not here to judge you."

"Oh really, then why are you?"

"Why am I here?"

"No, why are you judging me?"

"I'm not."

"You might not think so, but you are. I can tell from the condescending tone in your voice that you don't think I'm good enough for your friend. That if he hadn't made you promise, you wouldn't even be here talking with me. Women like me are good enough to bed, but have a conversation with, or marry, heaven forbid! Well, you have given me the message. Now, kindly remove yourself from my presence."

"There is more," he whispered.

"Finish then."

"Kevin wants you to accompany me to his home. He is waiting for you. He still wants to marry you."

"You and I both know I cannot go," sobbed Kathleen as she turned and ran.

Gabrielle could not believe her eyes. Although she was unable to make out their conversation from this distance, she had clearly heard Kathleen say, "Oh my Kevin," before falling into the man's arms. Was he THE Kevin? If Kevin had finally come for her, what had made her run from him? Kathleen, an old hand at this seduction game, must be up to some ploy. Well, now Kevin would take Kathleen away and she could quit moping about him. Still, Gabrielle couldn't help but wonder what had happened.

Not wanting to be seen, Gabrielle remained in the shadows. The moonlight was just enough that she could make out the man still standing by the railing. In one swift motion, he took off his mask and wiped his brow. She recognized him! It was her handsome stranger. Kathleen was his desire? Was this man HER Kevin? Oh, no! She stood in stunned silence. As the tears streamed down her cheeks, she had to face reality. She loved the man that loved Kathleen.... In that moment her heart broke.

As he wiped his brow, he played things over and over in his mind. He had made a muck of things. How had everything become so complicated? He couldn't leave without Kathleen. He had promised Kevin, and even if he had to steal her away, he would get her to him. But now, there was little hope of finding the girl that had fascinated him. He would have to concentrate on getting Kathleen to Scotland. He would have preferred finding the beautiful woman who made his heart race. She would be perfect to spend a few nights with. As he turned, he caught a glimpse of movement in the shadows.

He turned towards her. *He can see me,* she thought. *What should I do? If I can never have him and never see him again after tonight, can I kiss him once more?* Is that being a trader to a friend? She stood in indecision. Again, as last time, her body took control and without conscious thought, she moved toward him.

As the shadow moved forward, it took on the shape of a woman. The moonlight captured her slight form. She seemed to be covered with a blanket – no, a cape. She walked closer. As she neared him, he caught the light scent of violets. She remained silent and so as to not frighten her, he too said nothing. She stopped in front of him, then without hesitation she brought her right hand up to her throat to unclasp her cape. All time seemed to have stopped as the garment dropped to the ground. The moonlight no longer

89

captured a bulky form, but a slim silhouette. Her shape was perfect; she seemed very small, but still perfect. Her long black hair, left loose, seemed almost decadent. He could not help thinking Helena's certainly did provide everything one could desire! Yet, the woman seemed vaguely familiar. Without thinking he took a step closer. He reached for her and then pulled her to his chest. He then leaned down and kissed her. When his lips touched hers, it was a sort of déjà vu. The taste, the style and the smell, all attacking his senses at once, trying to get him to remember something or someone from the past. Something so familiar it just didn't connect. Finally, after several moments, he stopped. He looked at her and then without warning he reached up and discarded her mask. Like a bolt of lightning, it hit him. He knew that face. In the sea of strangers, in a castle this size, he had found her! He found himself shaking with desire. He ran his hands down her sides, over her hips, then back up again. He couldn't seem to get enough of her. There was nothing to the dress she was wearing. She was practically naked, standing here with him in the moonlight. Only her exquisite face overshadowed her alluring body. He ran his hands across her breast, down her sides, then behind her back. He pulled her tight, molding her closer and closer to his own firm body, just to hold her and prove to himself she was real. Embracing her, he leaned down and crushed her enticing mouth again. His masculine hands, sensuous mouth, and firm body all conspired to work their magic on her. Causing wild sensations, which ran through her body. He kissed her so thoroughly and with such intensity she was shaking.

Gabrielle poured her heart and soul into that kiss. Her arms reached up and wound around his neck. She molded her body to his. Her whole body trembled with emotion. She finally understood desire. Raw hunger. These were feelings she couldn't control. He was kissing her neck, her shoulders and her lips. He created sensations she couldn't explain. When he tore his lips from hers, she could barely stand on her own. Finally, she pushed away. Lingering only a moment, trying to memorize his face. Kissing him on the cheek and then grabbing her cape, she quickly turned and ran into the crowded ballroom.

He was still standing there, confused and bewildered. He started to follow, but by the time he reached the entrance, she was already lost in the crowd. He was alone! What the hell had just happened? He saw her and then he lost her. He found her, she ran, he lost her again. Damn, she hadn't told him her name again! Boy, they sure trained them well here; he had never ached for a woman before in his life!

She was long gone. There was no reason to attempt a search in that throng. So he decided to take a moment and collect his thoughts. Moving over to a bench he sat down and lit a cheroot. The chill in the night air began to cool his adore. The combination of the fine tobacco and nippy atmosphere allowed him calm down.

Chase after her? What was he thinking? She was a whore. Taught the art of seduction. He was not about to let her know how much she affected him. After all, she was merely part of the menu, he would order her up tomorrow. Remembering the tear he had felt running down her cheek as she kissed him, he turned sullen. What was that about? Maybe this time he wouldn't even look for her. What the hell kind of a game was she playing anyway?

Gabrielle raced through the ballroom, up the stairs, down the hall. She was two floors away from him before she even began to slow down and three floors until she could no longer control the tears. She couldn't believe the irony. Kathleen was her best friend, Kathleen loved Gabrielle's handsome stranger. Kathleen had known him first, so now Gabrielle would have to bow out. Another thought occurred to her, this must be Kevin. That is why Kathleen had run off, she had been mad that Kevin had let her down.

He had announced earlier that he was going to the party to be with his heart's desire. He had been there with Kathleen. It didn't take long to add up the facts. Kathleen was his heart's desire! She was not with a customer, but with her one true love. Not an illusion.

This must be Kevin. No wonder she always bragged about him. How the heck had Kevin gotten back here anyway? She still couldn't believe out of all the men in the world, they loved the same one. Well, the next time Kathleen bragged about how wonderful her Kevin was Gabrielle would not be able to argue with her. As her sobbing subsided, she reached the costume room. She quickly disrobed, hanging the cape on a hook nearby. She fondled the silky, sheer, web-like dress. Recalling how brazen she had seemed, she still could not believe she had dropped that cape and had stood there practically naked. Even still, how bold she had been to kiss him like that! She just couldn't help it. With him she seemed to have no control. She had known she could not give him up without tasting him one more time. She needed to spend those few moments with him before she could purge him from her system, for her friend. Yet she did not believe she had ever done anything this hard before. She hung the garment with the cape and left the area, walking slowly to her room, to spend the saddest night of her life.

Chapter 7

The next morning, James was a man with a mission. He sent a message to Helena requesting an audience, then ate his breakfast and awaited a reply. While sipping on his tea, a knock came to his door. "Enter," he simply stated.

"Good morning, sir, may I have a moment of your time?" Maude questioned

"Certainly."

"Helena was up quite late last night and asked if you could come to her room, as she will be quite a while yet. Your message did say it was urgent."

"It is rather urgent to me, as I have an errand to complete. However, it is not urgent as in life or death. If Helena would prefer a lunchtime meeting, that would be fine." With a large sigh he added, "Though I am not opposed to being pampered while I wait. Who is available to give me a massage?"

"That can certainly be arranged sir. My mistress will appreciate your compromise. After your massage, I will guide you to Helena. You can enjoy lunch with her. Would that be satisfactory?"

"Yes."

"Do you have a preference for bathing attendants, or can any of the girls be of service?"

"I prefer Kathleen"

"Kathleen is already working a fantasy this morning. You can watch if you like."

"Watch?"

"Yes, we do have Viewing Chambers from which you can watch any of the fantasies and their participants. Some people prefer to watch. Would you enjoy that?"

"I think I prefer to stay out of other people's fantasies and create my own."

"Would you prefer to indulge in an illusion? Or do you prefer a simple massage?"

Feeling just a bit wicked, he said, "What do you have in mind?"

"Oh, I don't know, your preferences. But you can pick the girl and she can dress as a princess, a maid or a tavern wench. She can wear anything, or nothing. You can decide."

"I would save the planning to include Kathleen. I would prefer she dress as a servant girl. Instructed to obey my every command. Is that possible? Also, for the rest of my stay, I would like her available at all times. She can stay with me. I will pay you handsomely for her continued service."

"That is not the way it is usually done." Maude frowned.

"I won't work her that hard, it's just that both times I have wanted her, she was unavailable. I would prefer her at my beck and call while I am here. After all, I do expect to be gone by the end of the week. So let's get everything arranged for later. I'll have my massage, then talk to Helena," he said, dismissing any more discussion.

Maude murmured, "The maid will be here shortly to take you to the baths. I will return for you shortly before lunch." She turned and left.

"Oh, I just remembered seeing a beautiful brunette last night, would it be possible to have her attend me in the baths?"

"I will try to get whomever you request, who would that be?"

"I do not know her name, but I could pick her out if I saw her again."

"You have quite a chore ahead of you, but I guess you could start with the book. That may help you."

"The book?"

"The *Book of Illusions*. It is in the main entryway, where you came in. Located in the corner, near the front desk. The book contains fantasies, positions and miniature portraits of all the girls. If you find the one you're looking for, you only have to tell one of the girls at the desk, she will arrange everything. How would that be?"

"That would be perfect. I am ready now, you may direct me."

Afterwards Maude returned to Helena's suite and was pacing back and forth as she complained. "He is a arrogant."

"You already said that," Helena replied.

"Well, he is."

"Where is he now?" asked Helena

"I left him in the main hall. He was going through the book and Millicent was sitting on his lap, explaining everything." Maude grinned wickedly.

"That is very naughty of you. If he mentions he is waiting for Kathleen, Millicent will do everything in her power to have him for herself. You know how those two compete." Knowing full well that Millicent would enlist his participation, Maude nodded in agreement. "Then again, I'm sure that one can handle Millicent." Helena laughed.

"What should we do about his request?" asked Maude

"Go to the chart room, change any engagements already on there. Mark her out for the next week. You'd better give her a few extra days afterwards, just to placate her. Make sure Esmerelda understands she is not available to anyone for two weeks."

"So you're going to let him enjoy her for a full week?"

"If his fantasy is to own a woman for a week or so, who am I to complain? Besides, I will charge him a fortune!"

"What about Kathleen?"

"When you take her up to him, explain this fantasy will last longer than usual. Don't make too much of it, Maude, she doesn't often complain."

"He wants to talk to you, I explained lunchtime would be better. Would you like to eat on the north terrace?"

"Yes, that would be perfect."

Helena turned back over to grab a few more winks as Maude left to find Kathleen.

Downstairs James had his hands full. After looking through the *Book of Illusions*, every muscle in his body was taut. He still could not believe he had browsed through such an erotic book so quickly. James was not sure if it was the girls at the desk watching him for a reaction, or the girl on his lap trying to seduce him. Maybe it was just the ideas in the book itself. But right now his whole body was tense. He needed relief. He wanted the girl from last night, but having never found her picture in the book, he finally agreed to let Millicent take him to the baths. He followed her up the staircase and into a door on the left side of the corridor. It was a perfect place to relax. He stood there while Millicent explained to the other attendant that he had requested her. Is that what he had done?

Anyway, he stood there while she undressed him, washed him and then rinsed him. Feeling slightly awkward, he lay down upon the massage bench in an effort to relax.

He turned his head and saw Millicent pouring oil all over her own naked body. And what a body! She was tall and had the longest legs he had ever seen. Her skin was creamy white, and her smile inviting. Her hips were a little large, but so were her breasts. She created a pretty package. Her dark, curly, brown hair fell to her shoulders, and matched the thick hair between her legs. After dousing her body with oil, she smiled a most wicked smile and climbed upon his back. She lay down parallel to his own body, rubbing her chest against his back, her body slick with oil as she began moving, back and forth, up and down. The oil slid off her body and onto his own as her already hard nipples teased as they pressed against him. Now, Millicent was not an ugly woman, in fact, she was attractive and very skilled. By the time she had finished massaging his whole body, he could not have denied her if he tried.

However, refusing her never even occurred to him. His body was screaming for release. Brusquely grabbing her, he entered her, fast and feverishly. Without romance or foreplay, taking her right there on the massage table.

Physically satisfied, he was eager to go on about his business. Yet, she continued to nuzzle him as if believing the dalliance were to continue. However, he was no longer interested and became impatient as she washed the oil from his body. Finally clean and in an effort to dress more quickly, he gave her a gentle shove from the room. Easily dismissing her, as he had countless others, from his mind as well as from his service. But now that his body had gained release, his mind had gained guilt, but why?

Suddenly James recalled the sweet smell of violets that had surrounded the mysterious maiden of yesterday. Shaking his head, he just could not decide why she kept popping into his thoughts. He did not know the woman, did not even know her name. There sure as hell were no future plans in his life for her. He was certainly not going to fall for a little whore like his friend Kevin. So why the guilt? Subconsciously maybe he had expected the attraction to go away by taking Millicent. That sure hadn't worked. Earlier, he had been determined that the alluring woman from last night was not going to absorb his every train of thought. Nevertheless, so far, she had.

Helena was already at the table when James walked out to the terrace. He walked up to her and kissed her hand and smiled. "You look radiant. You should have a birthday every day."

"Flattery will get you everywhere. Come sit down. Would you care for some wine?"

"Indeed, madam, I would be delighted. The last time we met, you were a brunette. The second meeting at the ball, you were blonde, as you are now. Is this your natural color then?"

"I often enjoy changing my appearance, usually to fit my mood. This is my original color, as I had little time to prepare before our meeting."

"I was not exaggerating when I said you are beautiful. How you have not been captured yourself, I will never know. However, from what I have observed, it seems appropriate that you reign here."

"You flatter me, but I relish it."

Drawing his eyes away from Helena, he admired the surrounding area. "The view from here is quite grand!" He announced. "Not only is your home a fascinating design, but structurally sound. It is quite the fortress. It seems you have it all. Beauty and safety."

"You seem to be investigating more than female forms, Lord Armstrong. Is there any reason for this?" Helena stated.

"No, just an observation."

She let it drop. "Our dinner will be here in a moment, I trust you like salmon?"

"I am very easy to please, madam."

"So I have heard," giving him a smug look.

"Something tells me, you know of my business in the baths?" he choked out.

"This is my home, this is my livelihood. Nothing goes on that I do not know about. And because I like you, I'll give you a pointer. Millicent is Kathleen's rival. If you're trying to woo Kathleen, I wouldn't let her know you have shared your favors with Millicent. I will not be to blame if she tries to scratch out your eyes. Now, let's get some business out of the way, before dinner comes. Shall we? I have decided to allow you total possession of Kathleen, while you are here. It is quite a unique fantasy, however, I like to accommodate my customers. Before I agree I would like to ask you a question."

"Feel free, madam," he responded.

"I would like to know if you are up to something?"

He certainly couldn't tell her his plans. He could hardly respond by saying, 'Yes, I'm up to something; I'm about to drag one of your best moneymakers away.' Stalling for time he simply repeated, "Up to something?"

"Yes, having total possession of one of the girls may be your fantasy, but it is highly unusual. So I was wondering what you are really up to."

Then an idea struck him. Deciding to be upfront he dangled a bit of truth and announced their departure. "I guess I can give you fair warning. I am planning on asking Kathleen to run away with me. If she says yes, will you allow her to leave?"

"You have a funny way of showing your devotion. You want to run away with Kathleen, yet if she's unavailable, anyone will do. Not very romantic."

"Your business would hardly be making a profit if men were monogamous," he answered snidely.

"Monogamous? Men?" she said, astonished. Then she erupted into laughter.

"Or happily married," James returned.

"Men are rarely that." Addressing his earlier statement, she added, "Did I say I was making a profit? However, after you pay me double the usual fee, I will hardly be able to deny making a decent living."

"I think it fair to say this place is every man's fantasy. You have done a wonderful job with your illusions and your staff. Yet after such a thorough training, you can't possibly want to loose your investments. What do you do if they want to leave?"

"Contrary to what most people think, my girls are here by choice. They stay if they want to and they go if they choose to. I do not hold them. I will not stand in your way, nor will I convince her to go with you. She has not had an easy life, but she has been safe here. Will you protect her?" Helena demanded.

"I will protect Kathleen with my life," meaning every word he said, for he had already promised the same thing to Kevin.

"Such loyalty in such a short time."

He did not respond.

"However, I do feel I should warn you, she has recently lost the love of her life. I do not anticipate her leaving with you, as she has not yet gotten over him."

"Really? And how do you know he was her great love?"

"Not feeling a need to convince you, suffice it to say she glowed when he was here. Her feet simply never hit the ground. When he left, she sobbed for weeks. When I say sobbed, I mean the bells in the bell tower are quieter than that woman was. I could go on and on, but I think you understand my meaning."

"If I convince her to leave with me, there are no repercussions?"

"No, why would there be?"

"I'm not sure of her term of service. Does she owe you money?"

"Her money is not your concern, the money you will pay me is. You do realize the price will be enormous? Good luck in convincing her."

"That is why I need the total possession of her. She cannot argue at first, as she will be my slave. Then, after I convince her of my sincerity, she will be glad we had our time together." He thought the story a bit melodramatic, but women all loved to hear that drivel.

Helena would have him watched. She did not believe a word he said, but was willing to let him believe she did. She then changed the subject. "Ah, here is our food," she said as the server entered with the large tray. "Let us enjoy our dinner." During dinner they talked of many other things, except Kathleen and of course Gabrielle.

Later that day, the door to his chamber opened very slowly. It was Kathleen. She didn't knock, she didn't enter, she just stood there on the threshold. "I thought it would be you," she said.

"Come in," James said.

"Why are you doing this?" she whined.

"So you can't run someplace I can't find you. I need to talk to you. I need to make plans. I need for you to hear me out."

Slowly she entered and then shut the door. "So make your plans, then go."

She was standing there, looking more forlorn than any woman he had ever seen. She really was very pretty. Her long thick hair had been put into a bun at the base of her neck, but rather than give her a demure look she appeared haughty. The outfit she wore did not flatter her figure and the bodice was a bit tight, emphasizing her huge assets.

"I promised Kevin I would bring you home," James said simply.

"I guess you'll have to break you promise."

"Why all of a sudden have you changed your mind? Do you no longer love him?" he taunted.

"I have come to my senses," she responded.

"So you will not come?"

She merely stood staring at him.

He was so angry he could hardly stop from throttling her. He stood clenching his fists to his side. The vein in his neck stood out. Then he hollered, "Fine, then take your clothes off and get on the bed." Damn tired of dealing with her attitude, he thought to shock her and embarrass her into admitting she only wanted Kevin.

She hoped her surprise did not register on her face; after all, she was a professional. There were no emotions involved in this, just plain sex. Walking over to the bed, she slowly sat down. She took off her slippers and then rolled her hose down, one leg at a time. As she was undressing, Kathleen couldn't help thinking. She didn't want to go through with this, because he was a friend of Kevin's. However, this was her career, this was her livelihood. This was something she was good at and she was not ashamed. He should be ashamed. If he were such a great friend to Kevin, he would not demand to sleep with her. Maybe that was his plan. To screw her, then tell Kevin. If that was his plan he could go to hell, because she had already decided not to go to Kevin. She really was not good enough for a man like him. She didn't even know how she had let Kevin convince her that things could work out. Maybe this James fellow's plan would serve her purpose as well. It would be easier if Kevin didn't want her than for her to try to turn away from him.

James' hair was standing on end, as he kept dragging his hand through it. Pacing back and forth, he kept trying to come up with something. How long was he going to let her undress? Why didn't she just say no? Or tell him to go to hell? Did she want to sleep with him? If she would sleep with Kevin's good friend, could she ever be trusted? He kept thinking she would beg off, maybe start crying or something. How long would this go on? Good God, she really meant to go through with it. Was she bluffing? Looking out the window, reality hit him like a thunderbolt.

She would not cry off, as she had been ordered here. She had been requested by him and sent here by her employer. She would not stop. So much for his request shocking her! He turned around to tell her to stop. Only then did he see she was already naked. Shit! Well, she was one very pretty woman. And he could honestly say he had never seen bigger tits on any woman in his life. Taking two long strides across the room, he angrily pulled the covers down off the bed. Wrapping the covers around her, he tried to apologize. "I didn't think you would really undress. I'm sorry I requested you do so."

"You didn't think I would do my job?"

"I didn't think you would sleep with Kevin's friend."

"Well, now you know better."

"Look, it's not my job to convince you to marry Kevin. It's not my job to judge this harebrained relationship. It is my job to get you there. After you get there if you choose to break your promise, that's your business. Just know this. You are going!"

"You can buy me for the week, mister. But you can't buy me for a lifetime. You can't make me do anything I don't want."

"Fine, if your word is no good, I'll just go back and tell Kevin my version. How you never believed in him. How you never really meant to marry him. How you don't even care that he was hurt. Then, how you wanted to sleep with his friend!"

"Tell him anything you want, I don't care!" she hissed.

With that answer, his temper began to boil. James did not think he could stay in the room without shaking her. So he walked out the door, slamming it behind him.

Meanwhile Gabrielle had just come from the chartroom, after locating Kathleen's whereabouts. She needed to find her and talk to her. One of the girls had mentioned Kathleen was with the handsome stranger from the ball. Gabrielle finally found the right room and rapped on the door several times. It appeared as though no one was inside so Gabrielle decided to would wait for Kathleen's return. Slowly turning the handle she eased the door open.

There was no way to know that Kathleen had finally worn herself out from crying and had simply fallen asleep in the big bed. As she peeked through the doorway, Gabrielle put her hand to her mouth to muffle her cry of dismay. There, lying on the rumpled bed, was a naked Kathleen. Peacefully sleeping, blankets in disarray. Gabrielle believed Kathleen to be the picture of a woman after sex. She didn't see Kevin anywhere, but was not staying to investigate. There was no longer any doubt, Gabrielle now believed the handsome stranger was Kathleen's beau. She had been right all along, assuming Kevin had returned for her. Gabrielle ran from the room as tears streamed down her face.

Later that evening Helena sat dining with Sheriff-Constable Muden. He sat at the opposite end of the table stuffing his face. He had thin lips that always seemed to be shaped in a sneer. He had dark curly brown hair, and long porkchop-shaped sideburns. His nose and ears were very large and his eyebrows thick and bushy. His voice sounded gruff and demanding. There was simply not one attractive feature about him. Helena even knew the size of his penis. She had heard from Isis after the last time the sheriff had visited. They had certainly laughed at that. Another feature as unwelcome as the rest of him. He was wearing a waistcoat, too small for his bulging stomach. With his puffy, sallow skin he looked repulsive.

"I'm glad to see you managed to have my favorite foods," he said.

She gritted her teeth and responded, "I was happy to. What brings you here, sir?"

"I've been after a thief. I've been on quite a chase. I was going to be in the neighborhood and knew you would pamper me."

"Humpf," she snorted.

"I am looking for a young woman, maybe I should have you line up all the women here so I can take a look at them all." He grinned, showing his black, rotted teeth.

She tried to smile without sneering, eager to change his ideas. "I retained the services of the girls you requested."

"Yes, the little eastern girls." He nodded.

They were interrupted by a knock at the door. "Enter," she hollered.

"We heard our favorite customer is here. We could not control our enthusiasm any longer, mistress." Both Isthmus and Isis ran over to the sheriff's chair. One hopped into his lap. The other stood behind his chair. Both began to kiss and hug him. His smile was enormous.

He stood up. "I will be here for two days. Have my money ready by the time I leave." Pulling a girl into each arm, he accompanied them out the door. "Don't disturb me until then," he bellowed.

Helena sat back down and sighed a huge sigh of relief.

"I trust that was good timing?" asked Maude

"Very good timing. It was all I could do to sit here and create polite conversation, while he stuffed his face. See if there is anything in his pockets, before they go to the laundry. Maybe there is something we can use against him."

Two days later Gabrielle was about to knock on Helena's office door, when she heard voices within. The male voice sounded familiar, but she could not place it. It sounded like they were walking towards the door, so she hid behind a huge potted plant on a pedestal down the hallway. The voices were muffled until Helena opened the door, while standing at the entrance she politely muttered, "Good-bye, and have a pleasant journey."

Who knew he'd start chatting. "I'm off to Northumberland. Friend of mine got married a few weeks ago and I promised I'd check up on his property while he's away. They are on an extended honeymoon and he didn't want the servants getting lax in his absence. So I volunteered to stay while he is gone. You remember him; we've been here together, Viscount Herrington?"

Helena did indeed remember him, his fantasies were aggressive and he had a tendency to salivate during intercourse. "Oh, yes. I haven't seen him in some time though. You say he got married?"

"Yes, just a small wedding mind you, yet he is married just the same. I'll probably be at Herrington House for a while." She realized immediately that rather than giving his location, he was really bragging about the fact he would be lazing about, reaping the benefits. "I'm sure going to miss those two little girls of yours. Last time I was up there I had to use a brothel closer to his home. The girls are not nearly as beautiful or talented as the girls you have here." As though reconsidering his answer he cocked his head to one side, then he laughed and said, "But in a pinch, any girl will do."

"Well, good luck in your travels," she said hoping to speed his departure. And it worked, for moments later she stood in the doorway watching him depart. As he neared the end of the corridor, Helena motioned to young Tim to follow him and make sure he left the castle. Funny, until Helena had signaled him, Gabrielle hadn't even noticed Tim standing nearby. As Tim walked past Gabrielle to follow the sheriff, he turned and grinned right at her. He had known she was there all along, so much for being inconspicuous, she thought. She walked to Helena's door and knocked.

"You may come in," answered Helena. "Gabrielle, come in. What can I do for you?"

"Originally I came to talk to you about something else, but now that can wait. I could not help overhearing part of your conversation with the man that just left. Do you know who he is?"

"Yes, I do. That was Sheriff-Constable Muden. He was just finishing up a visit. Why, do you know him?"

"I don't remember him being a sheriff. He was a thief-catcher, back home. Only he had a reputation for arresting innocent people. As a thief-catcher he became very wealthy because people paid him to keep from being arrested.

He once had an argument with my father. I cannot say as to the subject, I only know, from all the shouting, that they disagreed. Shortly after, Father had him shown to the door. I still recall my father saying he is very corrupt and not to be trusted."

"Oh, yes, I know better than to trust him," Helena agreed.

"I'm sorry, for eavesdropping, but now I must ask for a favor."

"What would that be?"

"The viscount, the man he mentioned, is the very one I ran away from. If there was a wedding, he must have married my aunt. While they are away on their honeymoon, I must take the opportunity to return to my home and get the information I need. Can you help me?"

Helena took a few moments to consider her options. "Captain Anderson is leaving in two days. I think he said something about sailing down to Plymouth. Maybe he wouldn't mind taking you to Teesdale, but if he has already made other plans I will simply send you by coach." Taking a moment to ponder her options, she announced, "Either way I will have to find you an escort. After all you were very lucky the first time not to have been abducted by rogue bandits, we cannot take the chance of you traveling alone again."

"Do you think he will take me?" Gabrielle asked anxiously.

"He lives to rescue young maidens." Helena laughed at the young girl's expression. "Give me some time to arrange things. I will find you when I have the details worked out."

Helena sat there thinking. Henry had just left to go back to work in Bristol. He would have made a perfect escort. Stuart would know whom to send. So off she went to find him. Instead she ran into Maude. Explaining her intentions, she passed the errand of finding Stuart off to Maude. Turning in another direction, Helena went to find Derek.

After locating Stuart's room, Maude knocked and then pushed open the door. She stood rooted in the doorway, laughter had died and spontaneously three people sat up. Astonished, at Maude's entrance, the women blushed. Slightly embarrassed herself, Maude tried to hide her surprise at his choice of entertainment. She avoided looking in their direction and averted her eyes to the open window instead. She quickly blurt out "Stuart, you will have to finish up, Helena needs you. Ladies, good day." Pulling the door shut, Maude headed down the hall, her head shaking in disbelief. Before she reached the end of the corridor, Stuart, still tucking his shirt in his breeches, caught up with her. She couldn't contain her mirth as she looked up at him and grinned. He sheepishly smiled in return. "Both of them?" Maude inquired.

Stating that he valued Maude's opinion and did not want her to think him a cad he volunteered his plight. "Well, first I was sleeping with Molly and

102

enjoying myself immensely. Later, the women played a trick on me and I was sleeping with Polly instead. Seems like when one was busy the other took over. It went on for some time before each became jealous and they started to argue over me." At that he grinned. "I was more than a bit taken aback, that I had not noticed a difference. After they confessed, the girls wanted me to choose between them." He became indignant. "I can tell you that was not going to happen! So I said, 'I'll take both of you or neither of you. I have done nothing to warrant this situation and I'll be damned if I will be the one blamed.' Seems like I made the correct decision because it's been both ever since. It works…. I'm happy, they're happy."

"It is not up to me what any of you do in your off time. I am glad you have found an arrangement you like." She genuinely liked Stuart and they worked closely together to maintain order within the castle. "Sure won't be a cold winter for you, that's for sure." She cackled.

He laughed along with her and eagerly changed the subject. Stuart said, "What does Helena want?"

"She is in need of an escort for young Gabrielle. Do you have a man among them you would trust?"

"My men are all good. If I had to pick only one, I would pick Terrance Russell. He is young, strong, and dependable. He will be able to take care of her."

Maude instructed Stuart to track down Terrance and inform him.

Helena stood in the Viewing Chamber connected to the Tavern. The serving wenches had just finished with him and were exiting. Derek was still trying to catch his breath as he lay on the bar. She exited the Viewing Chamber and strolled into the Tavern. Lounging on the bar, without a stitch of clothing, she could tell by the sound of his breathing that he was not asleep. Lying still drenched in sweat his golden tan seemed to glisten. His stomach looked like that of a washboard, his muscles were so toned. He rested with both arms up above his head, though one was bent at the elbow and laid across his eyes to shield the light. She reached out to rub his dark already mussed hair as her eyes began to roam his lower half.

His eyes opened immediately, as he said, "Helena, you were watching?"

Helena giggled. "I instructed my servant to inform me when you had finished. She must have believed you done, or she wouldn't have come for me. Yet when I arrived you had begun again, so I but waited."

He sighed and waited for her to continue. "If you bother me when I am bedding your women, it must be important. Or did you come for instruction?"

"I hardly think so!" she said indignantly.

"Forgive me, my sweet, I know better. Just ruffled at your presence. You are like a sister to me, it is a little disconcerting to have you watch me with others."

"You lie. You are never embarrassed when on display. You cavort with wild abandon." She sighed. "I came neither to watch nor to pester you. I came to ask a favor."

"Anything you wish," he replied as he sat up.

"You are so sweet."

He hopped off the bar and looked for his shirt. "What is the favor?"

"What is the direction of your next route? Did I hear you say you were going to Plymouth? Is your route planned?"

"After just returning from that last ocean voyage and all the troubles we encountered, I'd like to stay a bit closer for a while. Now that we have entered into war with the colonists, I will be avoiding that travel route for some time. I do have tobacco and spices to deliver and now after playing cards last night with one of your clients, I have also included Edinburgh to the list of ports. Why do you ask?"

"I would like to request a favor."

"Done."

"You treat me too well. You haven't even asked what it is."

He smiled and stroked her cheek. "You would never knowingly put me in danger. You will certainly give me the details and you compensate me fully. Why do you feel the need for an interrogation? Have I ever not done as you wished?"

"Never. But remember that pendulum swings both ways. I too, have done many favors for you."

"Yes, we are friends for life. There is nothing we wouldn't do for the other."

Helena held his hand and sighed. "I value your friendship and devotion more than you will ever know. You are the only man whose opinion I appreciate." Turning from the serious conversation to lighthearted banter she giggled, "You sure I can't talk you into marriage? We would have a perfect relationship. We love and trust each other and you can sleep with hundreds of women under my very nose!"

As he buttoned his trousers and looked for his boots, he responded. "I would like you to sing another tune, for this one hurts my ears!" He grinned, back at her. "You are selfish! You think to use me for your own selfish plans. To keep me as a figure head because you seek no real husband. One day, we will both find appropriate mates. I personally am not nearly ready to settle down. Now, I have had enough of all this foolish talk. Next time you even whine marriage to me, I will simply turn around, get aboard my ship and sail away. Isn't it enough that I am utterly devoted to you for a lifetime?" He pulled her into his arms and hugged her. They stood there holding each other for a long time.

Finally she pulled away and sat down on a chair. She changed the subject. "Would it be possible to take one of my girls with you? You could stop off some place like Teesdale."

"That's right up the coast and certainly on the way. What's the story?"

As he finished dressing, she filled him in. Then they continued on to Helena's chambers. Helena and Derek spent the next few hours together. It wasn't until later that evening that Derek mentioned Kathleen and James were also included on this voyage. That's why the trip to Edinburough had been included.

She mentioned to Derek that the less people that knew of Gabrielle's whereabouts, the better. She told him the story of Gabrielle's arrival and subsequent living arrangements. Helena informed Derek that the viscount Gabrielle was up against was good friends with Sheriff-Constable Muden. The same sheriff that had made their lives hell several years before. Even though they had foiled his efforts, neither could stand him. They had learned to deal with him, but they didn't like it. Everything was best kept confidential, even from the crew. So the next two days were spent in a flurry of activity.

Kathleen was in the baths on the second floor when Gabrielle entered. Gabrielle had been unable to talk with her about Kevin. This was because Kathleen had been in his room since he arrived. Gabrielle couldn't leave without saying good-bye to Kathleen, they had shared too much. More than even Kathleen realized, thought Gabrielle glumly.

The room was filled with women today, some playing in the water, others lying upon tables receiving massages. Each appeared to be enjoying the relaxing atmosphere. Kathleen was sitting in the pool of water, trying to think. James had been hounding her for days now and she just couldn't take it anymore. She had agreed to accompany him, but she knew it was not right. She knew that she really wasn't good enough for Kevin. It had all seemed so possible with him here, convincing her to believe her past didn't matter. Assuring her they could indeed be happy. With him here, she had even come to believe it seemed possible.

Yet, in reality, she knew it wouldn't work. She would never be good enough for a man like Kevin. To have one more opportunity to see him, touch him or hold him. Around him she was weak, she could no longer pass up the temptation. Not to mention the peace and quiet it had gained her once she had agreed to leave with James. She just couldn't figure out what to do from there.

She was just staring into space when Gabrielle came to sit near the edge of the pool. Though Kathleen looked sad and forlorn, Gabrielle mistook it for a love-struck, dreamy look. Gabrielle said, " I came to say good-bye."

Though Kathleen hadn't had the opportunity to explain what had been going on the last few days, with Gabrielle coming to say good-bye, Kathleen believed Gabrielle must have heard about her leaving with James, to travel to Kevin. After all, James had already worked out the arrangements and gossip spread faster than fire around here.

"Yes, I am glad for the opportunity to say good-bye," murmured Kathleen, yet she didn't smile.

"I hope you will be happy with Kevin," said Gabrielle.

"I am not sure what to do about Kevin. I am so undecided. I do not think I am good enough for him. But I love him so desperately, I am tempted to throw caution to the wind and marry him anyway."

She was right! It was Kevin! Now Gabrielle's worst suspicions had been confirmed. After she heard Kathleen say she loved him desperately, her heart shattered. "I want you to know how much your friendship has meant to me. I will miss you terribly," choked out Gabrielle.

"I will miss you also," Kathleen responded. "I will send a messenger, letting you know what happens with Kevin and me."

"Good-bye," Gabrielle whispered. She embraced Kathleen. Kathleen had been the best friend she had ever had. She had been there to explain everything, she didn't judge or complain. Gabrielle could not believe it would end this way. She just could not trade secrets. For her secret would hurt Kathleen. Gabrielle was so overwrought that she could hardly continue their conversation, let alone tell Kathleen about her plan to go home. Gabrielle hugged her tightly and then turned to go. Leaving as quietly as she had come.

Kathleen stood up, toweled dry and put on a wrapper. Something was wrong with Gabrielle. Gabrielle was much too quiet. Usually she was rattling on about something. However, this time, Kathleen just didn't have the heart to listen to someone else's problems. Hers were just too big. And definitely too complicated to explain! She was being dragged across the country, by a mean, arrogant creep. She was being taken to a home where her man was ill and his family would hate her. Worst of all, she was going to back out of the marriage. What a situation! She tried to enjoy a leisurely massage, which would be her last if she stayed in Scotland. She was tense and upset when she dressed and was ready to go. Her future was so uncertain.

Helena's gracious and sympathetic attitude was rewarded with respect and admiration. Yet the fact that she also ran a strict household and business caused the staff to remain a bit aloof. After all, she was the boss.

Helena couldn't believe all the commotion. James was taking Kathleen and Derek was taking Gabrielle. She would definitely feel the void with Kathleen gone. For somewhere along the line, between tears and shouts, they had become true friends. Gabrielle, her innocence and utter charm, had somehow snuck past her defenses also. Helena almost wished she were going on the voyage too. Helena knew the trip would have its dangers, but she also knew it would be full of adventure for them both. With Kathleen and Gabrielle both leaving, Helena felt a little sad. Leaving a house full of people behind, Helena would be far from lonely. Yet a special bond had been created between these women and Helena would really miss them.

Helena had finally received a response from Lucas Fenwick. Helena had convinced his superior that the sheriff was a traitor to his country and Lucas had been immediately put on the case. In his job the need for anonymity was important, so Lucas rarely met anyone personally. Helena had secretly supplied him with information and sources, yet it had been some time since the investigator had been in touch with her.

Only today, a message from him, found on her desk, confirmed that things were progressing as expected. The note had been brief, without names or signatures. For only a moment did she ponder the fact that a message had been placed among her private papers, upon her desk, in a castle she was sure Lucas had not visited. Realizing she would never figure out how he left the note, she shrugged it off and returned to other tasks. The sheriff had friends in high places; still she was convinced that Fenwick was the one man who would be able to catch this criminal. And upon reading the reply Helena was immediately filled with hope.

Life in the castle continued at a hectic pace. There was the packing, the planning and the arrangements to contend with. Helena also had an elaborate party to plan for a prince. Not to mention the leaky boat in the pirate fantasy and the ripped tent in the carnival fantasy; both to be repaired.

Such was the complex life of a fantasy provider. Helena heaved a sigh, she would miss her friends terribly, but work must go on. Thankfully they all departed at different times, so Helena was able to say good-bye to them all separately.

Chapter 8

After descending the final step and opening the solid door, they walked onto the portico. James quickly turned around to assist Kathleen into the small rowboat. Kathleen looked lovely in her dark traveling suit, but with the expression she wore on her face, one would think she was shackled to an ugly ogre. Instead, he had done everything he could to make her comfortable. He had apologized over and over and had given in to all her other requests. He even agreed to go by sea most of the way, so the long trip wouldn't be so hard on her. As he reached to put his hands around her waist and lift her in, she said, "Stop taking every advantage to touch me."

"I was merely trying to be courteous and assist you," answered James.

"I appreciate your assistance, just stop touching me. Now that I have left the safety of the castle, I must look out for my reputation. You have seen me naked. You are Kevin's friend. You must not touch me so easily. I would not have it look as though we are familiar to each other!" She appeared indignant.

James thought she was making too much of it. He was only treating her like he would treat any woman. He was being polite, not forward. Women!

After reaching the ship and climbing aboard, Captain Anderson himself greeted them. "Welcome aboard," he said.

Clasping his hand, James said to the captain, "Derek, great to see you again. I would like to introduce you to Kathleen Dunbar. Kathleen, Derek Anderson, our captain."

Familiar with Derek, Kathleen said, "Thank you for giving us transport."

"Well, after fleecing James out of his money the other night, I could hardly turn you down. No, no, just kidding. It was on my way anyway. However, I have added one stop to our route. It should not delay us longer than a day or two."

James laughed. "I hope you brought a deck along, I'd like the opportunity to get some of that money back. Turning to Kathleen, he said, "I ran into Derek in the study the other night. We had a couple drinks, played a few hands of cards and traded several stories. Anyway, he took me for 100 pounds."

Derek had to laugh at the pout in James' voice. Turning to Kathleen, he said, "There is another young lady traveling north with us. James will have the cabin next to you, and her protector will have the cabin next to her. Do not come up on deck too early, the deck belongs to the crew. My men are good, but there is no reason to tempt them. I hope you enjoy the trip." With the short, firm statement complete, his mind was once again on business. Derek turned to his first mate and said, "Conor, will you take them below and show them around?"

"Aye, Captain." Then directing his gaze to James and Kathleen, Conor said, "Follow me."

As Kathleen continued to walk behind Conor, Derek held James' arm, a gesture to hold him back. "A moment of your time?" he said as James stood still. Derek sighed, "I hesitate to even acknowledge this, but it must be said. "Keep track of the girl." When James gave him a confused look, Derek continued. "I know she is the woman you are taking home to marry. But if you have a spat, you still must know where she is at all times. The men are good, but they are not saints. If she goes to them for assistance and promises her wares, I won't be able to control the outcome. I do not say this to be mean, only to warn you. You are responsible for her and this is a small area. Nowhere to run, if you understand?"

James was totally annoyed. If this had been his real love, and not just for pretend, he would be insulted by this speech. Kathleen had done everything to conduct herself as a lady. Now he was annoyed. The captain was not aware of her occupation from this short meeting, yet he did know. That meant either Helena had told him, or he had slept with her himself. Would it never end? Would they always run into her old lovers? He said to the captain, "How do you know her?"

"I have been visiting Helena's since it was opened. I know of them all. I enjoy them all. I am not judging. I am glad she has left this life to start another. Yet a beautiful woman causes problems on a ship. Now go to her, get her settled. Come up and have a drink later."

Unsure of a response, James turned and silently walked away. Is this the way he sounded to Kathleen? Nice, but insincere? Mulling this over, he crossed the deck and found his way below.

Just as James went below, Gabrielle and Terrance rowed up to the great ship. The name *Deception* was boldly painted on the rear of the ship, she noticed as they approached. Thanking Terrance as he assisted her to the deck, Gabrielle then took a long look around. Spellbound, she simply stood there, with her jaw hanging open. Absorbing the sights and sounds of the large merchant ship, she was in awe. Watching the crew carry on their activities, she couldn't help but admire their hard, well-toned bodies, exerting such strength and stamina.

Looking about the deck she was impressed with the cleanliness of the deck and crew. The galleon was built with a high sterncastle that housed elaborate living quarters. She was aware that it was a cargo vessel but was still surprised by the number of cannons running along each side. The ship had been built with a special hull to carry the added weight of the heavy cannons, for any unarmed cargo vessel became a favorite target of pirates. The foremast and mainmast each carried three sails and the mizzenmast carried two. This specially designed ship was faster, more maneuverable and better armed than previous ones. And Derek ran a tight ship. He expected his ship clean and dependable and his men reliable and loyal. His ship and the sea were his home.

The powerful ship was magnificent. Strolling the deck Gabrielle continued to stare in amazement at the activity surrounding her.

"You're going to catch flies in that mouth if you don't shut it!" laughed Derek as he hollered down to Gabrielle, from the upper deck.

Gabrielle smiled. "I could not help but find your ship fascinating. This looks to be quite an impressive ship, after all."

Derek couldn't help but be enchanted with Gabrielle. She was a beautiful young woman. Black hair piled on her head, covered by her bonnet, except the few tendrils that had loosened surrounding her face. Her large, dark, soul-filled eyes were very expressive. Most beautiful women were more interested in themselves rather than their transportation. She had at least two things in her favor. She was attractive and she adored his ship.

Derek made quick work of descending the short stairway and shook both Gabrielle's hand and Terrance's. They chatted for a while, as he explained his rules. He took the opportunity to brag about both his ship and his record. Eager to be off, he turned and instructed Conor to see them to their cabins. With a twinkle in his eye he said, "I will talk with you later!" Then turning his attention away from his passengers, Derek commanded, "Patrick, pull anchor and lets be off!"

At the railing as they sailed away, Gabrielle stood staring at the castle atop the cliff. If anything was to happen and she didn't return, she wanted to remember exactly what Helena's looked like. Although the sheer size was intimidating, the shape and design gave it a storybook appearance. The cone-shaped roofs on all the towers added character. The pink coloring was so feminine and unusual it added to the fairy-tale effect. From the outside it looked like a place fantasies could come true. In her mind, she pictured the two courtyards. First, the large one for customers, containing flourishing green ivy, cobblestones pavements and hand-carved flowing fountains. The second, smaller, one with barracks, workshops and stables. In her mind she went over the kitchens, pantries, laundry and scullery. Upstairs, the chart room, the counting room, the sewing room. Included in her memory was the array of makeup cluttering the tables in the cosmetics room. Not to mention the decadent amount of gems strewn about waiting to be cleaned, fixed or worn. She easily recalled the abundance of beautiful garments and accessories available to the women and the whirlwind of continuously changing costumes and props. She could go on and on. Inside the main castle, the ballrooms, the dining rooms, the hall, the fantasy rooms, the viewing chambers, the servants' quarters and the baths.

A visitor would only see the perfect setting. Feel the ambiance, participate in fun and games and find relaxation. A place where every whim is performed, every dream fulfilled. No wish denied.

Yet, as one who had lived there, she realized how hard everyone worked to accomplish that goal. The charade of an easy lifestyle and carefree atmosphere was the image they all worked so hard to achieve. Truly, this place really was all an *illusion.*

Looking up at the charming castle she became misty-eyed. Here, she had been taken in by strangers and been kept safe. She had been allowed her freedom to grow and learn and yet been protected from those who would harm her. She loved the people inside and would think of them with fondness. She would always remember the magic of this beautiful place.

She must have fallen asleep. She woke to the gentle swaying of the ship. She just lay there on the bunk, thinking. Finally she sat up and stretched. She had a blanket covering her, and her shoes were off. Funny, she didn't even remember leaving the bench near the large porthole. There was a knock at the door. A crewmember announced dinner. She allowed him entrance. He informed her that as she had slept through dinner, he had brought her a tray. He lit the lamp and assisted her to the chair. The air had become chilly, so she kept the blanket around her. He would pick up the tray later; she could ring the bell near her door if there was a problem. Then he bid her goodnight.

She sat there for the longest time, just feeling the loneliness. She thought she had forgotten that feeling, but it appeared to be back again. In all the time she was at Helena's, she had been *safe* and never alone. She had been *safe* and happy. She had been *safe* and busy. She had simply felt SAFE. Now she was about to travel by ship, break into her own home and get the information she needed. She would have to hunt for her guardian, and then get the authorities to look for her father. Maybe she should have stayed at Helena's, where no one would hurt her. Sitting there worrying, the problems seemed insurmountable. Tears ran down her cheeks. The sadness and the loneliness were burdens almost too much for a young girl to bear.

Again, there was a knock at the door. "Enter," she murmured.

"Good evening, we missed you at dinner. Are you feeling well?" asked Derek

"I'm fine. I must have dozed off," answered Gabrielle, wiping the tears from her cheeks.

"I know, I checked on you earlier," he said

"Oh, then you covered me? Thank you."

"No need for thanks. You had fallen asleep on the bench and you looked so uncomfortable. I simply carried you to the bunk and covered you. How are you now?"

"How much do you know about me?" she answered a question with a question.

"I know you are in trouble." He smiled kindly.

"I am aware that you have met me. I mean how much do you know about me?"

"I think I know all I have to unless you feel the need to tell me something."

"I was not one of the girls that slept with the men at Helena's," she stated.

"This I know."

Looking into his somber eyes she was overcome with relief. "Oh, good. I wasn't sure if you expected...." She seemed to breathe easier. "Not that I object to that lifestyle. I just didn't want you believing I am something I am not."

"You think I'm here looking for companionship?" He just laughed. Then his laughter became louder and louder. Finally his shoulders shook and he began to laugh in earnest. After a few moments, the laughter subsided.

She had always felt plain compared to the exotic women that entertained at Helena's. Still, he did not have to laugh at her and confirm her own inadequate feelings. "You don't have to laugh! I could be if I wanted to. I could do it if I tried," she stammered.

My God! He realized she didn't even know her own worth! "I'm not laughing at the prospect of your abilities. I'm laughing because what you say is absurd. I just spent the last week on my back, surrounded by the most beautiful women. I am satisfied for the moment. I like and respect you and would never treat you in any manner you didn't like." Switching tactics, he smiled. "However, if you were one of Helena's girls, I would certainly pick you without a qualm."

She knew he was bamboozling her, but she didn't mind being sweet-talked a bit, now that she knew he was safe. He was very good-looking, not as devastatingly handsome as Kevin, but still very attractive. Most important, she did feel quite safe with him. "Thank you, I think. Would you care for something?" She motioned to her tray.

"No, I just stopped by to check on you." With a quick pat on her back and a simple squeeze of her shoulder, he added, "I will see you in the morning." She was easy on the eyes and fed his ego with her dependent nature. Soft and alluring without realizing her own appeal, he felt the sudden need for air and immediately departed. Whistling, he went to his own cabin. Following the narrow, dimly lit corridor, he entered his cabin only to find he was not alone. James was sitting in Derek's favorite chair, smoking his cigars.

"I hope you do not mind." James gestured to the drink and cigar. "I was waiting for you, when I noticed them." He grinned.

"I'm not really up to a game of cards," said Derek. "Help yourself to anything you wish. Why aren't you with your fiancée?"

Remembering that everyone at Helena's and everyone aboard believed him in love with Kathleen, he quickly came up with, "She is in her cabin, seasick. Not much fun to be with. I came up to go over the itinerary. All right?"

Derek told him they should only be in Plymouth for two days, if everything went according to plan. One day for unloading, one day for loading. He had already made arrangements. As for London, that would be approximately three to five days. Derek could promise nothing until they arrived. Then a short stop at Teesdale and last Edinburgh.

"A little longer than I first anticipated," stated James

"You could have taken a coach. With ships, we have the weather to worry about. We have loading and unloading to deal with. We have customers. I can go on and on with reasons we can't hurry," said Derek

"No, please don't. I'm just being impatient. I have something I'd like to see to, after this trip," said James, thinking of the little delicacy, back at Helena's.

Derek said, "If you can tear yourself away from your fiancée, you can tour the London haunts with me."

"Sounds good to me," James readily agreed.

Again Derek wondered if the woman in his cabin would be able to captivate James for very long. He certainly accepted going out and about without a second's hesitation. This situation would bear watching. Maybe he had just better have a chat with Kathleen later. Turning the conversation to other topics, they sat smoking cigars and sipping whiskey.

Plymouth's port was a hub of activity; men scurrying back and forth, shipments being loaded and unloaded, ships coming and going. Located in southwestern England, Plymouth possessed a natural harbor. Here they unloaded the wool they had picked up in Bristol. And half the tobacco and spices collected on their ocean voyage. After loading some tools and weapons, they sailed for London. Before long they were following the continent to the English Channel.

Unfortunately Terrance had become violently ill from their voyage and Gabrielle spent most of her time in his cabin, nursing him. Captain Anderson suggested he disembark in London and stay at his parents' townhouse until he was able to return to Helena's. Both Gabrielle and Terrance took exception to that. Gabrielle didn't want to be abandoned and Terrance would not leave his post. Derek took over the duty of escorting Gabrielle on deck for a short stroll each night. On just such an excursion they reached the side and spotting something off in the distance, she stopped and stared. The golden-rust sunlight reflecting on the water seemed to dance across the surface, creating a warm, sparkling, picture. The rhythmic waves lapping against the ship produced a sweet, melodious song. The combination of sight and sound enabled Gabrielle to feel at peace. It was the most colorful sunset Gabrielle had ever seen. Her face was lit with happiness and her joy apparent. Instead of the sunset, Derek's eyes fastened upon her. Her innocence and genuine honesty drew him to feel overly protective towards her. He constantly reminded her of this and teased her into an easy camaraderie.

Shortly after Derek and Gabrielle had finished their walk, James and Kathleen came on deck to do the same. James held Kathleen's arm as he escorted her about and though he nodded in response when she spoke, he was merely going through the motions of being polite. For something else had already claimed his attention. He swore he could smell violets. And of course, the scent reminded him of the woman he left behind. Wasn't that silly? The woman he left behind, indeed. A brief flirtation was all it was! Why did he keep thinking about her? He needed to have a diversion; he couldn't get that little trollop off his mind. He fully intended to join Derek in London and pick up a bit of fluff. While kicking up his heels, he would then forget about her … he hoped.

Heading up the Thames River they approached the Port of London. The next day they moored midstream in the river and waited for the smaller boats to transfer the cargo to shore. Once the cargo had been loaded, Derek and James boarded one of the little boats and headed into London. The girls were well protected with the crewmembers guarding their safety.

Agreeing to meet up with James later in the day, they each headed in different directions. James used the opportunity to meet with Lucas Fenwick. Then he took the time to stop off and look for his brothers.

The first place Derek needed to go was the Bank of England. He carried a packet full of bank drafts and desperately needed to make a deposit. After which he stopped home for a brief visit before heading to the small district of St. James. Entering his club he easily found James playing cards in the back room. With a gel on his lap, a cigar in his hand and a smile on his face, James waved to Derek. Derek gave a low appreciative whistle when he spotted the amount of money piled on the table in front of James. Not wanting to change James' luck, Derek announced he would play at another table. As the evening wore on, both men experienced a streak of good luck.

It wasn't until dusk the next evening that Derek's luck started to change. He shifted the beautiful serving girl on his lap and announced to the players that it was his last hand. He no longer felt like playing cards. The voluptuous, young girl was distracting. Also he rather suspected she was sending signals to one of the gents at the table. He was not in a fighting mood and after drinking for two days, didn't figure he would fare to well. Instead he decided to bow out of the game. Derek signaled James that he would be in the lounge waiting. He gave the wench a through kiss good-bye and went on his way. By the time James finally caught up with Derek, Derek was properly soused, with James not far behind. Both realizing they should get to the ship, they cautiously headed back.

When they finally got aboard, Derek remembered that he should check on Gabrielle and Terrance. Gabrielle had been nursing Terrance almost single-handedly. Derek also had to admit he really wasn't in shape to do much more than get to his bunk. Derek knew he should visit Gabrielle himself, but the way the room was spinning, he finally had to admit defeat. Derek knew that before James retired, he would check in on Kathleen. So Derek begged James to check on both women. He knew James could be depended upon to take care of any problems that may have come up. Without hesitation James agreed to check on all the passengers. So after getting Derek to his cabin, James stopped in front of the cabin next to it. James knocked on her door, but didn't receive an answer. He went on to Terrance's door and heard a low moan. Along with the moaning, he heard a woman's encouraging voice. The female voice, along with the male groans, was enough confirmation for James. He had promised Derek to check on his passengers, not interrupt them. Deciding those two could look after themselves, he continued on to Kathleen's room.

Kathleen had been bored to tears all evening. She was not one to appreciate being alone. She was becoming cranky and in desperate need of companionship. So when James pounded on her cabin door moments later, she invited him in. Even he was better than no one, she decided. So Kathleen offered to share a bottle of scotch and some lively conversation.

Rather than retire to his cabin, he accepted. His intention was to ply her with alcohol. Then question her about the woman he could not forget. Maybe a name or some information would fall into his lap. In this manner, she would not remember his questions and would not connect his motives. Thinking to drink her under the table, he had forgotten how far ahead of her he was. Shortly after entering her room, James fell fast asleep in his chair. She couldn't help but laugh as she threw a blanket over his loud, snoring, form. Now that she was not alone, she felt comfortable enough to find her bunk and relax. She was no longer alone, though he was hardly in shape to converse with her. Yet, his mere presence in the cabin was enough to ease her tension. Feeling somehow content, she finally fell asleep.

Shortly before dawn, Kathleen woke to hear someone crying. Then she heard a heart-rending scream. Then gut-wrenching sobs accompanied footsteps pounding along the corridor. All at once there were more voices and more footsteps. She decided to find out what was going on. She dressed quickly and then ran into the hallway. While Kathleen made her way to the galley, trying to find out who screamed, Gabrielle staggered out into the hall. As Gabrielle stumbled down the hallway, she saw a cabin door ajar as she went past. She stopped short. She just couldn't believe it! There, just inside the cabin and sound asleep in a chair, sat her perfect stranger! His shirt off, his breeches completely undone, a blanket piled at his feet. His appearance was disheveled, yet endearing. He had more than a day's beard growth, giving him a devilish look. Without uttering a sound he had captivated her once again. Simply by being here. Her heart began to race. If he awoke and spoke to her, she would be charmed all over again. Then reality hit. What was she thinking? This is Kevin! If Kevin is here, where is Kathleen? She spun around and as she turned she could not believe her eyes. There, standing at the end of the narrow entrance, was her best friend. She was stunned! Recognizing each other simultaneously, they both began to screech, immediately rushing into the other's embrace. While they were jumping up and down in excitement, Gabrielle suddenly froze in horror. The crewmen came out of Terrance's room with his covered body. As Gabrielle began to cry again, Kathleen tightened her arms around her. Silently, the girls followed the men carrying Terrance's body, up the tapering stairway.

They gave Terrance a burial at sea. It was a brief ceremony. None of the crew had known him; even Gabrielle's time with him had been brief. Kathleen had seen him around the castle, but was unable to call him more than an acquaintance. It was truly sad. The captain said a few humble words. Then, after dropping his body into the vast sea, it was over. Afterwards Kathleen followed Gabrielle to her cabin. They were both a little numb. Death had a way of making reality come marching home. On the flip side, their happiness at finding each other aboard the same ship could not be measured! There was so much to talk about. Gabrielle explained that the scream Kathleen had heard this morning had been when Gabrielle realized Terrance had died. They talked late into the morning. Gabrielle even explained about going home to find the missing information. Kathleen then shared her plan for going to Kevin's home. The only thing not explained was James. Kathleen thought Gabrielle knew about James taking her to Kevin. Gabrielle still thought James WAS Kevin. At least now, they had each other a bit longer, so neither of them felt so isolated.

Long after the body was gone, James finally woke up. Shipboard routine continued. As the day passed, no one really realized James didn't know Terrance was no longer on board. James had no way of knowing anything untold had happened.

A few nights later, Derek announced to James that their other female passenger would be joining them at the captain's table for dinner. James recalled the moaning coming from the cabin a few nights before. He had concluded that the young lady in question was just some tart. And after Derek had the gall to make sure he watched Kathleen. He couldn't believe it! So in response to Derek's announcement, James said to Derek, "Do you think that wise?"

"I certainly do not think dinner with us this evening will be a problem. She could use the nourishment. She has been chained to that bed for days," he answered.

"Exactly what I mean. Do you think it wise to flaunt this woman?" James now believed Derek had taken up with the other woman.

"I am not flaunting her. I am offering her dinner."

"Do not deny you have stepped into Terrance's place."

"I do not deny that I have taken over her protection from Terrance. But why are you so upset that I have taken over the position? You would think by your tone I had asked you to take care of both ladies."

James simply stood staring. Again a mistake in communication, yet he was unaware. "You have the audacity to point out that Kathleen stay away from the men. Yet it doesn't bother you, that the other girl spends her evenings with a man?"

"You suddenly seem very prudish. Who else would have taken care of him?"

James could hold back no longer and his answer came back in a roar. "Why is it you demand I keep my woman under control and away from the men and you do not have to do the same with yours?"

Derek could not believe the hostility coming from James. Yet with the crude remarks hurling from him, Derek had no choice. Derek's answer was in the form of a left hook. Little did he realize Kathleen and Gabrielle had been just behind him. In time to both hear James' statement and to see Derek's response. Also in time to see him fall. "Leave him there!" Derek bellowed the order. "He will come to, soon enough." He held out both arms and said, "Ladies." They each grabbed an arm and went to dinner.

When James awoke, his jaw hurt, it was dark and he was all alone.

The next morning at breakfast Kathleen and Derek were the only ones eating. Gabrielle was sleeping late. James had yet to show his face. Kathleen informed Derek that she now knew all about the plan to sneak into Gabrielle's home. She also explained about James really being only her escort. That he had preferred not to tell others for some strange reason that he was taking her to Kevin. Still it was better for all of them if Derek knew the truth, for Kathleen could barely tolerate the man at times. They talked for some time before she demanded that he allow her to be included. They began to argue. Derek knew it would be risky enough having Gabrielle along, let alone Kathleen. He tried every persuasive argument he could think of, but she wouldn't budge. She insisted she would be an asset. Derek reminded her that James was to take Kathleen safely to Kevin, that in all likelihood he would deny her also. She merely pointed out that if James didn't know anything, he couldn't stop her. For Derek it was useless to argue. Kathleen reminded him they should not delay, as there was no telling how long Gabrielle's aunt would be gone. Derek said they had finished loading their cargo this morning and would sail with the tide. They both commented on Gabrielle's endearing personality and James' alienating one. After breakfast Derek had much work to do and Kathleen went to find Gabrielle. The day passed quickly. Kathleen and Gabrielle both helped mend the crew's torn clothes. This was a tedious chore that helped to both pass the time and keep them busy. The kind act endeared them even more to the men, for there was plenty for all to do. James whiled away his time helping to repair the rigging.

When James sat down to dinner at the captain's table, he was not surprised to find only Derek waiting for him. It was about what he deserved. By now he had learned of Terrance's death and felt like a heel.

"The ladies are not joining us this evening?" he inquired.

"No, they have spent more time in your company, than they wish." He sighed. "What was all that about yesterday?" Derek asked.

"I really am thickheaded. I certainly didn't mean to offend anyone. I was not aware at the time anything had happened to Terrance. I didn't realize you had taken over her protection because of necessity."

"You didn't realize you were rude? Talking about them as if they were not even present. I realize men from our class barely acknowledge, let alone aquatint themselves with the lower class. Yet you are so condescending. Did you have to speak crudely in front of them?" Said Derek

"What? Are you saying you told them what I said?"

"No, they heard you loud and clear."

"No. I did not realize they were within hearing distance. I will apologize."

"You should only apologize if you are sincere. Do not apologize if you do not mean it. Then you will have to add hypocrite to that list of endearing qualities you have."

"Of course I would mean it. I never show bad manners," insisted James.

"You are spouting about manners, when I have told you that you hurt those girls feelings," hollered Derek.

"What a servant or woman thinks never enters my mind. Though I would hardly injure their feelings a purpose."

"Really?" Derek said sarcastically.

"I never spend much time with either." He sighed dramatically.

"Your line of reasoning is ridiculous! It's not as though I have asked you to befriend them. Just be civil! You are absurd. You sound like a religious fanatic. Just refrain from sharing your comments. I don't want you to upset them."

"You think I do?"

"I don't know, but I have seen no compassion so far." So saying, Derek got up and left James sitting at the table. James racked his brain; he just could not remember the last time he had had to be compassionate. Now, loyalty, he understood that, and commitment was an emotion he had long dealt with. Love was simply the way he felt about his parents, grandparents and brothers. But compassion? Hardly cold-hearted, he must have at some time, right? He tried to think of many different situations. Finally he tried to imagine being uneducated, untrained and unhappy. Even he knew it was a far stretch to imagine all that. However, he was determined to be polite. He had been taught better than that. He would not treat these women, any women, less than his good manners allowed.

As the days went by there had been little opportunity to have any serious conversations with either lady. They had been taking trays in their cabin and staying to themselves. James had tried unsuccessfully, to coax them from their cabin, several times. Yet, James knew eventually they would have to come out and when they did, he would find a way to make it up to them. Still the situation chipped away at his pride, for James had never lowered himself to worry about women's feelings. They came and went through his life as little more than an evening's entertainment. It was almost embarrassing that he had allowed these two doxies to have him jump through hoops. This ridiculous situation would not last much longer! He would apologize as Derek suggested, he would escort Kathleen as Kevin had asked, and he would walk away without a second thought to both. Or so he thought.

Chapter 9

Something woke him up. Listening, he lay there becoming accustomed to the gentle swaying of the ship, trying to figure out what had startled him from his sleep. There it was again, some sort of scraping noise against the ship. He lay there a moment, trying to think of obstacles that could have drifted into them. Then there was a splash! Had someone fallen overboard? He silently got out of bed. A man of previous military experience, he was an expert at dressing quickly. He threw his pants on and was buttoning his shirt, even as he was running out the door and up the stairs. It was dark and there wasn't much of a moon to give light, but he could make out the small boat in the distance. The clouds parted and the moonlight was suddenly enough to make out the shapes of the figures in the boat. Several figures. How many? He just couldn't be sure. Damn! It looked like two small figures. Women? Not one, but two. Kathleen had to be aboard. Even though he knew there were only two women on the ship, he ran down to her cabin, in the event he was wrong. He wanted to prove himself wrong. He was hoping to find her safely sleeping on her bunk. But she was gone all right! His worst suspicions confirmed. He ran to the other girl's cabin, quickly flinging open the door, no one there either. He went to look for Derek. Were these pirates? Though he had only seen the one, there could have been more boats. The women were in danger. Spending precious time searching, he realized he'd never be able to find Derek. The ship was huge and Derek could be anywhere. James ran back up to the railing. Their shadows were getting smaller. They seemed to be going in the same direction as the small lighthouse in the distance. He had no choice, no time to plan, no time to think. He stood atop the railing and dove in.

Thank God he was a good swimmer. He slowly followed the slow-moving dingy. He moved quietly through the water, finally getting close enough, to observe the situation. When he got tired, he flipped over and floated. The boat he had been following finally reached the beach. The larger figure got out, to pull the boat ashore. James stayed in the shadows, drifting in as close as possible. There were only three of them! That was great, one man would be easy to overpower. As he waited, the man helped the ladies out of the small boat. James could see no weapon and again wondered what was going on. He decided to follow them and find out. They walked up the sandy beach towards the lighthouse. Either they had come this way before, or had very good instructions. Was Kathleen trying to escape? Had she changed her mind? Who was with her? What were they after? His mind raced through all the different scenarios. Still he had no clue. He simply followed. Running up the sandy shore his foot hit a sharp shell partially buried in the sand. Pain! As the seashell bruised his foot, he suddenly remembered jumping into the water barefoot. Great! He continued running over the endless dunes even though his foot was throbbing. He quickly regained some of the distance lost, after he had hurt his foot. Looking up at the lighthouse, he noted it was taller and less wide than most he was familiar with. He climbed over some boulders reaching the side of the lighthouse. He followed them down a short, grassy slope to the small barn. He could hear voices as he approached. He couldn't make them out clearly. The noises, however, sounded like they were hitching a rig to a horse. He stood waiting. Without warning, the door to the barn was flung open. The occupants were already in the carriage as it exited the doorway.

Stay or go, a split-moment decision. He couldn't be left behind. He would never keep up. He jumped onto the rear of the carriage and held on. Dangling from the rear of the carriage, with little to support him, was a struggle. Discussion he overheard was limited to a few grunts and gestures. After leaving the beach, they seemed to stay off main roads. Traveling the bumpier, less traveled paths. They had left the coastal plain and headed inland, continuing on through the hills and moors. They had been driving at a frantic pace for some time, when they pulled off the road, into a thicket of trees. It was here that James jumped off, more like fell off, and blended into the foliage. The Tees River ran just below, in a series of cataracts forming a long rocky stairway. Cauldron Snout's vertical distance from the first cataract to the final one is two hundred feet, making this waterfall not only noisy, but the highest waterfall in England. And the noise made eavesdropping almost impossible.

Gabrielle was standing off to the side, watching Cartwright Manor for signs of activity. With the bright light from the moon she could clearly see the outlines of the buildings. Everything looked so familiar, yet that seemed a lifetime ago. Looking past the stone wall encircling the manor, she could see little movement. Although she could not clearly see her gardens or the ivy covering the structure of her home, she knew they still existed. Located on a hill above the river, the manor was a high-quality home, with equal designs for protection and comfort. Her grandfather had used the best materials and masons available. The result being a large, secure, country home. The back kitchens had been made of timber and had burnt down a few years earlier. Gabrielle still remembered the chaos when the rebuilding took place, this time with stone. Her earlier life had been predominantly quiet and peaceful. Even now she wondered how she had adapted to the fast paced, hectic, life style of Helena's. She stood there continuing to watch for movement and thinking of days past.

Kathleen and the man were arguing AGAIN. With the surrounding noise, from the waterfalls, James could not understand the muffled tones. Instead relying on body movements and impatient hand gestures. Then the large male figure went to grab the taller woman, the one James believed was Kathleen. As the man held her arm she shrieked "ouch". Somehow, over the dull roar, James recognized Kathleen's voice. He jumped out of the bushes and attacked the man. A short time ago he had been soaking wet, after the wild carriage ride he was nearly dry. Still, the dampness did nothing to help and everything to hinder, his efforts. They rolled, they punched and James got in a few good wallops. The other fellow gave as good as he got and the scuffle continued. The women frantically tried to get James off, the captor. Didn't they realize he was here to help? Finally something hit him from behind and darkness engulfed him. He awoke a short time later.

"Finally!" Kathleen sighed. "I wasn't sure how hard I hit you."

"You hit me?" James said incredulously

"Yes, why were you attacking Derek?" she asked.

He could not believe her response. No heroes welcome here. He looked around. Derek? What was he doing here? He saw a small hooded figure, kneeling next to Derek. Though he had never seen her face, which even now was covered by her cloak, James assumed her to be the other female passenger. Turning his head to look at Derek lying on the ground across from him, James saw that he was not smiling.

"What the hell are you doing here?" shouted Derek

"I thought someone was kidnapping the women. I thought I was rescuing them. What are you doing here?" he said accusingly

"You have ruined everything," muttered the hooded figure.

"What have I ruined? Tell me." demanded James

Kathleen said, "We made plans to help Gabrielle. However you have barged in where you don't belong."

"I belong any where you are. I am to protect you. I will help you all, then we will be on our way that much sooner." James grinned, "No harm done, just an extra partner.

"Yes, harm was done. You attacked me. Now I've twisted my ankle. I won't be able to hoist Gabrielle up through the window or follow behind."

"Surely, you're all right. I barely–"

"I said I twisted my ankle and can barely put weight on it. We will have to think of something else." Derek interrupted sternly.

Looking at the faces of gloom, James volunteered, "I will simply have to take your place."

"That is impossible!" whispered Gabrielle, her heart racing.

Derek looked at the shrouded figure. "We are already here. We do not know how long they will be gone. He is as strong as I. Surely we can't turn back."

Gabrielle knew he was right. She also knew it would be almost impossible to resist Kevin if they were alone. She didn't know what to do. She looked at Derek, then at Kathleen. This was her only chance to get into the manor without the viscount or her aunt knowing she had been there. Just great, her only chance depended on the man she was deeply in love with and that same man loved someone else. A man that thought she was a whore. Just great! What else could go wrong? With few alternatives, it was finally agreed with Derek laid up James would take his place. Kathleen would still stay below the window, where she would warn them if someone were to come. James would now boost her inside and accompany her.

"Well, let's get started." said James. As he stood, his foot hit a sharp rock and he said, "Ouch." Too late, he remembered his bare feet.

"Are you hurt too?" asked Derek hopefully

"Give me your boots," James directed at Derek

"What?"

"Give me your damn boots. Your ankle's twisted, you're not going anywhere. I didn't have time to put any on, as I thought I was off to rescue the women. I hardly had the opportunity to throw boots on before jumping overboard. Now I've gone and stepped on a rock and realize I'll need them to finish this mess."

"Just remember nobody invited you. You bloody well poked your nose in where it didn't belong," Kathleen chimed in.

James turned to give Kathleen a long, silent stare. Then, as Derek handed over the boots, James sat down and quickly put them on. "Fill me in," he announced.

They explained the plan, so under cover of darkness; they headed to the large manor down the hill. Gabrielle had to admit, as a stealthy partner Kevin fit the bill. Earlier she believed he would mess it up and that she'd constantly have to tell him to be quiet or hurry up. Instead he was as close as a glove and as quiet as a mouse. His presence made her a bit anxious and uncomfortable. Yet, as the plot unfolded she had to admit to herself his being there also made her feel safe.

Once they had both climbed in through the window, Gabrielle noticed nothing much had changed. She couldn't see if the house had been redecorated, as it was too dark. The basic layout of the furniture seemed to be the same. Exiting the library and moving along the corridor, she identified other rooms as they passed by each door. When they passed the fourth door, she explained that if they became separated for any reason, this would be the door to find. It was connected to a wine cellar, which contained an outside entrance. Emerging from the wine cellar through that doorway would also give them an advantage, as that entry was located on the other side of the manor, closer to the woods. If an emergency were to arise, this would be the exit to take. They rounded the corner, reaching the main hall, with only the moonlight filtering through the windows for guidance. Gabrielle had no time for reminiscing as they passed the family portraits, hung along the way. They swiftly stole up the staircase and quietly entered her father's room.

Immediately she could tell this room had been redecorated! With such little light she could not tell the color or style. Yet, she could tell the furniture was new and different. This must be the room the honeymooners had decided to use. The idea made her cringe. Every time she thought of her aunt and the viscount, she remembered the scene in the library the night she left. A quiet click caused her to turn her head around. Gabrielle watched as James carefully closed the bedroom door, soundlessly lighting a nearby lamp. She smiled, and then turned around to cross the room. She sighed as she opened the door to her father's dressing room. Suddenly her heart stopped! What used to be a wardrobe was now the entry to the bedroom next door. The old closet area was now a small hall adjoining the two rooms. Shelves filled with boxes and bed linen lined either side. It was simply a corridor rather than a dressing chamber. The room it used to be was just missing. Why would someone need to get to this bedroom, from the master suite? Her mother's suite was located on the other side of the room, with a separate entrance. She was baffled. Her breathing became labored; she started to feel lightheaded. She wasn't sure what to do; she looked at Kevin in confusion.

"I don't know what to do." she whispered, "this used to be a dressing chamber." She sounded anxious.

James tried to sound lighthearted, so she wouldn't worry. Good-naturedly he offered, "He probably wanted easier access to his wife, men are like that" he grinned. "Do you remember approximately where to look?"

"The back right corner held some loose floorboards. But as you can see, there is no real corner anymore." She hesitated. "Why would he need another door? There is already a separate entrance for the viscountess over there." She pointed across the room.

He could barely make out her face, with the darkness and the hood. But he could hear concern in her voice. In an unusual gesture, he took a moment to pacify her and said, "Little one, did you not learn at Helena's that a man is rarely satisfied by one woman?" He thought to ease her distress. "He probably uses this entry for a mistress or serving maid," believing he had smoothly placated her sensibilities by answering with honesty, uncommonly pleased by his display of tenderness.

Of course! This was no longer her father's room. It was now the room of that vulgar pig, Viscount Harrington. The answer was her NEW uncle's lack of fidelity. Oh, her poor aunt. How easy Kevin had come up with that answer! Gabrielle felt Kevin's answer also reflected his own personal habits. It surely indicated another reason not to fall for his charms. Though Gabrielle still had no idea that he had not recognized her, she kept a safe distance from him, trying to remain unaffected by his presence. "It would be just like a man to have a woman on the side and he is newly married too! I hope my aunt does not find out about it, she will be hurt," Gabrielle huffed.

"Maybe it was from before they married.... Maybe he does not even use it." he replied. "I was merely answering the question you posed, referring to the door. I didn't create the door or the situation. I hardly think your surly tone is appropriate." Her act of outrage began to irk him, so he added. "Why are you so zealous in your idea of fidelity? You're the one that works in a house of ill repute!"

She couldn't even answer him, she was so mad, again the mention of being a paid woman! Well, what if she had done what he thought? What business was it of his? He certainly didn't hide his attraction to women like that. He made her so darn mad! He would never understand. In a fury, she turned away from him. After ignoring him for several moments and regaining control of her emotions, she continued inside the old closet area. Leaning down, she said, "Maybe if you could help me move this chest, I could...." She stopped as he pushed her aside and picked it up as though it were weightless. She dropped to her knees and began pulling boards loose. Yes, there it was! Removing the last plank, she pulled out the small container, hidden within. Inside, sealed in a leather pouch, was a journal. Here was the information she had been looking for. She didn't take time to read it or even examine it. Instead she stuffed it down her blouse and into the safety of her corset.

Carefully she put the box back and replaced the boards. As she backed out of the way, James swiftly put the chest back in place. In the closeness of the small room he unexpectedly caught a whiff of violets. As they shut the door, he decided it had to have been something already in the room. Extinguishing the lamp, they both realized the need to hurry. Light was slowly beginning to sneak in through the windows as dawn approached. James just couldn't get the smell of violets off his mind, where had the aroma abruptly come from? He followed the girl out into the hall.

There, in the large open hallway, at the top of landing, hung a new picture. A portrait of the viscount, standing beside him was a pale, mousy-haired young girl. Gabrielle stared at it for a few moments, wondering why she didn't recognize the girl. She did not believe the viscount had children from any other marriages. Yet what other explanation?

Moving down the corridor and as she headed down the staircase, he was right behind. They heard a noise in the back of the house when he whispered, "No time to go out through the study, just use the front door." They had just walked out and shut the front door behind them. A noise from inside made James realize they would be caught at any moment. Without hesitation he said, "Just play along," as he grabbed her and pulled her into his arms.

Skillfully, he wrapped his arms around her, crushing her close to his body. Did he say just play along? Just play along!! She had tried so hard to steel herself against his charm. How could he do this? Yet the moment he held her in his arms again, her determination melted. He began kissing her, assaulting her senses. Instantly her legs turned to jelly. She couldn't get enough. She knew it was a rouse. She knew she would have to give him up to Kathleen, but for just a moment, she could pretend. Her heart overpowered her head and she kissed him in return. Conquered by her own emotions, she began to devour him. Her attempt backfired, as her own senses reeled. When he finally broke apart, she was literally hanging on for dear life.

This was something James could never have anticipated! The simple act of kissing this woman produced an unexpected impression. There was no reason for this female to affect him in this manner. He had never in his life been influenced by a simple kiss. Then suddenly two women, in two weeks, filled him with desirable cravings. That was impossible. Something wasn't right. Then the smell of violets overwhelmed his senses. Still holding her, close to his body, the hood of her cloak fell. With the smell of violets lingering in the air, he could almost hope, no, that was impossible. As her hood slid lower, he couldn't resist opening his eyes, taking a closer look. He couldn't believe it. It was she! No one else had such beautiful, dark velvet eyes, or such tender lips, now swollen from his kisses. No wonder the second woman affected him the way the first one did. They were one and the same. Eventually he would have figured it out, without even opening his eyes. For he had never felt like this before, his passion ignited by mere moments in her company. No one else appeased him so well and so quickly. He wanted to grab her hair and loosen it from whatever hairpiece contained it. No wonder he thought he smelled violets all along, he had. He greedily began to consume her. He couldn't get enough, he was amazed. Each was as devoted as the other, trying to absorb every delight. He had to force himself to pull away as he felt her unsteadiness. It only made him happier.

"It's you!" he practically shouted.

Reality suddenly reared its ugly head as she immediately tried to pull away.

He held on even tighter. "I have never met a woman who so controls my very thoughts. I was going to come back for you."

"I'm sure you were," she scoffed. That he thought she would really believe such a story meant he thought her completely naïve.

He smiled "I didn't even know your name and yet you never left my mind."

"You have to stop this," she said, stomping her foot. "I am too easily influenced by you and you only toy with my affections. I am Kathleen's friend and I know you have plans for her."

"Yes, I will have to deal with Kathleen first, but then I will have all the time in the world for you," he grinned. He was elated. She was jealous of his time spent with Kathleen. It proved she must care for him.

She was mortified. Did he think to share them? Just as an evil retort was to escape her lips, the front door swung open.

"I thought I heard something, what can I do for you?" The tone of voice that confronted them was bitter. "Though I say it's much too early to be paying calls. The sun is barely up. The staff hasn't even started breakfast so please state your business, as I've plenty to do," said the servant, standing in the doorway. Gabrielle was startled, and then breathed easier when the servant didn't recognize her. In turn, Gabrielle could not identify the servant either.

James replied, "No need to trouble anyone, just passing through and took the liberty of helping ourselves to a drink from your well. Thought to thank the owners, are they about?"

If James had taken only a moment to look at the expression on Gabrielle's face, he would have known that the last thing Gabrielle wanted was to see the owners. But he hadn't looked, so he didn't know.

The young girl answered, "They are still on their honeymoon as far as I know. However, Lady Penelope Cartwright is due back this morning. She was over visiting Herrington House. Do you want to wait for her?"

Gabrielle was very confused. She had thought the viscount had married her aunt. So she said very quietly "Oh, we must be confused. We thought Lady Penelope married Viscount Herrington."

"The servant laughed. Oh, no. Lady Penelope is the aunt of the young bride. As I said before, the viscountess is with her husband, still on their honeymoon.

"The bride's na … na … name?" stammered a completely baffled Gabrielle.

"Why, her name is Viscountess Gabrielle Herrington.

At that moment, James could tell Gabrielle was falling apart, because she was like dead weight leaning into him. So he said "No need to wait. Just traveling through, one of our horses threw a shoe and the other took off. We simply wanted to thank them, for the use of their barn. It was late when we arrived, we didn't want to disturb anyone. Though it's very early we must be on our way, please thank them for us." He squirmed, waiting to see if the servant would buy the story.

"That would be grand, stop on your way back. Maybe the whole family will be back by then." Shutting the door the servant could not help but to sarcastically add, "Try to come by later in the day, next time round." Then with a loud thud, the door slammed shut. At that same time Gabrielle fell into a dead faint and Kathleen rounded the corner of the front porch.

"See you still have them falling all over you," she sarcastically muttered.

"We have to get out of here, fast," he urgently whispered.

Quickly lifting Gabrielle into his arms, he and Kathleen scurried up the road. Reaching the top of the hill, they ran for the cover of the trees. Gabrielle was still unconscious and yet they couldn't take the time to stop. James helped both Kathleen and Derek into the carriage, and then gently placed Gabrielle in Kathleen's arms. Then they drove like bats out of hell. About a mile down the road, James veered into a shaded glen. He tied the horse to a tree and took Gabrielle from Kathleen's arms. He situated both invalids in a thickly shaded area and directed Kathleen to sit down. Resting on the ground, he viewed the surrounding location. Over to their left was a large patch of violets. Looking at the flora he thought perhaps the abundance of the unique flower was what first attracted her to the scent. After breathing in the gentle aroma he changed his mind, deciding she was simply drawn to the light fragrance. The scent was so perfect for her, enchanting and enticing. The more time spent in her company, the more he learned about her character. As they tried to get comfortable, Derek announced, "She is awake." They all leaned over her and as her eyes fluttered open, she was greeted by the staring expressions of her friends, each offering comfort.

Gabrielle turned her head from one, to the other, to the other. Finally she softly said, "Thank you," as a single tear fell from her eye. She was so happy. Although they had almost gotten caught and it had been dangerous, they had been successful. Now, she could find her guardian, look for her father and go back home. In fact, "thank you" barely seemed adequate enough.

As Gabrielle sat up, James demanded, "What the hell happened back there?"

"What do you mean?" she wondered

"That young maid talked about the bride and groom and suddenly you act strange. Then she mentions some aunt and you stiffen up. Some girl's name is the same as yours and you barely wait till the door closes before you swoon. Now, please explain."

Gabrielle looked at each of them and responded, "I'll try. While still at Helena's I overheard Sheriff Muden say that Viscount Herrington had recently married and would be on his honeymoon." Turning to look directly at James, she said, "As I had been his intended victim, I deduced that he had married my aunt instead. With Cartwright Manor empty, I figured I could sneak in and get the information needed to find my guardian. What I don't understand is, if he didn't marry my aunt, who did he marry?"

James was confused, delighted, and speechless, all at the same time. He was first confused because he hadn't understood the relation of all this to Gabrielle. Realizing if she had lived here, she was a member of gentry, delighted her station in life was no longer in question. Though given her chosen profession, the highest position she could hope to achieve would be that of his mistress. An appointment he definitely intended to bestow upon her. James remained speechless because now he had both time and opportunity on his side to plan his conquest. However, he kept those thoughts to himself as the discussion continued.

They tossed around ideas for a bit, when James stood up and said, "This is getting us nowhere. Derek and I are going to find out what is going on. Try to stay out of trouble." Unlike Derek, James was not going to argue with the women. He merely went about putting Derek in the front of the carriage. He untied the horse and said to the women, "It is in your best interest to stay out of sight. We will be back as soon as possible. If for some reason we are not back by nightfall, you get to the beach, then to the ship. I don't care how long it takes. Do not deviate from the plan." He stared at each girl for a moment, with such intensity neither wanted to argue.

Jumping into the carriage, James said, "I'll need your coat too, old man."

"What?" asked Derek in disbelief.

Misunderstanding, James continued. "I know it will be a tight fit, but I

130

believe if I leave the buttons undone, slit the seams under the arms and not move about too much. I will be able to make do."

Derek was speechless.

Then James started to explain his plan to Derek as they moved down the road. "I will simply use my title with the old bat. It has always been handy to be the son of a duke. I will say I am passing through, needed to freshen up and a bite to eat. I'll get her talking and see what I can find out."

"I'm to be your driver, I don't even have on boots!" whined Derek

"Then stay in the damn carriage!" snapped James "We only have one pair between us and I have to go inside."

"Fine, I'll see what I can do," Derek pouted.

When they pulled up to the front of the house, James hoped the lady was in and the servant that had seen him earlier wasn't. Finally a bit of luck on their side, as the footman opened the door. He announced who he was and that it was imperative he see the Lady Cartwright. Lady Penelope Cartwright. He was shown the drawing room and instructed to wait, as the lady would be with him shortly. James was very surprised when a gracious, older woman entered. She was nothing like he expected. She had a warm smile and a friendly demeanor. She was dressed in elegance and style. She led him into the dining room as soon as they had exchanged introductions. The table was set for one, although the serving girl was adding a setting. To him, it seemed rather silly for just the two of them to be eating at such a massive table. The formal dining room was huge and dark but at least the place settings were next to each other at one end, rather than at each end. He would not have been able to convince his host of his charming personality if he had to shout from one end to the other.

Convincing him to stay and eat had not been terribly difficult. Besides being hungry, it provided ample opportunity to judge Penelope. They exchanged polite conversation, right up until the food arrived, when James pressed for another topic. "I had rather hoped the viscount would be back from his honeymoon by now. It's a shame I missed him."

Lady Penelope patted his hand and replied, "Dear Herbert, I miss him so." Quickly catching her mistake, she said, "I mean I miss them both." With a sigh, she continued, "But they will not be back until Herbert has accounted for all of my niece's holdings. They have been left unmanaged by the death of my brother. We decided, I mean he decided, to combine his honeymoon and his taking inventory into one trip."

James said, "So this was an arrangement your brother had made?"

She was surprised by his curiosity, yet Lady Penelope continued on with her fabrications. "No, it was not arranged by my brother. After his casualty at sea, we were two lost and lonely females. Viscount Herrington came to console us and Gabrielle immediately fell in love with him. I really do not know if my brother had any plans for a husband for Gabrielle. If there were, he never mentioned them to me. As they were in love, I, as her only relative, gave my consent."

"Wasn't it a bit soon after his disappearance?"

Here Penelope became dramatic. "You have never been responsible for a young girl in love. I was afraid if I denied them marriage that she would insist on spending time with him anyway. It was really quite frightening how quickly she had grown close to him. I worried about her shaming the family and becoming with child. Gabrielle was always a greedy child. Wanting everything immediately. She didn't change as she grew. She fell head over heels for dear Herbert and there was nothing I could do. He could not have fended her off much longer, so I gave my consent." Here she smiled.

James decided to use his magnetism, "Please do not take offense. I have never been in the position of having to make decisions for young girls. I am sure you did what you thought best. It just seems odd that she would fall for one so … old."

"The viscount has many attributes and can be most delightful. She needed someone mature to take care of her. You know, young girls are easily impressed. One smile, one kiss, they are mesmerized. They truly make a wonderful couple. She caters to his every whim and he seems satisfied with her." Then Penelope inquired, "Have you ever met Gabrielle before?"

"Alas, I must admit I have not. Her father bragged about his thoughtful daughter from time to time, though I never had that opportunity," he answered.

A smile lit her face before responding. "She was often more than thoughtful, she was a handful. I was the one left in charge of her and she was quite spoiled. Thoughtful, now that was her father's opinion." Her voice quivered. "She was very temperamental and headstrong. It was one of the reasons I decided she should marry and become the viscount's responsibility. What she lacks in beauty and brains, she will more than make up for by being his companion and providing his heirs." Her face contorted as though in pain. Moments later both her face and voice were back to normal.

James asked, "How long has your brother been missing?"

"It is almost a year now, God rest his soul," she replied, believing she had given a perfect performance. "The viscount and my niece should be back in a week or two, will you be in the area by then?"

"No, I will be back in London. I am merely scouting some land myself. My driver must have taken a wrong turn, for we found ourselves upon your doorstep. I can't thank you enough for your hospitality. Perhaps I will run into you if you intend to travel? Will you be moving some place else, when they come back?"

"Certainly not! I am needed here," she huffed.

"Well, with a new mistress and them being so newly wed, one would think you would feel as though you'd be intruding, Lady Penelope," he offered kindly.

"My niece is far too young to run this household. Not to mention the fact that she will probably carry his heir before much longer." Here she winced again, just the thought of someone else carrying Herbert's child caused her immeasurable pain. Then remembering the plan, Penelope knew it wouldn't be much longer until Herbert was hers again. She smiled. "The viscount needs me to teach his wife everything she needs to know, to please him. Running the household, I mean. She is very young and untrained; maybe someday she will be able to take over. For now, I am in charge. When the viscount is away, that is."

James continued to ask leading questions, and she continued to answer diligently, with her prepared answers. After dessert, James announced, "I have dallied longer than I intended and need to be off. I must go and inspect that property." Leaving, she held out her hand to him, remembering his manners, he leaned over and kissed it. "Everything was delicious, please tell your cook the salmon was superb. However, it is you, my dear woman, I shall miss," he said, oozing with charm.

She sighed; she was a bit lonely these days, what with the viscount gone. She walked him to the entryway. Just as they reached the door, the serving girl brought a sack with fruit and sandwiches to take along. She shut the door behind him and Lady Penelope turned to go upstairs. She was quite satisfied with the performance she had given. It was truly unbelievable how easy it had been to substitute Gabrielle.

James hopped into the carriage and said to Derek, "Let's go."

Derek snapped the reins and off they went. He could hardly wait to tell James about the information he had been able to gather. Though both anxious and fatigued, they continued on, in companionable silence. Finally reaching the women, Derek and the girls ate the picnic lunch acquired by James. As they relaxed in the shaded glen, they chatted a bit, but decided to get to the beach before getting into any lengthy discussions.

Making their way back to the coast, the soft glow of the lighthouse came into view. Though the sun had risen, the dark clouds did not let much light filter through. The day was going to prove damp and wet. Reaching the small barn, James assisted Derek to the soft pallet as the exhausted women sat close by. Though James was just as tired, he first took care of the horse and carriage. Moments later, they were suddenly in danger of being discovered, as they heard a horse approach. Quickly jumping into the pile of hay, in the last stall, they hid as far back as possible.

The barn door creaked open, allowing an old man and his horse entrance. As he tied his horse and supplied him with oats, he murmured he would return after turning the lantern out. By the time he finally returned, the group had become restless. They were afraid they would be found out. However, the old man went about his business of feeding the horse they had so recently returned and cleaning the stall. Though it had been a rather close call when the last pitchfork full of hay had torn Kathleen's dress. Lying there in silence until the man had finished and left had been a torment. At last, the old man had concluded his chores. The barn door closed and off he rode. After breathing more than a simple sigh of relief, they all began to talk.

"Who was that?" asked Kathleen "He almost took off my backside. Tore my dress he did." She held it out for them to see.

"That is the man that lights the lantern for the lighthouse. I guess he cares for the animals too," informed Gabrielle.

"That was too damn close," whispered Derek.

Gabrielle said, "Shouldn't we get back to the ship?"

Derek said, "I think it would be better if we wait till dusk. Remember, we were supposed to do all this in one night. We could never have anticipated James following us, causing injuring to my foot, then proceeding to interview our suspect." All three turned to stare at James. The unrepentant dictator stared right back as Derek continued. "If we are seen on shore, or going out to sea, the incident may be recalled at a later date. Better not to alert others by keeping a low profile. We'll just rest here till sundown."

Gabrielle said, "Others may have use of the horse and carriage. If we are to wait all day, we will be safer in the lighthouse."

Before Derek could argue, James picked him up and told Gabrielle to lead the way. The whole time, Derek complained about being treated like a baby. Ignoring his comments, James followed Gabrielle, up the hill and through the doorway. By the time Derek was finished whining about his treatment, James was setting him down, with a little good-natured teasing.

"I suppose I should say thank you," said Derek.

"I'm not the one who preaches about good manners, you are," James said, with a twinkle in his eye. "However, it was no trouble."

Derek winced at the reminder of the times he had mentioned manners to James. "You're a right good fellow, I appreciate the help. Even if you are the reason I need help in the first place."

134

James laughed. A great big heart-pounding belly laugh.

Then Derek joined in, followed by each of the girls. They didn't even understand the jest; they just got caught up in all the exuberance. Finally the tension and adrenaline seemed to ebb away. James dropped the latch on the door and looked around. The only form of furniture contained in the large spacious area was that of a table a chair. There was a stairway that started on the left side and spiraled the wall, all the way to the top. Standing in the middle of the room you could see straight up to the glass-enclosed ceiling. Kathleen investigated the cupboards along the wall and shouted in delight when they were found to contain several blankets and pillows. They all settled down to relax in the center of the floor, the pillows adding the much needed comfort which enabled them to relax. Before long each and every one of them had fallen asleep.

Gabrielle was the first to awaken. She sat up and stretched. Not wanting to disturb the others she tiptoed towards the stairs. She had climbed, and climbed, until she finally reached the floor at the top of the lighthouse. The lamp in the center of the room was unlit, as it was daytime. She went past the light, to the door on the side. The door opened onto a balcony that encircled the entire lighthouse. It was high and open and private. She simply stood watching the sea. The surf pounding against the rocks, the water gently sliding up the sandy shore. The birds flying overhead, the fish occasionally sighted beneath the frothy waves. Only the soft blowing breeze to keep her company. She couldn't define freedom any better than this. She would now be able to seek out her guardian and start a search for her father. The desperation of knowing all along where the information lay, then the agony of being unable to retrieve it suddenly at an end. It had been well over a year that she had patiently waited for the right opportunity. She was giddy with excitement and bubbling with enthusiasm. Now that such a huge burden had been lifted, she could return to her simple life.

Suddenly two arms reached around her waist, at the same time soft lips trailed up her neck. His kisses caused her whole body to tingle. She admitted to herself that she was young and naïve. She realized this situation was exactly what the girls had warned her about, at Helena's. Her head knew better, her heart simply overruled. Her resolve melted like butter. She couldn't seem to push him away. Grabbing her by the shoulders, he turned her around. Again he mercilessly attacked her senses. Kissing, nuzzling, caressing. Sometime later, it was again he who tore away. James had to summon the willpower, for he was a master in the games between men and women, she a simple novice. He realized this girl was different. Never before had there been trouble walking away. His lust for women was legendary.

135

However, so had been his control. Not this time. This time, a small chit seemed to unman him, with very little effort.

This time after tearing his lips away, he continued to hold her. She just seemed to fit so perfectly there. He felt happy and alive. He felt satisfied. He had dreamt of her for so long, now she was here.

Although he created a feeling of euphoria unlike she had ever experienced, she had to think of her friend. Now she could certainly understand the buckets of tears Kathleen had shed when she had thought Kevin was not returning for her. Gabrielle knew she, too, would be crying nonstop when this adventure was over. This romance was just not meant to be and the sooner she admitted it to herself, the better for all concerned. Yet for a few more moments they just stood there, arm in arm. Content simply to be together.

Watching the sea's pulsating waves creep farther and farther up the shore. The feeling of tranquility overwhelmed them. Yet they barely spoke. There was still too much to do, too much to fix, before putting any definition to this relationship. Later, their heads overruled their hearts and they pulled apart and returned downstairs. With each step down, the weight of depression, getting heavier and heavier. Both seemed to be feeling a sense of loss and foreboding, each for different reasons.

Gabrielle immediately sat next to Kathleen, so as to ward off Kevin. She was thinking she was protecting herself from unwanted advances. Gabrielle believed Kevin would never show interest in her in front of Kathleen. The guilt she had been feeling was growing unbearable. Damn him for putting her in such a position! Kathleen was her friend. She was too inexperienced to fend him off. She needed help…. She would stick to Kathleen like glue.

James, on the other hand, thought it amusing. His first impression with her choice of seating was that she was trying to remain proper. Then he thought perhaps she was being a tease, which only made him grin.

James began, "It seems like everything Lady Penelope says is correct information. However, she has a haughty air about her. She seems to feel she is indispensable. Anyone want to guess about her relationship with the viscount?"

"I believe we have found the owner of the dressing room door," whispered Gabrielle. "For my aunt and the viscount were lovers before I left."

"Amusing," he answered.

"I too, have information," insisted Derek

"Let's have it," said James

"There are no servants living there that have worked longer than six months. The entire staff had been let go and completely replaced. Isn't that unusual?"

"Where did you get that information?" questioned James

"A pretty dairy maid, coming from the milking shed." This time it was Derek with the wide grin. "She stopped to talk and I slipped in a few questions pertaining to Gabrielle."

"Slipped in?" questioned Kathleen "Is that before or after you kissed and flirted?"

"Hey, never mind my methods, the information received is important," Derek said. " The household was turned upside down approximately eight months ago." Turning to Gabrielle, he said, "That would be shortly after you had run off, I would imagine." Then he continued, "Everyone, from the gardener to the upstairs maid, has been replaced. Including, I fear, our own dear Gabrielle. I would guess that they decided to replace Gabrielle, and then realized too many servants knew what she looked like. So they replaced all the staff."

"You are saying they substituted me?" Gabrielle was astonished

"That is what I believed happened," said Derek. "It would fit with everything else. Your father disappears; they try to get you to marry the viscount. You foil their plans and run away. They follow and try to find you, to no avail. Your aunt can't marry him or they lose your assets. Instead they have an impostor take your place, none are the wiser. They gain control of your property and your money. If he impregnates the girl posing as you, they even have their heir."

"Well hell!" said Kathleen. "That should be easy enough to fix, let's go find someone that will recognize Gabrielle. Then we will expose them for the impostors they are."

James looked totally bewildered.

Sadly Gabrielle looked up and said, "Who would it be that would recognize me?" She sighed, "All the servants are gone, my father may have drowned at sea. My aunt will deny me. Viscount Herrington would be a fool to acknowledge me. And I've yet to find out who my guardian is."

"What do you mean? You can think of no one that would vouch for your identity?" questioned Derek.

"What about girlfriends? Beaus? Neighbors? You cannot be without any of them?" asked James

"Although my father often joked about having a beau hidden away for me," she said sadly, "I now believe, it was just his way to make me feel better."

As Gabrielle was shaking her head no, to all of the people mentioned,

Kathleen offered more. "Dressmaker, teacher, relatives?"

"Unfortunately, I lived a very sheltered life. Occasionally I was able to travel with my father, but that was usually by ship. I had only servants to converse with and only my aunt as a relative. Viscount Herrington is our only neighbor to the north. With the Pinnine Mountain Chain to the west, few travelers venture our way. An old sailor operates the small lighthouse on the east coast. Unluckily, he has poor eyesight, barely recognizing me most of the time. There is a fishing village down the coast. There is also the small town of Darlington, south of Cartwright Manor. However, I have never been to either. Servants made my dresses here and my tutors traveled. " Here she stopped, took a deep breath and continued, "As we are so far north and very reclused, I have not had the opportunity to obtain a beau. I was to go to London, last year, for my coming out party. However, you know how my first season turned out. I have not had much opportunity to attract a man," she said as her cheeks turned red.

"What about you?" Derek pointed to James. "You are the son of the Duke of York. Marquee of Scarborough, Earl of Richmond, Viscount Helmsley and Lord Armstrong, with all these titles you carry, is there nothing you can do?

Gabrielle was speechless. How could Derek embarrass her like that? It was as if he were dumping her problems into Kevin's lap. She needed to distance herself from Kevin as it was. It was getting harder and harder to focus on the fact that he was Kathleen's beau. "This is not his problem!" she exclaimed.

James looked over to see Gabrielle's reaction, for he didn't want another woman falling at his feet, merely because of his wealth and title. Yet little reaction came his way. Was he really expecting Gabrielle to fall at his feet? Strange as it seemed, he was definitely the one doing the falling in this relationship. He answered, "Without witnesses there will be little anyone can do. Title or no title." They sat around glumly, trying to come up with an idea. Suddenly James remembered, "Gabrielle, where did you put the stolen information?"

Jumping up as James finished his sentence, Gabrielle suddenly turned her back to them.

He thought, not for the first time, what an unlikely trollop she made, instantly becoming hard just watching her toss the cloak to the ground and tear at her blouse. Her hair had become unbound and fell well past her hips. Her cheeks were flushed and her eyes bright with excitement. He began thinking about what was under that outfit and changed his mind once again. Oh yes, he would have sought her services. She was unforgettable.

Turning around, away from the group, she was frantically tugging at the top of her blouse. Gabrielle was having difficulty as she dug down the front of the corset. How could she have forgotten the whole reason for going home in the first place? She produced the pouch containing the journal, while turning around and saying, "All the answers I need are here. Some place in this book is the name of my guardian." Nervously wringing her hands, she quietly spoke. "Though I'm not even sure I would recognize him, for I only met him once and that was a very long time ago. I do recall his name being William something, for father instructed me to call him Uncle William."

Silently they all sat on the ground, taking turns looking it over, flipping the pages and skimming through the journal. After lists of property and possessions, both in Britain and in France, came several pages about a place called Ceylon. This was followed by page upon page of investments made in the East Indian Company. The next few pages contained instructions regarding his ward! That seemed to surprise Gabrielle far more than anything else. Followed by lists of property and possessions in India. Quickly paging through the information not pertaining to their quest, it seemed a plantation in the West Indies was the final piece of property listed. Last, but not least, they finally found what they had initially been looking for. Under the heading confidant and guardian, in bold scroll, it listed the name William Pitt, First Earl of Chatham.

"Why you can't mean THE William Pitt? He's bloody famous," said Derek. "Though my father has known his family for years, I am more familiar with them because of business." Looking directly at Gabrielle, he said, "Do you realize the significance of having a man as important as he for a guardian?"

The air was heavy with silence until Kathleen stammered, "You know, one of his sons is also named William Pitt? They call him William the Younger. How do you know he is not your guardian?" Kathleen questioned.

"The paper lists him as William Pitt, First Earl of Chatham. Pretty specific," retorted James. "Besides, William the Younger is a just a youth of seventeen or eighteen. Too young to be named guardian by her father." He sighed. "I have heard The Earl of Chatham speak in the House of Lords. He his both a formidable opponent and a strong alley."

"Isn't it strange that you are both familiar with my guardian?" asked Gabrielle.

"Some of us are a bit more familiar with him than others," laughed Kathleen.

Slightly perplexed, they all stared at her until they comprehended her meaning.

139

They exchanged amused looks among themselves and then turned to look at her once again. Suddenly they could no longer hold back the hysteria as they burst into laughter.

"Though it has been years since I have seen him, he was a kindly old gent," Kathleen added.

"What are the odds that the four of us all know the same man?" asked Gabrielle.

"The man was prime minister, for crying out loud! Who doesn't know him? And even though he is no longer prime minister, he is still in the public eye and his views constantly quoted in the press," huffed James incredulously."

"Actually, I don't think it is uncommon at all. It just goes to show what a small world it really is," commented Derek.

Frowning, James inserted, "That Kathleen has run across William Pitt in her business is slightly more surprising.... I'd have thought he was well past those activities by now. However, being a man, it is quite normal to seek entertainment." Stopping, he glared at Kathleen before continuing, "Please refrain from telling us each and every time we run across a previous client, however!" He grimaced. "I hardly feel we need to be privy to all your information."

Turning, Derek spoke directly to Gabrielle. "Who knows? If things had turned out differently I may have met you at your coming out. Suffice it to say I would have asked you to dance immediately and we would have become great friends.... Wait a moment ... and so we have. A shortcut, if you will." Derek smiled. "You see, it is not so unusual that we know the same people, yet for different reasons."

Both James and Kathleen rolled their eyes in exasperation at the kid gloves Derek often used when speaking to Gabrielle. James became irritated and his interest returned to the paperwork at hand. Ignoring the others, he reached for the pouch containing the journal, at the same time feeling a lump through the lining. Realizing something still remained inside, he pulled the journal back out and tipped the bag upside down. Spilling out was a beautiful sapphire ring. The dainty ring itself was made of silver. Though the ring itself was not very large, the magnificent sapphire stone was a good size. The gem appeared solid and clear yet so blue it seemed almost icy. Sparks of silvery brilliance streaked within the stone with slight movement when bathed in the light. The silver was twisted in a rope design and ended underneath the stone setting, as though in a bow, or a knot. It was beautiful and unique.

After staring at it for some time, the group became curious.

"Why was this in the pouch?" asked Kathleen.

"Was that your mother's, Gabrielle?" whispered James

Gabrielle looked into Kevin's eyes for a few moments and then turned to the others. She believed it was her mother's, yet she could not be certain. She had no answers. She was under the impression that her mother's items were still in her box at Cartwright manor. This had not been among them. "Surely she had more than one item of jewelry, this one must have a meaning behind it. Don't you think?" suggested Derek.

Sensing the confusion Gabrielle felt, James asked again, "Gabrielle, is that your mother's?"

Finally she shrugged her shoulders. "I honestly don't know. I don't recall ever having seen it, yet it must have been. It is really peculiar. Maybe it was to have been a gift for me, maybe upon his return father would have...." Her voice trailed off.

"Well, it must mean something, either put it in the pouch or wear it. But whatever you do, don't lose it," announced Derek. Suddenly Kathleen and Derek began to squabble between themselves about what to do with the ring. Meanwhile, James took the ring and picked up Gabrielle's slim hand, easily sliding it upon her small finger.

With all eyes upon her, Gabrielle began to feel flustered and tried to back away.

As though he had read her mind, James' attention was entirely focused on Gabrielle. They both seemed to tune out Kathleen and Derek, who where involved in a deep discussion of there own. James gazed into Gabrielle's eyes and smiled. Manipulating her with his charm, he melted her resolve. "Do not fear, we will find your guardian and perhaps even your father."

Tension created by his nearness caused her to pull her hand away. "I can not thank you enough," she murmured. Her blouse was still askew after first hiding, then dislodging the journal. Several buttons remained undone and he could not help but look at her revealing form. Admiration of her cleavage caused his pants to become just a little snug and his breath a little short. He was drawn to her like no other! Her eyes gazed into his revealing passion and desire. Her mouth was tender, warm and willing. She attempted to play this damn teasing game, sometimes allowing him close, other times ignoring him completely. Yet it only amused him to watch her efforts. Her every mannerism invited him closer, easily yielding when he complied. She wanted him as badly as he did her, then as though struck by a sense of propriety she would quickly withdraw. He would press her to submit to his passions now, had they been alone. Damn, did she have any idea of her effect on him?

Staring into his eyes she could not seem to take her eyes off him. Her breath became a bit ragged, her eyelids heavy. She felt as though she was in a trance whenever he was near. Standing next to him she wished he would pull her to him and kiss her again. To taste his lips and feel his soft kisses trail along her skin once more. To be held in his arms and feel safe and warm and wanted was all she would ever ask. His male scent filled her nostrils, her heart fluttered uncontrollably. It appeared as though he was leaning towards her, all the while attempting to pull her closer. Had he read her mind again?

Kathleen's sudden screeching at Derek startled both of them, causing James and Gabrielle to grudgingly return to reality. In unison they turned their heads, trying to focus on the problem. James was furious to be interrupted yet again, while Gabrielle only blushed, appearing upset.

Oh, my God! thought Gabrielle as Kathleen railed away. *I almost kissed Kevin in front of Kathleen. How does he do that? How does he make me forget my resolve to dissuade him? How does he make me forget my very surroundings? I have got to stay away from him or I will lose total control. The attraction is just too strong. I am not experienced enough to remain unaffected. What can I do but stay away from him? Kathleen is my friend. I will not be the one to hurt her. I must be strong. I must think of how he is hurting my friend. He is a cad, a rogue, and a fiend! How can he treat both of us so callously?*

Without a word, she quickly moved from his side and once again sat close to Kathleen, for safety's sake. Silently James straightened and moved to join the circle. With both Derek and Kathleen between them, Gabrielle felt only slightly better. And once again James watched as Gabrielle attempted to withdraw from him, both physically and mentally. He decided to let her think she had succeeded ... until another opportune moment was at hand.

Returning to the earlier discussion, the group spent the remaining time arguing about what to do. One suggestion was to continue on and bring James and Kathleen to Edinburgh. Then Derek would take her back to London and use his father for an introduction and get her in to see the earl. Kathleen and James totally disagreed with that idea. Kathleen stated emphatically that she would not be going to Scotland until dear Gabrielle was safely in the care of her guardian. James totally agreed with that idea. Derek, however, had to be talked into the idea of going south again, instead of following his original itinerary.

They were still arguing when the sun started to go down. Gabrielle grew concerned and reminded them that the old sailor would be coming to light the lamp. They had to hide. So they tidied up, leaving no traces. Quietly they crept back into the barn. Sitting in the loft and staying silent, they finally heard the coming and going of the old sailor.

Finally it was late enough and they made their way down the beach. By now, the crushing waves and high tide had pushed the boat up farther and deeper into the sand dunes. This trip, Derek was happy to have James along, as it was not easy to dislodge the dingy from the sand. Finally they pushed it loose and jumped aboard, joining the ladies. They seemed more subdued and kept to their own counsel for most of the trip back to the ship. They had short, quiet discussions, but none returned to the previous topic. They got to the ship, climbed aboard and tied the small craft to the hull. Tomorrow, with the help of the crew, they would pull it up. Saying goodnight and heading toward the cabins, the ladies hoped to discourage the men from further discussion. Staying topside, the men hoped to converse without the women's interference. The women raced down to Gabrielle's cabin and, after cleaning themselves up, spent half the night trying to come to a decision. The men stayed on deck and smoked and drank and did the same.

The next morning they all met in the captain's cabin for breakfast.

After finishing the last of her tea, Kathleen began "Gabrielle and I have discussed this and we hope you see the wisdom of our plan. We are set on this course of action, but would like your agreement also." Kathleen looked at Gabrielle and continued, "Gabrielle would like us all to stay together, until she feels safe, with or without the consent of her guardian. She also wants to hunt for her father, once again with or without the aid of her guardian. What do you think?"

"I think it is a practical plan," said James, not mentioning that Derek and he had already made the very same plans. "We will go back to London, stay in my townhouse and find your guardian."

"I don't think we should impose," said Gabrielle. She was already filled with guilt for betraying her best friend. She had tried several times, last night, to confess. Yet, every time she tried, she cried. She couldn't even breathe, thinking about staying in his home and being so close to him. It would be too much! Not only did her best friend's beau infatuate her, but also she believed she was falling in love with him. Things couldn't get much worse.

"You could stay with me and my parents," Derek eagerly suggested.

James gave him a dirty look and said, "The less people that have any idea of what we are up to, the better." Looking directly at Derek, he said, "We have already discussed this. I have the home, I have the space. Now, I suggest this discussion is over.

Gabrielle said, "Unless you have someone living with you, we will not be able to stay," she huffed. "Our reputations would be a shambles."

"Your reputations!" laughed James. "You girls come from a brothel! What the hell can happen to your reputation?"

Gabrielle picked up her bowl of porridge and threw it across the table, some landing in his hair, some stuck to his face, most landing on his lap. Then she stood up and said, "I will stay with you when hell freezes over!" and she fled the room. The sight of him covered with porridge would have been enough by itself, but added to the look on his face, it was priceless.

Both Derek and Kathleen could not stop laughing, the scene was so funny. They both realized, at exactly the same time, that James thought Gabrielle one of Helena's girls. Really, it was too rich! Anyone with an ounce of brains could see that Gabrielle was as innocent as she appeared. Finally, after they stopped laughing, they informed James of his misconceptions.

James could not believe how he had blundered. How in heaven's name was he going to fix this? He had never given a moment's thought to the running of a house of ill repute. He simply thought all the women inside were for sale. He should have caught on when Gabrielle told the story of living here, in Northumberland. He should have at least been suspicious when she explained about her flight from her aunt and the evil viscount. He had gained the knowledge of her heritage yet had not caught on to the fact that she was still an innocent. At first he felt guilty ... then his mind began to pull her story apart....

Innocent, hell, he had kissed her, hadn't he? She sure was not innocent. Maybe even Kathleen didn't know everything. It wasn't like there wasn't ample opportunity for experimentation while living at Helena's. Hell, he could have had her himself, a couple of times. Maybe someone else had. She sure hadn't learned to kiss like that on her own! First he thought he'd have to apologize, for judging her harshly. But after thinking back to the seductress he had met on the balcony at Helena's, he had second thoughts. She had manipulated him too easily for her to be totally innocent. Maybe, he thought he'd just observe her and decide if he owed her an apology, at all. For now, he would wait and see.

Meanwhile Gabrielle was pacing back and forth in her cabin. She was stomping actually, the whole while calling James vile names. She was furious. If he thought she was that kind of girl, maybe she should just act like that kind of girl. She could simply watch Kathleen and mimic her every move. She would be damned if he was going to treat her in such a manner. The sooner she found her guardian, the sooner he would be out of her life.

However, by the time Kathleen joined her, she was calm and quiet. So quiet in fact, Kathleen knew she was up to something. When Gabrielle took out her sewing kit and a few dresses, Kathleen became curious. Gabrielle began tearing and ripping clothing as she sat in the corner. No longer able to contain herself, Kathleen could not help but question her. After Gabrielle explained her intention to make her dresses more revealing. To act the part the vile man upstairs believed her to be. A seductress, a temptress, she would show him! With a dramatic flair she strolled across the cabin with an exaggerated sway of her hips and a sultry expression on her face.

Bursting her bubble, Kathleen informed her that they had already told his lordship the truth. Telling him what a fool he had been, how if he had but opened his eyes he would have realized Gabrielle's true nature. Kathleen had hoped by revealing this information Gabrielle would be happy. Instead this foiled Gabrielle's intentions completely. So without comment, she neatly folded the dresses back up and put them in the trunk. Gabrielle would have to fix them later. Unresolved issues weighed heavily upon her and she knew she would get no rest until Kevin agreed to stop tormenting her. He needed to concentrate on Kathleen and leave her alone. She went in search of Kevin to straighten everything out. She found Conor, the first mate, and asked him to send Lord Armstrong to her cabin. He didn't come to her cabin till nightfall. By then Gabrielle was livid that he hadn't bothered to respond to her request. She simply felt he no longer cared about her feelings. Of course, he shouldn't care about her feelings, he had Kathleen. Yet it did hurt. Finally, after many hours, a knock sounded at the door.

"Come in," called Gabrielle

"I'm sorry it took so long to answer your summons. Derek and I were up to our ears in ropes and masts, as the rigging had come loose. I was in a precarious position hanging on one of the ropes and couldn't come sooner. What can I do for you?" James explained.

"Come in, sit down, care for a drink?" she asked in a hurried voice. She was giddy now that he was here and hadn't ignored her.

"Fine," he muttered

She gracefully slid into the chair across from him at the table. They silently sipped wine, eyeing the other.

"You requested my presence for what reason?" he asked

"As there seem to be a few misunderstandings, I wanted the opportunity to clear them up," she said.

"Go on," said James

"First and foremost, I believe there has been a slight misconception of my reputation. I am not a woman of ill repute, as you so willingly categorize me. I am only seventeen and still a virgin. I would appreciate your snideness to disappear. Second, I am of noble birth. I am able to travel in society and meet people and question whomever I please. Which leads us to number three, I don't need you for anything. I certainly do not have to do what you say, nor do I need your permission to do anything, if I so choose. I expect to be in on

145

all decisions we make as a group. Not the men decide and the women follow. It would certainly be different if I were your sister, your ward, or your wife. As I am not any of them, I expect to be consulted!" she shouted.

He watched her carefully before answering, "You are one of the most beautiful women I have ever seen. After tasting your charms and watching the display of your appeal, I have been blinded to all else. I should have realized you were young and innocent. Yet when you kissed me, you were so aggressive, I thought you wanton. You seemed to have experience. I didn't take the time to properly assess your true character. For this I am deeply sorry. Even after we had raided your home and you had shared your past with us, I didn't associate you with the girl from that manor. On some level, even hearing that you were from the gentry, it just didn't register. Maybe it was because if you were the young innocent girl from that country home. I wouldn't be able to think of you as that seductive, irresistible, alluring, beauty. The woman I met at Helena's. However, I know now that you are as innocent as you seem. Again I am sorry. As for my assistance, there I must disagree."

As she started to protest, he held up his hand and said, "Stop," before she could even get a word out. "Let me have my say." He reached over to the sideboard and grabbed the carafe of wine. Refilling both their glasses, he continued, "It is impossible, if you think to go somewhere without me. First you need my protection. Both my size and my title will come in handy. Until your guardian takes over, I feel it is my duty to step into the role. Third, although this is all new to me, I will make the effort to listen to your suggestions when we are making our plans." Here he hesitated. He stood up and walked over to her. Pulling her out of her chair, his arms encircled her. His mouth crushed hers with a powerful, hungry energy. He craved her liked he had craved no other. He wanted her, and without having to admit it, he needed her.

She was spinning out of control again. His smoldering gaze and soft caresses started a fire under her skin. He pressed his body close and claimed her lips as prize. His mouth had left hers to explore and was leaving a trail to her ear, down her neck and back again. His mouth repeated the sensual torment started only moments before. This time it was she that pushed herself away. She stiffened her arms and held him at bay. Finally, she said, "I can't do this." Thinking of Kathleen.

He kept forgetting she was as young and innocent. This time it was her trying to be in control. "It is best you stopped us now before we had gotten too caught up to stop," he said to encourage her decision, thinking it would please her to have him compliment her so.

"You conceited ass! Why is it up to me to control you? Don't forget Kathleen. You have prior commitments. Leave me alone!"

He was confused. Had he rushed her? He decided she needed space. He would give her more time. He stepped back, saying, "Forgive me." As he sat back down across from her, he thought to himself, *She is upset about starting a relationship with me, merely because I have previous travel arrangements?*

She dropped back into her chair. Oh, he had given a pretty little speech all right. All about him taking care of everything and what she could and could not do. Yet, he had mentioned nothing about his feelings for her, nothing about loving her. She was not even sure what she would do at that point, not wanting to hurt Kathleen. But she wanted to hear the words, not even knowing if she could stand being loved by someone who already pledged his love to another. She was so upset.

Her hair was mussed, her cheeks were flushed and her eyes were bright. She was beautiful. He couldn't stop staring; even though he knew he was devouring her with his eyes. Now that she was not a prostitute he would have to think of some other way to keep her close by. How a mere slip of a girl wreaked such havoc within him, in so little time, he would never know. He had come to the conclusion that he was not going to let her go. He could provide her with everything she needed. He could give her the comfort and security she wanted. Suddenly, like a bolt of lightning, the realization hit him. James was thinking of her on a permanent basis. He was considering something he had struggled valiantly to stay away from. MARRIAGE! But knowing he wanted her in his future and accepting it were two different things. Struggling with his emotions, he changed the subject.

Suggesting different avenues to take while looking for her guardian, "Your guardian will either be at the townhouse in London, or his country estate in Somerset. As it is early in the fall, he could be at either place. However, as we are closer to London, we will first check there. I deem it more likely, with his poor health, that the baroness has him safely ensconced at Burton Pynsent." As soon as James had mentioned her guardian's health, Gabrielle expressed concern. "Gout," he said simply, as though that explained everything. Eyeing her speculatively for conformation, he began pacing until she nodded her head affirmatively. Then he continued, "We can stay at my home in London." Here he stopped, because she was shaking her head no again. "Why not?" he demanded.

"The same reason as before. Our reputations. I assume you care about Kathleen's as well as mine," she stated

"I will bring in someone to chaperone."

"No, that will not work," she sighed

"My parents' home?" he mentioned, hoping she wouldn't like that idea either.

"That would be perfect," she responded.

"Oh, great, you would agree to that. Now we will be involving more people, when I told you the less people that knew the better. Suppose we run into someone that knows your aunt or the viscount?"

She hadn't thought of that. There had to be a way to fix all that. Then a brilliant idea occurred to her, "Aha, I've got it. I can marry Derek and use his name. Then when I'm introduced I can be the Lady Anderson. How is that for a great scheme?" she asked.

The green-eyed devil sitting on his shoulder made James shout, "Great, just great," as he turned and slammed the door. Why the hell hadn't she come up with the idea of being his wife? After the passionate kisses they had just shared. The information they had shared. The time spent together. Did he really mean so little to her? Even if she thought it only temporary, she should be his, not Derek's. He was going to talk to Derek about this.

Oh bother! He says I can help plan and use ideas. Then he slams out, after only one idea. It suddenly occurred to her. Maybe he wanted me to ask him. That would put him in a pretty silly position, being engaged to Kathleen and all. Oh well. Not giving it another thought, she went about her toiletries, and readied herself for bed.

The next two days passed in relative compatibility. The men plotted courses, looked at charts, and made plans. They practiced swordsmanship on the deck or they worked on the rigging, which was forever in disrepair. The ladies sewed, read, and planned. After the suggestion of marrying Derek, James had been a bit distant. Except the last night aboard when he came to her and blurted out, "The plan to marry Derek is not sound. I would be the better choice, as I have the better connections to have it declared invalid later. It was wrong of you to impose upon Derek in this manner. However, as the captain, he could marry us tonight. Then we could stay in my home without hurting your reputation. This plan is also more practical because we would not have to include strangers in on our schemes."

She had simply stared at him. Couldn't he understand how hard this was for her, even temporarily she couldn't be the wedge that drove him and Kathleen apart? And if it didn't drive them apart how about her own feelings, what about the despair she would feel, later? How would she react after the sham marriage was over and he returned to Kathleen? Didn't he know what this would do to Kathleen? Did he really care for either of them? She simply stood staring at him, unable to respond. Finally he turned on his heels and returned to his duties.

She went below to find Kathleen. But Derek had reached Kathleen first and had explained James' plan. Kathleen was delighted, as she had long ago thought James and Gabrielle perfect for each other. She was sure once they were married, they would work out whatever differences they had. Kathleen also knew that even if they thought it temporary, they were only fooling themselves. If they needed time to see it, so be it. But for now there was a wedding to plan. So when Gabrielle found her, she was pulling the sheer white gown from her trunk. Gabrielle insisted that she couldn't possible wear a garment of Kathleen's. She also was dumfounded by the fact that Kathleen was not the least bit bothered by the situation. Was Kathleen so secure in her knowledge that Kevin loved her then? Gabrielle continued to shake her head no to the whole idea. Kathleen merely chatted away, completely ignoring Gabrielle's arguments. In the end, Kathleen finally wore her down.

Still Gabrielle was so confused. Why could neither of them understand how devastating it would be for her both to have him and to lose him?

Next, Kathleen proceeded to persuade Gabrielle into trying on the gown. When she did, the front neckline fell to her stomach. The girls fell into peals of laughter. What had they expected? It was Kathleen's dress after all and she had a huge bosom. Kathleen pulled and tugged and pinned. With continuous effort, the dress finally seemed to fit her body. They fell to work sewing and planning. Then Gabrielle said, "I want to thank you for all you have done for me. Are you not uncomfortable with me being first to marrying? Tell me true?"

"I'll have to admit I thought to have been in Scotland and married to Kevin by now. Yet I could not go to Scotland without finishing this adventure we have started. Besides, you are my best friend. We will do anything necessary to protect you. Whatever happens happens to all of us. After you are safe and with your guardian, I will travel to Scotland and be with Kevin. For now it is a grand experience, one I will someday tell my grandchildren.

Tossing and turning in her bunk later that evening, Gabrielle simply couldn't sleep. Giving up, she tossed on her wrapper and tugged on her slippers. She quietly made her way down the narrow corridor to Kevin's cabin. She knocked quietly, yet no one responded. As she eased the door open, a small shaft of light fell onto Kevin's sleeping form. Sliding quietly inside, she shut the door. Making her way by memory, she stumbled her way through the darkness. Finally she reached his bunk and sat on the edge. She softly shook his shoulder.

He seemed a bit groggy, but she repeated several times if he was awake. Having heard two affirmative answers, she began the speech prepared only moments before in her cabin. The speech about how she thought she was falling in love with him. Reminding him of the importance of taking care of Kathleen. How she could not marry someone as a pretense. She promised not to argue with him over where to stay while in London, if he promised not to argue with her about coercing her into marriage. She rambled on and on. Finally she thanked him for all he had done and all he would continue to do. Letting him know that when the time came to let him take Kathleen to Scotland, she would just accept it.

Then she leaned over and kissed him. It was just a sweet, gentle kiss on the lips. Not one of passion, but of simple gratitude. She inhaled his masculine odor and caressed his cheek with her hand. Then retreated from the cabin.

So, his little dove did not want a marriage in name only. She could only marry for real, with someone she loved. She wouldn't argue anymore. He didn't believe that for a moment. However he was not about to let that boon slide by. He would get her into his home, get her to marry him, and then get her in his bed. As his door shut, it was fortunate that Gabrielle had not glanced back. If she had, she would have caught the devilish expression on his face and become concerned. As it was, she left lighthearted and slept with contentment, the whole night through.

The next day, they once again found themselves sailing up the Thames River. Standing on deck the three of them watched the activities on the riverbanks. They admired the scenes as the entered London Port. London's was a very hectic harbor. This time they did not have a cargo to unload. So after mooring his ship, Derek immediately joined the group.

Now all four of them stood together, waiting for the small craft bringing them ashore to be lowered. There was laughter and excitement among them. Everyone had an optimistic attitude and a happy expression. The day had started out clear and sunny. Whereupon they had all shared a bountiful breakfast. Derek, of course, recalled the flying porridge story. Sending each and everyone into peals of laughter. All through breakfast everyone had been eager to share stories and compliments. After all their trials and tribulations, they had bonded, forming a unique friendship. They made plans to attend the theater. To visit the museums, attend the art galleries and go out to dinner. The women wanted nothing more than hot baths and endless shopping. The men were eager for a hand of cards, fine alcohol and bed sport. The mood remained festive and jovial. Their joy and infectious laughter stayed with them right up until they docked. Agreeing to wait near the pier, while James hired a carriage, they surveyed the surrounding activities.

Near the docks the crowds were thick and noisy. All around were people rushing about, busy at work. From the vendors displaying their wares to the sailors unloading cargo. The smells of sewage and fish and gin assaulted their senses. Noise seemed to accompany every activity as women selling fruit or buns on street corners haggled and spirited young boys hawking newspapers shouted. Buggies rushing to and fro, wagons loaded with items for delivery. Crewmen all headed to the nearest tavern, groups of people waving to passengers as they disembarked the ships. Noise and commotion surrounded them.

As they stood waiting, the mass of people seemed to push them up closer and closer to the street. As a man jumped out of his carriage, trying to catch a friend, another man was shoved into Gabrielle.

"Oh excuse me, madam, I must apologize for so rudely bumping into you," he supplied.

"With all this activity I can hardly blame you, sir," she laughed. "I was not injured or insulted, I can assure you." Gabrielle smiled.

"Are you staying in London then?" he inquired with a grin.

"Yes." She took a moment to look him over, realizing he was very young. "For the moment anyway." He was just a lad really, probably not even twenty. It was his etiquette and speech that led those around him to believe he was older than he really was. His face was flushed, as though embarrassed to have run into her, yet he had a caring manner, which put her immediately at ease. Gabrielle beamed up at him.

Derek could hardly believe the coincidence. What are the odds that they would run into her guardian's son? "Excuse me, William, it is I, Derek Anderson," said Derek, diverting his attention from Gabrielle.

"Derek, you old hound. Haven't seen you for quite a while. How is your father doing? Still trying to talk you off your ship and into marriage? You must stop up sometime. Do it soon, though. Father hasn't been feeling quite his old self."

As Derek began to answer, Gabrielle interrupted and blurted out "William? William Pitt?" she asked hopefully.

He nodded affirmatively.

As he was a young man, she again confirmed "William the Younger? What a coincidence! We are here looking for your father."

Derek said, "Now Gabrielle, you're not following the plan." Pulling on his collar, which suddenly seemed too tight, he envisioned James' reaction to the untimely exchange. Derek wished James were here to handle Gabrielle. He was having trouble stopping the flow of conversation.

Looking at Derek, she failed to understand how this was failing the plan, when they had just moved from step one to the finish line, instead of weeks of investigation. She continued on, "I have just come to seek the protection of your father. My name is Gabrielle Cartwright. Lord Cartwright is my father. He is missing and I am in a predicament. Will it be possible to visit him?" she rushed.

"Not only will you visit, but you must remain with us. We will get everything straightened out." Signaling the driver to come forward, William turned to Derek. "This is my coach," he said, opening the door. "I insist upon giving you a lift also."

Gabrielle said, "Oh, I couldn't impose in this manner. We do already have plans, couldn't I just visit him tomorrow?"

"My dear, my father is not in the best of health. He has very good days and also poor days. Today is he feeling quite chipper. As you are his ward, he would become very agitated if I were to fail to bring you directly home. Your friends are certainly invited also."

Gabrielle looked at Kathleen and Derek anxiously, not sure what to do.

Kathleen stepped in to say, "I'm certainly going wherever you go, Gabrielle."

Derek mumbled, "I'd better stay and give His Grace the news." What he really meant was, somebody had better wait for James and explain. And boy, I wish it wasn't me. He walked over to the carriage and assisted the ladies in. Explaining to them that the men would be in touch very soon, he wished Gabrielle luck with her guardian and told Kathleen to behave. Both girls responded with undignified huffs. William's carriage pulled away and it couldn't have been five minutes before James appeared. James hopped out of the coach after spotting Derek, immediately inquiring where the ladies had gone off. After hearing the answer, his temper flared. Upset over the abrupt change of plans, he couldn't help shouting at Derek in frustration. He simply could not believe that he was gone approximately ten minutes and everything had gone haywire.

Finally getting through to James, Derek reminded him that it was an act of fate. That it was hardly anyone's fault that William had bumped into Gabrielle. After all, what were the odds? And to her credit, Gabrielle had insisted she had another place to stay. Yet once William found out she was his father's ward, nothing would sway him. Derek also explained to James that William's father was not in the best of health. That possibly it was good timing to have run into him. After all, they were still in town. Realizing what Derek said was true, James calmed down a bit. Then James apologized and suggested they might as well go home. So sharing the carriage, they left the docks. James dropped Derek off at his family's home before continuing on to his own.

Suddenly all alone, after days of commotion and chaos, he felt edgy and restless. At first, he had been uncomfortable with the entire fracas that traveling with two women provided. How quickly he had become familiar with it. Now he felt uneasy in his solitude, even a bit lonely. As he slowly climbed the stairs of his house, James recalled his plan. Escorting Gabrielle into his home and watching her fascination in delight. Observing each expression as he guided her through his home and shared his possessions. He had fully intended to pamper her and extend her his every hospitality. So she would wish to linger. He had certainly been in no hurry to find her guardian! How different the homecoming had turned out to be.

As the *son of a Duke*, James was unaccustomed to circumstances falling beyond his control. As a *spy*, it was unfathomable to believe he had failed in achieving his goal. As a *man*, it was damn frustrating to be out-maneuvered by a woman.

Chapter 10

By the time they pulled up in front of the townhouse, the three of them were talking as though they had been friends forever. William was a gifted speaker and had the ability to put them at ease immediately. He explained that if indeed his father were her guardian, she would lack for nothing. Gabrielle informed him there was a long story to tell. She also included the fact that after dinner would be soon enough for the telling. They emerged from the coach laughing and talking. Upon entering the large foyer, they were greeted by the family butler, who promptly assisted them with their wraps. He was of slight build, with barely a hair on his head. The expression he wore was warm and friendly. The butler quickly settled them in the salon and then went to the kitchen for tea. William, on the other hand, went in search of his father.

When William returned, an elderly man followed him. Gabrielle rose from the settee, looking to see if she recognized him. He was familiar, yet not exactly the same. Looking at both of them standing in the doorway, she compared them. The earl appeared frail, but though he used a crutch, his carriage remained dignified. It was easy to see he dressed much more elaborately than his son. Both men had long, narrow faces with hawk-like features, though William the Younger possessed the advantage of youth. Beady black, expressive eyes brought out the resemblance of father and son. Dressed in black velvet, William the elder was wrapped to the knees in flannel. Suffering from gout, he leaned heavily on his crutch.

However, it wasn't until William 1st Earl of Chatham smiled, that Gabrielle recognized him. It wasn't a grin or a small smile it was a huge smile. A smile that covered his entire face, causing large crinkles near the corner of his eyes. Suddenly she remembered that smile, she remembered him. Though it had been almost ten years, she ran to him like a small girl. "Uncle William!" she shouted. Hugging him and jumping up and down, Gabrielle squealed in delight. She finally slowed down, realizing she had practically knocked the man over. Apologizing, she dragged him to the nearest chair. After some of the excitement had faded, Gabrielle remembered her manners and introduced Kathleen. Though a fleeting smile and a brief nod was all the attention William the Elder gave to her. The old earl had a twinkle in his eye as he observed Kathleen but he assumed the others were completely unaware. Gabrielle wondered if he did indeed remember Kathleen or if he simply appreciated the beauty of her companion.

William the Elder treated Gabrielle warm and tender and was very responsive to her inquiries. Yes, he remembered consenting to be guardian to Gabrielle Cartwright. Happy with this answer, she smiled.

As to a positive identification, though it had been years since he had last seen the young girl, he was convinced of her identity, insisting she was the image of her mother. Looking in Gabrielle's direction, the earl said, "In fact, Richard presented me with a miniature of you last time we were there." Looking back and forth between the girls, the old earl continued, "I can't recall offhand where it is at the moment. However, if you require proof, I shall send a messenger to my wife. She will know where to locate it and take the proper steps to sending it to us."

Here Young William snickered, "More than likely Mother will have a good laugh at your expense and we will receive a message saying it is some place in this very house."

William the Elder blushed and then returned his gaze upon Gabrielle. "Occasionally I misplace things. I'm sure it has been well protected, for that is my nature. Odd, that I can't remember exactly where.... Never mind, my wife will save the day, she has an eye for detail."

The earl was ready to accept his responsibilities as Gabrielle's guardian, both emotionally and legally.

Gabrielle continued to question him, determined to find answers.

No, he had not heard from her father. Gabrielle frowned at his response.

Nor had her father's solicitor notified him. She felt only ambivalence with that answer. Her aunt had not yet contacted the earl. Which could only mean Gabrielle's aunt still had no clue as to the identity of her guardian. That was one point in their favor. As Gabrielle chatted on and on, William the Elder noticed her unique sapphire ring and made mention of it.

Her demeanor changed, suddenly quiet. Slowly she answered, "I believe it was my mother's ring. Though I am not certain. I found it among my father's personal possessions." With a heavy sigh, Gabrielle recalled the romantic moment Kevin had slid the ring on her finger.

Kathleen had remained rather quiet, watching the interaction between the Pitts and Gabrielle. The gentlemen seemed sincere in their hospitality and concern. Gabrielle seemed comfortable, relating with ease to their inquiries. She was finally able to believe that they would be able to effectively look after her.

A servant arrived with the tea, interrupting their conversation. So, they talked of mundane things, such as holidays and weather. Yet even after the serving girl had left, they continued to talk of other things, while enjoying the crumpets. The earl decided that after dinner would be soon enough to sit in the study and listen to Gabrielle's tale. He wanted a full accounting, yet felt she should rest, clean up, and get comfortable first. He wanted to ensure Gabrielle all the necessary privacy for her story.

William the Elder sat in his chair sipping tea, yet his mind was already miles away ... planning. He would first need to send for his barrister. Then he needed to send a message to a friend, enlisting aid to his young ward's plight. Gabrielle's position required immediate action. If the rest of her tale proved as upsetting as what he had gathered thus far, he would need strong assistance. Henry Fielding was a personal friend, with an outstanding reputation; he would not betray the earl's confidence. Henry's men would assist them, assuring both protection and caution. As allies they would direct them toward the correct actions. It was imperative to keep Gabrielle safe, so he needed the secrecy provided by Henry's men. These fearsome fellows were also known as The Bow Street Runners.

Still in his seat, his thoughts returning to the present, the earl tried to focus upon the ensuing conversation. Gathering it was something about fashion he immediately desired escape and clumsily got to his feet. He had decided that rather than offer the girls an explanation or raise alarm, he would exclude them from his plans. "Enough of this chatter," he announced. "I feel the need for a nap, I suggest you all do the same. I will see you at dinner." Then he proceeded to exit the room. Reaching the doorway just as the butler was entering, he muttered to the butler, "Show them to their rooms, we will dine at the usual time." Then William Pitt 1st Earl of Chatham vacated the room.

All three were stunned at the abrupt change in the earl. He had been comfortably drinking his tea and well settled before the fire. Seemingly relaxed and at ease when suddenly he stood up, ending the conversation and exiting the room. Gabrielle and Kathleen both looked to young Will to explain. He returned their stares with a blank expression of his own. Shrugging his shoulders, he murmured, "I guess he really needed a nap!" At that comment Gabrielle and Kathleen exchanged glances and grinned.

After being shown to their rooms, Gabrielle would have sworn she wouldn't be able to sleep at all. Yet a couple hours later she awoke, feeling delightfully well rested and safe. Sitting upon the edge of the bed, her first thoughts were of Kevin. She well understood now how Kathleen was so enamored of him, for she too had fallen under his spell. Valiantly she reminded herself that Kathleen was too good of a friend to let the man come between them. So Gabrielle remained more determined than ever to put Kevin from her mind. She would focus on becoming reacquainted with her guardian and trying to find her father. Moving to the dressing table, she finished her toilette and then went in search of Kathleen.

She found Kathleen and Uncle William, sitting on the window seat, in the drawing room. They were huddled together, deep in conversation. For William the Elder had indeed remembered the compelling young woman from Helena's. After all, beautiful women with creamy soft skin, huge bosoms and light Scottish accents hardly fell in his lap every day. That this particular one had previously done so could not be forgotten. And her appearance needed to be immediately addressed.

As Kathleen had descended the stairway, the old earl had not allowed a moment to pass by before accosting her. He had verbally berated her for associating with a young innocent such as Gabrielle. William the Elder attacked her character and maligned her intentions, at the same time complimenting her beauty and accomplishments.

Such was the way of men! Kathleen thought.

William the Elder complained that she was hardly an adequate friend – let alone proper chaperone – for Gabrielle.

The whole time he protested Kathleen sat there as if immune to his insults. She would be damned if she was going to tolerate being threatened by the likes of him. He had participated in a few lascivious acts of his own and he should agree to put their pasts behind them. Yet, she remained seated, letting him continue to voice his arguments. It wasn't until he made mention of removing Kathleen from the premises that she rose and calmly performed her rebuttal.

First and foremost Kathleen informed him that she was no longer associated with her previous occupation. Second she explained that she would only be in London long enough to see Gabrielle settled before going on to meet her fiancé in Scotland. Third, that although it may be a trifle uncomfortable for him to have Kathleen in so close proximity, he did not have to share their previous liaison with anyone. Lastly, she reminded him that if he wanted any kind of relationship with his ward, he would be smart not to openly attack her character. Gabrielle was a very good and sincere person and would be greatly upset if the earl were to reject Kathleen.

"You believe she would see it as cruelty to you, rather than saving her reputation?" demanded William the Elder.

"Yes. I suggest you pretend you do not know me." Kathleen was not about to tell him that Gabrielle knew all about her; instead she thought to use it to her advantage. "I will be leaving shortly and then you will have her to yourself. The alternative is to chastise me, upset her and embarrass yourself."

"Embarrass myself?" he questioned.

"Won't you have to tell Gabrielle how you know I'm such a wicked influence?" she smiled.

Taking a moment to think, he let out a long dramatic sigh. "I realize it would be the best course of action. Though it galls me to no end that you are to remain her chaperone."

"Have anyone you want chaperone her around." Kathleen laughed. "Then it will only upset you that I remain her friend." Kathleen became sincere. "You take this too serious. I mean her no harm. I am hardly evil, after all. Simply let this go."

Moving closer, he smiled. "I know that, my dear. You are a lovely and talented young girl. A woman, kind to a man in his waning years, who must now show his appreciation rather than his disdain." Then he insisted. "However, because of your previous experience, it is unseemly for you to guide Gabrielle."

"I realize you are only concerned with her reputation. I meant what I said earlier. Have anyone you want chaperone. Remember though, upon occasion I will accompany her and you must not panic. Few people even know me and those that do may not come forward. I will be gone before you know it. I will not flaunt myself but remain in the background and inconspicuous."

He laughed at that for a man would have to be dead not to notice her. Then after a heated debate, followed by a laugh or two, they were finally able to come to an agreement. By the time Gabrielle entered, they were sipping on sherry and enjoying themselves.

"I hope I'm not interrupting anything," Gabrielle said warmly.

"Not at all, my dear. We were simply chatting while waiting for you and Will. Shall we go into dinner?" questioned the earl.

Both women nodded agreement. Running into William in the hallway as they proceeded. During dinner, Uncle William had explained that his wife Hester, his daughters Hester and Harriet, and his sons John and James Charles had already left for the country. Having an audience, William the Elder dominated the entire conversation. He proclaimed that his daughters would be delighted with Gabrielle's arrival. Giving them a reason for an unexpected shopping expedition. Insisting his wife would be upset if they didn't bring Gabrielle with them when he and young Will returned to their manor in Somersetshire. His wife, too, had greatly admired Gabrielle's father.

When they had finished eating, they gathered in the study to share the evening. The room itself was appropriate for either relaxing or working. A huge fireplace sat in the center of the wall on the left side upon entering. The spacious rosewood desk in the center of the room was directly across from the fireplace. Nestled in-between the fireplace and desk were two wing-backed chairs and a settee. Though late in the season, the day had been warm, so the window had been left ajar. A slight breeze caused the curtains to sway. The fire gave a warm glow as it crackled in the fireplace.

Upon entering, Gabrielle and William both sat upon the settee. Kathleen had chosen one of the large brown chairs. The earl was seated at his desk and during Gabrielle's narration he would scribble a note or two. After she had concluded her tale, he had informed her he would check into the situation. Having finished their drinks and the sad story, they were now more relaxed. The soft light from both the fire and the oil burning lamps added a touch of solace.

The conversation had been interesting, the atmosphere relaxed. The old earl looked at Gabrielle and William, sitting close together, deep in conversation. He studied them for sometime. They looked very good together, in fact, a rather charming couple. Suddenly an idea struck him and he immediately acted upon it.

"Gabrielle, I had not thought to mention this so soon, yet I can hardly keep such information secret." He paused. Hoping, if her father turned up alive, he would be able to explain his current actions. Trusting that his good friend would understand. Yet as her guardian, it was his job to provide for her future. The solution was obvious.

After receiving everyone's attention, he continued. "I really don't see any reason to put it off any longer." He hesitated, hoping they would approve. "Your father and I had planned on you and William getting married. Though he is not here to look out for you, I see no reason why we shouldn't carry on with the original plan." Watching for a reaction, he thrust the final blow. "I know you wouldn't want to disappoint your father," he concluded. He sat back, waiting for an argument.

Gabrielle could barely breathe. She couldn't possibly marry someone she barely knew. What about Kevin? Then she looked at Kathleen. What about Kevin? Loving Kevin was only going to lead her down the path of heartbreak. She wanted to do what was right, for everyone. She looked at William. He was a very nice young man; she was very comfortable with him. He seemed friendly and interesting. However, he certainly was no Kevin. Her heart did not race when he was near. Her breathing was not labored or ragged. Her skin did not have goose bumps, or tingle with delight. Nor did his eyes gleam in a wolfish fashion. His hands did not roam and cause sensations throughout her whole body. He was not charming in a devilish way. Yet, William was kind.

She couldn't believe this was happening! Yet maybe this was the solution after all. This was the future her father had planned. This was the opportunity for her to let Kathleen and Kevin go to Scotland and save face. Kevin could no longer assault her senses and would have to be totally committed to Kathleen. Kevin was a rogue for having started all this in the first place! If she couldn't keep him, at least they would all remain friends. She looked at Kathleen again, but couldn't read her expression. William's face looked full of apprehension. Uncle William's face was full of concern. She took a deep breath and slowly nodded.

The earl was immediately elated! He could barely hide his grin. He congratulated them both and suggested they get a special license, so they could be married immediately.

Gabrielle was mortified. When she questioned him as to the rush, the earl reminded them of his ill health and went on to mention how fortunate he would feel if he could see his son married. Tossing guilt like that in their laps, they could hardly argue.

Kathleen was dumbfounded. She wondered what actions James would take when hearing this news! She would have to contact him immediately. She couldn't understand what Gabrielle was doing. Anyone in his or her right mind could see she loved James. Standing in the room with her and James for only a moment, even a stranger would be able to tell. All hell was going to break out when James heard this news.

William the Younger stared intently at his father. Trying to figure out what his motive was. He knew that Gabrielle was not his intended. Only last month, he and his father had been discussing the Landenbergs' daughter. Yet Gabrielle was sweet and compatible. He did not feel she would burden him with undue attention, as he had many political aspirations. He finally smiled and nodded to both Gabrielle and his father. This was a sound idea, he agreed.

The earl watched each participant in the drama as it unfolded. Gabrielle had been surprised. She had at first looked uncertain, but then loyalty to her father won out. He watched her face, with first a fleeting moment of disappointment. Then squaring her shoulders, holding her head high, she had smiled and agreed.

The earl also kept a close eye on his son. He was momentarily unsure if his son would go along with his plan. Young Will was so absorbed in school and politics he often wondered if he would ever fall in love. The earl watched his son as he absorbed the idea his father had thrown out. William the Elder

160

looked for some sign of disagreement, yet none appeared. His son had decided it was a worthwhile venture. The old earl let out a sigh. Until that moment, the earl had been unaware he had been holding his breath, watching Will for a reaction.

He also observed Kathleen, mostly because she was dazzling. Not so much because she was a key player. However, if she voiced a negative opinion, it could hamper Gabrielle's reaction. Her expression gave away little, yet he somehow knew she did not agree.

Manipulating them all, the earl sat back to let the chips fall where they may. Did he feel remorse? Not in the slightest. Now, Young William would have someone to look after him. He barely took time from his work to eat; he would need a wife to attend him. William the Elder was on top of the world. He leaned back and smiled.

At that moment, Gabrielle looked at Uncle William. He was smiling that huge, fascinating smile. She had made him very happy. Glancing at William, he too was wearing a little grin. Again, the only person she couldn't read was Kathleen. Boy, she couldn't wait to get upstairs, alone with her. They sat a bit longer, content with each other's company. She had even agreed to visit the House of Commons with William tomorrow. Finally, they all retired.

After the house had quieted down, Gabrielle quietly knocked on Kathleen's door. She slipped inside and sat at the end of the bed. They both chatted on and on about the turn of events. There they listed the pros and cons of marrying William, neither of them bringing up the only person who would have tipped the scales. Kathleen didn't mention James, because Gabrielle truly believed this was what her father wanted. Gabrielle didn't bring up Kevin, because she still believed he was going to Scotland and marrying Kathleen. They laughed, they argued. It wasn't till the sun was nearly up that they gave up trying to change the other's mind and went to bed.

The next day, William was delighted to have someone to accompany him and share his viewpoints with. A young maid was sent along as Gabrielle's companion for the day. So off they went to the House of Commons.

It had already been decided that until Gabrielle married, she would use her grandmother's family name. This way, when she was introduced, there would be no connection to the Cartwright name. They also intended to simply present Gabrielle as William the Elder's ward. No mention of upcoming nuptials would be leaked until the completion of the ceremony. Absolutely no unnecessary information was to be supplied. There was really nothing to suspect. With these precautions in place, they hoped to deceive the scoundrels jeopardizing Gabrielle's safety. Anyone even remotely familiar with either her aunt or the viscount would be unable to link even a shred of similarity in passing conversation. Any link to her real identity merely a coincidence. The Earl of Chatham believed he had thought of everything.

Sitting in the gallery, Gabrielle had spent the better part of the day, observing the chaos often accompanied with the House of Commons. Listening to William explain events, mindful of all the different speakers and paying attention to the crowd, she had sat uncomplaining for hour upon hour, while William had droned on and on about all the changes being planned. As the dinner hour neared, she couldn't take any more. Finally there was a break in the action, so as courteous as possible, Gabrielle informed him they were about to depart.

With Gabrielle's life in danger, William the Younger could hardly let two women rush off alone. So, grimly, he attended to them. No matter how polite he seemed, William was agitated at having to leave. They had just come to a critical juncture when she had complained about leaving. This was only one of many reasons he had not intended on marrying for some time. He would no longer be able to bring her to the House of Commons or he would not enjoy his time here. She would be fine as a hostess or companion. However, she had not shown the enthusiasm he had hoped to share.

While Gabrielle and William were away, Kathleen used her time to look for James. She had traveled to both James' townhouse and Derek's parents' house. Asking the driver twice to go to the docks and check Derek's ship also proved unsuccessful. She even sent messengers to several men's clubs, not knowing either man's preference. Completely unsuccessful in her search, she returned to the Pitt home.

Meanwhile, James and Derek had gone to the Pitt household early that morning. Upon finding both girls already gone, the men were willing to wait. After an hour or more, the butler suggested they make a return visit. Uncomfortable leaving without talking to the girls, James felt little better after leaving his card with the butler. That way they would know he had been by. It was the best he could do at the moment.

Kathleen had already returned and was lounging in her room when William dropped Gabrielle off. When she entered, the butler did indeed show her James' calling card. However, it was now on the silver platter with several others. Gabrielle looked at the cards, Lord Somebody, Earl of something, Lord somebody, Marquee of something else, blah, blah, blah. Unable to distinguish any one in particular, she simply placed the cards in her reticule, immediately forgetting all about them.

The next day Uncle William suggested giving a small luncheon. He indicated it was to be for the following day, asking Gabrielle to play hostess.

After the menu had been planned and the invitations sent, Gabrielle went to the dressmaker.

So, the second time James arrived with flowers in hand, that's where she was. Trying on a dress for a fitting. She had selected a golden yellow dress. It made her long black hair appear even darker; it seemed to have hues of blue. Her expressive dark eyes seem even larger. She looked radiant. She had also included matching gloves and kid slippers. As she was no longer at Helena's, a crinoline was once again part of her ensemble. She had now developed more of a bust. With the corset tight, even a respectable neckline had become more than a little enticing.

Gabrielle had been so busy since the moment she had come to reside with the Pitts. Everyone was more than accommodating to her and gave her everything she desired. Still, something was missing. There was emptiness. She sometimes felt totally alone, even in a room full of people. Yet, she did not complain, she forged ahead. She was ready to meet her destiny.

The luncheon had gone off without a hitch and everyone seemed to adore Gabrielle. The ladies were charmed, the men captivated.

Kathleen had been absent, but had spied from the kitchen. She had secretly laughed at many of the couples, recognizing some of the men. As Kathleen watched, she understood why so many of them came to Helena's in the first place. Some of those matrons were downright scary-looking! Even the stoic, young wives may provide perfect lineage, but little recreation. Gabrielle was unaware of Kathleen's escapades and carried off hosting to perfection. Several couples at the luncheon were visiting from India. Their stories added to the already colorful atmosphere.

Though sufficient in funds, the Pitts were hardly rich. Their true wealth consisted of friends, colleagues and acquaintances. While still prime minister, William the Elder had been successful in having the British government take over the task of governing in India. Several of his current guests were indebted to him. Others, seeking wealth for themselves, required advice. Investments, the leading topic for men, fashion for women.

Gabrielle thought them all very interesting. Uncle William had been in such deep conversation with one of the gentlemen that Gabrielle suspected the earl was still dabbling in some venture or another.

As the day went on, she grew weary of the inane chatter and boring conversations. As she was presented throughout the day, Gabrielle remained well mannered and continually smiled. She catered to Uncle William and his associates, while secretly keeping an eye that he didn't overdo. Overhearing a brief conversation between William the Elder and Lord North, she became curious. The name of her father had popped up and a trade route to Asia.

Hadn't Derek said he had often traveled that route for William the Elder? She would have to remember to ask Derek, for it seemed possible. Returning to her duties as hostess, the day quickly passed. She had been a hit, making many new acquaintances and acquiring many compliments and invitations.

The next day, William Pitt, 1st Earl of Chatham, was to give a speech in the House of Lords. Though he had resigned his office in 1768, he continued to make speeches in the House of Lords. He urged conciliation of the American colonies, yet he somehow believed peace could be achieved without granting the colonies independence. Bidding Gabrielle to come, he later urged her to decline his invitation and remain home. Yet, she insisted on accompanying him. Secretly, he was delighted to have her as a companion. After her excursion to the House of Commons with William the Younger, the earl was well aware it was not her interest in politics enticing her to go. Just another reason she delighted him so.

Gabrielle listened to his organ-like voice, accompanied with perfect gestures. She was as overwhelmed, as the rest of the onlookers. She was simply mesmerized by his ideals and true genius. Gabrielle would have preferred to decline the offer of a second performance in the arena of politics. Yet she had seen the gleam of anticipation in his eyes when he had asked her to accompany him. Truly enjoying his company, she did not want to disappoint him. Maybe the real reason for her prompt acceptance.

He had just recovered from a bout of gout. She wanted to be nearby if he should need anything, or have a relapse. Both he and his son were always so immersed in politics that they never took proper care of themselves. So she enjoyed doing the little things that made them feel special, as much as they liked receiving the attention. That night the earl took Gabrielle to the hotel restaurant and they dined in style. Over dinner he tried to fill her in on some of the missing pieces of the friendship between her father and himself. He shared some family antidotes, of when the children were younger. He leaned back, enjoying his port, and told her of his wife. By the tone of his voice you could tell he adored her. Soon everyone would be in Somerset for Christmas. No longer would she be alone, but part of a very large family.

The evening afterwards, Young William escorted her to a reception given by Lord and Lady Blenkinsopp. The evening was filled with wine, music and dance. Gabrielle developed a fondness for Will. He was a wonderful companion and friend. As they were only one year apart, he being eighteen, he felt more like an older brother than a beau. He was a mature and sophisticated man, with eloquent speech. One often forgot how young he really was. She enjoyed spending time with him, yet was not interested in a romantic relationship. However, as she could not follow her heart, for that meant Kevin, she would do her duty and be a decent wife to William.

The following day James decided to wait until later to call on Gabrielle and Kathleen. He felt as he had tried the early hours, on several occasions, the evening hours might be luckier. So that evening he arrived, flowers in hand, fully believing he would see Gabrielle. Unfortunately, when he arrived, they had already left for dinner and the opera. The earl, William, Gabrielle and Kathleen were a foursome. Out on the town and ready for a good time. Again, James was left alone. His mood turned sour and he decided to head over to the club instead. After several hours of some very good brandy, he was feeling sorry for himself. He decided then and there that he had paid his last visit to Gabrielle. He was no longer going to chase the woman. What the hell was going on anyway? Women were supposed to chase him, that he had fallen so far so quickly was embarrassing.

Several days later, Gabrielle and William went on a picnic with some friends of William's. It was at that time that Kathleen begged off and remained at home. After they had finally gone for the afternoon and the earl left to go to the House of Lords. Kathleen too, left the house, taking the opportunity to look for James and Derek, once again. This time luck was on Kathleen's side. After days of trying to track him down, James was finally home.

Sitting in the library of his townhouse, James first poured them a drink. This time they both drank whiskey, neat. His library had a very masculine appeal. Everything was large, thick and dark. It had thick carpet and huge, book-lined shelves through out. The paneling, woodwork, furniture and fireplace mantel were all dark mahogany. Roaming about the room, she noticed several family portraits decorated the wall of the fireplace. Kathleen remarked how alike he and his brothers looked, and then only commented on the handsomeness of his brothers. Laughing, she moved away from the portraits. James had a twinkle in his eye and a smirk upon his face at the indirect compliment she had given him. The table and chairs were off to the side. With six chairs about it, more than likely, where he entertained his card playing buddies. Another smaller table and two chairs were located in the corner, between window and fireplace. On the table was a finely crafted chess set. The only splash of color in the whole room were the crimson drapes covering the windows on the far wall. Kathleen and James helped themselves to another drink, and then sat in the two huge chairs facing the fire.

Without Gabrielle about, the atmosphere seemed somber. Kathleen informed James of the last few weeks' events. At first he ranted and raved about the fact that it had taken her weeks to meet with him. Kathleen explained over and over that the Pitts were monopolizing all their time. Accepting invitations, scheduling appointments and insisting the Pitts escort them. She had tried several times to find him, without luck. Turning the tables on him, she demanded to know why he and Derek hadn't tried to visit them. Finally, after a heated discussion, Kathleen understood that James had indeed been trying to see them. James also conceded that Kathleen, too, had been trying to connect with them. Understanding they both had commitments they had to work around, it was agreed to work together from this moment on. However, after informing him of Gabrielle's upcoming nuptials, she thought she was going to have to find smelly salts, as James turned three shades of gray. Again, they argued, each blaming the other, with neither one accepting responsibility for the circumstances. He said he was going to go over there and demand she refuse her guardian's son. What a farce of a marriage. He raged on and on about how she had told him she would only marry for love. He paced back and forth, nearly wearing the carpet bare.

Kathleen explained, "You will have to remember she is marrying for love, the love of her father. His memory. The hope he will be found. The marriage he intended for her. You will have to have a strong argument to convince her if you want her to go against that. Her guardian, her intended, her father, these are all strong motives to continue this chosen path. Think long and hard about what you will do and say, for you may only get one chance!" They tried to come up with a scheme to divert the plans but were unable to come to an agreement.

As the dinner hour approached, Kathleen needed to leave. She did not want to have to explain where she had been. So she intended to arrive home before the others. When she left, she told James she would do everything in her power to keep Gabrielle from marrying William. Gazing into James' lugubrious eyes, she said, "Gabrielle loves you, though she doesn't seem able admit it for some reason." She sighed. "You, on the other hand, seem to enjoy her company. Yet, if she is merely a distraction for a young marquee, let her go. Let her go now quick and clean. It is better for her to never start something that will break her heart, rather than be a fling for you. She needs stability. William may never fulfill her romantic aspirations, but he will never leave her. Before you rush into this, you'd better know what your doing!" Their conversation over, she extended a short embrace and departed.

James sat back down. Why was he so enamored? What was it about Gabrielle that drove him to insanity? Staring into the fire, his mind wandered. Remembering the expressions on her face during embarrassment, anger, excitement, danger, pain, joy, fear and romance. He recalled his own feelings whenever she was with him. Was this love?

He recollected seeing her at Helena's, from the magnetism of her dress to each and every movement that she made. The ocean voyage, thieves in the night, the lighthouse. There was as much static in the air when they fought as when they held each other close. No other woman was as unafraid or unimpressed by his titles as she. She loved and hated the man, she knew and wanted the man. Every memory made him smile. The sensations she created every time she touched him were like no other. No other woman had ever wreaked such havoc with his emotions. Coming to the conclusion that indeed this must be love was not easy. Now, what to do about it?

Over dinner that evening the earl informed everyone at the table that the wedding was to take place the following evening. Reminding everyone it was still a secret, he explained his plan. His friend, the good Reverend Sutherland, was coming for dinner. After dinner, William the Elder would call in a favor. The simple request coming from him would be enough to assure the Reverend's agreement to conducting the service. Though the banns had not been posted, he did have the special marriage license required to expedite the procedure. Sharing his scheme, his face radiated the joy he was feeling. Looking around at one smiling, one dumbfounded and one disbelieving face, he continued. Following their original plan of secrecy, there would be no strangers, friends nor even relatives invited. A quiet, intimate wedding is what was planned, including only those now in the room. Will's new suit had arrived this afternoon. The dress had been created by the same dressmaker Gabrielle herself had picked out. He had sent instructions to the seamstress, informing her to be creative and original. Using only the measurements previously provided by Gabrielle's previous visits.

Now, the time had come. All the key players available, all details tended to. The Reverend was available, the special marriage license obtained. The dress was finished, the menu planned. The date was set!

Young William seemed elated. He had long ago come to the conclusion that having Gabrielle for a wife would be a huge asset, forming that opinion after one of the many balls they had attended. Though there had been dancing, he had only danced with Gabrielle once, as she had been surrounded by young men the entire evening. Holding her in his arms on the dance floor was astonishing. He had almost forgotten politics.... Almost. She was charming, beautiful and a pleasure to hold in his arms. As he was much taller than she, the bountiful charms beneath her dress, though cleverly concealed, were viewed by his advantage of height. He did not feel he would have any trouble warming to her after the marriage.

However, it was not his new awareness of Gabrielle as a woman that most enticed him. It was her entrance to all the other women's confidences which made him realize how valuable she was. So after every event they attended, he quizzed her on the way home. He compared his earlier conversations among the men with Gabrielle's version of what the women had shared. When the stories conflicted, the women's stories shared by husbands in confidence seemed more often correct. She really had no idea what an asset to his career she was going to be.

When Gabrielle chatted on and on about what went on in the salon, or who said what to whom, what the topic of conversation was at the dressmaker or gossip she had picked up while shopping, he always listened. She truly believed William cared about her and her activities. He had grown fond of her. He didn't enjoy riding as much as she, so they hadn't been. She could sit for hours watching a fire, a starlit night, or a sunset. But he didn't care for idleness. So they hadn't done that together, either. He spent most days at the House of Commons, or attending lectures. At night he went to his club. Yet he always stopped if she had interesting news to share. He listened to her squeals of delight and her rambling upsets. That, decided Gabrielle, was William the Younger's greatest asset. His ability to listen, showing genuine concern for those he cared about.

As dinner came to a close, the earl suggested to William the Younger that he take Gabrielle for a walk in the gardens. So while Kathleen and the earl went to sip brandy, they went for a walk. They sat on the bench near the gazebo and William asked if she were nervous or if she was excited. She explained that she was both. He told her he was glad for their alliance, that she would make him a splendid wife. With no warning, he suddenly turned and sheepishly asked if he could kiss her, in celebration. She could barely refuse, tomorrow being their wedding day, after all. Yet she couldn't help but compare his asking for a kiss to Kevin's taking a kiss. Will's kiss was formal and dry. She didn't appreciate the feel of his lips or the chill of his caress. Again her mind wandered, weighing the differences between William and Kevin. He was very polite and proper and it was over before it had begun. However, though he seemed satisfied, his kiss hadn't stirred any emotion in her. Maybe something was wrong with her. Didn't she appreciate all they had done? Why didn't his kiss cause any sensations? She began to worry. They slowly moved into the house, meeting up with the earl and Kathleen.

After finishing her sherry, Gabrielle excused herself. She was exhausted! She informed both men that she was retiring for the evening. At the foot of the steps, the earl stopped her. He gave her a warm hug and smiled at her. He told her he was proud of her and would be pleased to have her in their family. This created more anxiety for an already uncomfortable Gabrielle. Then, wishing both her and Kathleen good night, he departed.

168

When she opened the door to her room, a lamp was already lit. In the center of the room stood a dressing dummy wearing the most beautiful gown she had ever seen.

It was a white satin and lace wedding dress. The scooped neckline was fully encrusted with pearls. The puffed lace sleeves closed about the wrist with a row of pearl buttons. The satin skirt was wide and elegant, covered by a lace overskirt of intricate design. The train and the veil were also made of matching lace. She stood staring in awe.

Kathleen reached the landing a minute or two after Gabrielle. Seeing Gabrielle just standing in her doorway, made Kathleen go over to her. She saw the same sight as Gabrielle. They both stood there in fascination. After a few moments, Kathleen pushed Gabrielle inside and shut the door. She then walked over and lightly touched the garment. "Gabrielle, you have to feel this!" she said.

As though in a trance, Gabrielle walked over and fingered the object. The lace was so delicate, as though woven by spiders. Kathleen said Gabrielle should try it on. Gabrielle insisted she couldn't. Kathleen reminded her that she was getting married tomorrow. If anything needed to be fixed, they would need time to do it. Gabrielle argued again. Once again, Kathleen won by bullying.

This was definitely not your excited bride! Kathleen assisted her undressing, and then she slowly slipped the creation on Gabrielle.

Gabrielle didn't understand why she couldn't allow herself to be happy. The dress really was the most fabulous gown she had ever seen. She turned to look in the mirror. Her flushed face gave her an excited glow. Her long black eyelashes fluttered with tears. Sad tears? Happy? She had never been a vain girl. Yet looking at herself in the dress, at that moment, she allowed herself the compliment of beautiful. It revealed the appealing cleavage and tiny waist, Gabrielle attributed to her corset. As Kathleen picked up the veil and added it to the ensemble, they both stared at her reflection, spellbound.

Gabrielle looked like a princess. She was elegant, beautiful and charming. However, the picture staring back at them was marred by the sadness in her eyes and the grim expression of her mouth. While staring at herself like this, she pictured Kevin at the end of the isle waiting for her. She pictured Kevin holding her hand. And she pictured Kevin holding her close, his mouth crushing hers with a kiss of wild abandon. She shook her head, as though to clear her thoughts. She turned and looked at Kathleen. With a cry of distress she pleaded with Kathleen to help her out of the dress!

Gabrielle was behaving like a caged tiger! She was tired and on edge. She was not really happy and she couldn't pinpoint the reason.

Kathleen would have happily informed her, if Gabrielle would listen. She had not seen James the entire time they had been at her guardian's and she was beginning to miss his attention. But Gabrielle would not listen. Finally Gabrielle sat at the foot of the bed and began to sob uncontrollably. Kathleen placed an arm around her, trying to comfort her, yet Gabrielle continued. It was really pathetic that Gabrielle was marrying one man and loved another. But Gabrielle was committed to doing what she thought her father wanted. Poor little Gabrielle, she was so loyal. Loyalty.... Suddenly an idea occurred to Kathleen!

Kathleen started to talk. In fact, she was rambling on and on. Gabrielle was still bawling. Finally Gabrielle jerked her head up and tried to stop crying. In the mist of the noise and the tears, she thought she heard Kathleen say she was leaving. "What did you say?" sniffled Gabrielle.

"I've had enough of this London hospitality, I'm headed for Scotland. I told you I would stay with you until you found your guardian and now you have. So I'm leaving in the morning." she bit her lip, holding her breath, hoping Gabrielle would take the bait.

"You can't leave before the wedding," she responded.

"I want to get to Scotland, I'm tired of hanging around here. I'm going alone, by coach." Kathleen confirmed.

"Please don't go yet, I need you."

"Everything can't always be for Gabrielle. This time, I'm doing this for me. I need to leave." Then she tossed out, "It's too bad you couldn't get married later, you could go with me."

Kathleen's casual statement kept going over and over in Gabrielle's head. Why couldn't she wait? What was the rush, after all? There really was no hurry. Uncle William seemed in better health. If something were to happen, she could hurry back. She needed some more time. She felt rushed. She felt crushed. Suddenly she had an idea. She would go to Scotland too. She would leave both William and her guardian a letter, explaining how she felt. She would hardly be leaving a broken heart, for William thought of this match as more of a partnership. Nor would she be causing a scandal, for no one was even aware of the wedding plans. In her letter she would explain that she felt the need to accompany Kathleen and it would allow her time to reflect on her decisions.

They would have to get ahold of the men. She mentioned her plan to accompany Kathleen, but Kathleen pretended to have none of it. Then Gabrielle said they would need time to prepare, find the men and ready the ship. That they simply wouldn't be able to leave in the morning, as they did not know how long it would take to make arrangements. But Kathleen insisted she was leaving ALONE, in the morning. Then she promptly left Gabrielle's room. After she was alone, Gabrielle cried again.

Early the next morning, no one was up when Gabrielle came downstairs. Writing her note the previous evening, Gabrielle had also included repeated thanks for all the Pitts had done for her. She wished them well, trying hard to explain her reasons for leaving. She told them she would be in touch soon and not to worry. Leaving her letter on the desk in the study, she started to have second thoughts. Upon hearing a noise on the steps, all thoughts vanished and she quickly hurried to investigate. Entering the foyer, with a valise of her own, she met up with Kathleen. Kathleen pretended to act very surprised to see her up.

"Where are you going at this hour?" Kathleen demanded.

"I am going with you," she answered firmly. "Who is that?" Gabrielle questioned, spotting the man standing behind Kathleen.

Though he was a footman Kathleen had bribed into escorting them to the boarder, she would be damned if she would tell Gabrielle that. So instead Kathleen said, "His name is Brandon. He is visiting relatives and headed in the same direction. I suggested he travel with us, for propriety's sake. We will simply pretend he is our brother." Kathleen grinned.

They bantered back and forth for a few moments and then Gabrielle reminded her that they would wake up the household. So they threw on their capes, grabbed their bags and out the door they went. It was still dawn; the sun was just on the horizon. Early morning had a look and smell all its own. It appeared as though there was hardly anyone about so the girls did not need to hide. Instead, as they strolled down the walk, Gabrielle began to hum. This caused Kathleen's head to turn in her direction. What she saw was Gabrielle wearing a dazzling smile. When Kathleen saw that, she knew immediately she had done the right thing enticing Gabrielle away from the plans that had been made for her. It had been days since Gabrielle had looked so happy and carefree. Kathleen knew Gabrielle would never have refused to marry William. Even now, Gabrielle probably believed she would come back and honor her father's wishes. But Kathleen knew Gabrielle loved James. Kathleen was giving James time to get to her. So they walked to find a hack to get them to a station. There they would wait for a coach to get them to Scotland. They both walked and smiled and hummed. Neither could remember feeling quite this giddy. Brandon, very quietly, lumbered behind. Later upon entering the coach, heading north, Kathleen said to Gabrielle, "I guess we are off on another adventure!"

Chapter 11

The butler led Derek out to the patio, where James was having lunch. James insisted he have a seat. While one server poured the wine, another added a place for Derek. After filling both their plates and covering the remaining dishes, James waved them out, signaling he would call if necessary.

"Derek, you look a bit piqued this morning. Whatever is the matter?"

Derek had no idea how to begin. Why was he always the one giving James bad news? He knew James' temper would fly. Derek also knew James loved Gabrielle. How did one explain she'd gone missing? He began, "I received a caller early this morning. My only complaint was the bloody inconvenience, as I had just returned from the club barely an hour before."

"Yes, I saw you last night. You were with that actress. Very pretty, is she new?"asked James

"She is new to me, but not to town. She has been here for some time. However, she has recently left the protection of Lord Brett Neville. She seemed a little lonely and clever devil that I am, I assisted as best I could." He chuckled. "However, I digress. After I left Miss Bitterfield, I went to the club. Stayed till about seven this morning as I was trying to recoup my losses. Anyway, long before nine o'clock William Pitt the Younger is banging on the door. Of course, by the time I entered the drawing room, he had worked himself into quite a snit. He wanted an explanation as to the whereabouts of the girls, you see."

"Which girls?" interrupted James, filled with dread.

"Why, Kathleen and Gabrielle," explained Derek

"You mean he does not know where they are?" James was astonished.

"Exactly," said Derek. "Both Gabrielle and Kathleen are missing."

"Give me the details, if you please," James said tersely.

"It seems at dinner last night. Gabrielle, Kathleen and Young William were informed the wedding was to take place, tonight! It seems the earl had arranged everything. Unfortunately, it also appears as though the girls have taken flight. Gabrielle left a letter explaining her actions, though she simply said she was accompanying her friend home and would be back and not to worry. Needless to say, the men are extremely troubled.

"William remembered my earlier association with the ladies and he immediately assumed I was involved. However, as I was home, about to go to sleep, he really couldn't blame me. Yet, he is worried and now I am too. So, I rushed right over. What do you think happened? Where can they be?"

James thought a moment. "You say The Earl of Chatham announced the wedding date?"

"Yes, it was to be late today," replied Derek

Shaking his head, he said. "So, she took flight instead of calling off the wedding. Any indication where they were headed?"

Derek said, "Gabrielle's letter was simple and straightforward, stating Kathleen wanted to leave immediately and go home. That she was going to accompany her and that she would return as soon as possible. She also said not to worry." Derek sighed in frustration. "It seems to me that two women traveling alone cause nothing but worry."

James was franticly trying to remember all that Kathleen had told him. What was it she had said when she left the other day? Something about doing anything she had to to stop the wedding? This was the only plan she could come up with? Some plan! WOMEN! "I guess we are going to have to follow them. One would suppose they are headed to Scotland. Though with our luck, by telling us they are going home, it could also mean Helena's. You may as well get comfortable, we have a bit of planning to do."

Meanwhile, finally reaching the first stop, the girls had certainly tired of travel. Brandon, their companion, had chosen to ride up top with the driver. He seemed a bit shy and rarely talked, preferring the open air and peace, as opposed to the stifling, fully packed coach.

Dreading the idea of climbing back into the crowded conveyance, they were happy to wait till morning to continue. With no real itinerary, Kathleen and Gabrielle requested a room. Their meal that evening was fresh trout from the nearby stream, accompanied by an abundance of wine. While dining, they enjoyed the local entertainment and observed the neighboring gentry. The atmosphere was jolly and the evening quickly passed in amusement and relaxation. With no private rooms available, they were shown to the women's quarters. One and twenty females found comfort in the wide chamber provided. The brick floor was swept, the bedding fresh, a blazing fire for warmth. The accommodations furnished all the requirements two weary girls needed. Brandon was quartered with the men, his area, less comfortable, yet consistent with most inns.

Crossing through Essex, the following day passed much the same as the day before. The picturesque landscape had been full of thatched cottages, timber-framed windmills and castle ruins. Passing through the large, dark, forest, they finally stopped at The White Horse Inn. The interior was clean and simple and the deer stew and warm bread hit the spot. Then they retired for the evening, planning the following day to continue north to Ipswich.

The plan that James and Derek had come up with was simple; follow them. However, as they were not sure exactly which way the ladies would pick to travel, they decided to go by two different routes. So after sending a messenger to Helena's, they left. James was going to travel by land, Derek by sea.

James had taken little time to prepare. In his satchel were the necessary items he would need when he found Gabrielle. Also, he made sure to send a dispatch to his ancestral home in York, thus, informing his family of his current plans. He included a change of clothes and the necessary currency. Their trail should be an easy one to follow. Two beautiful women alone, headed north.

He took the same roads as the girls had taken earlier, believing he would catch up to them in less than a day. Their coach was slow and heavily burdened. He was unencumbered, riding one of his brother's fastest horses. However, leave it to the ladies to disrupt his plans, yet again.

The girls had not taken a very direct route, on the way to their destination. As danger increased with darkness, the girls only traveled by day, seeking shelter in the evenings.

The smaller inns simply provided food and lodging, the larger hotels were more extravagant. Furnishing entertainment, private rooms, fine linen and beds hung in silk. Though large or small, all the innkeepers were friendly and accommodating, though it certainly didn't matter which abode they descended upon, for by evening they were exhausted. Usually food, drink and rest were all they required. Each morning, after a hearty breakfast, they would be on their way.

After several days of traveling by coach, Kathleen had finally had enough! She was adamant about never stepping foot inside another carriage. Though public conveyances had been much improved, the roads were still in unbearable shape. The ruts were deep and the routes poorly planned. She was tired of fat, smelly men, crying children and mean women. She was weary of each and every bump and jolt experienced along the way. She convinced Gabrielle that as they were both excellent riders, they should simply ride horseback the rest of the way. Gabrielle argued it wasn't safe. Kathleen bullied. Gabrielle finally agreed to Kathleen's request, so long as when they grew fatigued, Kathleen would again agree to return to a coach. Kathleen agreed only too quickly.

Thankfully, each girl had included riding outfits when packing. Simple split skirts with matching jackets. Each of them were competent riders and chose not to stand out by riding sidesaddle. Not wanting to cause attention to themselves, the girls had chosen to stay away from the colorful choices. Kathleen wore dark brown, tan for Gabrielle. Each wore white linen shirts, with their hair fashioned back into a single braid. Emerging from the hotel, their hair well hidden under their hats, their simple outfits, unassuming. At first glance and from a distance, they could pass as three young boys. With a second look, under closer inspection, they could not fool anyone. Knowing they would often be riding hard, the women had bound their breasts. However, there had been no possible way to camouflage Kathleen's huge bust. Even after binding their bosoms, Kathleen's had been prominent. The best they had been able to do was loosen their shirts and keep their jackets on. Yet, the motion of the horse inadvertently put them on display. While in town, they kept their pace at a walk to cause as little attention as possible.

The best way they could think of to remain undetected was to take the less traveled roads. Kathleen had figured James and Derek would follow by ship and she wanted to follow the coast north. So they headed north to the city of Norwich. Keeping her plans to herself, Kathleen hoped to be soon spotted by the crew of the *Deception*. Gabrielle was blissfully unaware that all of this was just part of Kathleen's plan to enable James to find them. Unfortunately, by discontinuing travel by coach, they no longer followed a popular route.

After Ipswich, James lost their trail. No one had seen them aboard any coaches. Not one man could remember seeing the two women. Both women were beautiful and alone, someone should have seen them. He could not do anything but continue north. He headed northeast, in hopes that Derek would be signaling from the ship.

The trio reached The Wash inlet and decided to rest there for the evening. It was dark and they only had the blankets from the saddle for warmth. Despite their lack of creature comforts, they were happy and carefree. The next morning, while Brandon stood watch, they found a secluded area and bathed. Cleaned up and feeling better, they stopped at a public house. After eating a virtual feast for breakfast, they continued on their journey. The owner informed them there was a ferry available for the crossing of the inlet. Also that on the other side boats gathered to take passengers upstream. If they wanted to have a break from riding they could take a boat. With little convincing the girls went in search of the ferry to cross the inlet. After they had crossed, there were indeed many boats going upriver to hire. They picked the largest, safest-looking vessel and booked passage. That evening and most of the next day were spent sightseeing. They chatted, they rested and they ate. The following evening they docked in Lincoln.

This time when they left the stable, all of them had matching standardbreds. These fine animals had finished their illustrious career at the Richmond racetrack. The owner of the Black Stag, where they had spent the previous evening, was eager to let them go. He had felt guilty not allowing them the running they deserved. So he gave the group a good deal and with little ado, they were off once again. Kathleen kept watching and hoping to see their rescuers. The strain of traveling on their own was beginning to take its toll, always being on guard against highwaymen and constantly looking over her shoulder. So far they had not encountered any villains, nor had they been rewarded with the sight of James or Derek. Kathleen had really hoped they would follow once they knew the girls had left. Assurance in that quarter had not arrived. But by choosing not to include Gabrielle, Kathleen was unable to share her fears and worries.

James found the remains of a camping area near The Wash inlet. It wasn't until he found a ribbon, caught in the branch of a tree that he was convinced the girls had been this way. Even still, it was a long shot. Yet what else did he have to go on? Locating the hoof prints, he followed. Arriving at the same inn where they had recently stayed, he began his inquiries. Luckily the same serving girl was working and did indeed remember the ladies. Yet, the young girl had not been informed as to their destination. Fortunately, the owner admitted to instructing them to use the ferry, and then continue on by boat. So, finally on the right track, James breathed a sigh of relief. Taking a few extra moments, he also had a marvelous breakfast before continuing on his journey.

The girls crossed the Hull River, traversing the beautifully created stone bridge. Watching the construction of docks, extending for miles along the river, they entered the town of Hull. Past the University, the grammar school, and the museum. Slowing down to view the Trinity House and Art galleries. Leaving the horses at the stable, the trio ventured inside to get rooms. The proprietor immediately escorted them to their rooms and ordered up hot baths. He informed them of the dinner that would be waiting for them downstairs at their leisure. Unfortunately for him, the girls requested trays in their room. He was very disappointed. They were very lovely; he would have appreciated them spending the evening in the taproom. It would have assured his customers a pleasant view and himself a prosperous evening.

The girls were soaking in two wooden tubs, both set in front of a blazing fire.

"Is this heaven?" inquired Gabrielle

"No, Helena's baths are heaven. This is a tub of hot water!" she laughed.

"After riding, camping, and swimming. This is heaven! What is our plan now, Kathleen?" questioned Gabrielle

"I propose we spend the evening pampering ourselves. We'll fix each other's hair; eat a wonderful, hot meal. Sleep in this soft bed. Share stories. And tomorrow, head north again. How does that sound to you?" Kathleen asked.

"I'm not so certain I can do much with your hair. How about doing some shopping?" asked Gabrielle.

"We could, however, we have no way of carrying our purchases. I believe we should forge ahead and shop at the end of our destination." There was a knock at the door. Kathleen sheepishly looked at Gabrielle and said, "Are you ready to get out?"

Gabrielle replied, "I know what that means!" She grumbled, "That you are not!" Kathleen simply laughed. Knowing that Kathleen would not budge from the tub until the water became frigid, Gabrielle climbed out of her tub, threw on a blanket and went to the door. "Yes?" she inquired. After hearing the serving girl mention their dinner, Gabrielle opened the door. The serving girl placed the food on the table and asked if there would be anything else. Gabrielle gave her their clothes to launder and sent her on her way. Their leisurely evening continued.

Leaving the next morning, they passed a group of men riding into the courtyard. One, travel-weary, man stared rather intently at Gabrielle. Unknowingly, Gabrielle cantered right past and continued on her way. Intent upon their own destination, Kathleen had also paid scant attention to the group of men as they rode away.

One man jumped off his horse and quickly strode inside. He demanded rooms and hot meals, for himself and his men. The household scattered to prepare these services. It wasn't until after his nap that he recalled the girls leaving earlier. After harshly questioning the innkeeper, he received little information. He continued with more and more questions. Still, the owner had few answers. The rest of the staff also had little to tell. However, after piecing together the fragmented stories, he marched into the taproom. There he announced to his men to enjoy themselves tonight, for tomorrow they ride! He went on to say they had a change of plans and instead of chasing the mouse, the mouse was headed for their trap. The men laughed and cheered in unison. Tonight, the drink and the money all flowed. The proprietor was torn, happy for the income, sad for the two young women. Tomorrow would be soon enough to wonder what the sheriff and his men were up to.

Spending the next day on horses, they were tired and grumpy. They stopped around dinnertime just to appreciate the view. They enjoyed watching the ocean pound the rocky shores and shared amusing comments on the nose-shaped peninsula. Flamborough Head was a warm sunny spot on the coastline, where they stopped to reflect and take a brief nap. Soon after their brief rest, they headed north again.

By the time they had reached Scarborough, even Gabrielle had to holler, "ENOUGH!" She was saddlesore, tired, and achy. The riding through forests and along shorelines had been both adventuresome and breathtaking. Now, though, she wanted a break. She reasoned and argued with Kathleen until finally Kathleen relented. This time they would stay at the King's Lantern, for more than one night. It was a huge friendly pub, attached to a boarding house. They had a large, bright, open room with a wide balcony. The furniture was sturdy and comfortable, the carpets plush, the four-poster bed made with only the finest linens and thickest coverings. As the fire burned in the hearth, the two women ate, drank and relaxed to their hearts' content. The balcony provided the perfect place to share early-morning breakfasts and late-night dreams. It was just the place to view the town below, yet remain detached. On the last night, after sightseeing and simply wandering around town, they strolled down to the beach. Brandon once again stood watch, as the girls discarded their slippers and waded in the surf. As the tide began to come in, they laughed and pushed each other in. Like two small girls, they giggled and frolicked.

It was while they were walking along the beach that they were being watched. They had not detected the man observing them, nor did they feel his presence. They ran and jumped in the ocean in gleeful abandon. The water caused the material of their dresses to stick like a second skin. The dark-haired one, the one called Gabrielle, was a beauty. Her bosom, like melons, plastered to her skin. His breathing became ragged. Yet it was the taller, auburn-haired girl that really enticed him. Her breasts were not merely tempting, they were irresistibly huge. Her legs were long, her skin the color of alabaster. She had a playful grin and tiny waist. She was the one who set his loins burning. Watching the two young women run up and down the seashore, bouncing, jumping and splashing, he decided then and there, even if the girl in question was not the one he had been searching for, he was going to procure these women and keep them, anyway. He would teach them everything they would need to know to please him. He would use them separately, or together. He had no favorite position or woman, his preference was variety itself. Yet, he was willing to change his habits and keep these two. The one thing he was determined not to do was share them with anyone else. If the girl called Gabrielle turned out to be the one he had been pursuing, he would have to release her into the viscount's custody. Still, he would keep the redhead for himself.

He put the eyeglass back in his pocket, walked down the rocky hill and joined his men. Climbing silently upon his horse, he turned and headed down the road. Instantly, the men also jumped on their horses, galloping behind Sheriff Muden.

The girls settled on their blanket, to soak up the last of the sunshine and to dry off. As twilight descended, they sat nibbling on fruit and chattering away. Kathleen mentioned going on to Whitby, all agreeing it was time to leave. Returning to their rooms, they ate dinner and retired early. The next morning they were on there way north again.

James was on their trail once more. After two misleading tips he was finally headed for Scarborough. There he would stay at the family home. He was tired, he was crabby and he was worried.

As the girls and their young escort rounded a bend in the road, they unknowingly rode straight into a trap! And it was just outside of Whitby that all three were apprehended.

Rapidly assessing the danger, they turned their horses around, to make an escape. However, the group of men closing in from behind made them realize they were pinned in. With the men in front and behind, there was little they could do. The circle had quickly formed as everyone moved in. The girls held their heads high, trying to keep a civil tongue, demanding to know their intentions! The men offered no excuses nor supplied any answers. They simply informed the girls they were to accompany them. If they tried to escape, they would risk being harmed. The threat of being thrown over their horses and finishing their ride on their stomachs ultimately quieted them down. The girls looked around, yet didn't recognize one single face. Then they turned and looked at each other. They silently cursed themselves for being so lackadaisical about their safety. Their abductors quickly tied the women's hand and blindfolded them. Kathleen and Gabrielle's horses were led up and down hills, across moors and over rough roads, before stopping to make camp. The girls had been plenty tired approaching Whitby. Now they were exhausted. They could hear whispering; unfortunately they couldn't make anything out. After seeing to their necessities, they were tied to a tree and left there. The next morning they were given some hard biscuits and helped back into the saddle.

As they continued on their way, the loud sound of crashing water sounded in the distance. As they journeyed it became louder, the violent sound of water colliding against rock. Louder and louder until you couldn't even hear your own voice. Gabrielle thought the sound of rushing water reminded her of her childhood home. Kathleen thought perhaps they had been led to an inlet, where the ocean crashed against the cliffs. Worried that they would be taken to sea....

Each girl was disoriented and remained confused as to their location yet they tried repeatedly to figure out where they were headed. As they trotted along, the deafening sound of water falling was to their right. Gabrielle again compared these similarities to those of her neighboring countryside. Kathleen didn't know what to think, only that they were near rushing water. Shortly that too changed as they slowly ventured away and the noise of the water faded in the distance.

After riding a bit farther, they suddenly stopped. The women were carelessly dragged off their horses and carried down a narrow stairway, only to be tossed to the ground and locked in a room. Abandoned, tied, blindfolded and scared, they contemplated their plight. Without word or direction, both girls worked frantically to get the blindfolds off, both finally succeeding in pulling them off their eyes, the dark blindfolds remaining loosely around their necks.

"Do you have any idea what this is about?" Gabrielle asked quietly once she had looked around.

"We have been abducted for any of the following reasons; servants, white slavers, prostitution or ransom. Take your pick. What the hell were we thinking, not riding in a coach?" grumbled Kathleen.

Gabrielle began to cry. Kathleen embraced her. "Look, Gabrielle, I could be all wrong. There may be some mistake, they may just let us go."

Gabrielle responded, "When pigs fly! They can't let us go. We know who they are. How can we get out of this mess?" They looked around at the small, airless room. They had enough room to stretch out and so they did. As their eyes adjusted to the dim lighting and she was able to look around, Gabrielle gasped, "Kathleen, we may be in more trouble than we first anticipated."

Kathleen responded, "Worse than servants, prostitutes or being sold to white slavers? What could be worse?"

"If I'm not mistaken," she muttered, "this is our very own wine cellar. I believe we have been hauled back to Cartwright Manor."

A baffled Kathleen still did not comprehend.

At Kathleen's blank expression, Gabrielle continued. "Don't you see? We have been taken back to my home! The people I ran from are now holding us!"

"What are you saying?" Kathleen paused then sputtered, "How did we get in this mess?"

"I can only imagine that the men that found us were hired by the viscount. The same sadistic viscount I was to marry. The how and when are a little fuzzy, but the who is definite. Who else would want to capture me?"

180

"What I don't understand is how they found you. We have been on the move for days. We didn't even know where we would be or for how long. And the men we wanted to follow us haven't found us. How did these men?" screeched Kathleen.

"I don't know if it's logical or not, but I think we found them. I think we simply rode into their encampment," said Gabrielle.

"Heaven help us! No one knows we are here. No one will find us!" moaned Kathleen. Unable to untie themselves or each other, they sat in silence. A routine began as they worried, slept briefly, only to awaken and worry some more. The evening finally passed and sunlight appeared through the crack of the door. They were afraid and starving. With the morning came the answers to their questions.

The door suddenly opened and a man, presumably their guard, led them up the stairs. The light was bright and after being in the dark room their eyes had trouble getting accustomed. Even with her eyes more shut than open, Gabrielle could recognize her own home. Her suspicions were confirmed! Though that made her even more anxious. The girls were then led into the formal dining room.

"Girls, you may sit down." The servant instructed them to eat and their host would join them presently. Both girls took advantage and filled their plates, eating with speed, not manners. The food was both hot and delicious. After clearing their plates and devouring most of the ham, the girls were arguing over the last tart when their host unexpectedly joined them. The girls became silent, immediately turning to glare in his direction. Paying little attention to their blatant hostility he snidely said, "Don't stop eating on my account." Then, with an exaggerated wave of his hands, he added, "You may continue to eat until we have our discussion." Instantly delving into his own breakfast of kippers, he easily ignored them.

Gabrielle could not stop herself when she said, "How dare you do this? How dare you steal my home, my fortune, and now me!"

He leered at her. "How dare me? How dare you!" he retorted. "You were to be my bride, you were trying to leave me at the altar! You little slut! Do not think for a moment that I'm not aware of the way you must have used to support yourself. Were all your little escapades really better than becoming my bride?" the viscount hissed.

Gabrielle merely gaped at him that he should treat her in such a manner. "Where is my aunt?" she questioned.

"Sit down and eat. My bride and my lover are upstairs getting dressed. We have had a rather busy morning." He grinned. "We were informed of your return this morning and your aunt will follow directly. We will continue this discussion when she joins us."

"But I–" started Gabrielle.

"You look pale and thin. I suggest you eat." He stared at her bosom and began to salivate as he added. "However, you have grown quite ample in other areas, haven't you?"

Kathleen was trying desperately to think of a plan of escape.

Gabrielle was furious. If she had been thinking rationally, she would have been frightened. Deep in thought, the girls silently picked at the food in front of them, while the viscount continued to shove both food and drink in his mouth at a rapid pace. Approximately fifteen minutes later, Gabrielle's aunt made her entrance.

She walked into the room as though not even seeing the two young women seated at the table with the viscount. She walked directly over to his chair and curtsied. The she leaned over him, letting her well-endowed bosom caress his face. Then she leaned in and received a long, noisy, kiss. Straightening, she received a swift pat on the rump and a little giggle escaped her mouth as she fluttered her eyes in response. She turned and walked to her seat at the other end of the table.

"Gabrielle, so good of you to finally come home. Where have you been?" asked Aunt Penelope.

Gabrielle could not believe her aunt was acting as though Gabrielle had been gone a day or two. Taking the time to really look at her aunt, Gabrielle realized there had been some changes. Her aunt, who had before looked matronly, now looked very handsome. She seemed thinner. Her hair seemed shinier and was arranged differently, a style which made her look much younger and friendlier. Her face practically seemed to glow. Her eyes radiated a happiness the likes of which Gabrielle could never remember seeing. Her dress was of blue silk and her bosom was on complete display. Her impersonation of a fine lady was belied by the array of so many jewels dripping off her form, which instead caused her to appear gaudy. Huge rings on every finger, along with a four-roped pearl necklace around her neck. Bracelets matching her jeweled hair combs. Although everything about her aunt had changed, the real change had been in her attitude. Her whole personality had become regal yet snobbish.

"Aunt, I demand some sort of explanation!" started Gabrielle

"You demand?" she repeated in a haughty tone. "I can't think why you should get to demand anything," was the reply.

Gabrielle tried a softer tone. "Aunt, I realize things haven't gone exactly as you planned, however–"

There her aunt interrupted. "Things have gone exactly as we've planned, haven't they, Herbert?"

Bringing the viscount back into the conversation, he responded, "Yes, my dear. Everything has gone exactly as planned."

Gabrielle said, "What is going on?"

"Gabrielle, I remember telling you our plans. I also remember you leaving us high and dry. What were we to do? As you were not willing to cooperate and your disappearance created a problem, we had to come up with an alternative plan," said Penelope "Didn't we, darling?"

"Quite right, quite right," the viscount replied gruffly. "Now, the choice is up to you. You may stay and become my wife. You may rule my household and sleep in my bed," he invited. "Or you may pass and I will sell you into servitude to a friend of mine. The choice is yours."

"Aunt, how can you let him do this?" whined Gabrielle

"Gabrielle, you are such a selfish girl! I told you before that arranged marriages are done all the time. I told you that having to share a marriage bed is wonderful. I explained to you that if you didn't enjoy the intimate part of the arrangement, you would no longer be expected to participate once you provided an heir. You are young and beautiful. You have your whole future in front of you. I have sacrificed my entire life for you and your father. Staying to raise you and provide a family when he was off on his trips. Neither one of you ever thought of me and now my turn has come. Herbert loves me. He married you to provide all of us with an income and a future. However, if your duties in the marital bed abhor you, you need not feel guilty, as I am quite prepared to entertain him. Now, you may stay and be Viscountess Herrington. Or you may go and be the sheriff's servant. Either way, you will end up in bed with some man, I suggest you choose to be a viscountess." At the end of her little speech, she poured a glass of wine and held it up in a silent salute.

At this time Kathleen interjected, "Can I clear something up?"

"And you are?" inquired the viscount in an insolent tone.

"I am Kathleen Dunbar, a friend of Gabrielle's. I'm just wondering if letting us go is an option? Say Gabrielle agrees to give up her inheritance and disappear into the wilderness of say, Scotland. Wouldn't that also be an answer?" she questioned hopefully.

"Well, Kathleen," sneered the viscount. "I certainly hope Gabrielle intends to stay, that way you can remain as her maid." He licked his lips. "Our maids are kept well satisfied and I'm sure you would be quite happy here."

The hairs on the back of Kathleen's neck began to stand on end. She couldn't think of a worse idea than staying. She sat there going over and over their options. They would have to escape, she finally concluded. She would have to talk Gabrielle into pretending she would stay, to buy them time.

Penelope gave Kathleen a scathing look and condescended to respond in a very chilly voice. "That ridiculous idea is not an option! She fled the last time we depended on her. Her word is hardly enough to inspire confidence. And you, my dear, will stay out of matters that do not concern you," she stressed.

Gabrielle was having none of this. "I can't believe you think you will get away with this!" she exploded.

The viscount turned on her, his beady eyes centered on her. "But my dear, we already have. At this very moment, my viscountess is upstairs. Would you like me to introduce you?"

"How did you talk someone into this plot?" questioned Gabrielle

"Maybe you don't realize how many homeless women and children there really are? It took a while, but I finally found a young woman that fit the part. Ironically, she was employed as a governess." He smirked and looked directly into Gabrielle's eyes. "Your aunt had a list of things the young girl needed to have. My only prerequisite was finding a virgin. For although you had run away, I was not going to be cheated out of one." He paused. "Not that it's really any of your business, but I feel you should know that I have gone to great lengths to achieve my goals."

He began, "Though at first she pretended disinterest, I finally persuaded her to become our alley." Watching both Kathleen and Gabrielle's expression he became smug and told far more of his evil plot than was necessary. "After deciding on this particular young woman, I immediately set to work destroying her character." Gruffly he continued. "Yet it turned out to be relatively simple, by having a simple little conversation with the lady of the house. Letting her know that her husband had mentioned what a tasty morsel the new governess was. I incited distrust and discord within the household. Reminding her as we chatted that if her husband had his eye on the governess, she could easily send her to me." Here the viscount grinned. "For some vague reason, shortly after my discussion with her, the wife immediately had the little slut thrown out.

"Of course, I didn't tell the young chit I was the reason she lost her position in the first place. I simply sat back to watch the drama unfold. After several weeks, lacking sleep and nourishment, she began to get desperate. Without employment, shelter or funds, her only alternative would have been as a prostitute above a seedy saloon. I appeared, offering a position too good to resist." He laughed. "She is not educated enough to realize she has entered into anything unsavory. Nor will you be around to claim differently."

Looking at Gabrielle, he added, "My wife thinks of me as her knight in shining armor. It will certainly not be a hardship to keep her over you."

"You really are a beast!" exclaimed Gabrielle

Pretending outrage, he exclaimed. "Maybe I should withdraw my offer. For it is I that will definitely be ending up with the worse end of the bargain. You are an obstinate and complaining creature."

Gabrielle jumped up from her chair. "Threatening to withdraw your offer is a favor, not a punishment. You will never get away with this!" She shook her fist.

Penelope said in a hushed tone, "Gabrielle, you are getting yourself overexcited. Please use the manners I have taught you." She huffed, seemingly oblivious to Gabrielle's predicament.

Gabrielle looked in horror as her aunt rattled on about manners and etiquette, while at the same time keeping her prisoner.

The viscount interrupted Penelope and said, "Gabrielle, I can not have both you and the other Gabrielle staying at the house. Someone will find out and you will ruin everything. I will allow you one day to decide your fate. You and your friend will remain locked in the wine cellar until you have made your decision. By the time the sheriff arrives tomorrow, if you still refuse to do the right thing, I will have no choice but to allow him to escort you off the property. At which time, he will become your lord and master. You will be his servant, responsible only to him. If you choose incorrectly, your life will change forever. Life here will remain much the same. For I will keep my fake wife, with none the wiser."

"Gabrielle, please choose to remain home with us," Penelope interjected. "The other girl can be sent to the sheriff in your place. I have missed you. It will be like old times. The only change is that Herbert will live with us. We can travel; we can buy anything we wish. Please do not reach a hasty decision, give it plenty of thought." She looked over at Kathleen. "You may even keep your friend." With that she rose and excused herself. The viscount met her halfway and they exited the dinning room, arm in arm.

Gabrielle looked at Kathleen. "Now what?"

Kathleen motioned for Gabrielle to move. They quickly went to the door, slowly, cracking it just an inch, to see if they were guarded. Just as they peeked out, a man grabbed each girl by the arm, dragging them back to the wine cellar. With the slamming of the door, gloom once again surrounded them.

James felt so much better. He had information that led him to believe he knew which way to go and that meant the women were headed to Scotland. After losing the ladies' trail near Scarborough, he had visited his home instead. He spent the evening being pampered and loving every minute of it. His brothers had not been in residence, but his parents had. His father had understood, swearing that his mother had also led him on a merry escapade or two. His mother had been practical and amusing. She tried to get him to see the humor of it all. He had a long hot bath and slept in his own goose-lined bed. He had a new mount; clean clothes and a good night's sleep behind him. He was cheerful and happy when he rode out.

As he rode the countryside, going north, something seemed peculiar. He couldn't quite put his finger on it, as he hadn't rode this far north of the family estate in some time. The hair on the back of his neck stood on end. Something was causing an uneasy feeling. Finally approaching an area secluded by trees and bushes, he heard the sound of people and smelled something cooking. Leaving his horse to edge closer, he tried to eavesdrop. He heard a few bawdy jokes and some very humorous stories before the conversation turned interesting. They commented on the loveliness of the two girls that were captured and taken to Teesdale. Teesdale! Two girls! Could it be Gabrielle and Kathleen? He began to break out in a sweat. The discussion turned to other things, providing him with no more information. One by one, they drifted off as the snores accumulated. James quietly eased out of hiding, immediately changing course. Heading towards Teesdale, he was now in a quandary. What if he lost track of Gabrielle and Kathleen riding in the opposite direction? What if these abducted women were not his abducted women? As his horse galloped down the lonely roads and through the moors, memories of Gabrielle flashed through his mind. Gabrielle. The thought, the feel, the scent of her, permeated his brain. He made his decision. First rescue these two women, if they turned out to be someone else, he would then continue after Kathleen and Gabrielle. With any luck, they would be the same women he sought.

That evening they were brought upstairs and questioned by the viscount.

He told Gabrielle she was beautiful. He told her she could have anything she wished. He went on to inform her he was a wonderful lover, that none of his women had ever complained. He told her he would be gentle as she was a virgin. Then he had turned vicious as he continued. She was a virgin, wasn't she? he had suddenly demanded. When Gabrielle realized it was important to him, she simply smiled. She refused to tell him. Angry and frustrated, he sent them back downstairs.

The next day, the pattern remained familiar. They had been fed, questioned and then returned to the cellar. Kathleen figured they would be questioned one more time before the sheriff arrived.

Later, the viscount said they were to be given baths and a change of clothing. He had decided that if indeed the sheriff were to take them away, it would not do to have them looking so offensive. So after dinner, they were ushered upstairs and primped and cleaned for the sheriff. The maids even combed and styled their hair. Gabrielle had picked her favorite violet soap and Kathleen smelled like lemon. However, the only dress that would fit Kathleen was one of Aunt Penelope's. Even though Penelope was quite buxom herself, the dress was very tight across the bosom, because Kathleen was so well endowed. Fortunately they found a suitable dress and finished their toilette. Clean, dressed and fed, the girls were led into the back study.

With a guard standing in front of the door and another below the windows, the viscount felt it was safe to see to his own needs. Shoving them inside and locking the door, the viscount gave strict orders to the guard. Little did anyone know the room was already occupied.

As soon as the door closed, they both raced over to escape out the window. Immediately they spotted the guard.

"Now what?" whined Gabrielle to Kathleen.

Plopping down on the settee, Kathleen answered, "I think this is the first time I am at a loss for ideas. Unless we can escape the guard, we'll never get to the horses."

Sitting in the large chair behind the desk, the plain young girl realized she was no longer alone. She often sat there, in the huge overstuffed chair, facing the windows. She remained stiff and quiet as she slowly shut the book on her lap. She was loath to turn herself and the chair around. For although she would learn the intruders' identities, they would also realize they were no longer alone. So she meekly sat on the large, leather, chair, behind the great mahogany desk. Listening for even a shred of information that would give her an idea of what to do. Finally she had heard enough to guarantee they were no threat to her, so she carefully spun the chair around and waited for someone to notice her.

As soon as the chair began to move, Gabrielle noticed her. The unpretentious young woman simply sat observing them. In turn, Gabrielle took a long look, wondering what it was about the girl that seemed so familiar.

Kathleen finally followed Gabrielle's gaze and she too, stared in return. Then, Kathleen demanded an introduction from the girl.

Without preamble she answered, "Gabrielle Harrington."

Now, Gabrielle remembered where she had seen her before. It had been the night she and Kevin had come here to gather information. The portrait of the viscount and the young girl had been spotted at the top of the stairs. Gabrielle slumped back on the settee! At first Kathleen thought Gabrielle had fainted again, until she realized Gabrielle was merely overwhelmed.

The girl pretending to be Gabrielle was probably only thirteen or fourteen. She was small, pale and certainly no beauty. It appeared there were few requirements to impersonating the real Gabrielle Cartwright. Obviously any female with dark hair willing to submit to the viscount fit the bill.

"You have to help us! Your husband is holding us against our will." announced Gabrielle.

Kathleen joined in. "We are his captives! He is a brute!" Then changing her tactics she suggested, "You are the only chance we have of escape."

The fake Gabrielle responded, "You do not look like you are here against your will." She sighed. "If you are here to spend time with my husband, I will step aside without complaint. You do not have to fabricate a story, I am quite used to his tendencies. I suggest you do not make him mad though, he often gets mean and hurtful." Standing, she moved closer to the door before she said, "Enjoy yourselves." She turned to go but stopped dead in her tracks as Gabrielle began to shriek.

Absolutely dumbfounded, Gabrielle shouted, "You know he has other women? He does not treat you kindly? Then why do you stay with him? Maybe we should be helping you," groaned Gabrielle.

She stared down at her folded hands and replied, "I am only here due to the graciousness of my husband and my aunt. It is not your concern. You must carry out your business."

As soon as the word *aunt* was out of her mouth, Gabrielle and Kathleen exchanged looks. In silent communication, they realized the fake Gabrielle did not know the real Gabrielle was now in front of her. With a slight nod to each other, they agreed to keep it that way, both feeling she would share more information if she were at ease with them. After the short acknowledgement, they turned their attention back to the young woman as she continued.

Kathleen tried again, "You must help us. We are not here to spend time with your husband, we are being held captive."

The fake Gabrielle raised her eyebrows in question to that remark.

Kathleen continued, "You hardly look like you enjoy being here, why can't you just believe us and give us aid?"

"Though it is surely none of your business, I will take the time to explain," said the fake Gabrielle. "I have been given a home and security. I am taken care of and treated with respect. In return all I have to do is comply with their wishes." Her look implored them to understand. "You will never understand my plight. I will do anything not to go back. I am sorry for what ever problems you may incur, but I cannot help you." She looked at them solemnly. "I just cannot jeopardize my own safety."

They understood all too well that the young woman had neither the power nor the opportunity to afford them any help. They simply gave each other a knowing look, admitting to a hopeless situation.

Suddenly the door opened and in strolled the viscount. He was licking his lips in anticipation. He boldly marched right in, facing the girls on the settee. Not noticing that his wife stood just inside the door and well behind him, he declared his intentions. "Girls, the sheriff has been detained. It is lamentable for you. However, it is good news for me! I will have you both in my bed this evening!" He leered. The viscount ignored the looks of contempt and disgust, along with the obscenities and denials they were shouting at him. He continued by describing the erotic fantasies he had planned for the evening. Realizing the viscount was unaware of her location, his wife darted out the door unseen. She flew up the stairs, only to stop in front of Penelope's bedroom door. Trying to catch her breath, she waited a moment and then knocked. Since moving in, the viscount's wife had become a very good actress, now was the time to see how convincing she could be.

Penelope's maid answered. After gaining entrance, the fake Gabrielle calmly strolled over to the chaise where Penelope reclined. She plopped down on the end, near Penelope's feet, and began, "Aunt Penelope, would it be possible for you to help me with my embroidery this evening? I fear I am at a loss for something to do."

"It has already been decided that you are spending the evening with Herbert. He wishes you to become pregnant as soon as possible. You must not shirk your duty," began Aunt Penelope in her lecturing tone.

"It is hardly within my power to cancel an evening with my husband. I know my place." She sighed. "However, I overheard his lordship talking to someone in the study. He said something about teaching two new students lessons, this evening. So I don't think he will have time for me after all." She added a little pout. "I thought you and I could do a little needlework this evening and leave him to his business."

At little Gabrielle's announcement, Penelope's eyes widened and her lips compressed to a thin line. "What?" she asked, perplexed.

Suppressing a smile, the fake Gabrielle innocently said, "I'm sure he will tell you later what has him so excited. After all, he tells you everything."

"Excited?" Penelope whispered.

"Yes, though why work would make him act that way is beyond me. He seemed happy and shouting at the top of his lungs what good pupils they would be."

"W … wh … who?" she stammered.

"Whomever he is talking to, downstairs. Haven't you been listening? That's why I won't be with him. Even though he stressed over and over that it was imperative I not shirk my duties. I want you to remember it is not my doing, he is the one downstairs...."

Penelope interrupted by jumping up from the chair, and saying, "I simply cannot help you, my dear. I already have plans for this evening." She turned to give instructions to her maid and then once again her attention fell to little Gabrielle. Trying to remain calm and pretend the conversation had not upset her, Penelope continued, "I have told you before about eavesdropping. It is not polite. Your position requires perfect manners. You may go to your room and reflect on your dismal etiquette. Stay there until one of us comes for you." Taking a breath, trying to seem as nonchalant as possible, Penelope added, "You may go now!"

Following instructions, the fake Gabrielle walked out of the room. However, she waited at the end of the hallway, to see if Penelope would take action.

As soon as she had departed Penelope flew from the room and ran down the stairs. The fake Gabrielle could not contain herself and a huge smile appeared upon her face. It was a wonderful feeling to be able to manipulate others! She had been sure that the only way to foil the viscount's plans was to immediately inform Penelope of his intentions. Penelope's feelings for the viscount were clearly visible, however, her jealousy was not comprehendible. No matter, Penelope would find a way to curtail the proceedings. With a feeling of satisfaction, the fake Gabrielle went off to bed, realizing Penelope had indeed taught her well.

Waiting outside the study door for just a moment, Penelope easily confirmed the viscount had indeed changed the evenings events. As the viscount bragged to the women inside of his virility, Penelope became more and more outraged. Though she was well aware of his greedy nature and knew he spent time with other women, that didn't mean she liked it. She often ruined his plans by pretending ignorance, yet many times she could not. She had learned long ago to swallow her pride and look the other way. She had even gone so far as sharing the evenings with both him and his wife, hiding her discomfort and shame, in order to receive even the slightest attention. All because he claimed he loved her and she believed him. She certainly didn't think because he cheated, he loved her any less. He was simply a healthy man, a man, not unlike all the others of his station. She was not a stupid woman, yet there were still times she simply could not comprehend why he had settled for her. At fifty-one years old she had finally discovered the wonderful feeling of love. An emotion she had never before experienced and now that she had, she was bound and determined to do anything within her power to keep him.

So, as jealousy pierced her heart, she began her strategy. She wrote a short note, giving a servant explicit instructions. Then she opened the door and waltzed inside. "Oh, I'm sorry. I didn't realize anyone was here. Herbert, I thought you had gone riding," Penelope said, acting surprised.

The viscount was clearly upset, the surprise at her entrance evident. He had wanted to spend the rest of the evening with the two women. He did not want to explain his actions. He had been in the process of verbally arousing their interest and passion. He assumed he had been well on his way to achieving his goal, when Penelope had walked in. He sighed, and then said, "I thought you were upstairs resting. Are you feeling better?"

In response she put her arms around his neck and kissed him thoroughly. "I feel much better, now," she whispered. "Why don't we go upstairs and I will show you." Penelope smiled.

Now that he realized Penelope was not going to cause a scene, the viscount was no longer upset. Instantly he had an idea! He could have them all! He leaned down and spoke softly in her ear, "I had thought to surprise you, my dear, and bring both of them along to share with you this evening."

She didn't answer. A few moments later, feeling her response had taken too long, he said, "If you want to feel my passion tonight, you will have to share me. You know I'd rather have you there to show them my preferences. Yet if you choose not to...."

She interrupted, "Herbert, I love you. I will take you any way I can have you. Yet I insist that if I have to share you, you will tell them that they are merely pawns, while I am your queen. That it is not that one woman cannot please you. Simply that you are so masculine it takes many woman to do so. You will do this for me and I will reward you by showing them how you favor being attended." She smiled sweetly.

Not dreaming for a moment that anything Penelope had said was anything but the truth, he had become immediately hard. Within the confines of his tight breeches the evidence of his belief and excitement was there for all to see. Herbert engulfed her in his embrace as he looked over her shoulder to the two speechless women. The hug was brief, though even after their embrace he continued to hold her hand. "You two girls are in for a treat. Not only will I share my vast experience with you, but also my love will guide you in the acts of passion. You will be going to bed with us both!" he shouted with glee. "You are just two women with which I will pass an evening, nothing more. She is my queen, and knows my desires. She will teach you all you need to learn."

If Kathleen and Gabrielle had looks of disgust on their faces earlier, it was nothing compared to the sheer horror on them now!

With all three women screeching and arguing, the viscount barely heard the knock at the door. Finally the loud banging penetrated his thoughts. Taking his message from the servant, he went and sat behind the desk to read it. He groaned. "Drats! Of all the luck! Seems the sheriff has changed his mind, he will be here posthaste." His crestfallen expression said it all. He was at an impasse. Which did he prefer, the sheriff's gratitude or a new conquest? With a look of disappointment and the sound of frustration, the viscount quickly made up his mind. Opening the door, he bellowed for the guard to take the women back downstairs. Following their departure, he easily dismissed them from his thoughts. Leering at Penelope, he said, "It seems we are to be alone and I believe you have some entertaining to do." She nodded obediently, yet as she accompanied him upstairs, her smile remained smug.

Chapter 12

The girls were both completely drunk. They had spent the rest of the day and the better part of the evening clawing, banging, scrapping, and pounding in their effort to break out. But no one came to their aid and all they had to show for it was filthy clothes, broken nails and cobwebs in their hair. With no success, still enclosed and left alone, they had gotten thirsty and opened a bottle of wine. So at first, they simply drank to quench their parched throats. Becoming a bit giddy and giggly, laughing and dancing, which enticed them to open a second bottle. The second one disappeared too quickly, causing them to continue. While drinking the third bottle, their attitudes became surly and whiney. They bellowed, cried, shouted and screamed, even mentioning the men that hadn't followed them. By this time, they simply continued to drink because they were already soused.

Suddenly the door flew open. There, standing in all his glory, was Lord Armstrong! Gabrielle couldn't believe her eyes. In her drunken state, she believed it was a dream. Yet his presence was so overpowering and seemed so real she tried unsuccessfully to stand. Finally, the third time, she actually made it to a standing position. She put her arms out in front of her, as she staggered over to him. When she bumped into his chest, she threw her arms around him. She started kissing his face, his eyes, and his neck. She couldn't help it. Then his arms reached behind her, pulling her close. He crushed his mouth to hers. He consumed her. He nibbled on her lips, slightly tugging them apart. Then he slipped his tongue inside her mouth, causing sensations too strong to be called anything but delicious. Gabrielle's kiss also had the flavor of wine and the combination was heady. Violets, he smelled violets! She had been riding horses for days, then imprisoned in a wine cellar. Yet she still smelled like violets. How did she remain unruffled and sweet-smelling? His tongue probed the recesses of her mouth, matching hers thrust for thrust. Moments later she was limp in his arms. He pulled his mouth from hers. Just as he did, Kathleen said, "And about time you were getting here, we were giving up hope!"

But as soon as Gabrielle heard Kathleen's voice, she froze. She tried to pull away from Kevin's arms. She didn't want to hurt Kathleen. She was pulling and tugging, twisting and turning. Still trying to get away. Tears were beginning to run down her eyes. Yet after finally finding her, James was loath to let her go. So he held her even tighter.

Gabrielle shouted, "Kevin, you have to stop this. You have to let me go! I can't do this to Kathleen. Please try to understand." Unfortunately, with all the wine she had drunk, it sounded more like " Kist lgo I cadth to Kaln! Peas tr stand." The whole time she was shouting she was still pushing and trying to get out of his arms.

"Gabrielle, it is I, James. You must have had too much to drink, little one." He could not understand her reluctance. He tried to remain patient, yet wasn't. He firmly grabbed her by the shoulders and shook her. He tried to get through to her. Although his voice was trying to soothe her, she continued to struggle. Gabrielle said something about Kathleen, sobbing louder and louder. James didn't understand a thing she was babbling; yet he continued to hold her. Then, in the midst of it all, she passed out. While still in his arms, she fell into his chest.

Kathleen laughed. "Still have them falling all over you I see!"

Easily ignoring her comment, he belted out instructions. "We have to move quickly. Here!" James said, thrusting the lifeless Gabrielle towards Kathleen. "Hold her a moment!" He turned and exited the way he came, returning once again with the unconscious guard slung over his shoulder. Stuffing a rag in the man's mouth as he dropped him in a corner, James proceeded to tie his arms and legs with the rope he had grabbed from the shed. He finished and looked at Kathleen, pulling Gabrielle back into his arms. He said, "We don't have time for either hysterics or explanations. We have to get out of here. How do you feel?"

"Never better!" she giggled.

James just rolled his eyes. "What an escape this is going to be!" he muttered. Motioning for Kathleen to go ahead, he re-latched the outer door, causing as little notice as possible to their escape. James threw Gabrielle over his shoulder and then helped Kathleen up the short, narrow stairwell. They moved quickly. James had no idea when they would change the guard. He just knew they had to hurry. This time, instead of making their escape by going over the hill and following the road, they slid down the hillside, towards the valley. They moved as fast as possible, which wasn't all that speedy, with the dead weight of Gabrielle on his shoulder and a fuddle-brained woman beside him. As they ran, the noise of the waterfall became louder and louder. James was trying desperately to put distance between themselves and the manor. Kathleen's staggering swagger and Gabrielle inebriated state did little to help.

While they were walking along the embankment of the cascading waterfalls, James experienced discomfort in his shoulder. Although Gabrielle was just a little thing, she was dead weight. He stopped, setting her down near a large boulder. Pondering the dilemma at hand, he removed his jacket. As the noise from the waterfall was deafening, he signaled for Kathleen to wait where she was. Kathleen was only too happy to rest and settled under a tree.

Upset because Gabrielle was still unconscious. James picked her up again and then jumped in the water. Wading through a low area, he walked directly towards one of the many cascading falls. Sliding Gabrielle down off his shoulder, he held her close for several moments as the water poured over them. Though her body remained limp, he continued to hold her. Finally, after what seemed an eternity, Gabrielle began to cough and sputter. She tried to stand on her own. She was screaming and her arms were flaying. He continued to hold her upright as the cool water drenched her. When it looked like the water had done its job of reviving her, he moved several steps to the left. Standing under the large plateau, they were now directly behind the falling water. His eyes twinkled, his smile devastating. As he watched her expressions, he hollered, "Gabrielle, are you all right?"

The noise was so loud she thought he said, "You are the love of my life!" she pushed away from him vigorously shaking her head no.

"Kevin, you have to leave me alone! Haven't you heard about William? What about Kathleen? We simply can not do this!" she bellowed.

She was shaking her head no, yet he thought he heard, "Don't ever leave me alone like this!" James could barely hear and not very clearly, with the combination of Gabrielle slurring her words and the water spraying all over them. The splashing and the noise from the falling water made it even worse. But Gabrielle's eyes sparkled when she looked at him. He knew she couldn't hear him, any more than he could hear her. So instead he pulled her close. She resisted and struggled at first, but he held her firmly. Nudging her mouth open, he kissed her, lightly at first. Passion overwhelmed them both and like before, the kiss deepened. Minutes later, she began melting in his arms. Standing there in the roaring cascade, their sight and touch took over where their hearing sense was unable to help. Holding her firmly with one arm, the other lightly stroking her body. Running up and down first her arm, then her back. Then his kisses moved lower. Down her throat, across her bosom and the anticipation of more causing her to tremble. Lightly caressing her nipple through the now translucent bodice of her wet dress. Her fingers dug into his shoulders, as his mouth worked its magic. She was responding to his attentions and began to moan with her arousal. His lips once again wandered to her mouth. She was shivering as he finally pulled his mouth from hers. She had a glazed expression on her face. He preferred to believe it was his kisses that gave her that look, not the wine she had drunk. Ultimately, good sense did prevail and he insisted, "We have to go! Will you be able to make it?"

Nodding her head yes, she responded, "Yes, I can take it. As long as I am with you, Kevin!" Again, with all the noise around her, she had heard incorrectly. In return, James had not heard Gabrielle's true response either, but he continued on. She was smiling and holding his hand as they trudged through the falls and wading over to the bank. Her wet clothes made her heavier and even slower than before. As he held out his hand to assist her up the embankment, she noticed the large grin on his face. She believed it was because they were finally on their way. If she had also noticed the gleam in his eye, it would have given her more of a clue as to his smile. Yet, even then, she would have no way of guessing. His grin was in response to her attire. His earlier stimulation was nothing compared to the view of Gabrielle in a dress, wet and plastered to her body. What a naïve temptress she was. When he pulled her up the embankment, seduction was once again on his mind. He had a twinkle in his eye and a grin on his face. He had never been happier. She responded in kind, with a huge, bright, smile.

There was Kathleen sitting near a tree, waiting for them. Kathleen didn't say anything; she simply got up and approached them. Suddenly, reality hit!

Immediately Gabrielle felt both nauseous and lightheaded. She wasn't getting enough air; it felt like she couldn't breathe! Without warning she shouted, "I can't take it!" She spun around and turned to face Kathleen. "I'm sooo sorry. I have loved him from the moment I set eyes on him!" James' chest puffed out in pride with this announcement. As Gabrielle poured out her heart to Kathleen, rambling on and on, about the guilt that consumed her. James and Kathleen were only able to comprehend bits and pieces of conversation. The noise from the nearby waterfalls added to the fact that Gabrielle's speech was still affected by the wine. Yet Gabrielle persisted in trying to explain. "He is the handsome stranger I told you about. I just didn't know he was YOUR handsome stranger." Kathleen did catch the part about a stranger, but the rest was too garbled to interpret. "I need him. Unfortunately, also just like you need him!" With that, Gabrielle burst out crying, tears streaming down her face. Sobs so loud they rivaled even Kathleen's worst outbursts. Then Gabrielle resumed her pleading, "I will give him up! I will give him up for you, Kathleen, I will! I'm sooo sorry!" With raised eyebrows, James looked inquiringly at Kathleen. Gabrielle continued bawling as Kathleen rolled her eyeballs.

James gave Kathleen a dirty look.

"Don't look at me," responded Kathleen. "I never asked her to give you up. We started on this journey so you could come after us. I saved your hide, for crying out loud! Otherwise by now she," pointing to Gabrielle, "would be a married woman!" emphasized Kathleen.

So, it had been as he had suspected. Kathleen had talked Gabrielle into fleeing to escape the marriage with William. James owed Kathleen. But what the heck was Gabrielle shouting about? Why would she be mistaken, thinking Kathleen did not approve of them together?

With Gabrielle drunk, the answers were not clear. The conversation had been confusing from the beginning. The more Gabrielle said, the more he became confused. "Every time I turned around, I saw him. I tried not to like him, because I knew he was yours! You cry louder than I do. I just didn't have the power to resist him." Then her head fell upon his chest, as she began to sob uncontrollably. Added to that she was still wet and shivering. Before long, she would be ill. They had to get moving. James looked first at Kathleen, then down at Gabrielle, and said firmly, "We have to leave now or risk getting caught." That got him the attention he needed. Gabrielle started to quiet down. He picked up the jacket he had left near the stream and put it around Gabrielle's shoulders. He once again gathered Gabrielle close and then swung her up into his arms, deciding it would just be easier to carry Gabrielle in her condition. Kathleen, though still tipsy, was more agile. So between carrying one and pushing the other, the two drunks were making this getaway damn difficult. As they followed the path, James could not take time to try to figure out any of Gabrielle's tirade. Pushing Kathleen to move at a faster pace, he really had his work cut out for him. Then they started down the path.

As they walked along, Kathleen muttered teasingly, "I wasn't sure you were ever going to come out from that waterfall."

James grinned sheepishly. "If we were not in danger of pursuit, I can guarantee we would not have." Then he said, "We'd better keep moving. We have to get to Derek's ship."

"You did come for us," murmured Gabrielle in response to the comment about Derek's ship. Of course he had come for them, didn't she see him standing there? James looked at Gabrielle and was only more bewildered than before. He had no way of knowing her intoxicated comment was from a conversation she and Kathleen had had earlier. However, he had already decided to wait till they were safe aboard ship before questioning Gabrielle again. God willing, by that time, she may even be sober.

They scurried past the flora and fauna and made their way up the steep slope. James quickly untied both his horse and the extra one he had obtained.

Walking up the hill and over, they finally guided the horses to a stop. James assisted Kathleen upon her horse, and then he swiftly climbed upon his own mount. He positioned Gabrielle upon his lap and cradled her close. Then they rapidly left the area, heading east, hoping to find Derek.

Later Kathleen and James were sitting on a log, on the beach, huddled near the fire. Autumn was fast approaching, the wind turning crisp. Still fast asleep, Gabrielle's back was to the fire as she lay on the other side. Lying on James' jacket, she hadn't made a peep in some time. James was anticipating Derek would see the two blazing signal fires. If he didn't, they would have to move on to plan two. James much preferred leaving the area as fast as possible. James and Kathleen alternated between views. Looking at the stars overhead or staring out at the water. Though they couldn't see much in the murky darkness, the waves seemed to have a soothing effect.

"Kathleen, any idea why Gabrielle thinks you don't want us together?"

"I have to say I'm as confused as you are. She has never given any indication that would lead me to believe she thought I didn't like you." Laughing, Kathleen continued, "I even think I've complimented you a time or two. No, whatever ideas she has are strictly her own. You'll have to set her down and end all the confusion. You should do it quickly, we've no idea if William has someone on our trail," said Kathleen.

"I know you had her follow you to Scotland to stop that wedding. I'm forever in your debt," whispered James with heartfelt emotion.

"I couldn't let her marry that man, he was like a brother to her. She liked him, but he does not breathe passion into her the way you do. Why do you think she followed so easily?"

James grinned. "I know she loves me, she tells me with her actions. Yet she denies that we can be together. Something is not right!"

"After you straighten out your situation with Gabrielle, what is our next move? You are not taking her back to her guardian, are you?" asked Kathleen.

"She will never again be under anyone's protection but my own. I intend to marry her posthaste. Agreeing or not."

"She will argue, she feels all this loyalty towards her father, her guardian and her fiancé. I mean William."

"Yes," agreed James, slowly nodding his head. "She feels loyal to them, however, she loves me! She knows I love her in return. I will make it work," he insisted. His arrogance was in full force once again.

"What is the plan?" Kathleen again inquired.

"I am going to fulfill my promise and get you to Kevin. However, we have been gone much longer than he had first anticipated. Kevin will be concerned about our delay. Traveling by ship and breaking into Gabrielle's home began the downfall of our timetable. Afterwards we elected to look for her guardian, and what a situation that became. Not only did we locate him, but also he insisted that Gabrielle live with him. Not to mention your fleeing London, followed by your abduction.

"I'm not sure of how long Kevin was to be in Edinburgh. So, first I have to apologize and then I'm going to beg his forgiveness for the delay. After I am back in his good graces, I will convince him and his friends to help us with the little problem of Viscount Herrington. Gabrielle's father could even be alive with all the foul play at hand. Don't mention my hunch to Gabrielle, I have no proof and I wouldn't want to disappoint her if I'm wrong."

"That damn Sheriff Muden is involved, he is in cahoots with the viscount and the aunt. Kevin will help, I just know he will," Kathleen assured James. Then she sighed, "What took you so long to find us?"

"What took me so long was the fact that you did not travel by any direct route. If you had stayed on course and traveled by coach, I would have caught up to you days ago. It was pure luck which led me to you. If I hadn't run into a group of men camping nearby and overheard their conversation, I would be headed to Scotland even still and you would be sitting in the wine cellar."

"No, if you had not rescued us when you did, we would even now be servants for Sheriff Muden. Though I'm not sure it would be his rugs we'd be washing," she smirked.

"What are you saying?" he demanded.

"I'm saying the viscount could not have two different Gabrielles running around without arousing suspicion. He had to get rid of one. So he planned to give us to the sheriff." Then Kathleen cringed. "Worse yet, before being sent off to the sheriff, we were to spend the evening with him and his lover first!" She chuckled. "You should have seen Gabrielle's reaction to that!" Kathleen could tell by James' expression that he still did not fully comprehend the actual circumstances. So she continued, "Though it would have been dramatic for me, I have survived much worse. However, you must realize what a trauma it would have been for Gabrielle. I mean, Gabrielle losing her virginity to the count!" she huffed.

James finally understood. "The bastard! If I had known before we left, I would have made that act impossible for him in the future! I will have to be satisfied to take my pound of flesh, when next we meet. Still, I am appalled at his audacity!"

"Oh, there's more audacity than you think! He intended to deflower and share your precious Gabrielle with both me and her aunt."

"What?" he choked out.

"Just thought you might like to know exactly what the hell was going on. So you see how your timing could not have been better?"

Ever so softly he spoke, "He didn't hurt either of you, did he?"

"No, he did not have the opportunity. I believe Penelope, Gabrielle's aunt, has the viscount under control most of the time."

"Was Gabrielle able to fend him off?" he questioned.

"Yes, I told you. We came through unscathed."

In a quiet and firm yet menacing tone, James said. "I promise you, he will pay. He will answer for all his crimes. I will let Gabrielle know, I will not rest until he is brought to justice."

Conversation lapsed into companionable silence. The only breaks in the silence were the waves washing up on shore and the loud crackling of burning wood, being the only accompaniments to the intense quiet. Kathleen leaned into the nook of his shoulder, for both warmth and comfort. Time passed. After hours of waiting, they finally heard a piercing whistle, in the distance.

James jumped up, trying to see something in the inky, darkness. He answered with the proper response. Loudly returning the whistle, two short, one long.

Then someone hollered, "Who goes there?"

James answered, "Only a sad lonely man." Not daring to mention the girls if it was not Derek. The response came moments later, confirming it was.

Derek could not contain his enthusiasm. "Everything all right?" he shouted, hoping the answer would be positive.

James hollered, "Everything is as expected. Now hurry!"

Derek said, "The girls are with you?"

"We are!" shouted Kathleen.

Derek said, "We'll be there shortly. Come on, boys, man those oars." As soon as Derek had confirmed that it was indeed his friends on shore, they lit the lanterns.

In a short span of time, they were aboard the dingy and headed to Derek's ship. Kathleen, Derek, and James all with huge smiles upon their faces. Kathleen's and James' were from the gratitude of being rescued. Gabrielle's was more a combination of wine and sleep. They reached the ship, scurrying aboard as quickly as possible.

The masts were gathering a slight breeze and they would be far from there by morning. Gabrielle had nodded off again and James was carrying her when they descended the stairway. "Still have them falling all over you?" muttered Kathleen. As James was used to the common barb, he didn't comment. Kathleen argued with James about where to put Gabrielle. She wanted Gabrielle with her. She knew the morning would bring more questions than answers. She wanted her close by. James was not about to let Gabrielle go. Not ever again. Not even for a moment. Not even for propriety's sake. After all, he had decided to marry her. Whether she wanted to or not. So off they trouped to their cabins, Kathleen to hers, James and Gabrielle to his.

The next morning her throat was tight, her mouth dry, her head throbbed. When she opened her eyes, the bright light caused intense pain. As she lay there trying to get her head to stop moving, she realized she was onboard a ship. She quickly sat up, thinking the viscount had abducted her. She heard a groan as her arm hit the inside of a thick, muscular thigh. She recoiled in reaction. Looking towards his head, she confirmed her suspicion, Oh, no, Kevin! What had happened? Why was she in bed with him? Where was Kathleen? What was going on? She turned to accuse him, when in turn he said to her, "Good morning, my love."

"No, you can't say things like that to me!" Her head hurt to talk; yet she tried to climb over him and escape from the bunk. "Where is Kathleen? Why aren't you telling her those things?" she whispered.

"Gabrielle, I believe I'm falling in love with you but I must admit there are just some times I just don't understand you. Why in heaven's name would I say those things to Kathleen?" asked James.

"Because you were hers first. Because you are going to Scotland."

"Indeed, I am taking Kathleen to Scotland to be married," he confirmed. Unfortunately it was the wrong answer.

"I know!" she said, huge tears beginning to fall down her face. "I'm trying to do what is best. Although you make it difficult," said Gabrielle. This time she was able to lunge past him and slide from the bunk. She quickly ran out, slamming the door. James was confused, however, as he needed to straighten things out. He quickly threw on his pants, and followed. He didn't even knock; he simply barged into Kathleen's cabin. They were huddled together, Gabrielle blubbering on Kathleen's shoulder.

As he approached, James continued to talk soothingly towards Gabrielle.

"Gabrielle, what is the concern? Why do you care if I take Kathleen to Scotland? After all, you are going too. I don't want to lose you, ever again." smiled James.

"You talk as if you are allowed more than one wife. Even then, I could never share you. What am I saying?" she pointed to Kathleen "She should not have to share you!" screeched Gabrielle.

"Gabrielle, again I must say I am confused. Don't you love me?"

"Kevin, you just have to stop this! You are going to marry Kathleen and that is all there is to it!" Gabrielle said, folding her arms across her chest.

James stared at her in disbelief. He continued to look at her. In fact he couldn't stop! How did such idiotic reasoning come encased in such a beautiful package? Kathleen was already giggling, when he began to laugh. He wasn't really sure what was going on, yet he was positive Gabrielle had some goofy idea! Why was she calling out Kevin's name? "Gabrielle, who do you think I am?"

Gabrielle was not sure as to the answer he was looking for. Did he want to know if she knew his title? She remembered Derek shouting out a whole litany of titles. She couldn't remember even one. Did he want her to reply with his position? She didn't know that either. So she simply replied the first thing that occurred to her. "Kevin," she said.

James began to grin, again. Then the grin turned to a smile, the smile turning to a laugh. What had begun as a small laugh turned into loud, uncontrollable laughter. Kathleen, too, was flopping up and down on the bunk trying to control her laughter. Finally, after many minutes, he reached down and tipped her chin up. He looked into her beautiful eyes and said, "I would like to introduce myself. James, Marquee of Richmond. It is indeed a pleasure to make your acquaintance."

Gabrielle didn't have any idea of what to do. She couldn't comprehend the mistake she had made all this time. "James?" she repeated, "James, not Kevin?" she finally stammered.

She looked from Kathleen to James and from James to Kathleen, several times. She was having a tough time comprehending the huge mistake she had made. Kathleen and James just couldn't quit laughing. She had to stand there while they carried on. Finally, James inquired. "Where did you get the idea my name was Kevin?" he laughed.

She began at the beginning. When she and Kathleen were sneaking around the castle and she had spotted him across the hall. She had been enamored ever since.

Later, finding him in the baths, she thought maybe it was love at first sight. She reminded him of their encounter on the balcony. As though he needed reminding. He recalled quite vividly every experience with her.

She went on to remind him of each and every time it seemed he was Kevin. No one had really introduced them; they had all assumed she knew. How when she mentioned Kevin and Scotland, the conversation always pointed to him. After an hour-long explanation and all the extenuating circumstances, he finally had to agree. It had been easy to misinterpret his identity, she genuinely assumed he was Kevin. At that, James recalled leaving his calling card at her guardian's residence. What about that? Did she not receive it? That should have brought about an inquiry. She sheepishly replied that there had been too many cards from visiting gentlemen. She had felt guilty for not remembering any of the names. Gabrielle admitted she may have read the card, yet, unable to match a face with a name, would have added it to the ever growing pile without another care.

Though he knew she hadn't known who he was at the time, the telling still deflated his ego a bit. Finishing on a lighter note, he suggested this story would bring laughter for years to come.

James was deep in thought. Now her reluctance was understandable. Now that she was not betraying a friend, she would be able to accept what he had done. He tried the straightforward approach.

"Gabrielle, you spent the night alone in my cabin. You have been compromised, I intend to marry you and make an honest woman of you," he said.

"I rather thought I'd marry for love," she sighed wistfully.

"Oh, is that why you were willing to marry William?" he commented.

"You knew about William?" she asked

"I knew, and I was consumed with jealously. Maybe you haven't noticed that it was I, who chased you all over the country. That I did not hesitate to come to your rescue?" he responded. "Not once but twice."

"Yes, but do you love me as I love you?" she questioned

"Gabrielle, I must admit I thought my feelings for you simple lust. I found you very beautiful and enchanting. Yet I fought my feelings for you every step of the way. I truly didn't believe it was love. When I was unable to contact you at your guardian's, you were always on my mind. Every time I turned around, I would want to share things with you or just tell you something. Finally I had to admit to myself it was more than lust. I wanted you with me, at all times.

"I was on my way to shout from the rafters my intentions, when you fled. After that, I really knew I loved you, because I was beside myself with worry. You have turned a conceited, tough rogue into a bedeviled, love-struck fool. I love you with all my heart," he said. He reached for her and they embraced. As he began to nuzzle her neck, a knock sounded at the door. Without awaiting a response, Derek waltzed in.

"Has my cabin suddenly become the grand salon?" questioned Kathleen, still laughing.

Gabrielle had thought she had been embarrassed when James and Kathleen had found out how stupid she was. Boy, was she wrong. The height of embarrassment was telling Derek, for he was still laughing two days later.

Though Gabrielle was uncertain about proceeding, James finally convinced her. Derek would perform the ceremony the next morning.

So after breakfast, James retrieved the marriage certificate from his saddlebags. On that warm fall morning, they were all gathered on deck for the ceremony. Gabrielle did not have the traditional trousseau, or any accessories. Even without the finery, the flowers, the music, she rivaled any bride. Her long, raven hair, gathered atop her head, skillfully arranged. The smile on her face radiated her joy and confirmed her happiness. The sun was brightly shining; the sky was blue and clear. The reflection of the rays dancing on the water provided the only decoration they needed.

Standing on deck as Derek began the ceremony, holding Gabrielle close to his side, James could not be happier. He still could not fathom how all this had happened and so quickly too. Thinking he had his emotions well in control, Gabrielle had somehow chipped away the tough exterior. For a man who thought he was immune to affection she had somehow slipped past his barriers. Unconsciously he had succumbed to her charms and now he held her secure within his heart. All that mattered now was that she was his.

Gabrielle had this nagging feeling of guilt. She felt as though they were doing something wrong. She wanted to meet his parents, she wanted his family here. She wanted to talk to her guardian. Then all she had to do was look at James and all serious thought fled her mind. Gabrielle could not help but stare at James in fascination. She was helplessly in love. She had never felt so warm and content. Whenever he was about, she knew she was safe and secure. He made her believe she was pretty and alluring. Gabrielle realized at that moment how miserable she and William would have been.

While gathered together, there was a shout, from the crow's nest. "Pirates! Pirates off the stern!"

Instantly, the ceremony was forgotten, as everyone scattered. Quickly, the crew attended to their assigned duties. Moments later, the women were escorted downstairs and the men prepared to defend the ship. The women were huddled alone, in the confines of the cabin, for hours. Gabrielle and Kathleen took turns pacing, though it didn't help. After having just escaped, the fear of capture was all too real. Gabrielle made some new decisions while waiting to see the outcome. If the ship didn't explode, she knew James would! Thankfully it was over before it had begun. They had been lucky; their ship had been able to outrun the pirates.

Later, snuggled in the safety of his arms, Gabrielle began to talk to James. She tried to explain that the pirates were a sign, that fate had intervened.

He shouted!

It had stopped her from making a terrible mistake.

He hollered!

She truly loved and adored him, but she wanted to wait to marry.

He bullied!

She pleaded with him to understand.

He bargained!

She wanted her guardian to give her away.

He coerced!

She wanted to return to her guardian and receive his blessing.

He blackmailed!

She didn't intend to begin her marriage by betraying her guardian.

He cajoled!

She also felt she needed to be the one to explain everything to William.

He flirted!

She smiled.

At first James just did not comprehend. He certainly was having difficulty believing he was not going to have his way. Finally, after trying every means of persuasion and exhausting all other excuses, his suggestion was to marry now, for propriety sake, then later again for family.

This time, she demanded he understand her feelings! She was not about to back down. Gabrielle was determined to start this marriage off on the right foot.

He relented!

At the end of their lengthy argument, it was agreed they would marry when they got back to London. They hugged and kissed; with the discussion over, making up was the best part. James was not really upset to have the large wedding with all the whoopla. He was just upset at having to wait to have her, she belonged to him, and he wanted it confirmed. James did understand Gabrielle's reasoning and knew her arguments had merit. He also knew he was being a bit irrational, but where she was concerned, he couldn't seem to help it. Leaving the room, he stated, "Remember, the moment we are in London, you will be my wife!" To emphasize the point, as he left, he slammed the cabin door behind him.

It was at the dinner table the evening before they pulled into Edinburgh harbor that Gabrielle casually made a remark about anatomy. Her naïveté and confusion caused continuous laughter. Yet with such an innocent look about her, the teasing soon relented. Kathleen remarked, "No one would ever know you spent any time at Helena's, with that innocent look to you!" She giggled.

James stared intently at Kathleen and said, "And no one ever will! Will they, Kathleen?"

"Well, I won't tell anyone, if that's what you're thinking. It's just here amongst ourselves that we can hoot about it. You can't think I would hurt my own friend! I don't appreciate you insinuating I would. Now just take that surly tone out of your voice, Mr. High and Mighty. If you're not nice, I'll really stoke that fire you have burning and tell the tale of our trips to the viewing chambers," she teased.

Gabrielle's eyes grew huge. She was unsure where this conversation was headed. Yet she did not want James' temper to flare. So she carefully kept her eyes on her plate. Finally she looked up and everyone was looking at her. Then they all laughed. James finally relented and agreed that among themselves, they could indeed continue to share conversation about their experiences. He did impress upon them the desire to save his future wife's reputation. That's when Gabrielle remembered a very important clue. "James, we have forgotten a very valuable detail."

"What is that? Gabrielle."

"My guardian. I have the papers stating that the 1st Earl of Chatham is my guardian. I have met my guardian and he remembered me from my childhood. He even has a small miniature with my likeness. I have been introduced to his son. Now am I able to seek justice with the courts?"

James pondered a bit. He looked at Derek, then at Kathleen. "I believe we will now be able to pursue this. I will contact the magistrate. When we contact your guardian for his blessing, we will also inform him of our plans. Although he will surely be upset about your marriage to me in place of his son, I still believe he will help us, what do you think?" he questioned.

"I believe he is an honest and kind man. He was very good to me. He offered his protection and also Young Will's. William is very interested in politics and though he was always very nice to me, I got the impression he did not care for interruptions causing him to take time from his work. And James," she hesitated, looking a bit mischievous, "I'm afraid, I am a very big interruption." she smiled

James immediately agreed. Adding that as he was qualified to handle such interruptions, only he would be burdened in the future. The others all laughed.

"To answer your question, though. I do indeed believe Uncle William will help me. So where do we go from here?" asked Gabrielle.

"First and for most, we get Kathleen to Edinburgh. It has been well over four months since Kevin expected her delivered to him. I sent a message when we were delayed in London. Yet there is no way of knowing if he received it. First Kevin and Kathleen get married. Then we enlist the aid of Kevin and Scott and their clan to raid Cartwright Manor. If we have to go to Herrington House, we will do that too. If we have to track down that damn sheriff, we'll do that too. We will do what ever it takes to right the wrongs that they have done. Then we will all be able to go on our way."

"Not on our separate ways!" said Gabrielle sadly.

"We will all have a great deal to keep us busy, but you can depend on the fact that we will remain close," said James

Kathleen smiled. "Gabrielle, you can rest assured that we will spend plenty of time together. Your future husband and Kevin are already good friends, we will surely have many holidays together!"

Derek said, "I, too, will make every effort to continue our friendship. Let's just get this adventure over before you plan the next." He raised his mug of ale to his friends and said, "To friendship!"

The next day, as they pulled into Edinburgh harbor, Kathleen turned to question James. "I could have sworn at one time Kevin told me he lived in the Western Isles. He said the Clan MacDonald was a proud and fierce lot and was able to escape the clearances of northern Scotland because he was from the Isles. Isn't that right, what are we doing in Edinburgh?" she asked, suddenly worried.

James responded, "Kevin and his friends have been trying to get a law repealed. You may or may not have heard of the Highland Dress Proscription Act of 1746. If you have or have not, it does not matter. What matters is the Scots have been banned from wearing their kilts. No bagpipes, no Gaelic, no individual clan kilts. It was a cruel blow dealt by our government in order to destroy their identities, and they are desperately trying to restore their heritage. Kevin believes that in the next few years, he will successfully win an appeal for all the clans. He has been working hard for their cause. You know what they say, *Once a leader, always a leader.*"

Kathleen eyes widened. "I didn't realize he was in politics."

"Kevin does what ever is needed. It is necessary for their pride and happiness to see this law repealed. The economic structure has changed dramatically here in Scotland. Thirty years ago, the clans lost a lot of men in the Battle of Culloden. Where he would have once ruled as a chieftain, he now is only an earl. He may retain his property and land; he cannot rule the whole clan, however. Yet he does what he can to change the injustices." He looked at Kathleen with all sincerity. "You have a whole new life in front of you. You will do him proud. You will stand beside him and you will pick him up when he falls. I have every faith in you." He gave her a quick hug.

Gabrielle beamed. What a far cry from his insolent tones when he first talked about the loose women of Helena's. She was very proud he had come so far.

"You sure have changed your mind since the first time you judged me to be beneath the likes of Kevin MacDonald. Not that I don't appreciate the compliment, but why the sudden turnabout?" demanded Kathleen.

"Let's just say I have gotten to know and trust you. I told you all along, I have good manners. When someone makes an error, they should admit it. I am admitting my error. I am proud to call you my friend. You have shown great courage in helping Gabrielle. I will be forever grateful." Changing the subject, he added, "Make sure you are dressed warm, the weather has turned cold."

After they anchored and had gotten ashore, though Edinburgh was similar to any port in England, it still had a bit of a rustic feel to it. The first thing they had to do was to secure rooms. So they headed down the street to locate an inn. After they had found the establishment of choice, they were given rooms. As the girls owned nothing but the clothes on their backs, they wanted to go shopping. But the men had other plans. James talked them into enjoying the luxury of a bath and he would have a dressmaker sent to them. In that way, he could go find Kevin without worrying about the girls' safety. Kathleen squealed in delight and gave her heartfelt agreement. Gabrielle could not argue, as Kathleen was the reason they were here. However, she was tired of four walls. Wine cellars, ship cabins and inns. She was going to have James take her for a walk this evening, whether he protested or not!

James and Derek had been everywhere. They had covered miles. Checking every guesthouse, tavern and gathering spot available. Unfortunately they were not to be found. They seemed to have left a month ago, for that is when the trail ran out. No one had seen or heard from them since. All their sources repeated the same. After a long, discouraging day, they finally returned late into the evening.

James and Derek did not tell the girls they were having trouble locating Kevin and Scott. They were unable to agree on what to tell them. So they stayed in the taproom till the wee hours of morning. Every time they thought to go upstairs, they decided to have just one more drink. James just couldn't face telling Kathleen that they didn't know where her man was. By the time they went to their rooms, they were drunk and stumbling. Kathleen had given up and retired long ago, but Gabrielle had been determined to remain awake until James returned. She was unsuccessful in the attempt, as the men were so late. She had fallen asleep in the chair near the fireplace. Before going to his own room, James first stopped at Gabrielle's door, hoping to speak with her.

Without preamble, James opened the door and staggered in. The moment he did so, he was hit with the realization of his own stupidity. He felt so brainless. He had not wanted to be anywhere but with Gabrielle. Yet, he had spent the better part of the evening getting drunk and staying away from her. Next time no matter how unpleasant the task, he would tell her. Then he would not punish himself with the lack of her company. Observing her sleeping form, his heart swelled with pride. Picking her up, he tiptoed quietly across the room with her sleeping form. Carrying her to the bed and carefully easing the covers over her. For the amount of alcohol in his system, it showed great agility. He extinguished the light and turned to leave, headed for his own room. Stumbling, he fell, immediately passing out, landing across the end of the bed.

The sun was streaming in the window when James woke the next morning.

He didn't feel too bad, considering what he had consumed. Looking around the room he was quick to realize, he was in the wrong room. Gabrielle was gone. Assuming she had not woken him because she was angry. Although it had been an accident, again he had spent the evening alone with her. He didn't have to worry about Kathleen besmirching Gabrielle's good name, he was doing well enough on his own. Fortunately, both instances were not common knowledge. If she would just hurry and marry him, this would not continue to be a problem.

Why was he acting this way? What was the matter with him? To have changed so drastically in so short a period just didn't seem right. A man never bothered by convention, or the wiles of women. What had caused him to forego his charming bachelor status for that of man in bondage? The smell of violets wafted about the bed as he started to get up. Just the subtle scent of Gabrielle caused the answers to his questions to come flooding back. The answer to all his questions, answered in one word. GABRIELLE. Never before had any woman been able to entangle his heart. This one accomplished it without even realizing the challenge it should have been.

As he stood, he felt a bit lightheaded. His eyes burned, his throat was dry and his tongue felt thick. Trying to steady himself, he breathed in deeply. How much had he drunk? Running into a servant as he stumbled to his own room, he demanded coffee. Finally, after a quick bath, a lot of coffee and a shave, he regained his composure. Briskly striding downstairs, he located Derek eating breakfast in the main room. Passing on breakfast, James had more coffee as Derek finished eating. With vague information, garnished from their patron, the men headed out to look for the women. With two women alone in a strange town, they'd better hurry. Grabbing thick capes, as the frost was still in the air, they quickly followed, so as to not to lose the women. As luck would have it, they were still at the dress shop. The women were not as mad as they had anticipated; they had already vented their fury on James' pocketbook, ordering every unnecessary item they could think of. Derek laughed at the deed and James joined in laughing at their audacity. James did not want to get into a serious discussion there, so he suggested the ladies take their time and meet them at the restaurant around the corner in an hour.

James and Derek spent that hour at the Boar's Head, where they finally hit upon a piece of luck when bumping into a man by the name of Cullen McRae. Cullen went on to inform them that a friend of Kevin's had pulled into port, on the ship *Avenger*. Kevin had convinced Red to take Kevin and his men aboard. So last month, the Clan MacDonald and Clan McTavish had joined the Clan Ferguson and sailed away.

Disappointed, James and Derek quizzed Cullen about their destination. Over and over he repeated that he didn't know. Finally he admitted he had overheard someone say they left to go looking for a woman. But he wanted to make it clear he wasn't sure of that information, "Anyway, as you say you are the friend he was waiting for, I have to tell you. They left! You just took too long, laddie," said Cullen.

They thanked the man for his information and after leaving him a little something for his time and trouble, they left.

When they returned, Derek led the women off to the side, sitting in a secluded alcove. James shut the double doors behind them and sat to talk. "First of all, ladies, you look lovely today," he said, remembering to compliment them. "I want to apologize for our tardiness last night." Hoping if he didn't include their drunkenness, they wouldn't know about it. "We were very busy gathering information. Time slipped away."

Derek merely nodded in agreement. The ladies exchanged looks.

"Listen, James. We know you men didn't get in until the wee hours of the morning. We also know you were soused. So save your damn story for someone else. Don't go handing it out to two women that have enough experience with men to buy that sorry story. Now, where is Kevin?" exploded Kathleen.

Derek started, "First off, you have to realize we are later than anticipated." He tried to lengthen the explanation and soften the blow.

James interrupted, "Kevin is gone."

Derek shoved him in the ribs. "Again I must tell you! You have absolutely no tact!" he muttered. "Kathleen, it's not as bad as all that. Just that we have to go back to Helena's to find him."

"What?" screeched Kathleen

This time it was Gabrielle that was unruffled. "Gentlemen, maybe you need to start at the beginning." So they repeated the last two days' events.

They spared the girls nothing, then remained quietly seated until everything sunk in.

Finally Gabrielle said, "Tomorrow at first light we sail for Helena's. It is imperative Kathleen gets to Kevin." She blushed, exchanging looks with James. "I want Kathleen to be as happy as I am." With a piercing gaze she stared at James. "Tonight, you gentlemen are going to escort us to the festival." Changing her tactics, she batted her eyes at both Derek and James, saying, "It's the least you can do to make up for deserting us last night."

Derek said, "But we didn't desert you, we told you we were tracking down–"

"Save it," James interrupted. "Before they demand we take them with us next time. Believe me, we are getting off easy." He turned and smiled at the girls.

Later, they went in search of the festival, easy to find, as the music led them to their destination. Along with the drums, there was a pleasant, yet unusual sound. The others were familiar with the sound, for Kathleen had been born in Scotland and James and Derek had traveled extensively. Gabrielle alone was ignorant of the Scottish tradition. She was pleasantly surprised to discover the music originating from bagpipes. As they enjoyed the festive music, they were informed about its past.

"I'm glad that fellow explained about the kilts and bagpipes. I thought you had said they were confiscated and taken away from the people," said Gabrielle.

Kathleen answered, "Only the military are given permission to both wear the native dress and play the instruments. It usually precedes only tournaments, important ceremonies, war and a traditional fair or two. They can be heard for six miles around and the high penetrating notes can even be heard over the noise of battle."

"Well, I like them," announced Gabrielle. The others laughingly agreed.

The group continued to wander around. The pipers were a lively bunch, never seeming to run out of energy or spirit. After Gabrielle had gotten a good look at the haggis, she was not hard to talk into moving over to the games. So they left the food and music to go watch the contests.

There were several events. The first event they stopped to watch was a weight for distance competition. They joined the crowd, chanting for the favorite.

Later, they moved over to the stone put, again cheering for the favorite. This time both they and the crowd were disappointed. For a new man emerged victorious.

As they shuffled through the crowd, headed towards another event, a large, red-bearded man waved Gabrielle over to try the stone. They all laughed, watching her try to lift it. She struggled for a few moments, and then gave up. Needless to say, she did not enter the event.

Their stroll ended up near the caber-tossing event. The idea is to spin the log so that it falls straight ahead. This event requires timing and skill and is not just brute strength. Starting with the lightest, shortest caber, then if successful they go on to the next size. They are either eliminated or they win.

The group bet on the outcome. They laughed, they talked, and they drank. They spent the evening with no worries or cares. Over on the other side of the park was a game of cricket in progress, though they didn't stay to watch. Ending up back where they started, the music was in full force. Now dancers had joined the pipers and drummers. They stayed to watch the dances. Several dancers even grabbed them one by one to join in. One dance called the High Fling was a bit wild, with arms held up in the air. It was a dance of victory after battle. Although they lacked the skill and technique to be at all competitive, they did dance with enthusiasm. After they were thoroughly exhausted, they sat and watched the remaining dancers, dance the sword dance. The sword dance was more of a victory jig to the skirl of the pipers, using two swords to form a cross on the ground. When the crowd began to thin out, even the girls had to admit defeat and announce they were ready to go back. Scotland had been a delightful diversion. They had enjoyed the beautiful scenery, the pleasant people and the wonderful customs.

Chapter 13

Leaving behind Scotland's panoramic scenery and wonderful folklore, the next morning they set off for Helena's. They were going past the Thames when Gabrielle suggested she jump off and swim to her guardian's, so as to do two things at once. James took her below to keep her occupied and out of mischief. Kathleen agreed it was too bad they couldn't stop in London. After all, they were right here, how long would that take? Then she realized it would be even longer before she was able to see Kevin, so she kept silent. Kathleen rolled her eyes towards heaven as Derek explained how they had to get to Kevin first and lay the foundation of their plan. How they would backtrack and return to London. Leaving Derek standing at the rail, she too, went below.

They had finally pulled into the Bristol Channel. They docked well over a week after leaving Edinburgh. Derek had complained often that the turbulent seas were caused by the lateness of the season. Usually he was in a warm port for the winter. The air was turning cold, the water choppy. After entering the secluded cove and approaching the castle, no place had ever seemed more a home to any of them. They felt the security envelope them as they entered their safe harbor. Hurrying up the steps and through the doorway, they had a feeling of homecoming.

Maude was at the door directing as usual, when they were ushered in. Gabrielle was never so happy to see anyone in her life. They embraced and both Gabrielle and Maude had tears in their eyes. After all, Maude was like a mother to her. Everyone was trying to talk at once, everyone saying something different. The chaos in the foyer was deafening. Helena came down to greet them all. She immediately hugged Derek and then everyone in turn. She exclaimed how worried she had been. Especially after Kevin and Scott and their men had arrived, looking for them. Kevin had only arrived one day before, even though they had left Edinburgh weeks ahead of them. The Ferguson ship had been attacked, which caused them all sorts of delays. Kevin or Scott could explain later. The possibility that they had been sunk or captured had been the focus of concern. As Helena was explaining, James interrupted, "Last night? You mean to say they left more than two weeks ahead of us and they only arrived last night?"

"They had been attacked," she repeated. She put her hands up, motioning to stop. "Now before you all get crazy, they lost no lives. They also had no serious injuries." All around her, everyone was asking questions at the same time and the group was getting even more unruly. "This is not the time to go into it! Let's get to our rooms, get cleaned up and meet for dinner. That way the story need be told only once and everyone will be able to hear everything. As the rest of the group was shown to their rooms, Kathleen pulled Helena aside and asked the whereabouts of Kevin. Helena smiled, saying, "Your old stomping grounds, the baths on the first floor." Kathleen smiled in response. Then scurried off to find Kevin.

As Kathleen departed, James took the opportunity to speak with Helena.

"It's good to know they are all safe." Looking over at Helena, Maude sighed as everyone filed out.

"Dinner is at seven o'clock in the main dinning room. And dress for dinner, this is a reason to celebrate," shouted Helena as everyone headed off in different directions. Turning to Maude, she said, "Tonight we will all try to figure out what this is all about. Send for the minister, Kathleen will get married tonight. However, Kevin suggested it was to be a surprise if she were to return. So be cautious in your planning." They all dispersed to go about their own business.

Having followed the servant to their compartment, once in the doorway Gabrielle balked. Well aware of her hesitation and why, James pushed her forward.

Gabrielle and James had been directed to a beautiful chamber, with a large terrace. A huge central sitting room, filled with comfortable furniture, separated two sleeping chambers. Clearly designed for a man, the larger chamber to the left had a dark, somber, motif. Richly decorated in black and burgundy, the room contained a huge oak four-poster bed. The second, smaller chamber, to the right of the sitting room, was decorated in creams and lace. This bed had a canopy, with beautiful silk drapes. The soft glow of candlelight created a mood of romance.

Unfortunately the mood made Gabrielle feel apprehensive. "I should tell Helena we want separate rooms," she suggested.

James watched her. She was volunteering to do the right thing. He was having none of that! If he couldn't talk her into marrying him immediately, the least he could have was her companionship. Now, how to make it so she could blame him later? He smiled as he pulled her close and began to nuzzle her neck. "Take a look again, maybe you missed the fact that there are two bedrooms. The sitting room in between couldn't be any larger. Gabrielle," he whispered, "not long ago, you convinced me to wait to marry. I tell you now I simply will not relinquish your safety to anyone save myself." She began to pull away, feeling a lecture coming on. He held tight, changed his tactics and worked his magic. "Now it's my turn to share my feelings. If you had let us marry, we could share the bed. You have insisted we wait. I have not pressured you in any way to indulge in a liaison before marriage. I share all your beliefs. Let's share this suite and use the time to get to know each other better. I'm really not asking so much from you, am I? After all, we are to be married shortly."

It was the sad expression on his face that clinched it. She could not deny him. Nor could she deny her own desire to spend as much time in his company as possible. He really had been patient and kind, agreeing to wait. She had put him through so much. "As long as this is what you want, I'll agree."

He grinned mischievously. "Well, it's not really what I want. I'd really like to settle on that large bed over there," he pointed, "and show you all the different ways to make love to you. I'd like to truly possess you and make you my wife!"

She interrupted, "You are being difficult and after I agreed to stay too!" She stamped her foot.

"All right, all right. I was merely pointing out that it is hardly what I want, rather all I can have." Then he added, "For the moment."

She immediately felt she had been right to stay. Helena's was hardly the place to stand on ceremony. It would hardly affect her reputation. She renewed her kisses with vigor.

James knew he couldn't hold out much longer. He was more than a little tempted to throw her on the bed, toss up her skirt and have his way with her, regardless of consent. Her naïveté along with her restrictions were causing him immeasurable discomfort. Somehow they must make it to their wedding night, but James believed he was suffering far more than Gabrielle. He would work on that.

Gabrielle was currently experiencing her own distress because James was wreaking havoc on her emotions. As a virgin she was inexperienced with her new feelings and she was fast losing control against the onslaught of sensations. She wondered if it was unusual to feel this disoriented, for James never seemed as affected as she. And new to the game of love, Gabrielle was simply not aware that her feelings of frustration were looking for a physical release.

James knew she was on the verge of capitulation and joy surged through his body in triumph. He wanted nothing more than to have her yielding body beneath his.... Then unexpectedly he saw the expression in her eyes. The turbulent look in her eyes seemed to somehow question his intentions. With extreme difficulty, he pushed her from him in an effort to regain command of the situation. He would shatter her trust in him if he were to continue. Even now his honor demanded he retreat. His ragged breathing matched her own until finally they both calmed and he told her once again how much he loved her.

Joy filled her heart with that announcement, for when he had stopped so abruptly she thought she had done something wrong. Tension eased between them when he swatted her bottom, causing her to giggle. He laughed at her spontaneity and knew he had been right to wait.

Rather than have a tub brought to their rooms, Gabrielle suggested they attend the baths. James was quite agreeable with that idea until Gabrielle explained she would be going to a separate bath! She was simply not ready to share a bathing chamber, even with the man she loved. Causing her to realize for the first time she would never have chosen to become one of Helena's girls. She wondered what she would have picked as a position within the household. Shaking off her absent-mindedness, Gabrielle sent him to the bath down the hall, while she used the bathing chamber above the kitchens. He was loath to let her go, especially because he desperately wanted to share a bath with her. Yet he finally agreed that it was probably prudent for them to bathe separately, so he found himself walking to the baths.

James lay there getting massaged and he knew he had never felt so content in his life. Every sore muscle, every twinge of pain, were completely gone. The young blonde girl, Agnes, had massaged him from his toes to his neck. Little Agnes had fingers of magic. She had been very surprised when he had turned her down for sex. He had been a little surprised himself, for upon entering the baths, he had been extremely hard. After a thorough bath and a relaxing massage she had only moments ago left him to rest. He was practically asleep, when he felt someone blow in his ear; he smiled as he believed Gabrielle had come to him! He lifted his head to confirm his suspicions. Suddenly he was very awake! Although he recognized the woman, it was not Gabrielle.

"What are you doing here?" he questioned.

"Agnes said we had a customer in the baths only wanting a massage. Of course I informed her she must have inadequately prepared you." She grinned. "I had no way of knowing I'd run into you again this soon."

He started to get up, when she began a little massage of her own. "I'm glad she chose the sandalwood oil for you, I like that smell."

He didn't even respond. He just lay there. What did he care if Millicent came to massage him. He decided to relax and enjoy the added pampering. When she reached between his legs, attending his lower anatomy, he knew he should stop her before it got out of control. He decided he would, in just a few minutes. After gaining access there, she nudged his body to turn. Without even realizing he had moved, he now lay on his side. Moments later, he was rock hard, once again. He tried to push her mouth away, he thought he even muttered no. Then he just lapsed into easy acceptance, followed by enjoyment and finally achievement. His breathing still a little uneven after reaching fulfillment, he simply lay there, grinning like an idiot.

Looking up at him, she smiled.

What an evil smile, he thought to himself and he knew he was in trouble the moment he saw it. Naked, she strolled over to the doorway, creating a dramatic exit. "I'm sure your future wife will be happy to know it was I making you smile like that!" She laughed. "Are you going to tell her I was with you or am I?" her eerie laughter echoing through the hall, as she departed.

How had this happened? He had said no! At least he thought he had. Millicent had deliberately set him up, but why? He slipped into his robe and headed to his room, not knowing what destruction she had caused already.

Gabrielle was still in the baths above the kitchen. That bath was warmer than the others and still her favorite. She had been giggling and gossiping with some of the others. Now she, too, was lying contentedly on a massage table. After a glorious massage, she felt like a limp rag, yet completely content.

Still in another part of the castle ... Kathleen was on a mission of her own. There he was! With his tousled fire red hair he was by far the most masculine man Kathleen had ever seen. Though the handsome features of his face were covered by thick stubble, he was still fabulous-looking. One of his wide, strong shoulders scarred and red from the musket ball recently received. His had a taut, rippled chest, along with the thick bulging muscles of his arms. As he was sitting, you could not notice his six-foot frame. Yet she did not have to see his legs to be aware of his thick, strong, long legs. She had silently opened the door to the baths and come forward. The scent of jasmine was thick in the air. The steam swirling all around added a mystical fog. She simply stood there, as though frozen. He was sitting in a bathing pool surrounded by three beautiful women. One was washing his hair, the other was trimming his nails, and the third was splashing playfully in front of him. They were all naked; they were all touching her man! She couldn't even move. Kathleen just watched. She stood there glued to the floor while others cavorted with him. This was not how she pictured her reunion! She was trying to keep from shouting. After all, the girls were only doing their job. After all, he didn't know she was here. After all, he was accepting her after being with other men; she could hardly do less. After all, nudity and sex was not love. AFTER ALL, NOTHING!

She was starting to get angry. All she had been through to get to him, to find him so easily replacing her, made her heart hurt. Finally one of the girls noticed her, and then one by one, all the girls noticed her. They stood in a silent circle all around him, unsure what to do. Then Kevin noticed her. "Kathleen!" he shouted in his rough Scottish brogue. At the same time he shouted her name, he waved the girls away and stood up. Standing there with his arms spread wide in welcome, he waded over to the edge of the pool. She took small tentative steps over to meet him, suddenly feeling shy. "Lassie, where ha ya been?" he whispered. She looked up into his face, the love and concern evident by his expression.

She could hold back no longer, "Trying to get to you!" she sobbed as she jumped onto the ledge of the pool. Who could stay upset at this affectionate, kind-hearted, easygoing man? Throwing her arms around his neck, she began kissing his face, his neck, and his chest.

"Kathleen, Kathleen," he murmured as his mouth crushed hers. Finally, after a long, passionate kiss, he purred, "As I am already naked and wet, wouldn't it be better for you to be also?" She agreed, and then turned around to get assistance from him with the buttons of her dress. After that she created an erotic show of slowly, enticingly undressing.

He could not be any happier. The moment she had finished her game playing, he dragged her naked body over the edge and into the water. He embraced her in a mighty hug, wanting the feel of her body, once again, within his arms. He trailed kisses all over her body. He wanted her to know that she was precious to him. Usually a bit rougher and faster, he went unusually slow, showing nothing but tenderness.

She had never been this happy to see anyone in her life. She kissed him with every ounce of her devotion shining through. They splashed and played, then they invented several ways to celebrate. When they finished in the water, they massaged each other with oil, inventing yet another position. Later they grabbed the robes on the hooks and headed upstairs.

Approximately seven o'clock that evening, servants were delivering clothing for the guests invited to Helena's private party. The household had been alerted to not only the usual amount of customers, but to the intimate feast given by Helena. Following that would be a surprise wedding. Everything would go off without the slightest hitch.

"It is different to be with a lass when she dresses," stated Kevin

"You are the one that did not want me to go to my own room," replied Kathleen.

"I am no upset, it is just different to watch you dress. Usually I am undressing you. I did no realize so much work went into the preparation." He smiled.

"Before a gift can be unwrapped, you must catch the eye of the intended," she chanted. "Even when the eye is caught, you must inspire his advance." She licked her lips seductively. "Once the intended moves forward, you must provoke his desire." Her eyelids became heavy as her gaze became alluring. "Only when your intended is in your arms are you assured the gift." Then, with an erotic sway of her hips, she approached Kevin, temptation written upon her face as she stood before him. As her sultry emerald green eyes gazed up into his twinkling gray ones, she smiled and whispered. "From this moment on I am yours and yours alone."

He gazed down at her with true devotion in his eyes. He knew her past and looked beyond. He knew what this promise she had given to him meant to her. He reached and pulled her into his embrace. "You are not only a glittery gift to unwrap, but a worthy gift to keep. I will love and cherish you always." He finished by ardently kissing her.

Meanwhile, in another suite, James was sitting upon the bed, laughing at Gabrielle. She constantly continued to surprise him.

"You have to help me find it. Please!"

Getting up, James said, "What does this slipper look like? Why can't you just wear another? You have spent far too long on this!"

She rolled her eyes and looked at him. "This one matches my dress. I would think you would like me to be presentable," she huffed. "After all, it is your fault the dress and shoes got separated in the first place. If you hadn't mauled me again, I would be ready now!" she argued.

"I will not apologize for stopping to kiss you. After you are my wife you will probably experience delays many times." He grinned. "You make me wild with desire and instead of whining about your shoe you should be thanking me," he boasted.

"You have a big head!" she laughed. She was not really upset, for she would rather be with him than anywhere else in the world. "I just want to look nice and Helena took the time to gift us all with beautiful outfits, I want to wear mine."

"You could wear anything and outshine everyone there!" he exclaimed. "Hell, you could wear nothing and surpass them all."

She giggled. "So now you want me to run around naked in front of everyone? What happened to that possessive and overbearing man that wouldn't even allow talk of me being here?" She paused, and then seemed to relent. "Well, all right, if that's what you want." She started to pull the arm of her sleeve down a bit.

Immediately he stepped over and tugged her sleeve back up. Looking into her eyes, "I don't share what's mine!" he growled. "You know I was but teasing you. And though I believe you are too modest to proceed, I cannot take the chance. Especially here, where it would hardly be an uncommon occurrence."

She laughed at his discomfort, not admitting for a moment that she was indeed too shy to disrobe. However, noticing the disgruntled look on his face, she quickly sought to soothe his ruffled feathers and said, "I do not understand your worry. Have I ever given you reason?"

James answered, "I am very possessive; you will have to live with it. Though I first brought up the subject, I can only apologize. The moment it passed my lips I regretted goading you. Only I will see your charms, you will do well to remember that."

Gabrielle smiled. "I find I have a jealous nature also. For when other women seek your attention, it drives me crazy. So your possessiveness does not frighten me, instead I think it entices me all the more." Then she reached over and kissed him tenderly, stroking the side of his face with her hand.

He pulled her close, turning her around so her back was pressed up against his chest. "You have nothing to worry about," he muttered as he began to strategically place soft kisses upon her neck. Catching a movement across the room he realized where they stood. He pointed to the full-length mirror across the room and said, "Look in the mirror, tell me what you see."

Her gaze traveled across the room, but she only saw his reflection. Dressed in black and looking more handsome than ever. His bulging muscles were covered by the shirt and jacket, yet the fit of the suit coat reminded her they lay just beneath the surface. His cocky grin and shining eyes were staring back at her. His powerful hands used to tenderly caress her, held her even now. As she stood there gazing at him, she smiled in contentment. "When I look at you I am half afraid this is all a dream, that I will wake up and you will be gone," she whispered.

He smiled and watched her concentrate. He wondered if she saw the same thing he did. How truly well they fit together. He had never sworn to love another before. She touched his heart as no one ever had. She was stunning tonight. The long red dress she wore complimenting her hair and skin tone to perfection. Her long, ebony hair piled artistically atop her head. Though a petite woman, the style gave the illusion she was taller than she really was.

She had a regal look about her. She was a confident, beautiful woman. She was his. Her ruby lips and sparkling eyes seemed to entice him. Standing together, they looked like the perfect couple.

Finally, after staring at their reflection, she answered his question. "I see more than the protector you are and the lover you will be. I see a confident, handsome man that melts my heart every time I look at him. And I can only think, don't ever let me go!"

James answered, "I see a ravishing creature that causes my senses to reel every time I look at her. She drives me crazy and yet she feeds my soul. I see my one true love." He turned her around again and kissed her with unrestrained desire. "Yet beyond your image and personality I see us as we are together. We are perfect together."

She sighed. "You say the most romantic things." He held her tight until she muttered something about going down to dinner. With the real world about to come crashing in, he was hesitant to let Gabrielle out of his sight. He loathed the subject of Millicent, yet sought to somehow spare Gabrielle's feelings in the event of unkind remarks. So he said to her, "Gabrielle, you are not only beautiful on the outside, you also have inner beauty. You far outshine the simple man that I am. I have done many things in my life and often make mistakes. I want you to know that I am far from perfect." But he was not about to apologize for simply being a man, and his statement fell well short of a confession. Yet if Millicent was evil enough to say anything to Gabrielle and she came to him looking for answers, he would mention his earlier disclosure.

Gabrielle interrupted, "Stop. You are not accountable for your past. I just want you to love me."

He was truly astounded Gabrielle was so open and honest. Again he recalled Millicent's odd threat. Though hardly willing to justify his own actions, he would deal with Millicent if she tried to hurt Gabrielle. Extinguishing the light, they were finally ready to go.

Meeting at the dining room entrance, both Gabrielle and Kathleen squealed in delight as they embraced. At that same moment, James drew Kevin aside to talk. Gabrielle told Kathleen how beautiful the pastel, lemon yellow gown looked on her.

Having Kathleen's measurements on hand and frequent practice with Kathleen's bountiful form, the seamstress had once again managed a flawless fit. The girls conferred as though it had been days, rather than hours since they had seen each other. After a few moments, Kathleen grabbed Gabrielle's hand and dragged Gabrielle over towards Kevin and James, interrupting the deep conversation the men were having.

"Kevin, I want you to meet my very best friend, Gabrielle. Gabrielle is also to be James' wife. May I present Gabrielle Cartwright?"

With raised eyebrows and a questioning look in James' direction. Kevin leaned down; pressing a kiss against her cheek, he announced, "Any friend of my lass Kathleen is a friend of mine," in a thick Scottish tongue. When he was finished he wasn't aware he had said anything funny. But as soon as he had finished, the group was howling with laughter. By this time Helena and Derek had joined the group. Helena, Kevin and Scott were the only ones that didn't know Gabrielle had once believed James was Kevin. Now that she had met the real Kevin, the rest of the group could not restrain themselves from laughter. Derek was quick to point out, "With his thick Scottish accent and fiery red hair, you could never confuse him for James. Which is why it was so ridiculous in the first place!" This only brought more laughter.

Helena wore a black gown which was made of satin. It shimmered in the light, reflecting her beautiful face and form. Her lovely blonde hair was once again on display with decorative black combs holding the style. Derek, Kevin, and Scott all wore dark suits, similar to James'. All wore white shirts, yet remaining unique by different-colored neckerchiefs. Together the men characterized sophistication and style. Separately they radiated natural charm and unquestionable loyalty.

Finally, after the laughter died down and everyone had been introduced, they entered the dining room.

Strangers would never understand the amount of preparation that orchestrated an event. As a previous tenant, Gabrielle detected the faint smell of lemon and wax, telling her everything had been recently polished. Looking about the room, the high gloss on everything confirmed her theory. Every candle in the room had been lit, creating a festive atmosphere. The fire was going in the fireplace, adding warmth and appeal. The table had been previously set and looked wonderful. A beautiful wildflower centerpiece adorned the table. As they were seated at the table, the servant poured the wine.

After hearing everyone's comments and sharing compliments on everyone's apparel, the tales began to unfold. First and foremost, the hilarious explanation of Gabrielle's confusion, believing James was Kevin. It was by far the funniest story.

As everyone was talking about her embarrassing mistake, Gabrielle sat back in her chair, looking around, trying extremely hard to forget they were all laughing at her. As the dining room table was so large, the small group all sat down at one end, creating a more intimate meal. Helena sat at the head of the table, with Derek on the right and Kathleen on her left side. Next to

Derek sat Gabrielle and James. Next to Kathleen sat Kevin and then Scott.

Though Scott was the newcomer to most of them, with his warm smile and carefree attitude, he fit right in. However, he appeared to rub Helena the wrong way almost immediately. Nothing he said or did could be construed as improper. Yet she just didn't warm to him. During the meal, they learned of Kevin's injury and Scott's race to save his life. Telling tales of their childhood and how Scott, Kevin and James had become friends.

Derek was the newcomer to the group. His relationship was first with Helena. Later, when Derek picked Kevin from a group of men destined for the colonies, he had probably saved his life. By allowing Kevin to be placed within the castle walls, it enabled him to send home for the money to buy his freedom. And it was while awaiting his delivery that he had fallen in love with Kathleen.

If James felt he had been quick to fall for Gabrielle, he should compare notes with Kevin. For Kevin insisted it was like walking into a brick wall for him.

No longer were these separate individuals just gathered around the table for dinner. Now they shared a special bond uniting them as allies and creating a group of friends. They ate a fabulous meal, drank plenty of wine and shared all their tall tales and real tragedies.

Kevin went first by explaining how he had requested James to come down and fetch Kathleen.

At which time James interrupted and snorted, "Requested? You damn well...." As he looked about the table he stopped short and after a brief pause continued, "Yes, requested, yes, that's what it was." He grinned sheepishly at the lie he had just agreed to, even as the entire group laughed.

Ignoring them, James took over by taking his turn to speak. He shared his feelings about a mission that sounded easy and started out simple. "Stop for a night at Helena's, return with Kathleen in tow. How hard could that be?" he said. Then he went on to say how he had fallen for Gabrielle, but could not stay to seduce her because of his promise to Kevin. So he and Kathleen had boarded Derek's ship in an effort to get to Kevin. Later finding themselves acting as sleuths in Gabrielle's home. And if that stopover had put them behind schedule, the trip to London really set them back. Then he used the excuse of Gabrielle's confusion between him and Kevin as the crux of the rest of the delays.

As the laughter subsided, Gabrielle took up where James had left off. Explaining how it had been an embarrassing misunderstanding. Imploring the others to understand how she truly believed James was Kevin. How she had fought her feelings and tried to stay away from him. Going on to tell about her stoke of luck in learning the identity of her guardian, only to be pressured into marriage with his son. Tearfully she confided how difficult it had all been.

At which time Kathleen jumped in to explain how the two women had set out to go to Scotland on their own. As soon as the words were out of her mouth, the men all groaned in unison. She ignored them and went on to explain how she had come up with the perfect plan to save Gabrielle, prompting yet another chorus of complaints! She told of their travels and adventures. She informed the men that they had made it a great distance, with only a servant for chaperone. There was no way of knowing Gabrielle had men following her. If they hadn't been trailed, they would have shown up on Kevin's doorstep, in record time. This time, the men laughed in unison. After Kathleen completed the story of their capture and bondage in the wine cellar, James took over again.

Informing them of the trail that had led him to the encampment. He recounted the information he had heard while eavesdropping on the criminals. Reaching what he now knew was Gabrielle's home, James maneuvered around several posted guards. Knocking out the fellow guarding the cellar door as he reached them. He laughed as he told them about finding both women drunk and ridiculous. James told the entire group how they made their escape, following the path along the waterfalls and up the river, retrieving the horses and then heading to the coast to wait for Derek.

At which time Derek recanted how he and his men had been up and down the coast waiting and watching, finally seeing the signal fires and bringing the dingy ashore. Moving quickly on to Edinburgh, where after every stone had been turned they had finally had to face facts. "We were too late, you had already gone!" he sheepishly said to Kevin.

Just as Derek finished his recitation, Scott told everyone about the attack of the Ferguson ship. "That damn John Paul attacked us when we were only two days from here," stated Scott. "I can no believe that man was born a Scotsman."

"I'm telling ya, man, he is terrorizing the coast of England and destroying any vessels he believes to be British," Kevin insisted. So Kevin and Scott took turns informing everyone how they had come under fire. Trying to lose their attacker, they had changed course, only to be outmaneuvered time and time again. Before they knew it, they had been hit, causing added delay. While scrambling to put out the fire, another British ship had appeared and begun an attack on the opposing vessel. The villains immediately lost interest in the small, already injured ship. A fight between them ensued, allowing the Ferguson ship to quietly retreat. It had not been until after reaching the nearest port that they had learned how lucky they had truly been.

The commander of the attack had been none other than the famous fugitive John Paul. He had been wreaking havoc upon the British coastline and they had just been unlucky enough to run across his path. Even more unusual was the confusion he had created by adding the surname Jones to his name and cleverly escaping British justice. John Paul Jones had destroyed fisheries, vessels and countless lives. Kevin and Scott were both well aware how lucky they were to be alive and remained thankful. Then finally after repairs the men had been able to continue their journey.

An eerie silence followed the end of their tale, for all those gathered around the table realized the enormity of the situation. Then James proposed a toast to the brave men and with a unified cheer it became unanimous that the worst adventure of the group had been Scott and Kevin's. The mood instantly became less somber as they laughed and joked once more. Both the conversation and wine flowed freely.

Scott sat stroking his short, blonde beard with his hand, as though in deep thought. Turning to James, he said, "It seems you did indeed run into difficulties, trying to rescue Kathleen and Gabrielle. Yet if it was as time consuming as you say, how did all of you have time to break into Gabrielle's home? Attend luncheons and parties in London? Get both captured and rescued in Teesdale? Dance and sing in Edinburgh? And almost get married along the way?"

At that question Kathleen, James, Gabrielle, and Derek all looked at each other. With guilty looks and shrugged shoulders, they broke out in laughter.

James finally answered, "I guess we did take a bit of time to ourselves along the way."

This ridiculous explanation caused even more laughter and ribbing. They toasted one another, spoke of family, and continued with the meal. A servant had tapped Helena on the shoulder during Scott's questioning. So Helena excused herself to take care of the problem. Upon her return though she had only heard bits and pieces of the dialogue, she thought the large Scot extremely rude. Who did he think he was anyway? Helena definitely did not like this Scott fellow or his attitude.

Helena announced that she needed assistance with another matter and requested Gabrielle and Maude help her. So they left the room. Scott, James and Derek also excused themselves, leaving only Kevin and Kathleen. She turned to him and said, "What do you think that was all about?"

"Who cares? As long as I can spend time alone with you, it matters no the reason." He leaned over to stroke her cheek. "Shall we make our escape now too?"

She shook her head yes in response. Standing, he pulled back her chair and as she stood he grabbed her by the hand. "Let's sneak out this door," he directed.

They went through the door and entered a small antechamber. It was a small sitting room with a fire blazing in one corner. The other corner held a dressing screen, totally inappropriate for the room. Kathleen suggested they were walking in on a fantasy and hinted that they leave. Kevin was ignoring her plea. He sat down on the settee and patted the seat beside him. She slowly complied.

He smiled. "I ha a wedding planned in Edinburgh, but no bride arrived." As she started to offer explanation, he waved it off. He continued to smile. Gazing at her face he noticed the freckles across the bridge of her nose. To conceal them she had used powder, but he adored them. Kevin began again "You are the lass I waited my whole life to find. I want you to marry me, tonight."

"Oh, Kevin. I would love to marry you tonight. But it will take days for us to arrange everything."

"Just tell me this. Do you want to be my wife?"

"Though I am surely not good enough, I would like it more than anything," she answered.

"This place we are in, it is famous for what?"

"Kevin, you know it is the place of fantasies. However, even Helena can not marry someone." She sighed, "Or plan a wedding in one night!"

"This is my fantasy!" he grabbed her by the shoulders, pulling her close and eagerly kissing her. Then he stood and pulled her up with him, leading her over to the screen in the corner. As she protested he gently shoved her behind it, then waited.

Behind the dressing screen, lying on the chase lounge, was a beautiful wedding dress. She leaned back and poked her head out questioningly.

He smiled. "I ha told you before and after this day, will never again explain. I ha had women beneath me since I was a lad of fifteen. I ha known many women and I ha had my choice of many maidens as wife. I could no picture myself shackled to any of them. I was no going to end up like my parents, stuck in a loveless marriage. Therefore I was willing to wait for someone to steal my heart. It took a long time, in fact, it almost did no happen at all. Whether by accident or fate, I ended up here and you stole my heart." He caressed her cheek for a moment before continuing, "You do no count the women I ha been with, no do you hold such experiences again me. I know it is unusual, but your past does no bother me. The decisions you had to make were for your survival, they do no make me feel bitter. I was no there to assist you, no one was. You must stop thinking you are no good enough for me. You are the one I have chosen, the one I want to keep. This is my fantasy. Now get dressed!" With that he turned and strolled out the door, leaving her staring behind. As he walked out the door, the girls flew in. Gabrielle and Helena could not control their laughter and good wishes. As they helped Kathleen undress and dress, they could not stop giggling.

Finally she was ready. Kathleen had never looked more beautiful. She held a fragrant bouquet in her trembling hand. Her dress was thin and light. She had the tiniest waist for someone with such a huge bosom. The dress that had been made for her was white and the material was the softest of silk. She marveled at the bodice's impeccable ability to look delicate, while restraining its generous contents. The skirt was so airy she seemed to float as she moved. Matching kid slippers, with crisp white bows, completed her outfit. Soon they were ready, the ladies all headed towards the patio.

There they met up with the men, all of them ready to begin. Kevin was near the wall standing with the minister. Violins were heard playing in the distance. Candles of all sizes and shapes were lit, creating a romantic, elegant, ambiance. As James stepped forward to escort Gabrielle to their seats, her heart fluttered. He was so handsome, so polished, so charming; his simple presence seemed to soothe her.

They had not even talked about plans for their own wedding. Yet, standing there, waiting, a feeling of excitement engulfed them both. As they headed up the makeshift isle, both recalled their close call to marriage. There was no comparison with their hasty plans on the deck of Derek's ship and this fancy one. Still, this wedding invoked warm memories, overwhelming both of them with romance, as James guided Gabrielle up the isle. For a brief moment, James was glad they hadn't gone through with their own wedding. There was no reason for Gabrielle to forfeit her big day, simply because he was a randy, impatient bastard. He loved her enough to wait. Then and there, he decided to create the perfect wedding for Gabrielle.

Next, Scott reached for Helena's elbow to escort her to her seat. She shrugged it away. Scott was a bit bewildered and tried again. Just as she took a step forward, he realized she was going to walk up without his escort. Of all the bossy, pushy, stubborn females he had met in his lifetime, this one pushed past the limits. She was walking ahead of him, over his dead body! He grabbed her by the arm, not tight enough to harm, yet not loose enough for escape. Helena looked at him murderously, trying to pull away. The violins in the corner continued to play, even though the others stopped to watch the exchange. Realizing she was holding up the ceremony, Helena allowed him to walk next to her. If she started to walk ahead he just took larger steps. His legs were so long, she never pulled ahead. She was not a petite woman like Gabrielle. Yet standing next to this Scotsman, she appeared small. After they reached the front, there was no real reason for him to continue to hold on to her arm, except he felt a little mischievous. She had deliberately tried to make him look like an unmannered buffoon. He was looking to return the favor. So because she was uncomfortable with his attention, attention was exactly what she was going to get.

Finally Derek escorted a beaming Kathleen to the front of the group. He stepped aside and Kevin stood beside her. Derek glanced in Helena's direction. He could not help but laugh at her forlorn expression. Finally she had met her match. A man she could not control with her pouty expression or wily ways. Her demands had not been successful either. Too bad he lived in Scotland, he would be good for her, Derek thought.

The ceremony was beautiful but brief. The flowers and lit candles were a signal that this had been planned all along. After congratulations all around, the group was directed into the ballroom. Even though they were in the small ballroom, with only nine of them, including the minister and Maude, the room seemed huge. Finally Helena had maneuvered away from that Scot. She approached the happy couple, congratulating them. Then she pulled them off to the side. "Kevin, once you leave here Kathleen will be a respectable wife. However, knowing her past as you do, would you be upset if her friends were to come and dance and celebrate with you both?" questioned Helena.

Kevin did not even hesitate. "Everyone is more than welcome to celebrate the marriage of this wonderful woman and myself. Invite them all," he shouted. With that Helena signaled Stuart. He opened a partition, allowing the entire ballroom to be wide open. As he did so, the overflow of people from the other side came pouring in. Kevin laughed as they all joined the party. "What would you ha done if I ha said no?" he questioned.

Helena threw back her head and also laughed. "They would have had a celebration next door, as I had already promised them a party. But a man that can look beyond someone's past to the person they have become can't be all bad. I have liked you from the start and I felt you would say yes. They all wanted to say good-bye to Kathleen and wish her well."

As the music started and the happy couple began dancing, Helena stood alone. As everyone filed in, she greeted him or her. Later, when Gabrielle was dancing with Kevin, Helena drew Kathleen aside. "I want you to pretend to slip and say to Millicent it's too bad you have Kevin as you have your eye on Scott."

"Why do you want me to sic Millicent on Scott?"

"So, you realize what I am up to? Do you? Well, I just do not like the man. If Millicent sets her sights on him, he will be occupied for the evening. If you say something to Millicent and pretend it's accidental, she will pounce on him like a dog in heat. She always covets what you want," said Helena smugly.

"Helena, I have never seen you let a man agitate you. Why does he bother you so?"

"I cannot explain it myself. Only that he is so smug and arrogant. He seems to think I am here for his convenience."

"That is probably because he learned what kind of place this is. He has been full of questions. Merely supply him with a fantasy and he will leave you alone," stated Kathleen.

"You think I have not tried that? He said if it included me, he would most readily be of service. If not, he would decline."

"What?" asked Kathleen. "What single man would pass up an invitation to bed a woman?" She shook her head in disbelief. "Your answer is to send him to the harem. No man can pass up many women, all vying for his affection."

"That's just it. I believe, he thinks, he would be the one doing the favor for the women. Not the other way around. I told you he bothers me!"

As Kevin approached to drag Kathleen back to the dance floor, she quickly said to Helena. "I will find Millicent and start the ball rolling!" She smiled as she walked away.

Helena grinned. Now with Scott taken care of she could have a good time.

While enjoying the dance, Gabrielle leaned a little closer to James and said, "Isn't this the most romantic thing?"

"What?" James questioned

"This surprise wedding. The reception. The dancing. The friends. The food. All of it, it's just grand!" sighed Gabrielle.

"Are you hoping yours will be this way?" Now he was glad he had not cheated her out of her perfect ceremony. "We can have anything you want."

"No. I am not hinting for anything. I am simply in fascination of the surprise and the grandness."

"Why such surprise? After all, that is what Helena's is famous for." he laughed.

"This place is so magical. Once our adventure has come to an end, we will never experience a place like this," she said sadly.

"There you are wrong. I'm sure you will want to stay in touch with your friends. I suggest we celebrate our anniversaries here. What do you say?"

For an answer, she squealed in delight and rained kisses all over his face. He smiled, because most women would be insulted if a man so much as hinted at coming to a place like this. Let alone include his wife. Not this woman! Maybe she really was an illusion after all. All he knew is that she made him happier than he had felt in years. So he mischievously danced her out the door to the terrace and right into a secluded spot.

Everyone was here; the groomsmen, stable hands, gardeners, cooks, servants, carpenters, liverymen, masons, artists, painters, plumbers and guards. And the girls! The only people not in attendance were several guards and a few occupied women. It was a crush.

Gabrielle was surrounded by a gaggle of giggling women, sharing stories of her recent adventures. James, standing off to the side of all the dancing, drank his brandy as he observed the merriment. As he waited for Gabrielle to return to his side, Millicent solemnly sided up to him. Instantly his body stiffened, in anticipation of a verbal attack. Instead she surprised him by very softly whispering, "Have no fear that I will tell your future wife of our dalliance." Apparently that was all she was going to say because she immediately turned to leave his presence.

But before she could escape, James quickly grabbed hold of her wrist. "Millicent, a moment if you please." She struggled for only a moment before turning to face him. Lifting her eyes to his face she tried to gauge his mood. Oh, why had she bothered? While watching him this evening, he had never even seemed concerned. Yet, after she had found out it was that simpering, naïve Gabrielle he was betrothed to. She felt the need to absolve herself and relieve him of any doubts. "Why have you suddenly changed your mind?" he questioned.

Eagerly trying to explain her error, she said, "I thought you were engaged to Kathleen."

He did not wish to argue with her, he simply stared in response.

"Didn't she leave with you? You were supposed to marry her. How the hell did she end up with him?" she asked as her eyes traveled to the large, red-headed Scotsman.

Now James realized what had happened. Millicent, Kathleen's arch-enemy, had taken a notion to go after Kathleen's man. Once again, James was mistaken for Kevin, this time for very different reasons. Only now, Millicent had just come to realize she had been the one who had been duped. James could no longer contain himself, he laughed and laughed and laughed.

Embarrassed, Millicent said, "I should tell everyone you are no good in the sack!" she hissed. "Would serve you right!"

Which of course made him roar even louder. As the laughter finally ebbed, he once again asked her, "So you changed your mind because...." as he released his restraint.

"I believed you to be Kathleen's intended. She and I have been rivals for some time. There is nothing I wouldn't do to make her more miserable. She is a thorn in my side. On the other hand, Gabrielle is just an innocent, certainly no competition for me. She has never caused me any problems and I am not so heartless as to hurt her intentionally." She sighed. "So after I realized my mistake, I figured I'd let you off the hook, so to speak. Now, I'm not saying you would, mind you. But I didn't want you to do something stupid, like confess, or something."

Casually leaning against the pillar, he used his arrogant, mocking sneer as a reply.

"Fine, fine. What was I thinking? I'm sure you didn't feel you owed her any apology, or explanation. I just didn't want to be the cause of hurting her feelings."

"Not that I would ever say anything, but isn't that exactly what you did?" he asked.

"It was my intention to have something to hold over Kathleen. So when I thought you were engaged to Kathleen, I could not pass up the opportunity, of bed sport with you. With that information I would later antagonize Kathleen. She was an equal opponent. Don't feel too sorry for her, she gave as good as she got. However, I have no argument with vapid little Gabrielle. So I just wanted to clear the air."

"Not that I owe you any explanation, though it will no doubt come in handy in the future, for you to remember, a man in my position, never and I repeat, never talks about his paramours. Especially to innocent, young maidens." He took the time to look bored, flicking an imaginary piece of lint from his jacket, as he continued, "Nor do I ever explain, or answer to anyone. Your silly threat was simply that, a silly threat." Then he thrust one last barb "You were certainly not entertaining enough to even recall after finishing your task. Now be gone from my sight!" James seethed. Watching her melt into the crowd, James sighed, realizing all the things he said to Millicent had been true.

Right up until he had met Gabrielle. Hadn't he begun to change the moment he met her? Didn't he worry about her feelings? Wasn't he always nearby in case she fainted? Hadn't he taken precautions concerning her reputation? She was the first thing he thought of in the morning and the last thing at night. He would give his life to protect her. He would spend a lifetime loving her.

In any case, Millicent had been right on the mark. He had been inclined to warn Gabrielle. Thankfully he had stopped after telling her he was not perfect.... No, she had stopped him. She claimed his infidelities didn't matter. In fact, she didn't seem to care about the things that mattered so much to others. Not his past, his title, his wealth. She loved him as a man. He was a bit embarrassed that a man of his prestige and acumen had been hit so hard. Though still the pretentious, arrogant, aristocrat, he could not get past the fact, that he had never smiled this often, laughed this much or felt this light hearted. His character was tempered with strange emotions. It wasn't something that affected his smooth style, debonair manner or manliness. Yet, it was filling the void in his soul he never knew existed. He was content. Finished with her conversation, Gabrielle glided over to stand by his side.

Now that Millicent no longer had a worthy line of attack to bait her nemesis, she continued to circle the room watching and listening. James thought she resembled a vulture. Still working on a plan, Millicent spent the evening, drinking liberally and mingling with the guests. She was headed towards the terrace to get a bit of air, when she overheard a conversation too good to be true.

"I can't believe I'm married and can only sleep with one man for the rest of my life!" wailed Kathleen.

"You should have thought of that before you agreed to it then," answered Helena, with no pity.

"But I have spotted a perfect specimen of a man with long golden hair, streaks kissed by the sun, standing tall and firm. I would really like the opportunity to entertain him!" sighed Kathleen. "Won't you keep my husband company for a while? Won't you help me? Think of it as one last romp!" Kathleen licked her lips in anticipation.

"Kathleen, who is it that has you in such a tizzy?" whispered Helena

"That handsome Scott. He is huge! And I imagine the rest of him is too. His bulging muscles, his mischievous smile and those eyes! Those huge, mischievous, green eyes, which simply project his every thought, they secretly seem to be undressing me every time I look at him. Please? I want him! Please!" whined Kathleen.

Before Helena could respond, they heard a rustle on the other side of the door. Both women eagerly looked around the doorway. They were rewarded with the vision of Millicent headed straight in Scott's direction. Both Kathleen and Helena immediately tried to stifle their laughter at being so successful in sending Millicent on a wild goose chase. Kathleen had insisted on keeping Kevin apraised of events, even before Millicent had taken the bait. Now she went to share the highlights of the story with him, leaving Helena behind.

Looking around, James admitted it was the least socially correct, yet most entertaining wedding he had ever been to. He had never felt so relaxed. Of course he realized it was because all of polite society, along with its archaic matrons and malicious gossips, were not about. As one of the men most often in pursuit, he relished the comfort this setting afforded him. No young maidens fussing over him, no frosty mothers, no starchy fathers and no rules to follow.

Later, James and Gabrielle finished a dance. They had moved to the side of the ballroom with several settees gathered along the wall. Still holding one another close, they dropped onto the seat. James took the opportunity to fully embrace her and kiss her ardently. "Do you realize how strange this wedding is? In fact, an unusual gathering of any kind, for I would never be able to do this in public." Demonstrating, he began by trailing kisses along her neck and shoulder. "We will forever after have to adhere to the strictest of society's rules. I will never give anyone the opportunity to chastise your past, or reproach your good name." He smiled. "But here and now is quite another story!" laughing as his mouth closed over hers.

She sighed, and then snuggled closer. She breathed in his ear as her tongue teased it, "You will have to keep a close eye on me then, for I can think of no better way to spend my evenings than this."

"If you would marry me now, with the preacher here, I could show you better ways," he flirted.

Ignoring his comment entirely, she went on, "I meant, whether out in public or in private. I am always going to want you near. I don't think I can pull off the polite look of boredom that I have seen on *proper* matrons." She gazed adoringly into his eyes.

"I never dreamt I would fall in love. I always expected to marry one day and produce an heir. Yet I truly never expected to admire and desire the woman I married."

She could not help but giggle. "Funny how fate works. We both ended up at Helena's. If even one of us hadn't, we would not have met the other." She sighed.

As the late evening turned into early morning, their sighs turned to yawns. Though the wedding had been fabulous, they could barely keep their eyes open and finally agreed to head upstairs. Turning to leave, they observed many people still milling about. Gabrielle made mention that Kevin's friend was dancing with danger. Looking to see what she meant, James smiled as he too observed Scott dancing with Millicent. A clear sign of departure if he ever saw any!

As the crowd began to thin out and staff began to clean up, Helena took a moment for herself. She walked out to the terrace and sat on a beautiful hand-carved marble bench. She sat in carefree silence, gazing up at the moon.

The sky was pitch black, the stars shining with uncommon brilliance. It was easy to understand their comparison to diamonds. The moon was a radiant yellow in its crescent shape. She simply stared at the sky above and completely relaxed.

Destroying the silence, a voice boomed, "Why are you all alone? Do you no ha a fantasy to fulfill for someone?"

She recognized the voice immediately as her body stiffened. Scott walked from the doorway, only to end up facing her. She answered a question with a question, saying, "Why are you here?"

"I asked you first," he answered

"Not that I am required to answer you, but I run this establishment. I do not book myself!"

Answering her question, he said, "I am here simply because this is where you are."

"Why are you not with Millicent?" she inquired

He nodded as though in confirmation. He had thought Millicent had been sent to keep him busy. Now it was confirmed. What had started out as a fun game of teasing Helena, in response to her ill treatment, was now turning to genuine interest. "You did no dance," he stated

"What?" she asked bewilderedly.

"You did no dance with anyone tonight. Why?" asked Scott McTavish

"Why are you watching me?" she demanded.

"Again, I asked first." he responded

She huffed, trying to remember the question. "I was supervising. It is what I do."

"I like to watch new and different things. I am also drawn to beautiful creatures, you fit both categories," he responded. Taking a few steps closer, he stood staring down at her. "I observe, it is what I do." He paused. "I make you nervous for some reason."

She could barely breathe. How long had it been since she had felt this way?

"No you don't," she lied. "I think our personalities clash. That is all. Soon you will be gone, does it matter that we don't get along?"

"You lie and no very well when you say I do no make you nervous. Is it because everyone around you does everything you say, at all times? Finally you ha run into someone you can no order about. I know it bothers you. I can tell."

"If you can tell, then stop bothering me. Your observation is flawed. The people here are my employees. Most have become my friends. However, their positions require they follow directions. Is that too hard for you to

234

understand? You would do well to learn the difference. You are Kevin's friend, for that reason alone I will try to be polite to you. Otherwise, stay out of my way," declared Helena, standing up.

As she turned to leave, he grabbed her by the shoulders. Turning her back around, his mouth came down on hers. It was a forcefully firm kiss, yet his lips were tender and his breath hot. He did not harm her, yet he did not allow escape. At first she tried to wiggle free, after a bit she began to squirm in earnest. Still he continued the assault on her senses. He was a solid confrontation, chipping away the wall of her defenses. Finally she responded in kind. She clung to him and returned his kisses with abandon. She was shaking with desire as he pulled away. He looked at her swollen lips and glazed expression, nothing had ever pulled at his emotions more. Yet he knew if this were to go anywhere, he would have to be the strong one. As her arms fell back to her sides he said, "Maybe it is you who will ha to stay out of my way." Then he turned his back to her and walked away.

Sitting back down on the bench again, feeling dazed and confused, she took stock of her life. She could never really change her lifestyle; too many people depended on her. Yet sometimes she wished she only had to care for herself. That her days could be her own, with nothing to do but please herself. She sat on that bench a little longer. Finally taking a deep breath and squaring her shoulders, she put her defenses back in place. Well, she would simply keep away from a certain someone that had been able to get past her defenses. That someone had been Scott.

The next morning at breakfast, they talked about many things, trying to come up with a decent plan, agreeing on none of them. Later, the men secretly met in the study. Sitting around the table over drinks and cigars, one after one, they threw out suggestions about how to proceed.

James said, "First things first. We must get to London and talk with Gabrielle's guardian. He was going to look into Richard Cartwright's disappearance and Herbert Harrington's appearance. We need the information he has gathered in order to proceed. Not to mention letting him know Gabrielle is safe and about to be married," he stated firmly.

Derek laughed. "That is really what you want him to know, so his son can stop fantasizing about getting his hands on Gabrielle." With that comment, James frowned.

Scott interjected, "I think we will have to break up into two groups. Your small party can go on to London, but I will accompany my men north to Northumberland, to watch Viscount Herrington."

"That is an excellent idea," said Kevin. "I will send my men to find the sheriff. If we can get that taken care of quickly, we will rendezvous with you and attempt to infiltrate Herrington's home. It will be better to accomplish many things at once."

Derek said, "I will leave at once. I will sail my ship to London and meet you. We are running out of time. It will soon be winter, making travel by sea treacherous. You will make better time, riding horseback. Yet, we may need the ship and I would feel better already having it in port."

Helena, Kathleen and Gabrielle all walked into the study. Hearing the men discuss travel plans, the girls sat down on the furniture across from the table where the men sat. "What about all our baggage?" asked Kathleen. "I have recently been on a trip with few possessions. It was too rugged for me.

Scott said, "This trip will not compare to the other. You are going to London. Buy new clothes, outfits, and shoes. Spend some of Kevin's money!" Then he laughed at Kevin's expression.

Derek glared at Scott. He could tell from Scott's answer that Scott had not a clue, as to how long it took women to shop. So Derek responded, "Depending on how long we are there will be the answer to if you shop." He knew how long it took for women to even decide on a new hat. He was in no mood to pamper the girls until the problems had been solved. "I will simply carry the extra baggage on board. You carry what you need for now; I will meet you a few days after you get there. So have your trunks ready, after dinner I sail."

"First light tomorrow should be soon enough for us to start on our trek."

James hesitated. "Is anyone opposed to riding horseback?" He looked at them individually, centering on the two girls. Nothing. He breathed a sigh of relief. "Good, it's decided then."

"Tomorrow we are off!" said Kevin. The following morning would bring adventure, full of danger, excitement and travel. Tonight they had time for romance, as the two couples left to retire. Which left Scott, Derek and Helena. Helena suggested they drink and play cards. Derek announced he had plans with a certain brunette. He laughed at the expression on Helena's face. She clearly didn't want to be alone with Scott. As Derek passed Scott on his way out the door, he whispered, "There was more than one brunette in the baths." You're more than welcome to accompany me." Though Scott smiled at Derek, acknowledging the invitation, he did not reply. Derek nodded his head goodnight, waved to Helena, and then took his leave.

Scott turned to Helena, asking, "Now, how about that card game and drink?"

"You want just the two of us to play cards? Why?"

"Clearly the two of us can keep each other company. I thought you told me you could pull off the act of hospitality. If you're afraid of the competition, just say so."

Helena groaned. "I am impolite if I refuse and I am condemned to an evening of harassment if I stay. How will I ever decide?" she said sarcastically.

"I can see this is no going well. I thought perhaps as the two of us were alone for the evening, we could keep each other company. It certainly will no break my heart if you choose to go elsewhere. I simply agreed to a drink and cards as a favorable way to spend the evening. Either we call a truce or call it an evening, but I will no stay and trade barbs with you. I am really too weary," he announced.

Helena looked at him for a long time, trying to decide the right approach. What the hell? He would be leaving tomorrow. Throw out the white flag. She smiled and said, "A truce then." A moment later Helena rang for a servant. After giving instructions to a young girl, Helena walked over to the settee and sat down. "Do sit down, McTavish. I have ordered refreshments so make yourself comfortable." A few moments after he sat down on a chair at the table, the young girl returned. Helena dismissed her immediately and moved over to the table to take over the preparations. Scott watched as she poured hot water from the teapot into two brandy snifters. After several moments, she dumped out the hot water, refilling the snifters with liquor. She casually carried the two drinks over to the table and grinned. "This is the best damn brandy you will ever taste, Napoleon brandy. Artfully added to a warmed glass, it has no rival," she grinned. Sitting opposite him at the table, she put her money on the table. "Let's cut for the deal," she announced.

After more games of cards than he could count, Scott announced he was finished. The money had just passed back and forth all evening, the inconvenience of only having two players. Finally he had conceded that she was as good a player as he. A compliment, yet not quite a compliment. Still it was all he was offering. They wandered over to the settee, in front of the fireplace.

"You play very well. What other interests do you have?" he inquired.

"Are you being facetious or are you really interested?" asked Helena.

"Again, a question for a question. I asked, so of course I am interested." He sighed. "Why are you always so defensive?"

She should have answered the first question, which may have prevented the second question. She really preferred superficial interrogations, as opposed to deep personal questions. She replied, "I suppose it is my way of preventing others from getting too close. I relish my privacy."

That was all the answer he was going to get about her defensiveness, he tried another tactic. "So what are your other interests?"

"I'm sure you would find them quite boring. Most of my interests revolve around the smooth running of my business; how to have better-tasting foods, what scents to add to different oils. What different illusions to add to create yet another fabulous fantasy. How to soften and create smoother skin. Who to invite for a visit that will add to the coffers. How to get the lazy girls to work harder. How to stop ambitious ones from killing the lazy ones." She was on a roll and her eyes were twinkling. "How to keep food hot once it's brought in from the kitchens. What serving boy deserves a bonus or a punishment. Unusual things like inspecting the horseflesh or watching a new colt being born. Matchmaking interested young girls to a decent husband or listening to new methods of farming. Learning new recipes so the brewer can create sweeter-tasting ale. All these things and more are my interests. Anything and everything pertaining to the smooth running and profit of my business." She sighed, "Boring, huh?"

"Lass, your eyes light up, you smile continuously and your voice softens. All this and more happens when you start talking about your business. One can tell you are very proud of your accomplishments. Uncaring, greedy louts run most establishments such as this. Their only concern is making their money, whatever the cost. They hardly care about the health of their girls, let alone the condition of their establishment. What you ha created here is a home. You care and provide for them all. How you came up with the idea of a business such as this must be an interesting story."

"It is not only interesting, but long. That is a topic for another evening," she replied.

"I must commend you on your undertaking, most men would ha failed. That a women has succeeded is remarkable."

"You are complimenting me? Why? What do you want?" she demanded.

"Oh! Here we go again! A simple compliment, yet you are suspicious."

"Yes, I am. I happen to know you and I don't really see eye to eye. Suddenly you are trying to be nice. It leads me to be leery," she huffed.

"When one is complimented, the proper response is Thank You. 'Tis no as though I requested you as my fantasy, though if you were to offer, I would nay object." He laughed as her eyes widened. "After a nice dinner, an evening of cards and pleasant conversation. I am merely being polite. You, on the other hand, are too suspicious of my motives." He sighed. "Shall we just go to bed?"

"Agh, you are horrible! You are conceited, arrogant, and bossy. You don't really listen to a thing I say. You are rude, incorrigible and unyielding! I don't like you one bit! To think I was about to tell you what a nice man you are, that maybe I had been wrong in my first impression of you, that I enjoyed spending the evening with you. How could you possibly think I would go to bed with you?" she screeched.

"First of all, simply being in Helena's may lead someone to believe they could accomplish the goal." He grinned. "However, you ha overreacted yet again, I merely meant, 'Shall we retire for the evening?'" He chuckled to watch her cheeks turn from a furious pink, to a heated, embarrassed, red. He had indeed meant "Let's just go to bed" as an invitation. Yet he had made a quick recovery and had decided, then and there, that she would have to be broken more slowly. He assumed the role of a slighted guest. "Even though you assumed I would want to go to bed with you. I ha no agreed to go to bed with you and, madam, that will be required before any participation on my part will be supplied. So it will be you asking, no, begging me, to go to bed with you. No the other way around."

"You buffoon. Who do you think you are? Any man would be happy to be invited to my bed!" As soon as the words were out of her mouth, she realized what he goaded her into saying. She quickly tried to backtrack by adding, "I am not inviting anyone, least of all you! We should have parted company earlier instead of trying to get to know the other better. Good night!" With that she slammed out the door.

Scott merely smiled; he was not upset at all. He simply assumed she wasn't ready to be pushed. The more time he spent in her company, the better he knew her. The catch was, the more he spent time with her the more he knew he had to have her. Yet he would bide his time until he was able to convince her it was all her idea. She was too used to men falling at her feet. It was time her abilities were challenged. Was that arrogance? No, simply confidence.

Scott stood and stretched. Wondering if Derek was still in the baths. Well, it didn't really matter; he was headed there anyway. For even though he was intent upon pursuing Helena, he was not a stupid man. He would appreciate the comfort and attention offered here. Before settling down to a steady diet, he intended to sample the buffet. As he wandered the halls looking for the baths, he continued to form a plan pertaining to winning Helena's heart. Yet as soon as he entered the baths and the two beautiful eastern girls took charge of his body, all serious thoughts fled his mind.

The next day as they stood in the courtyard, the small group of friends embraced. The three men stood off to the side and suggested to James that he prepare Gabrielle for the possibility of never finding her father. They all agreed he should do it soon.

"She will ha to be prepared," said Kevin

"The sooner the better," said Scott.

"She needs to be able to act, no matter the outcome. You will instruct her," Derek demanded.

"I will talk to her this evening, she will be informed. Gabrielle is strong, she will do whatever it takes," said James. "Don't forget she has lived with that possibility for nearly a year."

"Yes, but Kathleen mentioned she secretly has hope her father is still alive," said Kevin. "You must make her realize that is not probable."

"Now you want me to tell her to give up hope? She will never do that! It will have to be good enough that I tell her to be very ready to face the truth, whatever that might be. But give up hope, that is too much!" huffed James.

Finally they all wished each other farewell.

After the men were finished shaking hands and doling out instructions, Scott left the group. He said good-bye to each lady in turn. First to Gabrielle, whom he complimented, second to Kathleen, whom he reminded was now his best friend's wife and therefore also his close friend, assuring her, in Kevin's absence, to come to him for anything.

Lastly, Helena, he grinned. His eyes twinkled. He kissed her hand, licking the inside of her wrist. Just to get a rise out of her. He leaned down and whispered in her ear, "I will send you information, when this is over. You will ha knowledge of my exact location at all times. You will send for me when you are ready to accept fate and beg me for my favors." He gently blew in her ear. "You know you want me. You wanted me yesterday and you want me still. You will contact me when you accept that you will have to do the asking." Pausing for effect, he added, "I will miss you, lass." He straightened.

She couldn't move, she simply stared up into his eyes. Her feelings were mixed, a cross between deep hunger and extreme anger. She craved attention from someone not intimidated by her. So her desire for him was growing. Yet she seethed with rage. For one moment he proclaimed he wanted her, the next moment he crawled into another's bed. He considered her ignorant of the way he spent his evening. How could he believe she wouldn't hear how virile he had been? Nothing went on in this castle that she was unaware of. Maybe he didn't care that she knew. So much for her believing any of his declarations. Standing next to him, the top of her head just reaching his massive shoulders, she could not bring herself to respond. His golden mane untied, fluttering in the breeze. She simply tilted her head up and stared at his face, watching his features for a sign of insincerity.

"Probably the first time in your life you are speechless," he laughed. Then he turned and walked over to his horse, ascending the horse with a grace and ease of years of practice. She continued to just stand there, watching him.

When Gabrielle tapped her shoulder.

"What was that all about?" asked Gabrielle

"What was what all about?" repeated Helena.

"I thought you didn't like him much. What changed your mind?"

"What makes you think I changed my mind? I don't like him one bit. He is too conceited and arrogant. He is bossy and demanding. He is a bully when he doesn't get his way." Waving her arm in a good-bye gesture, she said, "I say good-bye and good riddance." Changing both her attitude and expression she immediately smiled and exchanged pleasantries with everyone. After hugging everyone in turn, then wishing him or her well, she hurried into the castle. Climbing the stairway and finally reaching the balcony, she observed the final preparation for departure.

Gabrielle and Kathleen stood off to the side. Scott and the troops took off through the gate, creating a thunderous noise and cloud of dust. As the Scotsmen were all leaving, the two girls stood there trying to figure out the Helena-Scott situation. "Did you see the way they stood together, as though they were lovers? Yet when I asked her about him, she insisted she couldn't stand him. What do you make of the way she denied her feelings?" asked Gabrielle.

"That she was protesting a little too much for someone she doesn't like. She must have really fallen hard," said Kathleen. "She probably realized they had no future. Yet they sure looked good together," she sighed.

"You don't buy the I-don't-like-him-one-bit line?" asked Gabrielle

"Not even a little. You?"

"Me either," said Gabrielle. "We'd better hurry, we both have men waiting."

Helena watched them all leave. Derek, her dearest friend, Scott, who had almost destroyed her defenses. And the others she had grown close to, all leaving on an adventure. All destined for excitement and new experiences. As she stood observing the scene, a single tear slid down her cheek.

Chapter 14

After riding for days, staying at overcrowded inns and experiencing cold, dreary weather, they eventually reached London and were more than a little excited when James directed them towards his townhouse.

The air was crisp, the temperature brisk, yet on the day of their arrival the sun had finally decided to come out. Still in good spirits by the time they reached his impressive home, they eagerly descended upon a surprised staff. Moments after their arrival they were ensconced in the salon before a freshly stoked fire. Along with sandwiches, liberal amounts of both hot tea and brandy had been provided. Once their stomachs were full they sat back to relax and enjoy the heat. That everything had been done so quickly was a direct result of the efficient servants, who were even now preparing their rooms. The house itself was warm and spacious, the furnishings dark and masculine. No dainty, feminine or small furniture decorating his home. Everything was large and sturdy. A short time later, as everyone else rested, James began making plans for the most spectacular wedding of the century.

That evening, upon entering Gabrielle's room, James took Gabrielle in his arms. "Remember our discussion from last night?" he insisted. "Because I don't want you to get upset or hurt, it is more than likely your father really is no longer with us. With the list of characters involved, it is the most probable conclusion. You have a tendency for fainting. If you hear that your father is dead, I want you prepared. It is what we expect. Will you be able to carry on?"

With James holding her, it was easy to say she would be fine. She was already quite aware of the possibility of her father's demise. Yet she did not want to leave any stone unturned. Once the truth were presented, favorable news or not, she would have to accept it. If the news was bad, she definitely wouldn't like it, for she missed her father dreadfully. After holding her a bit longer she nodded affirmatively to the questions James had just presented. As he moved to step away she clung to him. He offered, "We don't have to go downstairs. If you prefer we could have dinner up here." Giving her a devilish grin, he pointed to the rumpled covers. "We could hop in bed and I could show you a little trick or two. After all, I'm in no hurry to see anyone."

This time he lunged in her direction. Her sadness quickly fled as she giggled and darted out of his way. Soon he was chasing her around the room, only to capture her minutes later. Laughing, he tumbled her back onto the bed. "You are now my prisoner. What will you give me for your release?" he demanded as he sprinkled gentle kisses upon her face.

She giggled. "I won't pay you for letting me go. Your reward will be in keeping me." With that she reached her arms around his neck, pulling his head close to hers in a warm embrace. Her lips fastened hungrily on his and suddenly playfulness turned to passion. He couldn't get enough of her scent, her supple form and her tender caresses. And she couldn't deny his masterful tongue, his firm body, and skillful hands.

This is madness! he thought as he pulled away. "Unless you want this to go any farther, we must stop. I'm barely in control now." He sighed and looked at her glazed expression and swollen lips. "Gabrielle, the sooner we see your guardian the better! I want to wed you and bed you and if this keeps up, it may not be in that order!" Wrapped in a warm cocoon of pleasure and still breathing hard, she was having trouble focusing on what he was saying. She was also finding it terribly difficult not to agree.

After a brief adjustment to their clothing, they headed downstairs. James thought about the events of the evening before. He had approached Gabrielle in an effort to prepare her for the worst. She had collapsed in his arms and for the first time he had held her without seduction in mind. She had clung to him, expressing her fears and concerns about her father. Holding her tenderly he had done his best to reassure her that he would always be there to lean on. Though she had cried softly for a long time, he believed she understood the situation.

As they descended the stairway, he was brought back from his daydreaming as Gabrielle began to speak. So he paid attention to her as she paid various compliments to his home and his staff. She also went on to inform him that there would be little to do to improve it. He patted her head and assured her there were many things for her to do in the effort to create a less bachelor-like feeling to the place. He must have said just the right thing for when they entered the dinning room, Gabrielle was beaming.

Watching her as they dined you would not even associate his gentle vixen of today with the tearful woman of last night. For all her small stature, she was a sturdy character. She was gracious and delightful as she easily fell into the role of hostess. James smiled as he watched Gabrielle coach Kathleen in table manners. Upon being seated he had noticed both Kathleen's discomfort with the elaborate place settings and Gabrielle's observation of the same. By using exaggerated movements she could indicate which glass or piece of silverware to use, allowing Kathleen to easily imitate her manners. James laughed because Gabrielle believed herself successful in the art of deception. Instead she was an open book. It was a warm and friendly evening for them all.

Earlier James had sent a note requesting permission to visit the Earl of Chatham, so it came as no surprise when a reply came during dinner. The butler brought in the message while they ate. The earl had indeed agreed to see them and rejoiced over Gabrielle's safety. It seemed William Pitt had no prior engagements and was able to receive them that evening. Because the missive was worded as a command rather than an invitation, they all became a bit apprehensive. Nevertheless, after dinner, they immediately took the carriage over to the Earl's home.

Shown into the parlor they were already seated when Old William entered. Gabrielle jumped up and scurried into his arms, giving him a ferocious hug.

"I am so happy to see you safe," he said gruffly. He pressed forward and though he was still holding on to Gabrielle's hand, he was now seated in a comfortable chair.

Gabrielle took a deep breath. "Before you start, I need to explain. I'm sorry if I worried you. It was never my intention. I felt pressured, I panicked and I ran. I should have come to you and explained, I just couldn't bring myself to do it. You had been so wonderful to me. Taking me in, helping me, loving me. I did not want to appear ungrateful. However, I realized Will and I just would not suit and I could not marry him out of appreciation. I know how upset you must be, but I love another." Here she took a breath. "Please try to understand."

He looked around the room, locating the two gentlemen. Finding both men roguish in appearance, the earl said, "Which one of you is it?"

James stepped forward and Gabrielle quickly introduced him. "Uncle, this is Lord James Armstrong. Lord Armstrong, this is William Pitt."

The old man acknowledged the younger one with a simple nod of his head. Then he puffed out his chest and pulled rank by adding "The First Earl of Chatham," to Gabriele's earlier presentation.

So, it's to be like that, is it? James thought. He nodded in return as he said, "I am Marquee of Scarborough and very happy to make your acquaintance." Grinning at the foiled attempt at one-upmanship on the old man's part, James dared not let his smugness show least the earl erect barriers in his suit for Gabrielle. Using perfect manners before her guardian, James exchanged small talk and complimented him several times on various speeches before attempting to get down to business. Hoping he had made a good impression, he finally got to the matter at hand. "I would like permission to marry Gabrielle. I am sorry for any upset of your previous plans, however, I am not about to let her go."

Knowing the entire arranged wedding had been his own fabrication, he had little recourse but to accept. He looked at the beaming Gabrielle and his heart went out to her. He could deny her nothing. He gave his permission for the wedding and offered Gabrielle the gown already made for her. The beautiful wedding gown was still upstairs, where she had left it. "There is more of a story here, I'm sure. But that can wait. I know Kathleen, but who is this other fellow?" inquired William the Elder. After being introduced to Kevin, he could not contain his surprise at Kathleen's capturing a title. Though he could not agree with her being in Gabrielle's presence, he was happy for the young miss. He was also very glad the giant Scot would now be responsible for Kathleen. Congratulations were passed all around both on the most recent nuptials and the upcoming event. Suddenly the front door slammed and in marched William the Younger.

He stood in the doorway with a look of quiet desperation. Focusing on Gabrielle he walked swiftly over to stand directly in front of her. Both hands fisted and placed upon his hips he began his tirade. "Young lady, the next time you decide not to marry someone, simply tell the person, instead of disappearing off the face of the earth! Has my father told you how ill he became? Or of the many searches I participated in? I had to interrupt serious business to traipse after you. I hope you realize some apologies are in order!" he fumed. James was about to move in front of Gabrielle and shield her from his verbal attack, when he decided to wait before intervening. After all, young Will's anger at Gabrielle was justified. At the time, he himself had been just as upset and worried, so he allowed young Will to vent. Even still, the lecture went on longer than James deemed prudent. But just as James was about to speak out and defend her, Gabrielle took the situation in hand. By walking over and hugging William close, she immediately took the wind out of his sails. This caused him to cease his criticism and calm down.

Forgetting all the others, she spoke softly in his ear, "I will always love you like a brother and who could be a better friend? Know this, I did not leave because I couldn't marry you. I left to find my father, I left to accompany Kathleen and I left because I had feelings for another man. Someday you will make a wonderful husband. Just not mine." She smiled. "Please say you will be my friend, that you will remain close as a brother, that you are not mad." Not allowing him time to respond, she pulled away and reached for James' arm. She pulled James into their semi-embrace and said, "Will, this is James, the man I love."

245

Will stood and stared in surprise.

James smiled. Gabrielle treated a simple gentleman and a Marquee exactly the same. To her titles were not as important as the men that held them. He shook his head and grinned. She was so unlike all the other women he had encountered throughout his life. The knowledge that she belonged to him gave him cause to be more than friendly. So in an effort to make the lad feel at ease he used his lesser title during the introduction. Reaching out his hand, he said, "Lord Armstrong, at your service. I am happy to meet you, Young William."

Young Will had heard of the Armstrong brothers and knew of both their outrageous pursuits and their more prestigious titles. As he shook James' outstretched hand, he asked, "Which Armstrong are you?"

Knowing well his reputation had preceded him, James laughed out loud, easily acknowledging that Will was no one's fool. "I am James."

"Ah, James, the eldest brother and heir. Marquee of Scarborough," he muttered. William the Younger's expression conveyed his feelings of doubt and concern at the wisdom of letting Gabrielle to be mixed up with this rakehell.

A heavy silence descended upon the room.

Looking at both of them, Gabrielle directed, "James, you know Will is like a brother to me." Turning to Young Will, she said, "And Will, he *is* the man I will marry. You both have a special place in my heart and I want us all to be friends." No one acknowledged her comment and moments later a frown appeared upon her face. Her stance became rigid as she next crossed her arms, and then tapped her foot impatiently. Clearly their stalling was making her unhappy. The men appeared disgruntled by her pushing, but finally agreed they had little choice, for both wanted to please her. Quickly shaking hands once again, they entered into a brief conversation.

Will wished them luck, and then directed his comment at James as he said, "She will drive you crazy with all her antics. I realize now I would have been upset every time she distracted me from my work. I hope you have better stamina," grinned young William.

James laughed. "I have already experienced examples of her antics. I am willing to tolerate all her distractions. But you are right about one thing, William. She does require a large amount of stamina." At that, both men laughed with exuberance.

"Now that you have shared laughter at my expense, it is time to discuss what Uncle William has found out," stated Gabrielle.

As they went to sit down, William the Younger muttered to Gabrielle, "You do realize it is all your fault I will probably never marry now."

Gabrielle felt horrible. She had never believed his heart was involved. Or that he would be hurt. "I'm so sorry, Will," she replied.

Trying to keep a straight face, he couldn't. He laughed, for it was not his heart but his head that had made him face reality. "I mean it!" he announced. "I will never marry, for the short experience of a fiancée has opened my eyes. A wife would take too much attention away from my work. My work is my passion. Given my short experience, I've decided women require too much time and energy." He looked at her expression and laughed again. This time, they all joined in and laughed at her expense.

The Earl of Chatham was not happy with that statement, but there would be time later to change his son's mind. "The first order of business is to relay the information I have collected. Let us all sit and get comfortable. Gabrielle dear, sit near me." He reached for her hand, in doing so; he once again noticed the unique sapphire on her finger. Something was familiar about it, greatly niggling him once again. Now was not the time, however, as he pushed that thought to the recesses of his mind. He sighed and then began, "I have had several men running investigations since you first came to me. Gabrielle, it breaks my heart to tell you this, but the ship your father traveled on, really did go down. It was confirmed by more than one man to have sunk with no survivors." He waited for her to absorb the shock.

Gabrielle watched her guardian as he spoke. She could see his mouth moving, yet could no longer hear him speaking. She started to take deep breaths to ward off the butterflies beginning to collect in her stomach. With every ounce of her being, she tried to maintain command of her body. She felt lightheaded, and looking quickly away from her guardian, her eyes fell on James. Suddenly, as though she hadn't tried to control her body at all, she lost the fight and fainted.

James knew the moment Gabrielle glanced his way she had lost the battle. Just as her eyes rolled back and her body slumped forward, he was there to catch her. Leaning her back and taking his handkerchief from his pocket, he wiped her brow. With everyone concerned and crowded around, he muttered, "By now, you would think I'd learn to carry smelling salts." But a few moments later, to everyone's delight, her eyes fluttered open.

"James, I'm sorry. I did it again, didn't I?" said Gabrielle

"No harm done, I caught you before you fell. I had hoped to avoid this, but you seem unable to handle surprises well. How do you feel?"

After giving Gabrielle something to drink, she seemed to feel much better. The men tried to go to the library to discuss the details, but the women strongly objected to being left out. Finally Gabrielle said, "I am sorry I fainted. I did try to hold my wooziness in; it just took over so quickly. I will try harder next time. Please don't shut me out because I seem to have a delicate constitution." She pouted.

James looked down into her eyes and was consumed by the depth of his feelings for her. He simply could not deny her. After moving her to the divan, so he could sit close to her, the conversation continued.

"Gabrielle, if you get upset, or feel ill, simply let me know and I will stop," insisted the Earl of Chatham. "Now, to continue, I sent one man north, to follow the trail from your home, and one man south, to gather information of the sinking outside Portsmouth. As I said before, there were no survivors." Here he stopped and watched Gabrielle. One by one, the others also turned to look at her. Gabrielle returned their stares with a fragile smile.

He continued, "The owner, himself, notified families of both crew and passengers. That is how your aunt became aware of your father's disappearance. It is still unclear if they came up with their twisted plot before or after the sinking of the ship." Hesitating, he looked at her closely before adding, "The marriage of Viscount Herrington and Gabrielle Cartwright has been recorded with your local parish." He sighed, "So we have our work cut out for us! For though it is within my power to apprehend them immediately, we would be no closer to knowing the truth." Looking over at Gabrielle's forlorn expression, he regretted having to continue, yet it was inevitable. "Gabrielle, have you the stomach to see this through? We need to give them ample time and space to implicate others and hopefully right the wrongs already performed."

Kathleen jumped up from her seat. "There has to be a way to restore Gabrielle's birthright! It is insane to think a legal document exists stating Gabrielle belongs to the viscount! What about the fact that they are illegally spending her inheritance?"

"I talked to a barrister, he said if we get them to admit, to knowing the Gabrielle he has married is an impostor, then we have a case. As it is, if they deny any knowledge and claim to have been duped, they will appear innocent. We must allow them the time to hang themselves. We have plenty of people watching and waiting for just the precise moment to arrest them. I must urge you to let the manipulators progress with their scheme," the earl insisted.

At this moment, Gabrielle was more worried about the document proclaiming her to be the Viscountess Herrington. Her stomach tightened, this time from anxiety. "This is not right! What can we do?" questioned Gabrielle.

"We have plenty to investigate. We will ferret out the information. In any event, neither your father's title nor properties were entailed. Your aunt very well may have been next in line to inherit. If we simply haul them in, which I'd be more than happy to do, the court could be easily convinced of their innocence," muttered William the Elder. "Though we know it's a crock, it will be hard to prove. You must realize how important it is to see what they are up to?"

Although Gabrielle was obviously distraught, with handkerchief in hand and tear-filled eyes, she demurely sat on the divan looking beautiful. Gazing upon her lovely features, James had to wonder about his own feelings. Not long ago a woman that often fainted and needed constant attention would have gotten on his nerves. After a romp or two he would have quickly headed in another direction.

Gabrielle did not whine or demand, or even expect any attention. Somehow without a request or plea he simply felt the need to rush to her aid. She was not a tease, or flirt. She did not try to draw reaction from any man. Yet many men, himself included, were lured by her innocence, her honesty, and her charm.

It simply made him feel better, manlier, and powerful, in control to comfort and protect her. To see her so upset made James' heart constrict. He just wanted to do whatever it took to see her smile again. *Damn these circumstances!* he thought to himself. Gabrielle had still not healed from her father's departure. To have to sit idly by, allowing the evil ones to continue perpetrating this charade, seemed too much to ask. Finally he returned to the conversation at hand and after listening for a few moments said, "Are you saying there is no recourse?"

"The devils had the lasses kidnapped and tied up in the wine cellar! They knew all along the real Gabrielle was alive!" muttered Kevin. "This must be stopped before it goes to far."

Gabrielle waited for all the shouting to come to an end before she voiced her own concern. "What about that girl impersonating me? Surely that is a crime?"

"Strangely enough her name really is Gabrielle. Everyone around there just assumes she is the daughter, of the previous Lord. No one had reason to question the validity of that claim, until now. It goes without saying that she will be found guilty but it is more important to get the masterminds of this charade. Somehow we will have to get them to admit they concocted this scheme to get their hands on Gabrielle's money."

"My aunt knew all along she could not inherit, even if I were not to survive. There is a distant cousin on my father's side that would receive it all. That is why the impostor was needed in the first place; otherwise she could have simply killed me. I'm sure that option would have been more appealing if they would have had a choice. Then she could have married the viscount. Yet, there was no money without me. That is why she bartered my hand in marriage. That is also the reason I fled. The key is getting her to admit to it."

A loud pounding at the door silenced their chatter. Not waiting for the butler, Young William went to answer it. Listening to the voices in the outer hall, they still had no knowledge of the identity of the late-night visitor. Entering the parlor, William the Younger announced, "You'll never guess who is here to help."

As the older man slowly entered the room, William identified him as Melvin Van Meter. The men all around knew of him, the women not at all. He was presently in command of the Bow Street Runners.

William the Younger introduced him. Van Meter explained that guards had already been placed around the perimeter of the house. Melvin also informed them that he had one of his best men, a Lucas Fenwick, working on the case. Following several leads, Lucas believed the connection of the viscount to the sheriff would provide the lead they were all looking for. As they nodded in agreement, Young William continued to introduce them all. With a wave of his hand he said, "Laird and Lady MacDonald, Gabrielle Cartwright, the Marquee of Scarborough, and of course you know my father."

First acknowledging James, Melvin said, "Your Grace." James smiled and merely nodded in response. Walking over to Gabrielle, he grabbed her hands and shook them. "Lady Cartwright, I was sorry to hear of your father's demise. I am even more sorry now that it has been hinted there may have been foul play. I knew your father well and with the utmost discretion, I will work on your behalf. It seems we are all after the same men, though for different reasons. It would be worthwhile to combine our efforts, don't you think?"

They talked well into the evening, exchanging ideas and making plans. Just as the four of them pled exhaustion and summoned their ride, a new problem arose. William the Elder insisted Gabrielle was to remain behind. After all, he pointed out, he was her guardian, mentioning how he had earlier been offended, because she had not been brought directly there. While voicing his indignation, his piercing gray eyes turned almost black, daring any opposition.

There were objections, most of the complaints coming directly from James. None of the arguments were convincing enough to sway the good Earl of Chatham, however. Expressing his sentiments to those surrounding him, Old William used both his majestic voice and theatrical airs. Standing his ground, he was simply not going to be defied!

Finally succumbing to both fatigue and defeat, Gabrielle tugged on James' sleeve, pulling James aside. The rest of the group continued to stand in the middle of the foyer, deep in discussion, while they had relocated to a corner. James longed to pull Gabrielle into his arms as he stood there, adoring her with his eyes.

Gabrielle's arm remained upon his sleeve, content to merely be near him, without realizing she was gripping his arm tighter as they stood there. Because she wished to be leaving with him, her gazed reflected her feeling of defeat. She whispered in a sultry tone, "James, I will miss you terribly. Yet I feel in this instance we should let Uncle feel he has won. He believes he is protecting my reputation, which is his right as guardian. We knew coming back to London would bring changes. I will miss you just as dreadfully." She tried to smile, unsuccessfully. Gabrielle continued, "It is only for the evening, we can be together again tomorrow. Uncle William gives the impression he could stand here all night and argue, yet he is not well."

James grinned. "Gabrielle, you know I love you and I would like nothing more than to be in your company. But that is not the reason I am hesitant to leave you here."

She looked bewildered.

He knew it was her confusion, yet her expression seemed to lure his protective nature. "Gabrielle, the reason I prefer you remain by my side is for protection. I am better able to keep you safe."

She sighed, smiled and nodded. She completely agreed. For she always did feel safe when she was with him.

"Yet, I have to give the old man credit and agree that for the sake of propriety, you should reside here."

Melvin picked that precise moment to remind everyone of the guards already in place about the grounds. Taking yet another complaint out of James' hands.

Finally, after getting Gabrielle to promise not to leave the premises unless he or Kevin escorted her, James relented. Still, James felt a premonition of imminent danger and was unable to shake the feeling. James remained hesitant to leave.

At that time Van Meter once again reminded him that guards were on patrol. That Gabrielle was going to bed and that no one was even aware she was here. He rolled his eyeballs at James and said, "She will certainly be fine for the night. Tomorrow you can once again voice your complaint. However, I am leaving." Making a sweeping bow, he turned to the rest and said, "Good night!" making a rather dramatic exit.

After several lingering good-byes, the footman appeared with the wraps.

With the doors firmly shut behind them, Kathleen, Kevin and James headed home. As they descended the stairs, each pulled their cloaks tighter about them as the cold wind began to blow. Kathleen was particularly grateful for the soft, heavy, fox-lined cape Kevin had insisted she wear. Though James' vehicle was well padded and sprung, a gentle sway ensued upon departure. Day began to break and as they crested the hill, the sun rose on the horizon. The familiar clip clop of the horses echoed along the pavement, providing the atmosphere of loneliness James already felt leaving Gabrielle behind.

Later, after their second bout of lovemaking, Kathleen snuggled close to her husband. He held her tight and as he did, she had never felt more protected and loved. They lay in silence for some time before Kathleen said, "I am afraid for Gabrielle. Last time we dealt with the viscount he threatened to sell us to some infidel. He didn't give a fig how we were disposed of. Now it is even more serious, because of our escape. We are a liability to him. He will be looking for us because he knows we can jeopardize his scheme. Can we really pull this off?"

"Have a wee bit of faith, lass," Kevin said to reassure Kathleen. Even being aware of the danger they were about to face, he did not doubt either the abilities of himself or his men. It was the untrained group about to accompany him he was unsure of. Though others believed in these Bow Street Runners, he could not spare the confidence.

Holding her close, he whispered, "Before long we will be headed home with all this behind us. Dinna worry. You are mine and there is nothing I would na do ta protect ya." Kathleen did not respond, for by then she had fallen asleep.

In an equally plush room, down the hall, James stared at the ceiling. He was well aware Gabrielle was under guard, her safety provided for. He simply wanted her close at hand. Maybe that was selfish, as the earl had pointed out. He simply justified his feelings by acknowledging the fact that he had the ability to protect her. He just wanted to get this mess behind them and have Gabrielle by his side. Moments later his thoughts became more provocative. Damn, now he really couldn't sleep!

Trying to think of other things rather than ways to get Gabrielle undressed, his mind wandered. Remembering how he had rebelled at the length of time involved when William the Elder announced his earlier plans. Again James had been hopelessly ignored. The wedding banns had been posted, they were to marry three weeks hence. James had even explained how he had already obtained a special license, insisting there was no need to wait. However, he had been firmly informed by her guardian that it was not to be. After trying unsuccessfully to reason with him, James' attitude became haughty and pompous. William the Elder understood James' passion and the hurry he was in. Yet William politely scorned the fact that James had not yet even informed his own parents of his plans. The Earl of Chatham was not going to bend on this issue, using little eloquence to silence James. Employing the boast that it would take at least that long to organize the flamboyant wedding James had implied he wanted. Even so, with only three weeks, they would be hard-pressed. So again James lost the argument.

The next afternoon, not long after Kathleen and Kevin took off to romp about town, James felt at loose ends. Wondering off to his study, James decided to catch up on some much-needed paper work. Re-reading the same list for the third time, he finally realized it was useless. He just couldn't concentrate on business. Standing up to stretch, his gaze focused on the portraits along the wall, smiling as he thought of his family. At that moment, he decided to go to his parents' house. Opening the door and hollering for a footman to have his horse brought around, he then quickly penned two notes, one to send to Gabrielle, the other left behind for Kevin. Grabbing his jacket from the back of the chair, he put it on while striding into the hallway. After leaving instructions with his butler, he headed to his parents' home.

Upon his arrival, the family butler greeted him warmly. Hearing the laughter coming from the dining room, the stuffy butler announced that the family had already begun to eat, as they had been unaware of his imminent arrival. James grinned at the tactics of the old butler, realizing an indirect scolding when he heard one. Following his lead, James said, "I really must apologize for not sending word I was coming, it was a rather impulsive gesture."

With that, the butler that had been with them since he was a lad smiled brilliantly. Though of course none was required, he accepted the offhanded excuse as an apology. Muttering something about manners and the younger generation, he turned and walked away. Then the butler added with resignation, "I'm sure they will be happy to see you, no matter the condition. I will have Sara set another place immediately." Still smiling, James turned around and headed down the corridor.

He paused a moment in observation. Casually he crossed his arms as his shoulder leaned against the doorframe. He watched the easy interaction of his family with one another.

The sturdy, large round mahogany table was the focal point of the whole room. Hand-crafted, his mother had loved it on sight. The mantle of the fireplace and the sideboard, too, boasted the same dark wood. The plush, hand-tufted rugs made from pure wool were from China. The zigzag patterns were reminiscent of the plaster found on the ceiling above. The colors of both the rugs and drapes were rich tan bisque, though the elegant curtains had been made nearby. Ornate brass pitchers, wine ewers and serving bowls cluttered the sideboard with a variety of items. Hanging on the wall above the sideboard was the huge brass branch wall sculpture. Early in his parents' marriage a skilled artisan had gifted this unique design to them. In the corner sat several different sizes and shapes of oriental vases, each overflowing with flowers or foliage. Painted with gold and tans to match the rest of the room, they added dimension. The room itself provided a tranquil and homey atmosphere. Exactly the effect his mother had tried to create when decorating.

Still standing there, he smiled. Coming home was not only a statement, but also a feeling. Only moments later did his mother notice him and wave him in. Following their mother's gaze, Jake and Jared turned around and saw him standing in the doorway. "James!" they shouted as they jumped up from their seats to hurry in his direction. It seemed whenever James came home he caused a commotion.

Slapping each other soundly on the back, they never really separated, creating a huddle. Standing as they were together, they were so strikingly similar in appearance. A stranger at first glance would think them identical, with their black hair, amber eyes and perfect white smiles. All good-looking young men, approximately the same height, with broad shoulders and tan faces. Upon further scrutiny, one may notice James being slightly taller. Jake's muscles appearing somewhat thicker, or the trace of a scar along Jared's jaw.

However, as they stood together, Frances Armstrong's pride in her sons appeared quite evident. Though they didn't think she knew about the skirmishes they'd been in or the trouble they'd helped one another out of, they were considered notorious rakes among the ton. However, they were also highly sought-after bachelors on the marriage mart. Frances knew their dispositions and personalities. Even though they were rogues and adventurers, they had never harmed anyone undeserving.

Of course, these were things she was not to have knowledge of, nor would she ever admit to knowing. If her husband and sons went to such lengths to protect her sensibilities, she would simply go along. However, the smile on her face radiated the love and joy she felt for her family.

Crossing the room, the duke gathered James in a great hug. Holding him at arm's length, he took an accounting. Observing the twinkle in James' eye, his father boomed, "You look good, son. Welcome home!" Standing there, good-naturedly pounding each other on the back, her husband joined their circle.

With her husband standing among them, it was apparent they had received their handsome features directly from her husband. Remaining seated, she contrived two simple words describing each of them. Her husband Donald was possessive and tolerant. Her oldest son James most often appeared arrogant yet charming. Her middle child, Jared, was solemn and sincere. Her youngest child Jake seemed continuously cheerful and tenacious. All the men in her life were dependable, loyal and loving. Upon observation strangers noticed only their common characteristics. Yet, each had different attributes, giving them a hint of individuality.

Laughing as they broke apart, returning to their seats, James leaned over and placed a gentle kiss upon his mother's cheek in greeting before taking his own place at the table. Again the ease of routine and the familiarity seemed to overwhelm James with contentment.

As they dined, the duke reminded everyone that in the spring Jared had a new contender running in the race at Richmond. "I know you are all grown men with lives of your own. However, seems to me a family should be counted on for support. We should be there to celebrate when he wins." Then Donald Armstrong muttered under his breath, "Or commiserate if he loses."

"Which horse is it?" questioned Jake

"She is the beautiful brownish red filly, I named her Ginger." As he spoke about his chosen pastime, the tone of his voice softened. His interest was evident. "She has run the best time of any of my horses. Hercules brought in several wins last year, but I fear Ginger will far surpass anything he has done. Ginger flies like the wind, remains high-spirited, and has taken to racing more quickly than I remember any other horse doing."

"Seems to me you had a chestnut-colored horse a few years ago that did pretty well. Is that her foal?" inquired James.

"Your memory is correct. A few years ago, the mother went lame. She was almost destroyed before we realized she was breeding. I could only hope to have another mare so suited to the sport."

Jake laughed, "That's not Ireland's foal? Is it?"

"So you remember her too?" Jared was astonished.

"I can't believe you are so amazed that we remember, Jared. That little horse covered that track so fast I blinked and almost missed the race," laughed Donald.

His mother said, "I, for one, can't wait!" They all laughingly agreed. "We will all rendezvous at Rose Hill and spend some time. I love when the whole family gathers together. I especially love the Richmond house in spring. Though it is not our most unique home, the gardens are unsurpassed." With the conversation revolving around home and hearth, James would not find a more opportune moment.

"I am happy to hear you speak so warmly of family support, Mother. Because I also have an upcoming event I would like you all to attend." Holding his breath in anticipation, he said, "I am getting married." However, rather than the congratulations and cheers he had expected, the room became utterly silent. Looking from one family member to another, each had a more blank expression than the one before. No one was sure how to proceed; they all simply sat there, speechless. Finally he said, "Well?"

At first, each person at the table had been stunned. James had been more than just a defender of a bachelor's lifestyle. He had epitomized it. He was a rake and a cad, always popular with the ladies. His father and brothers knew he took what he wanted and damn the consequences. Even his mistresses had been epic, his romps legendary. He had emphatically opposed marriage until having an heir was absolutely necessary. It was only because they knew him so well that they didn't believe him. Within moments, all the men came to the same conclusion; James was pulling their leg. They looked at him, smiling or laughing in response.

Now, James was the one confused.

Again he tried. "Three weeks from yesterday we will be married at St Andrew's Church." Looking at his brothers, he said, "It would be an honor if you would stand beside me as witness."

Now the silence was marred by discomfort. Fortunately the duke gathered his wits about him and said, "I do believe you have stunned us, James."

"Who is she?" questioned Jared

"Why haven't we heard about her before this?" asked Jake

"When did you meet?" inquired his father

His mother was the one that truly knew him best of all. Knew that marriage had been a sore point with him. As the eldest, he had felt unfairly burdened with responsibilities all his life. She was sure it was a subject he would never use, even in jest, unless it was true. Believing him all along, she waited, in suspense with the others, for his explanation.

James began his long story. Explaining how Kevin had squeezed a favor out of him. Defining the mission for Lucas and how it had intersected with that favor. Revealing his meeting and falling in love with a beautiful woman. Defining the twist of fate which had changed his opinion of marriage. He expounded upon the fact that she did not immediately want him, so he had had to try even harder to get her attention. He went on and on about their adventures. Detailing how she had almost been forced to wed another. He accounted for his time spent going to Scotland and back. He spelled out all the confusion they had been through. He even unraveled the mystery of

Gabrielle's past and current situation. The only thing he never mentioned was Helena's.

With his mother present, it was a topic he preferred not to go into. He was not inclined to explain just what Helena's was and he didn't want his mother's opinion of Gabrielle to be prejudiced by it. He would not allow that, as he fully intended both the women in his life to get along. James would clarify his omission later, presenting the entire situation to his father and brothers over cigars. His evasion was merely to shield Gabrielle.

Afterwards, his family had indeed congratulated him. Including the hoots and whistles he had expected earlier. They had respected his decision and his choice unconditionally. They also demanded to be introduced immediately.

As the evening wore on, Frances retired and the men withdrew to the study. Located in the rear of the residence, this room boasted no female fripperies. With a roaring fire and fine brandy, the men settled in comfortably.

Pulling two chairs closer to the hearth to join the two already positioned there. The men were companionably close and discussion could be kept low. Before continuing with his story, James was adamant about them promising to keep the rest within the family. Only after their agreement did he go on to explain about Helena's. It was late in the evening before the men left the comfort of the warm study to head upstairs for the night.

Meanwhile, having just finished her toilette, Gabrielle was snuggled in bed with a good book and a cup of hot chocolate. She had worn herself out, trying to answer questions without actually lying or revealing any improprieties. Uncle William had promised her a shopping expedition on the morrow, so she had been anxious to rest. Gabrielle quickly drifted off, sleeping quite soundly. She barely noticed the temperature drop or the slight breeze created by the opening of her balcony door. In her dream state she simply pulled the covers a little higher and continued sleeping.

"You reckon we should pack her a bag?" asked the short fellow named Bart.

"Naw, he plans on keepen her in bed anyway," the taller man snickered.

"How we going to get her around in her nightgown? Just let me grab her some clothes," whispered Bart.

"We don't have time for you to be playin lady's maid. I'm tellen ya, there's nothin ta worry about. After her maid left, I slipped some laudanum in her chocolate. She'll be out cold for a long while, but we have to hurry." The man called Slim continued, "Now grab the corners and just wrap her up and we'll have her out in no time." As they struggled out the door and down the dimly lit hallway, her arms or legs knocked against the steps going down.

"Will you pick up your end?" Slim hissed. "She won't even be in shape to bed by the time you're done with her!" The short fellow strained to lift his end of the blankets higher.

Without any exertion from their captive, they encountered very little deterrence in capturing Gabrielle. The man at the front door was still standing watch. Yet the man who had been posted to watch the back had left his post hours ago. Until scurrying through the house, the villains had no idea where he had wondered off to. Taking the chance he had retired for the evening, they thankfully spotted him with a buxom young maid in the rear of the kitchen. Both the man and woman had been too busy divesting each other of their clothing to pay any mind to the kidnappers. The one and only guard that had attempted to stop them remained unconscious in the gazebo.

So, in the middle of the night, after the house had settled in for the evening, Gabrielle was off on another adventure, this time destination unknown.

Chapter 15

Their quarry still in sight, Scott and his men now found themselves traveling south. Neither the chilly air nor the dampness of the weather seemed to bother them, but the eerie patches of fog often made following the villains difficult. Just after dawn the viscount and the sheriff had parted company, so Scott had broken his group in two. Kevin's men trailed after the sheriff, while Scott and his men followed the viscount.

Over an early breakfast, Kevin read the message from James, explaining his visit to his parents. The message included a request that Kevin check in on Gabrielle while he was away.

Finding the instructions no great imposition, Kevin and Kathleen attended to it straightaway. As Kathleen and Kevin entered the foyer of the Pitt home, they could hardly be aware of the envelope on the table. Nor could they have knowledge that it was Gabrielle's note from James, still awaiting delivery.

By the time they were ushered into the earl's residence it was late afternoon. Requesting a visit with Gabrielle, they had been informed that Gabrielle was still abed. This concerned Kathleen, who immediately headed upstairs to check on her, while Kevin headed toward the study, determined to have a short conversation with William the Elder. Knocking softly when Kathleen came to Gabrielle's door, she waited for a response. Knocking a bit more firmly also gained no answer. It wasn't until she began pounding on the door that a maid scurried down the corridor. Kathleen quickly confronted the servant by saying. "Have you been called to Gabrielle's room today? Is she feeling all right? Have you helped her dress yet?"

Unfortunately, the young maid Kathleen stopped to interrogate turned out to be the same silly girl tumbled by the guard the evening before. Well aware there would be trouble to pay by acknowledging that either of them had left their posts, the young maid was not about to admit anything to Kathleen. Instead, she quickly lied, "The lady has a slight headache and has requested not to be disturbed this morning." Then before Kathleen could ply her with more questions the irresponsible chit pushed past her and made a speedy getaway. Kathleen thought about barging in, but changed her mind and decided that if Gabrielle was really that sick to still be abed, it would be better to let her sleep.

Gabrielle's note from James still rested on the side-table in the foyer, awaiting her descent downstairs.

Concluding their visit at the earl's, Kathleen and Kevin roamed about London seeing the sights. Though Kevin was accustomed to a more rigorous existence, he adapted to the leisure city lifestyle without incident. However, his huge frame hardly blended into the crowd without notice. The beautiful buxom woman and huge devil-may-care gentleman causing a bit of sensation among the crowd.

Kevin promised her jewelry, if they could pass the dress shops, when she hinted for a new one. She laughed at his bribery, yet acknowledged how well it worked! In return, she hinted to reward him later. Stopping to gaze into the window of a jewelry store, Kathleen was intrigued with an elegant pearl necklace. Pausing briefly to admire the large iridescent pearl, when she turned around Kevin was nowhere to be found. Turning around to look down the street she came full circle before he was once again standing beside her. He had a twinkle in his eye and Kathleen was immediately suspicious. Before she had the opportunity to question him, Kevin slipped the beautiful necklace around her neck. As he finished hooking the clasp, he nuzzled her neck and whispered, "I may not always pay attention to the rest of your ensemble," he smiled, "but I always notice what is or isn't accessorizing your breasts. I have been remiss in buying my wife baubles and next time you have only to ask." His gaze then fell to her necklace now nestled between the cleavage of her huge breasts.

Because they were in public she did not ardently hug and kiss him as she wanted, but instead whispered under her breath all the things she would do to him later to repay him.

He laughingly agreed to all her promises.

He agreed to take her to a coffee house for refreshments but when they passed the one near Saint James Park and didn't enter, she was quick to inquire. Kevin explained that he simply could not tolerate the clientele. That particular coffee house tended to be where most of the fops tended to congregate. He had little patience and their conversations were stifling and uninformative. Instead Kevin hailed a hack and they headed over to Will's coffee house, located between Covent Garden and Bow Street.

Though no one was excluded from any of these places if they had their money to put on the bar, everyone had a favorite local, for the customers created the atmosphere. Every rank and profession, every religion and political opinion, flocked to its own local. Stopping at Will's would not only be a pleasant way to spend an hour, but hopefully productive. For Will's was the place the press gathered. Wherever the press gathered, a small percentage of unsavory elements gathered also, either to hear or to create news. They sat at a small table with a polished wood top and iron framework scrolled legs. After ordering they remained upon their solid iron chairs, which were hardly designed for comfort. Kevin kept his ear to the ground, picking and choosing information. Most just gossip, some unrelated. Several men mentioned Viscount Herrington in passing, unfortunately the waiter intervened and Kevin was not able to hear what was said. Luckily, as they were about to depart, he overheard a conversation about the sheriff picking up a parcel that Herrington had discarded. Unluckily, that was all he heard as another group entered, ushering the men he had overheard out of earshot.

Kevin wanted to keep going, but Kathleen began to grow weary. Whispering in his ear, Kathleen suggested a playful afternoon if they could but take a break and return to James'. A wicked grin appeared upon his face as he listened to her plea. Hardly one to protest a lady's request, Kevin immediately hailed a hack. After a short ride and a quick race up the stairs, they were once again united in fantasy.

After dinner, Kevin had business to attend to. His suggestion that he meet up with her at the Pitt home afterwards was greeted with enthusiasm. Kathleen arrived at the Pitt home only to find neither William the Elder nor William the Younger about. Climbing the stairs after the butler had admitted her, Kathleen thought it odd that no one at all, seemed concerned Gabrielle still was not up and about. After checking in on her, Kathleen intended to go to the kitchen, to see what she had eaten so far. This time, without knocking, Kathleen simply entered Gabrielle's room. Standing in the center of the chilly room, she just could not fathom the sight in front of her. The room was in mild disarray, however, the bed was completely void of any blankets. Shaking her head as she entered the bathing chamber, she fully believed to find Gabrielle there. She stopped short. The room was empty. Retracing her steps, she quickly walked over to the balcony. Stepping past the open doors she scanned the surrounding area in all directions. There was no one about. Where the hell was Gabrielle? What had happened?

A premonition of doom settled over her as she ran through the house questioning the staff. The entire household was turned upside down in an effort to locate Gabrielle. Somehow she had disappeared without a trace. It wasn't until they found the guard still tied up in the gazebo that they realized she had been kidnapped. After sending messages to Kevin, James, both the Pitts and Derek, Kathleen poured herself a strong drink and sat down in the salon to wait.

Sitting there in a trance, she barely noticed the maid coming in to light the lamps. The first one to make it to the Earl of Chatham's home was Derek. He had been anchored in the Thames. When the messenger had caught up with him, he had been headed to his club. After his arrival at the Pitt residence, he was shown into the salon. Kathleen was sitting in front of the fire, deep in thought.

"Kathleen, if you missed me, you should have invited me sooner. What's this business of summoning me here without notice? You almost didn't catch me, for I was headed to the club for the evening. What is it you want?" he inquired as he entered.

"Gabrielle is missing." Fear made her eyes appear larger as Kathleen whispered. Derek noticed the unshed tears still in her eyes. She had done all the right things. First by instigating a search, then by notifying the men by messenger and lastly remaining calm under pressure. In fact, Kathleen had tried to be strong all evening. Now, he gathered her in his arms, assuring her she was not alone. Then the tears came, and with Kathleen that meant all the blubbering, crying and hollering that went with it. *No one cries like Kathleen, that's for sure,* he thought. Finally, she shuddered in his arms and he realized she was practically finished. It was at that moment that Kevin walked in. Any other man would punch first and ask questions later. However, Kevin was a man secure in his own masculinity and confident in his wife's adoration. He was sensible enough not to be upset and cautious enough not to accuse.

"What is this?" he questioned good-naturedly. "I leave you alone a few hours and already I am replaced." Smiling at Derek's apprehensive expression, Kevin laughed. Kathleen left Derek's arms and flew into Kevin's. As Kevin held Kathleen, Derek poured himself a stiff drink.

Finally Kathleen's tears abated. "Kevin, Gabrielle is missing. I have contacted everyone I can think of. Yet I don't know what else to do."

"Let's sit down." He motioned. "I have recently been in contact with my men. After we all left Helena's, Scott's men followed the viscount. My men followed the sheriff. They were near London earlier and have now settled in Bath. They have kept well out of sight. However, they knew something was about to happen. Obviously, this was it."

"The sheriff took Gabrielle?" asked Kathleen "Why?"

Derek and Kevin exchanged knowing glances. "Kathleen, you are wise in the ways of the world. You must realize Gabrielle is a liability to the viscount's position. In order for him to carry out his charade, there can only be one Gabrielle Cartwright, the other must disappear. She has been labeled expendable. In all probability, the viscount has chosen to leave Gabrielle's demise up to the sheriff's discretion. If that were the case, I would have to assume the sheriff intends to keep her for himself. How long is anybody's guess." He paused. "Surely you know why he wants to keep her, don't you?"

Kathleen became anxious. "Kevin, Derek! You have to save her! James is gone; he will not be back in time! She is an innocent! He cannot be allowed to ruin her!"

Trying to calm a nearly hysterical Kathleen, Kevin leaned over to whisper something in Derek's ear. Afterwards, Derek immediately strode through the door, hastening to do Kevin's bidding. At the same time, William the Elder, William the Younger and Melvin Van Meter all came bounding through. After Kathleen repeated her tale, plans had to be made. Van Meter sent several Bow Street Runners in search; the wheels were all in motion.

After hours of questioning all the employees, both the maid and the guard finally broke down, admitting to their rendezvous the night before and to the fact that Gabrielle had not made a request to sleep late that morning. With this new information they concluded that she had been abducted between late evening and early morning.

Kevin dispatched messengers to all concerned parties. Then he hastily explained to Kathleen that he and Derek were going after Gabrielle. Moments later he was striding out the door to meet Derek, who was already seated upon one mount. With little ado, both Kevin and Derek disappeared into the night.

Time being precious, they could not wait for James to meet up with them. He should be able to catch up soon but in the meanwhile it was imperative to act quickly. It was logical to believe that if they chose the route previously traveled by Kevin's men, they should at some time reach the sheriff. The only problem was if the sheriff was not involved. However, at this time, he was their only suspect and the obvious lead to follow. It was possible that even now, Kevin's men had Gabrielle in their sight. Still believing the sheriff was behind the kidnapping, Kevin and Derek picked up their pace. As they traveled, Derek said to Kevin, "If for some reason, we have no luck, you get to explain to James, that Gabrielle is missing, again."

Kevin belted out that great booming laugh of his and said, "Let me guess? You have had to give him bad news before?"

When Derek merely nodded, Kevin laughed again. Leaning over in his saddle, Kevin murmured to Derek, "Let's hope we are lucky enough to find her before we have to tell him then." Derek only nodded in response. "Though you are wrong to worry about his temper. For when James' disposition is fueled by anger, we are assured a victory." Leaving Derek to ponder his comment, Kevin galloped ahead.

This time it was Kevin and Derek's turn to spend days in the saddle. Stopping only to eat, rest and exchange mounts. With every day that passed, their hope to have Gabrielle quickly back home faded. Derek and Kevin faithfully followed the route they believed would lead them to Gabrielle.

Unaware that Gabrielle was missing. James was spending the day with his family. That morning, he and his father had had a little heart-to-heart chat, during which his father had implored him to have a long engagement period. Explaining how it was imperative for James to get to know the woman, to make sure she was not a fortune hunter.

James had been insulted and said so! He was well aware of the kind of woman most often after both him and his wealth. His father was doing a disservice to them both, thinking he could not tell the difference.

His father merely pointed out that James had never been enamored before.

Again James pointed out that, having been on the market for some time, he could currently identify every woman for miles around. The single women comprised two groups. One made up of conniving, ruthless, scheming, lying actresses, the other of insipid, frigid, unattractive virgins.

After meeting Gabrielle his father would understand. She was without guile, as unpretentious as they came. Gabrielle radiated beauty, yet remained unaware of her own allure. Though she was the most innocent of all the women he had lusted over, instead of her appearing inexperienced, the others seemed jaded. He tried to explain how it felt to enter a room, pinpoint her location, then breathe easier in her company. How his heart constricted when she smiled in response to his presence. How by her never having asked for anything, he was more than willing to give her everything! Last of all, James pointed out the fact that he was the one pushing for marriage. He did not want to lose the one woman who made him happy.

Then he turned the cards on his father, reminding him of his own marriage, a love match. A pursuit that included climbing trees, sneaking into private theater boxes and impersonating a carriage driver. These actions had all begun because his mother had declined his father's escort. His own parents certainly did not have an arranged marriage by any means. In fact, if not for his father's persistence, his mother may never have accepted him.

At that, his father had the grace to blush, pointing out, that while he had fallen for Frances, he did not have to decide between love and money, for Frances had provided both. Yet, after James had brought his own youthful indiscretions to light, the duke could hardly provide argument, concluding their private conversation by promising to be in his son's corner, no matter how difficult.

For, as an aristocrat, he was *arrogant* enough to expect a brilliant match, of equal status. As a businessman, he was *practical* enough to want the most advantageous marriage possible. Yet, as a father, he was *concerned* enough to want happiness for his son. Being a man, he could *understand* falling in love and wanting a woman, beyond reason.

James stood outside with his two brothers, explaining what he wanted them to do. Jake and Jared turned their heads towards each other, rolled their eyeballs in exasperation and returned their gaze towards James. Long used to each of them, James simply ignored them and continued, "Jake, I need you to travel north to see if Scott and his men have any information that would be pertinent to our efforts. They should still be camped outside of Gabrielle's childhood home near Teesdale. Scott McTavish and his men are watching Viscount Herrington. Jared, I would like you to travel west and seek information from a man named Stuart. He has worked with some shady elements and can probably help us."

Jared said, "Brother, there is nothing I would not do for you. Yet these seem like jobs any errand boy could do."

James took a moment. "To you maybe. However, depending on the information or the developments at hand, you may have to act quickly. If there are plans or serious decisions to be made, I would prefer the two I trust most to be the ones to act in my stead."

Jake and Jared both felt slightly guilty for feeling put out, though neither man felt contrite enough to tell James. Honored by his faith in them and their egos back in place, they returned to their good-natured bantering. As they worked out their plans, the afternoon turned to evening. Sifting through the information at hand, each man offered varied opinions to the mysterious puzzle. Later, even the duke joined them, hoping to help. He offered to send word to a discreet friend and see what he could dig up. Shortly after that, they moved their conversation to the study.

Jake held up a deck of cards and shouted, "Gentlemen?" They all eagerly complied as they pulled chairs around the table. A relaxed atmosphere accompanied the warm crackling fire as the long day of sleuthing changed into a night of camaraderie. The smell of tobacco wafting about the room, mixed with fine wine and brandy, created heady sensations. It was a carefree night full of competition and laughter.

By the next morning, the messenger from Kevin had caught up with James. Quickly reading the document, he shouted for a footman to see to his mount as he took the stairs up two at a time. Within moments he had hastily grabbed what he needed and was running out the door. With Gabrielle in trouble, he was eager to be on his way. What could have happened? Slamming his hand against the door in anger and frustration. He knew she would have been safer with him. Next time, he would have his way. Just see if he didn't.

Far from town Gabrielle has awakened to find her hands tied and her eyes covered. She remained perfectly still, trying to identify her surroundings. She instinctively knew she was in danger even though she was still disoriented and confused. Her head was pounding and yet she tried to concentrate in hopes of recognizing the voices coming from the next room. As one man mentioned meeting up with the sheriff, the hair on the back of her neck stood up. She became truly frightened and was completely baffled at what to do. A few moments later, the latch on the door rattled. The door was pushed open, slamming against the wall.

"Get up!" one of them hollered.

She did not respond, hoping they would think she was still asleep.

"If she ain't up, how are we going to get her to the sheriff?" questioned the other man. "You ain't makin me carry her no more!" he complained.

"Stop your whinen," the other fellow muttered. "We have to figure out how to get a nearly naked women through town and to the sheriff."

Suddenly she felt a hand on her stomach, lightly touching her. Perspiration formed at her brow and her hands began to tremble. She became terrified as the hand moved slowly, yet determinedly down until reaching the hem of her nightgown. A slight tug, then a cool breeze enveloping her, as the nightgown was pushed up towards her hips. She could take no more! Sitting up, she began to scream and kick.

"Ouch!" the younger man hollered. Spontaneously he slapped her in retaliation. Her head snapped back, tears pooled in her eyes. Remaining on guard, yet blindfolded, was near to impossible.

"Imbecile!" shouted the man in charge as he grabbed his partner by the collar. "You will get us killed if you mar her. Why do you think I haven't had her for myself?" As the reluctant man edged away, the older man continued, "Do not touch her again! Later, when we have made our money. We will find some women. Women with experience,eh?" Then they both began to chuckle.

At this time, it is unknown to either the kidnappers or the sheriff that Kevin and Derek have now caught up to Kevin's men. Dividing into two groups, Kevin follows the sheriff and Derek trails the kidnappers. Days later the sheriff becomes aware of the pursuit. He sends yet another message to the pair who have apprehended Gabrielle.

The sheriff's ever changing plans force the kidnappers to keep moving. The abductors drag her from place to place, trying to keep a low profile. However, after several days of wild goose chases, little money and no sleep, the kidnappers are becoming desperate. Realizing the sheriff may not show up at all, has given them reason to doubt their original plan. Not only is the promise of a handsome reward fading, but they are still saddled with the troublesome woman! She has brought them nothing but bad luck!

Even knowing they will be double-crossing the sheriff, the crooks just want to escape! In order to do so, they must dispose of their extra baggage. The kidnappers try unsuccessfully to get rid of her from town to town as they pass through. In one small village, they even tried to ditch her in the hayloft of a barn. Upon discovery, the villains pretended they had simply forgotten her. Once more, quickly moving from the area.

They constantly had to stop her from escaping, by feeding her laudanum. Then she was nothing but dead weight to drag around. Besides being exhausted, they became angry. The two men just want to get rid of her! The next town also proved to be unsuccessful. Neither of the businesses they approached were willing to pay the amount of money they needed to travel. The men pressed on. Again, they elude Derek's group of men. Sure that someone is pursuing them, they did not linger long in one place. Damn the sheriff for not showing up! What are they to do with the girl?

Later that day, after again drugging her water with laudanum, they placed her in a crate. Still dressed in the same rumpled nightgown since the night of the abduction, they covered her with blankets. The planks used for the cover bound together loosely, allowing air. Their plan was to appear simply as two men delivering goods to a store in town. No one would be the wiser. They took their wagon to the livery.

Afraid of becoming conspicuous, they left their wagon and walked about, not venturing far, so as to keep an eye on their possessions. The hours ticked by. Clearly in need of rest, they left the crate and wagon in the barn to find a place nearby. Locating the hotel, they checked in. The rooms were not fancy or spacious, yet they were cheap. Best of all, the back stairs faced the stable, where they could keep an eye on their merchandise. Slim offered to keep watch first, while Bart got some rest. Sundown was fast approaching when Slim woke up Bart to exchange places. Worried that the drug would be wearing off, Bart headed over to the livery to investigate. Without anyone's notice, he slipped in, checked the crate and slipped out. Quickly ascending the stairway and rushing into their room, he exploded, "She's waking up!" With the slamming of the door and the hollering, Slim woke up fast! They both swiftly retraced the steps so recently made by Bart. There was no other way to get Gabrielle to their room without being seen. So they had to carry the crate up the back stairs and into their room. Only the young stable hand was about and he barely acknowledged them. Striding from the livery to the back of the hotel and up the stairs, their only witnesses were the drunk near the gate and a burly shopkeeper. Each barely blinked an eye before going on about their business and no one else even noticed their unusual movements. After finally getting her in the room, they moved her from the crate to the bed. She tossed and turned as she began to come out of her drug-induced sleep."Damn! My back is killen me! We are not going to be able to do this many more times. What are we going to do?" whined Bart.

"Stop whining!" hissed Slim. "We should be fine, holed up here."

"What are we going to do?" muttered Bart.

What indeed? thought Slim to himself. It was a question he had not taken the time to worry about. Now, however, it was imperative to have an alternative plan.

"I'm going downstairs to have a look around. See what kind of arrangements I can dig up. Then I'll order up some food but keep her quiet." Then he added, "For God's sakes, don't even think about leaven this room!" With that Slim, took his leave.

Slim took the opportunity to study his surroundings. Wandering about town he came upon a rather dingy establishment. Choking on the thick smoke that lingered, he made his way across the dark room to order a drink. Standing at the bar he listened and observed. He also watched the scantily clad women parading about and was eager to procure their services. The bartender pointed out the owner so Slim headed in his direction. Slim offered to sell a young pretty whore in his possession and suggested the owner might be willing to purchase her. Trying not to give too much information, he merely wanted to know if the owner would be interested.

The heavyset, hairy man grinned a big toothless grin. "If ya got a whore you're trying to get rid of she must be no good, or you'd keep her. So you either want to get rid of this broad for some reason or she ain't really a whore, which is it?"

Astonished at the owner's keen intellect, Slim gasped in surprise, but with a quick recovery he continued, "I can't say exactly what she knows of men, but I can say I don't want her. What kind of a price can I get?" he inquired.

The big, greasy-haired man said, "I'll give ya one pound. If she's a rare beauty, I'll give ya five pounds sterling." Then he sighed dramatically. "Even if she's nothing special I'll still take her off your hands, but all you'll get is 50 shilling." Looking at the man's crestfallen faces at the deflated price he added, "And you'll be damn glad to get that!"

Slim responded, "You must realize how cheap the price is you're offering!" The owner wore a determined expression so Slim figured he might not be one to haggle. "If you throw in a woman for both my friend and myself, I'd be obliged to agree." He nodded eagerly.

"You have your own whore, yet you want one of mine?" The owner laughed. "She must be God awful ugly!"

"She's a very pretty girl, just not my type," he stammered, not willing to admit that she was to be Sheriff Muden's prize possession. Nor clue him in to the fact that her friends may be close behind.... More than that, he wanted to shout out that the damn woman was cursed, bringing them only bad luck. Yet that would defeat his purpose, so he stood there silently, waiting for an answer.

"You have yourself a bargain then! Come back tomorrow, bring the goods."

Thankful she was a pretty woman, Slim agreed. He would return tomorrow evening. After another drink, they parted company. Back at the hotel he ordered dinner to be brought to their room, then headed up to wait until the appointed time.

How to get her over to the saloon? In the end they simply tied up Gabrielle and shoved a rag in her mouth. Taking the rug on the floor of their room, they very neatly rolled her up in it. Carrying the rug on their shoulders from the back stairway to the backdoor of the saloon was much easier than any other way they had, thus far, transported her. Entering the back room, they simply waited to meet with the owner. Both men were aware they were not getting enough money to get away. However, the promise of this evening's delight was what was foremost in their minds.

The crooks stood transfixed on the scantily clad young gals coming and going past the back office. As a servant gal staggered past with a large load of clothing, she dropped several items. Bart picked up the articles of clothing for her. But by the time he stood up and looked around, she was long gone.

A few moments later the big, burly owner appeared along with a cloud of smoke as he chomped on a big old cigar. Demanding to see his merchandise, he easily pushed Bart out of the way as he entered. Quickly dropping the hand holding the garments, Bart hid them behind his back. Immediately, the evil crooks unrolled the girl from the rug. Viewing her from foot to head, the owner seemed impressed. Yet when he got to her still form, her sweaty forehead, her pale coloring, he suddenly became still.

"What's the matter with her?" he questioned.

"She's just sleeping," answered Slim.

"She's got something wrong with her," announced the owner.

"What are you talking about? She's sleeping. And she's beautiful. I expect you to stick to our bargain!" hollered Slim.

"I'm telling ya she's sick. She's got the sickness! Get her the hell outa here! I can't afford to have my girls get sick!" He huffed. "What the hell do you think you're pulling?" he shouted. As soon as the girl was once again wrapped inside the rug, he pushed them out the door. Shaking his fist, he said "I suggest you get out of town if you know what's good for you!" The huge barrel-chested man proved to be more agile than his weight suggested as he ran them away from his place of business. The two cagey villains took both his actions and words to heart as they sped away.

Fearing he and others would follow, they did not take time to check out of the hotel, but instead headed straight to the stable. Debating what to do, they noticed a large black trunk sitting near a carriage. Emptying the contents, they quickly unrolled Gabrielle from the rug and dropped her inside. The bright-colored clothing Bart had taken earlier had ended up inside the rug. Slim picked them up and looked questioningly at Bart, who merely shrugged his shoulders in response. Slim tossed the stolen clothing into the trunk along with several threadbare blankets found inside the livery. Gabrielle was now covered, so they moved the trunk to their wagon. Quickly hitching up their team, they needed to get away posthaste!

After driving in reckless abandon for quite some time they stopped to rest and make plans. However, their respite was brief, for they knew riders were breathing down their necks. Too many complications! They decided to get rid of her in the next town. NO MATTER WHAT!

By now Gabrielle was thoroughly unkempt and her skin puffy and pale from the laudanum and lack of food. Her breathing was irregular and shallow and she was barely coherent.

Finding a small hunting box, they spent the night. The next day, while divesting her of the tattered nightgown, exchanging it for the garments they had found yesterday, they proceeded to undress her. The unscrupulous men forced her lifeless body into the indecently tight lingerie. With time a precious commodity, they try to hurry. They unabashedly look their fill, wishing she were able to appease them. Unfortunately, she has brought them continued bad luck and they are loath to do more.

Pulling on the low-cut, bright blue, frilly dress, they were somewhat hampered by their own clumsiness after encountering the dozen or more hooks in the back. Finally, combing her hair into what they believed was a more comely style, she was ready. This time they decided, no matter the price offered, they would grab it and run! Carrying her into the back of another dingy pub, she is lifted from the trunk and set upon the couch. Moments later, a tall, sleazy-looking character enters. This owner has the face of a weasel but he doesn't ask any questions and pays the blunt without hesitation. The moment the cash exchanges hands, the criminals were quick to depart.

The owner wiggles his bushy eyebrows and a thin smile appears on his face. Thankfully, she is barely coherent enough to realize the trouble she is now in.

Leaning over the couch he thoroughly examines her. His bony hands eagerly caress her lifeless body. He believes she may look less disheveled and more exotic, after some food and rest. He decided to turn her over to one of his girls, to nurse back to health. Maybe he will initiate her into the throws of womanhood himself. He became erect just thinking about it. If he were wise, he would just auction her off. He would make a fortune and virgins were always high in demand. After all, he could find any women in this place to slake his lust upon. Her gaudy outfit and lifeless body did little to interest him at the moment. So he left her there, looking for someone to ease his discomfort.

Hester was picking up her clothes from the floor when the hair on the back of her neck stood on end. Turning slowly around she saw that he was awake and watching her. Quickly masking her true feelings, she smiled at him. He leaned against the headboard, smoking his pipe, his thin, unappealing form sprawled upon the bed. Approaching the bed, she sat on the end, crossing her legs; she began to pull her stocking on. He ginned, his evil, twisted smile.

"You are improving. You are a far cry from that lifeless, pathetic creature you used to be," he said.

"Thank you, sir," answering in her conditioned response.

"I have to leave town this week, I will not be able to properly see to your education. Therefore, I have a simple chore for you instead."

She tried to keep the excitement from her voice when she said, "As you wish, sir."

"Yes, I am indeed pleased with your attitude." He leaned down, stroking her shoulder. "Yet, you are still far too clumsy. Aware now, of a man and his needs, you will have to practice your new skills." Chuckling, he watched for any change in facial expression. Then he continued, "However, you will have a slight reprieve. I am putting you in charge of nursing a sick girl back to health." Noting her look of surprise, he went on, "She will be following in your footsteps shortly." Pausing, he suggested, "Maybe I will break you both in together." Here he laughed.

Still sitting on the edge of the bed, she could only hope he did not see her shudder. The girl named Hester tried with all her might to maintain her composure. It was really all she could do to protect herself. For if he even saw a hint of fear or repulsion, he would beat her again.

"I am leaving tomorrow, if all goes well, I will be back shortly." With her head held down and her eyes focused on the floor, he could not read her face.

271

"I am leaving instructions that you are in charge of the new girl, until my return. See that you do a decent job administrating to her needs. You are to be used by no one, so do not let anyone tell you different." Then he gave her a piercing look. "Currently you are totally inept. I alone will train you. Only when I am satisfied that you are no longer an embarrassment to my establishment or me will you be allowed customers. How long that takes is totally up to you." Then he noticed the upturned corners of her mouth. She had dared to smile. He became angry at the thought of somehow pleasing her. Immediately seeking to erase that smile, he continued to run his hand over her shoulder. Knowing her guard was down; he slowly, softly, caressed her bosom. Then, without warning, quick as a snake, he had her nipple in his hand. His grip was neither light nor playful. He twisted and squeezed until her water-filled eyes looked up at him. "You are a whore. You are my possession. You will do well to remember that!"

Tears streaming down her face had no effect on him. He droned on, "You were born to satisfy a man's lust. As your instructor, I will teach you all the positions and variations associated with your craft." He huffed, "Until I am tired of you, though, you will only serve me." Letting go as quickly as he had grabbed her he finished his tirade. "All the other girls have customers, you are the only one not contributing to my coffer. Therefore you will do a good job nursing this girl, or you will answer to me! While you're at it, convince her how happy she will be here. How her man no longer wanted her. How wonderful I will treat her." Taking her chin in his hand, his eyes burning with intensity, he announced, "Make no mistakes!" After letting go of her face, he gathered his clothing and abruptly departed.

Meanwhile the two kidnappers had slated their lust, filled their bellies, gotten drunk and then lost at cards. They were now on a coach, headed as far from town as possible. Gabrielle had been moved upstairs to Hester's room and remained fast asleep.

Derek, along with a few men, had ridden into town. The rest of the group he had accompanied remained camped just outside. They started at the barbershop, working their way through every store and restaurant. Later that day, standing at the bar, quenching their thirst, they had arrived at their last stop. Conversing with both the bartender and the patrons, they were convinced Gabrielle was not there. Earlier when they had entered the town Derek had been sure they would find Gabrielle. There was no mistaking the tracks they had followed. Where had she gone? Derek's heart was heavy as they made their way back to camp. "Maybe Kevin is having better luck," muttered Derek.

Smack! The cold harsh sound of fist against flesh, yet Kevin's face was grim as he sat on his mount observing the proceedings.

"You filthy heathens! When I get out of here, you will be sorry! You do not realize the power I have. You do not know the friends, that will come to my aid!" shouted Sheriff-Constable Muden.

Kevin gave a steel cold glare at the sheriff and then nodded to the man standing alongside the sheriff. The man nodded in return, again making a fist, he hit the sheriff again.

"I don't even know you! What the hell could I have possibly done to you?" cried out the sheriff, his arms tied around his back, his ankles suspended from a long, and thick rope, attached to the tree.

As the sheriff swung back and forth like a pendulum, he hollered out obscenities and threats! Impassively, Kevin gazed upon the man he had chosen to dole out the punishment and nodded. Again, the man struck the sheriff. This time with a bone crunching sound, as he made direct contact with his nose.

Even as blood spurted everywhere, running down his face, he continued to shout, "You can't honestly believe to get away with this! Do you know who I am?"

"I ken who you are," he said softly.

The man chosen to beat the sheriff had come forth willingly, at Kevin's command. He had been underpaid, overworked and abused, for years. Being forced to beat his employer was a gift, not a burden. Watching for the signal from the Scottish warrior, he hit the sheriff once again.

Kevin's men stood guard, in a closely-knit circle, surrounding the entire perimeter. It was imperative to gather as much information from the sheriff as possible. The sheriff had spent entirely too long in disbelief, then denial. Finally, it had dawned on him that he would go nowhere until the Scottish savage was satisfied. The sheriff could be quite talkative, when given the correct incentive.

After beginning his litany of offenses, he had become a fount of information. Listening to him babble, Kevin gleaned far more than he needed. Only moments ago had he begun some tale of committing treason, orchestrated to look as though an aristocratic family were to blame. He jumped from one partner and criminal act to another. Whining about his monetary loss due to an early mine explosion. Then off on a tirade about colonials and their confiscated arms, then he rambled off names, locations and histories. He divulged recently obtaining the whereabouts of a missing heir long ago forgotten. He admitted to blackmail, murder and mayhem.

When he started his recitation about sinking a ship, confiscating the booty and selling the survivors, Kevin paid special attention. By now, the sheriff had been hanging upside down for quite some time. His words came slower as he mentioned following two women. One for a huge payment, the other for lascivious purposes, while drooling at the prospect of bedding the buxom redhead, he became delirious.

Ranting and raving about being screwed out of the supple beauty because of his incompetent partner, droning on and on about his preference for the one called Kathleen. Wondering out loud if she would survive his rough sport. Declaring he did not kidnap Gabrielle, for how did one kidnap one's own property? She had been a gift from the count, in lieu of payment for another job. On and on he went, until finally, he became silent.

The tree limb crackled, the weight hanging from its branch a strain. Signaling one of his men, the servant who had done the physical damage was led away. Stoically, standing a few meters from the pathetic man, he took inventory. One eye hanging from its socket, the other swollen shut. Blood and bruises covered his entire body. His nose and jaw both broken, leaving his face twisted and contorted.

Kevin thought to end all this drama, by merely grabbing his dagger and shoving it deeply into the evil man's heart. Though it would give him immense pleasure, unfortunately it was necessary to handle matters differently. Kevin appreciated physical confrontation; he would have preferred a fight. Yet, the coward had kept running.

Kevin was well aware of both the stakes and the repercussions. Neither he nor his men would soil their hands. Later there would be a reckoning. There would be no killing attached to him, his men or Scotland. Though England and Scotland had long been united, the Scots were still considered savages. That was why he had so cleverly enlisted the aid of the disgruntled servant.

It was also essential that the sheriff have his punishment delivered before James arrived upon the scene. Kevin would not chance an impulsive reaction on James' part. Well aware of James' explosive temper, Kevin needed the sheriff to supply him with all the information before silencing him.

The sheriff must die a violent and painful death for his participation in these crimes. Hell, after hearing even a portion of his illegal activities, Kevin surmised the sheriff should have been held accountable years ago. After listening to the sheriff name the members of parliament and the number of aristocrats associated with his schemes, Kevin was convinced no trial would be fair. Therefore he would see that punishment was administered himself.

Every precaution taken, every loophole covered. There would be no implication here that anything other than an accident had occurred. No possible connection to the Armstrong family, no way to blame James.

Dismounting and covering the distance from his steed, to the tree, took only a moment, his heavy frame trampling plants, snapping twigs and causing pebbles to roll in his wake. The slight breeze that had been with them earlier had long since disappeared, leaving a deadly calm. As Kevin approached the beaten man, he grunted. Hanging upside down made it easy for Kevin to growl a simple effigy in his ear, "A man with no friends will never be missed." As soon as the words were out of Kevin's mouth, the sheriff's good eye popped open. Finally realizing there would be no escape for him, the sheriff stared at Kevin in horror.

Unrelenting and unforgiving, Kevin stood impassively, his arms folded, his legs straight as he continued, "Scottish law suggests a mon's death be swift." Here he grinned, "However, here we are in England and you an English mon to boot." Laughing, he hesitated. "Your death will be unpleasant and painful. As you have spent your life torturing others, so shall you be tortured," his effective announcement spoken with the Wisdom of Solomon.

Turning from the man, he returned to his horse. With a mere gesture of his hand, a guard let loose the rope. The man fell with a loud thud; headfirst, to the ground. "You will be left to the animals of the forest. They will rip pieces of flesh from your body for their meal. They will care not be you dead or alive." Mounting his horse, he trotted over to the group, holding the servant. "Six of my men will stay behind. When the animals have devoured the flesh from his carcass, you will be allowed to leave. You can tell of your participation in his death if you choose, I care not. I must tell you, however; it would be in your best interest to remain silent. We will be long gone, who would believe your tale? They would accuse you." He pointed at them. Then, throwing him a sack of coins confiscated from the sheriff, he continued, "You have had your vengeance and earned your freedom." Motioning for the rest of his men to follow, the group rode off.

Far from that scene, Gabrielle awoke. Her head was pounding and she seemed disorientated and felt nauseous. Opening her eyes did not help much, for the room was entirely dark. Lying there she heard a faint rustle coming closer. Then someone picked her head up and helped her drink some cool cider. Though more trickled down her chin than down her throat, she was grateful to have any. Gently, the hand laid her head back down. For some reason, Gabrielle grasped her situation had changed. After days of rough treatment and aggressiveness, she welcomed the mild manner.

"My name is Hester. I will take care of you," someone whispered in her ear.

Gabrielle tried to say something kind in return, however, her speech was not audible.

"Your man did not want you. He brought you here. You need not fear; I will nurse you back to health. Just rest. In the morning you can bathe and eat. You will like it here. The women are treated special. My master will take care of you. It is so sad, that your man no longer wanted you near him. For even though you are unkempt, at the moment, I believe after the dirt is removed, you will prove to be quite comely."

Trying to keep her eyes focused caused pain. Lying there, Gabrielle was trying to understand what had happened. Didn't she say James had brought her here? How was that possible? She heard someone humming as she drifted back to sleep.

The next morning, though her body ached and her head remained foggy, she was wide-awake as the young girl carried the tray into the room. Balancing it on one hip, she closed the door. Carrying it to the bedside table, she set it down. Gabrielle tried to sit up, but immediately became dizzy. Rushing to her aid, Hester said, "Don't try to do too much too soon! Here, let me help you." Grabbing several pillows from a small bed nearby, Hester proceeded to prop her up.

Spooning up some porridge, she hand-fed Gabrielle breakfast. However, as Gabrielle had not eaten much for days, her appetite was sparse. Pulling the covers back in place, Hester finished the remaining food. She sat on the edge of Gabrielle's bed, eating and chatting. Hester was in heaven. The food prepared for Gabrielle was sweet-smelling and delicious. She had been given only the meagerness of portions and those inedible during her own month-long captivity. The popover simply melted in her mouth. Returning from the kitchen after bringing down the dishes, Hester was at a loss of what to do. Her only job was to take care of Gabrielle and she was fast asleep. Hester shrugged her shoulders, reclined upon the other bed, where she too fell asleep.

That afternoon, Gabrielle again awoke. Spotting the young girl asleep on the next bed, she stifled a yawn. Taking the time to observe her surroundings, she was even more confused. The room itself was small and dingy. No place she had ever been before. The one window located on the far wall was covered by a torn curtain. There were no pictures on the walls, no rugs on the floor, a table and single chair its only furnishings. Looking at her own bed, she was covered only with a coarse wool blanket. Managing to sit up, she hadn't yet noticed the girl in the next bed, staring at her. Finally, Gabrielle noticed her. The young girl, now sitting at the end of the other bed, seemed about fourteen. Her hair was short and curly, the color of ripe wheat, her cheeks quite rosy and her smile infectious. Her chubby shape and lack of bosom led Gabrielle to believe she could be younger still. As Hester grinned,

Gabrielle could not help but smile in return. Though she was still stiff and sore, her head seemed less full of cobwebs.

"My name is Gabrielle. Where am I?"

"Gabrielle. Gabby for short?" she questioned.

"For short?" she answered.

"You know, a nickname," insisted Hester. "It seems friendlier, I'll call you Gabby."

"No … no, thank you," whispered Gabrielle. "I do not mean to be rude but I would prefer my own name. Now who are you and where am I?" she repeated.

"My name is Hester. You are at The White Wolf. My master's name is Franklin. He will treat you wonderful. I hope you will be happy here," recited Hester.

"I cannot stay here!" exclaimed Gabrielle.

"Oh, but you must!" interrupted Hester. "My master has purchased you. You must express your appreciation for rescuing you. You will have to repay him!"

"Again, I say, I cannot stay here! I was kidnapped from my home. Well, not exactly from my home, but from Uncle William's home." In her fear, Gabrielle began to ramble. "I know nothing but that I went to bed one evening, awaking from time to time, in utter confusion. When I did wake up it was while being jostled, pulled, thrown, pushed or carried. I tried to stay awake and distinguish voices or places, but I kept falling asleep. Now you inform me I must stay. I tell you I will not!" With that she threw the covers aside, in an effort to get out of bed. However, even the simplest of movements made her dizzy, rendering her incapacitated.

"Now, you've done it!" Moving quickly to Gabrielle's bedside, in one swift movement she lifted her legs back into bed and covered her up. "You will simply have to realize you are in no shape to argue." With a sigh, "My master will be back in a week and fully expects to find you totally recovered."

Ecstatic after learning she would be allowed a week to get well, Gabrielle realized she needed to make this girl her ally, immediately trying to calm the waters of dissention by befriending her. "I will do my best to make my recovery easy on you," smiled Gabrielle.

"That's better. You will learn to like it here, eventually. I have never heard any of the girls complain. You will be given new clothes and showered with gifts. The men will soon make your evenings unforgettable," Hester repeated the drill, with a voice totally void of any emotion, rendering her recitation unbelievable.

"Men?" Gabrielle shuttered "What manner of place are we in?"

"I have told you, The White Wolf. Are you not from around Clevedon? You have never heard the tale all mothers tell their youngsters? The horror stories made up to keep children close to home?" Hester asked in disbelief.

"I am not from Clevedon," Gabrielle repeated, thrilled to have gotten the name of the town out of her. "I have heard no such stories."

Sitting down alongside Gabrielle, Hester began, "I cannot say for certain how the old legend started. I only know each child has heard it a dozen times, if they have heard it once." She sighed and then continued, "Long ago, a girl from our village was born with remarkable beauty. Everyone expressed their joy, for her parents had believed themselves to be barren. Their daughter, Diana, was a tall, buxom woman with flaxen hair and limpid blue eyes. Although she loved her parents and was very helpful at home, she could not escape the restlessness within her. As she grew she became stubborn and willful, always running off into the forest. She loved to explore the creek that ran nearby, never being able to surpass the urge to jump in. She tried to explain to her family that it was the only time she was truly happy. However, her parents worried for her safety and when it became impossible to contain her, they begged the town to remain vigilant in their efforts to help protect her. Though her parents had warned her time and time again about leaving the safety of the village, she simply didn't listen. Her aging parents could never seem to properly rein her in, after spoiling her for so many years." Hester's eyes began to mist. "Then one day, as foretold, Diana disappeared. The entire village mounted a search, eager to help the unfortunate couple. Finally, after several days of being unable to find her, they admitted defeat and gave up. Months later, the mapmaker visiting their village deemed she had been captured by the white wolf. The story has grown and changed throughout time. Names added as other young girls disappeared over the years. However, in all versions, they all end up being the prey of the white wolf." Full tears like brilliant crystals were sliding down her cheeks.

Gabrielle found the tale sad, yet she thought crying over an old tale was a bit extreme. "The fable is genuine and sad. Yet it happened long ago. Why does it make you cry so?" questioned Gabrielle.

"It wasn't until the same thing happened to myself that I pieced the story together," blubbered Hester.

"I still don't understand."

"The white wolf was not an animal in the forest. It was where the girls that had been captured had been delivered. Though the townspeople do not know this, their warnings are very real. For if you are spotted alone in the woods by Franklin's thugs, they capture, abduct and sell you to The White

Wolf!" Now sobbing, Hester continued, "It is how I, too, will be remembered! My only consolation is that my family thinks me dead. Though I'd rather that be my memory than they know I am now a whore." As the girl broke down, she dropped her head into her hands. Her shoulders shook as she cried. Gabrielle reached over to hug her, clinging to her, until finally Hester calmed.

"What do we do now?" whispered Gabrielle, later.

"What can we do? We simply follow directions. In this manner we are fed, clothed and not beaten. After we are full-fledged prostitutes, we will be treated like queens."

Looking around, Gabrielle spoke. "The girls are treated like queens, yet they live like this?" She grimaced.

"Only because I have no status, merely a new whore. My status will not be elevated until I learn how to properly please a man. Until then I will receive no special treatment. I would wager your position would be the same. Besides, how can you complain, when your life has been saved?" Hester questioned.

Ignoring her comment, she answered, "Do you not want anything else?" demanded Gabrielle.

"Where would I go? I can't go home! What would I do? I am not a virgin. I cannot marry without shaming both my parents and myself. I have had no training but that of a shameful woman."

Quickly Kathleen's previous conversations came rushing back into her brain. How women often have no choices! How most accept their lot in life. Gabrielle would have to tread lightly here, for at present Hester felt indebted to her master.

Finally answering the question she had earlier ignored, she said, "No! I offer no complaint. It's just that you confuse me. My head is still foggy and I don't understand," wailed an acting Gabrielle.

Feeling pity for the sick woman, Hester said. "I am sorry you are bewildered, simply trying to explain, I think I mucked it up. I will try again." Then she shook her head, no, changing her plans. "Never mind. It is time for me to get your lunch. I will tell them to arrange for you to bathe, afterwards. When you are comfortable, we will chat more. Believe me, we have a week, with little else to do." She retreated quickly out the door.

Chapter 16

Slamming the huge door as he entered the great hall, James bellowed for Helena. Several girls rushed forward in an effort to calm him. When that failed, they ushered him into the nearby salon, quickly closing the door, explaining that even as they spoke, Helena was being sent for. Except the brandy already in his hand, he allowed nothing more to soothe him.

By the time Helena entered the room, James was quieter, yet no calmer.

"Helena." James brusquely nodded in acknowledgement.

"My Lord. What is it I can do for you?"

"I have been riding day and night since receiving the news of Gabrielle's kidnapping. The last trail faded with yesterday's rain. I am at a loss. Have you heard from Kevin or Derek? Has there been any word of her at all?"

Helena moved closer. "A messenger arrived this morning, bringing with him word that Kevin would be here tonight. He did not include anything referring to either Derek or Gabrielle. I am sorry. However, it will allow you time to rest and clean up before his arrival. Until then, there is very little you can do."

Pacing back and forth, he agreed, "I have been so distraught. I have had no control since the night I let William the Elder persuade me into letting Gabrielle stay in his home. If you thought I was determined and demanding before, wait until you see how unmoving I will be in the future!"

"You cannot blame yourself! That damn sheriff and viscount are behind it, I'm sure. We will find her!"

"You, madam, sound very positive. Have you any leads?"

"Not as of yet. However, Stuart and your brother have left to follow up on a clue." Observing the weary look about him, she immediately rang for a servant. "You look horrible! You have had no sleep and probably little to eat. You have been in the saddle for days and smell like your horse. I'm sending you upstairs, you need a little pampering," she instructed. Unable to help herself, Helena added, "Do you want me to have Millicent sent up?" She smiled.

Ignoring her teasing, he said, "I will take you up on everything, as long as you promise to send for me the moment either Kevin or my brother returns.

280

I don't care if I'm bathing or sleeping, damn it. The minute they return!"

"I agree. I will locate you promptly." Just as she finished her sentence, a young servant appeared. "Take his lordship to the baths. Afterwards, he is to eat and rest. Make sure you stay with him every moment, for he wants to be notified upon another's arrival." Turning back to James, she said, "I will handle everything, go now!" She hugged him, then quickly ushered him out the door.

Sheepishly, he apologized, "Helena I'm sorry I was so hotheaded upon my arrival, it's just that—"

She interrupted, "James, it is not necessary. I too, am anxious to find Gabrielle safe and unharmed. Now go!"

"Thank you for taking such good care of me," he muttered as he stalked across the room.

She laughed in response. "Though I worry for Gabrielle and you would always be welcome, my hospitality is not free. Try to remember your appreciation when I present you with your bill."

His booming laugh followed him as he exited the room and headed down the hall. How like Helena!

Lying on the massage table, feeling totally relaxed. James could not help but notice the young girl near the door, the same servant that had led him to the baths earlier.

Making small talk, he asked the masseuse, "What is her story?" motioning towards the girl in question.

"She is one of the castle children, my lord," was the response. "She is used to run messages and other errands."

"I don't understand," replied James.

"My lord, although every precaution is taken, occasionally pregnancies occur. She was born to one of the women that now reside here. Helena sees to it that all of them are treated well. Eventually, after proper training, they are old enough to work. Her name is Mary," smiled the masseuse.

James was taken aback. Never had he worried over the repercussions of any of his own indiscretions let alone anyone else's. But far worse ... was the idea that Helena was so.... Jumping to conclusions, he muttered, "Damn! Helena populates her own brothel. I can't believe it!"

The masseuse was a small woman, both in height and build. At nineteen, she too was the child of a prostitute. She had seen firsthand the bad side the life had brought for both herself and her mother. It was one of the reasons that while comely enough to entertain men, she had chosen not to. Her mother had never found work in such a fine establishment as Helena's, having died three years before. Gritting her teeth, she insisted, "You misunderstand, sir. Mistress Helena has certainly not been in business long enough to do that! No one here is ever forced to do anything. Children here are given an education and a home. When they find that which interests them, they are trained in that position. Though hardly surprising, many women choose to sleep with men." She grinned broadly at him, her supple hands vigorously kneading his body's stiffness away. James, naked, oily and newly enlightened, let the conversation die as he enjoyed the pleasure of her ministrations. Yet he had acquired a new understanding of both Helena and the tremendous task it must be to run this place. Afterwards, Mary led him to his sleeping chamber, where he made good use of it.

Several hours later, a small hand grabbed his shoulder, instantly waking him. Kevin had arrived! The burning lamp on the bedside table reflected the shadow of the servant. It was late. He dressed and then quickly followed Mary to Kevin's room. Reaching the doorway, James instructed Mary to remain vigilant outside. Upon entering, he found Kevin lounging, dressed only in a robe, having just come from the baths. Kevin motioned for James to join him at the table for some food and drink. As the meal proceeded, Kevin apprized James of recent events. They talked and planned long into the night. At first James had been angry and insulted that the sheriff had been put to death. Yet, Kevin once again, reminded James that they had discussed this option before. James agreed and then continued to grumble and complain that he should have been the one to see it through. It had been his right! Kevin agreed. However, time had been essential. Kevin insisted James remain focused on the real situation at hand, Gabrielle. Kevin knew in his place he would have felt cheated too. He also knew if the situation had been reversed, James would have carried out any necessary plans. Even though James occasionally raised his voice, the late- night conversation was fairly quiet. A gentle knock on the chamber door silenced their discussion. Moments later, footsteps sounded in the corridor. The gentle Mary stepped to the side as the man came and pounded on the door. Without waiting for a response, the door swung open. There, standing in the doorway, was Derek.

Both men jumped up in surprise, shouting his name in unison! They met him halfway, pounding him soundly on the back as he reached them.

"Derek! It is great to see you!" exclaimed James.

Kevin, too, was eager to hear any news. "Derek, mon! What news have you for us?"

Derek heard the anticipation in each of their voices. He heartily wished he could give them good news. Motioning for Kevin to fill his glass, he quickly downed the fine French brandy. After another drink, he felt fortified enough to explain. Just as he was about to begin, another knock at the door sounded. Kevin strode over to the door and answered it. A lengthy conversation ensued with the visitor. Finally, Kevin closed the door, returning to their conversation.

Derek explained how after his group split from Kevin's, they had followed the trail of the kidnappers. Pouncing on every clue, he had earlier been positive she would be found in the town of Clevedon. The trail had been obvious up until that point. He and a few men had entered the town, hoping to cause little attention and find out more information. He lowered his head as he declared he had not only had the trail gone cold, they had no new information on Gabrielle.

"Mon, can ya tell me why ya no had need o my men? Ya left them ta twiddle their thumbs outside o town. What happened?" inquired Kevin.

Wondering how Kevin knew the others had been left outside of town, he said, "Even the man you put in charge agreed it would cause less suspicion if we casually inquired about her."

Merely by looking in Kevin's direction and raising his eyebrows, James was able to inquire how Kevin had learned this news.

Kevin's response, "That was my man at the door. He correctly searched me out to report events before retiring. His story matches Derek's, up until the time of entering the town. They wanted to all ride in, search everywhere, then quickly exit. You are the one they listened to, because as an English mon you seemed to believe this was incorrect. They bowed to your digression."

Though Derek was not sure what made a difference, he nodded.

Kevin's lip curled in displeasure. "I'm sure you question people, then believe what they say. Is it so hard to believe someone could have lied to you?"

Derek was insulted. "I too have had to deal with scum. I am sure your men could have beat up everyone in town, but that too would have gotten us nowhere."

James knew these two could go back and forth for hours. Nipping it in the bud, he said. "Derek, I'm sure you did the best you could. Yet it is a peculiar quandary we find ourselves in." Turning to Kevin, he said, "You trust your men. They would not have adhered to Derek's elective if it hadn't been prudent at the time." He sighed. "Now let's share a drink and figure out where to go from here."

Another knock at the door, this time, Stuart popped his head in. "Would this be an opportune time to speak with you gents?"

Filling another glass as they waved him in, all nodding their heads in agreement. He pulled up a seat and eagerly welcomed beverage.

"What is the story?" asked Kevin

Jared and Stuart had only just returned from what had turned out to be a dead end. Upon Stuart's return a message awaited him. Circumstances were unusual and would bear investigating. Stuart told the others he should follow up the lead. "As soon as dawn breaks, I will travel to Bristol."

"I can accompany you," insisted James.

"I will be there and back before you know it, my lord. Henry, the lad that sent it, is more apt to give me information if no one else is about." He turned to leave.

As he was about to exit the room, James suddenly remembered Jared. Stopping Stuart from his departure, he asked, "By the way, where is my brother?" asked James

"He was having a bath, last I saw him. He promised to catch up with you in the morning. However, he had a pressing engagement and won't be joining us this evening."

Derek took this opportunity to mutter, "The only engagements here are the women." As soon as the words were out of his mouth, he slapped his forehead, aware now of his stupidity. "Which one has he chosen?"

Stuart started to laugh. "He was in heaven after he had been allowed to choose a fantasy. He chose the one called Warrior Trapped In The Tiger Pit." He laughed again. "I believe he thinks he has a fight on his hands, then afterwards waiting women rush into his arms."

James said, "I gather the assumption is incorrect on his part?" he chuckled.

Stuart replied. "He was so eager to be off he did not wait and hear the entire explanation." With a huge grin on his face, Stuart resumed, "Wait until he finds out the tigers are really five naked women painted to look like very authentic felines. Complete with tails and nails!" He roared.

"He will not be harmed?" inquired James.

"Indeed not. He is the master of his fantasy. He will first be filled with disbelief and apprehension. Yet as his illusion proceeds, he will become eager and even daring in his sexual games. In the end, his dreams of bedding more than one woman will come true. But all the women in this drama are tigresses in their own right. They will pleasure and torture him until he has fulfilled the needs of each of them, over and over again." Again Stuart could not contain his laughter. "He will be a puddle in the morning. I will run my errand and be back before he arises."

A servant found James later that evening and gave him a letter. The missive had come all the way from Wales, from Lord Cary Tredwell. It stated simply enough that Lord Tredwell had been lucky enough to find a clue and establish a lead. That he had passed that lead to a mutual friend and cohort, the young Knight Sir Brett Linwood. Even now Sir Linwood should be catching up with the group pursuing the viscount. Cary had added that both he and Brett would continue to search for both Cartwright and his daughter until further notice.

With no response necessary, James dismissed the servant. Then he fell into a chair, staring into the fire in the hearth. He was at a loss of what to do and beginning to feel despair. He had notified every friend, called in every marker and paid every detective he could find. He remained there in solitude. Every day that passed made finding her less possible.

At The White Wolf, Hester was in a wonderful mood. Today they would be allowed to use the bathing room, along with the gift of new clothing. She could barely wait until Gabrielle finished her breakfast. As soon as the last bite had been eaten, she pulled Gabrielle from the bed. Assisting her across the room and down the hall seemed to take hours. Though really only minutes had passed, it was taking Gabrielle some time to regain her strength. Shutting the door behind them, she slid the bolt. Hester then undressed Gabrielle and helped her into the old, wooden tub.

As Hester went about the business of washing their old garments in the small tub on the other side of the room, Gabrielle looked about. After growing up in her own home, then living at Helena's, she was appalled at the surroundings. The small room was hardly a bathing chamber. Someone had simply added two tubs and a wooden bench to the alcove under the stairs. The dank room had no ventilation and smelled musty. Both the floorboards and walls were warped, creating not only an eyesore but a hazard as well.

She almost laughed out loud at the idea of explaining what a real bathing chamber should be like, or expounding upon the tale and describing the baths at Helena's.

Realizing how cruel that would be, for although she was bound and determined to escape, Hester's fate remained here, unless, Gabrielle proved successful at convincing Hester to join her.

Finished with her task of washing their garments, Hester grabbed the lye soap and began to scrub Gabrielle clean. As she washed her back and neck, the harsh soap was abrasive to her skin. Unfortunately, even though it rubbed her skin raw, they were lucky to have soap at all. Finally, after toweling Gabrielle dry and assisting her into her shift, Hester motioned to Gabrielle to sit on the bench along the wall.

Quickly disrobing, Hester climbed into the tub just vacated by Gabrielle. With a sigh, Hester relaxed for a moment. As she waited for Hester to finish, Gabrielle began to pin her hair up to get the damp mass off her neck.

"Would you like me to assist you?" offered Gabrielle.

"Oh, no. I'll hurry. It just felt so good to rest a minute. It is not your place to wait on me," rushed Hester.

"Please do not hurry on my account. I surely have nowhere else to go, take as long as you wish. Would you rather I return to the room?"

A look of horror appeared on Hester's face. "Never go outside this room or our chamber, without me. I cannot protect you if you do not accompany me," insisted Hester.

Thinking to get a better idea of the layout, she really wanted to go alone, so she tried again. "I could hurry down the hall and be in our room in moments. This would allow you as much time as you need to finish your toilette," Gabrielle insisted.

"I left you alone, why do you begrudge me a few precious moments?" snapped an angered Hester as she threw one leg over the tub.

"Please take as long as you wish, I am trying to accommodate you as much as possible. I am trying to give you some privacy. You are too easily annoyed," she murmured.

"I'm sorry. I guess I am too used to taking orders and not used to anyone doing anything thoughtful for me."

Feeling guilty because she had merely wanted to plan an escape route, she answered. "The lack of understanding is mine. I too am sorry," smiled Gabrielle

"You cannot be alone in this place. It is not safe! Here it is a man's right to take you in the damn hallway if he comes across you. You have to stay hidden until you are trained," Hester announced.

"It is allowed to take possession of someone, merely by bumping into them in the corridor?"

"Yes. The man has paid for an evening if he is up here. He can have his fun with one gal and leave her room and head downstairs. If, by chance, he finds an unescorted female on the way, he can take her back to her room or right there if he so chooses."

Gabrielle was horrified. "I can't believe that is allowed. Who protects the women?" thinking of Stuart and the guards, back at Helena's.

"Protects?" questioned Hester.

"Yes, who puts these ruffians in their place?" wondered Gabrielle.

"You have strange ideas," replied Hester. "If you live here, you are the possession of Franklin. He controls where you go, what you do and who you're with. I would hardly say there is any protection involved."

"What if someone is harmed? Or they get a mean man?" Gabrielle seemed upset.

"This does happen upon occasion. Some of the girls have been hurt. Yet, after they mend, they return to servicing the customers. I'm not sure I comprehend your question, all that is part of the business."

"I'm afraid I'm not going to like this Franklin," decided Gabrielle.

"*Afraid* is the word for it," muttered Hester. Changing the subject, she said, "Didn't it feel wonderful to have a clean bath? The boys changed the water just this morning. It won't be changed for another month and we got to use it first. Now come over here, we'll get you dressed."

Her skin still damp, she struggled for several moments with the camisole. The gown she was given showed way too much bosom. Gabrielle truly believed if she bent over, her nipples would simply pop out! Even after she had Hester adjust it, she practically spilled out of it. Trying to tug the fabric of her bodice a bit higher, she remained unsuccessful. With her eyes focused upon her hands, she finally noticed the ring she had worn on her hand was missing.

Gabrielle was distraught. How had it disappeared? Had it been lost or stolen? Who had it now? Tears spilled from her eyes, she plopped back down on the bench and began to cry. Her beautiful sapphire was gone! A surprise from her father! She became hysterical. Hester was beside herself. She was unsure of what to do. Fortunately the matter was taken out of her hands when a pounding at the door interrupted them. The door opened and an older, heavy woman opened the door.

"You two bout finished?" snarled Shirley.

In the corner, on the bench, a startled Gabrielle began to subside, her eyes growing wide as saucers as she gazed upon the huge woman standing in the doorway. She looked like someone's grandmother should look, except she was wearing only her petticoats and camisole. She must be the cook or something; she couldn't possibly sleep with men at her age. Could she?

"We'll be right out. What's your hurry? You hate bathing!" Hester answered.

"I got a gent, what wants a bath. I am to play his handmaiden or some such nonsense. But he's got the coin and I got the time, so what the hell!" she laughed.

Looking at the two girls, dressed and finished, she said. "Your time is up!"

"I need to gather our things," Hester said as she grabbed their wet clothing off the line. "You know how things disappear around here!" she added.

"You two tiny little things don't have to worry about me. I couldn't get one leg in one of those outfits, let alone squeeze the rest of me into them."

She laughed.

"No, but you could sell them," muttered Hester. "I'll take them with me just the same."

"You can stay and watch if you want, he don't mind an audience. Everyone knows you two don't know anything bout men. I can teach you. The fellow comin in has a scarecrow of a frigid wife, so he loves all the meat on my body. He can do things I ain't never thought of." At the horrified expressions on their faces, the large woman shook with laughter. With no more warning, they took off at a dead run.

Just as the girls reached their room, a preacher turned the corner and entered the bathing room. Firmly shutting the door, he stood grinning as Shirley undressed him.

Late the next day, James finally caught up with Jared. Though he had eaten and dressed, he was one sorry-looking soul. James could not contain his mirth. He knew Jared had spent the evening trying to fulfill the pleasures of five women. He knew Jared was exhausted. He also knew it was probably the most erotic evening of his life.

Jared immediately thanked James for sending him in place of Jake. He had had an experience never to be equaled.

At that, James reminded Jared that for the right price, each and every evening, Helena's provided exactly that kind of experience.

Together they laughed as Jared provided details of the previous evening. How Jared had believed he was going to have a mock fight with fake animals and women vying for his favors. How he would look brave and fierce, later they would come running to his side. Instead he found himself with five naked women, all painted to look like wild animals. Locked in a pen, with women that looked at him, like an animal looks at raw meat. Each and every *tiger* demanding he slake his desires upon them, over and over again. His eagerness to accommodate went well into the night, until he appeared exhausted and drained. By then he had only wanted sleep. How they seduced and cajoled him into continuing, he still didn't know, wringing every ounce of unbridled passion from him they could. Only after each woman had been satisfied several times would they allow him to give up. It had been incredible. They had rubbed, pulled, licked, kissed, sucked, spanked and joined, in ways he had never imagined. Comprehending, as only a man can, how an evening of raw sex made a man feel. He was riding a wave of importance and virility.

James merely nodded as Jared's tale unfolded. After concluding their long conversation, he told Jared to take it a bit easier tonight. Stuart would be back or sending a message at any time. Barring any complications, they would leave at first light. Jared gave James a broad smile, for Jared now realized he had one more evening here. At that James returned the knowing smile.

Secluded away in the study, later that afternoon, James had been poring over a wide selection of maps. Unable to truly concentrate, he poured another glass of port, silently moving to the chair by the hearth. Though comfortable in the thick leather seat, he could not relax. Gabrielle's face and form, ever in his mind, continued to worry him.

A short time later, still wearing his cape, Stuart strode into the room. With a brief nod to James completing their greeting, he strode directly to the liquor across the room. Proceeding to pour a liberal amount of brandy, he quickly gulped it down and then poured a second healthy glass. Venturing over towards James, he stopped, then sat directly across from him. Stuart began, "Turns out Henry found his clue on a delivery!"

"And so?" said James

"Seems last week he ran with the lad to deliver some dishes and soap to a store in Clevedon. The weather turned bad, they decided to spend the night. After procuring a room, they headed over to the nearest pub for a drink."

James interrupted "Come on man! Get to it? Did he see Gabrielle?"

Stuart continued. "I'm getting to it." Then sighed. "Henry said it was near the end of the evening, when another fellow became looselipped, from drink. Seems the owner acquired a beautiful gem recently. This fellow tells Henry he knows it's tucked away upstairs. This guy rattles on about recently tumbling a tart that was green with envy." Stuart motioned for James to refill his glass, as James had gotten up to pace. "You are getting upset."

"Why did this Henry not do something? Why did he not realize?" James huffed.

"He did not know about Gabrielle's disappearance until he returned to Bristol. He also did not associate the recently acquired *gem* with abducted *woman*. But later when he got to thinking about it, he decided it was worth checking on. So he sent word to me."

James sighed. "You're right of course! Yet he had been so close! Please continue."

He looked James in the eye and said, "I know Henry. He is a good lad. Did you know he had met Gabrielle?"

"I did not realize."

"Henry often helps Mr. Fry with deliveries here. He met her several times, while Gabrielle stayed here. If he had suspected trouble he would have helped. He is saddened to know of her circumstances. He even volunteered to return, if necessary."

"Did your friend mention the name of the tavern?" asked James.

Interrupting their conversation, Kevin entered, fresh from the baths, his hair still damp.

"I see you have finished laboring with your men. Feel better?" questioned James.

"I feel wonderful! Nothing like an invigorating workout, followed by a heavenly bath and massage. I will be hard-pressed to endure the lack of creature comforts again when I return home," sighed Kevin.

As Kevin poured himself a drink, Stuart answered James' earlier question. "The tavern's name is The White Wolf. It is run by a real bastard named Franklin. He is notorious for having the place occupied by his own thugs. It will be difficult to infiltrate. I can guarantee there will be trouble."

"We can do nothing else! We will come up with a proficient plan. We leave for Clevedon immediately!" announced James.

Again Stuart felt it necessary to explain exactly what The White Wolf was known for. As Stuart talked, James' chest began to tighten. He was fast losing control. Stuart said, "My lord, it is best you know what kind of place this is before rushing in. Gabrielle may already be compromised. In fact, it is probably a certainty. Now that she has been soiled, are you certain you want her back?"

James looked at Stuart in panic. Then he took a deep breath and turned towards Kevin. Kevin's gaze was calm and sure. James was trying to come to grips with the information at hand. Kevin continued to remain steadfast. It hit James like lightning! Suddenly he understood what he had been unable to understand so long ago. How he had badgered and cajoled Kevin, for sending him to retrieve his whore. In the space of a mere moment, enlightenment showered over him. No matter what had happened to Gabrielle, he loved her. Unconditionally. He would accept what had happened and go forward. He would never hold her responsible. She mattered too much for him to allow his pride to stand in the way.

Moving closer to Kevin, his left arm slid around Kevin's shoulder and his right hand reached out and shook Kevin's. "I am sorry, old friend," said James.

Kevin had watched James reaction to Stuart's statement. The expression upon James' face had been profound when it first dawned on him what Stuart meant. He observed as James' attitude changed.

Yet pride was a lonely bedmate. He had found love and it would be all-consuming. "I knew one day you would understand. It comes to us at different times, for different reasons," stated Kevin.

Remembering all the vulgar things James had said about Kathleen when he had been sent to retrieve her, James felt compelled to say, "I said some horrible things. I beg your forgiveness."

"There is no need. The things you said were truths. You did not say them to cause me ill will, but to compel me to think. I have been in the place you have only just reached. You are and always have been my friend."

Now that they felt they knew where Gabrielle was being kept, it was imperative they move quickly. Stuart sent a servant to ready equipment and horses. Sending another to Kevin's men to deliver the message to prepare for departure. Though he too, would join the group leaving the castle in search of Gabrielle, he first had to see Helena.

Standing over the bed, one man on each side, both Kevin and James grinned. Standing with legs braced apart and arms folded across their chests, each man chuckled. The scene before them was familiar. Man and woman, in bed, having sex. This time, however, it was Jared. That they had seemingly just started and had not reached climax, could not be helped. Time was of the essence.

"You have to admire his technique," James chuckled.

"Indeed?" questioned the Irish man.

"You would think he would prefer to be on the bottom, letting this filly do all the work, after last night," said James.

"Some fellows always have to be in command," answered Kevin

Hearing their conversation above the boisterous panting girl beneath him, Jared stopped moving. It could not be! They were here watching? No he must be confused. Yet, he loosened his hold on the buxom redhead, raising his head in question.

"Oh, no! What do you two want?" he muttered.

"It is time to go," announced James.

"You said dawn," replied Jared, the wiggling figure under him causing sensations he preferred to deal with first.

"Plans change," said Kevin.

"Ok, ok. Let me finish, I'll be right with you," said Jared.

The two huge men, smiling from ear to ear, both said, "We figured you'd say that." They laughed as they lifted him off the sweet little morsel.

After grabbing him and carrying him from the room, they set him down in the hallway. Turning serious, James said. "Brother, would that we had time for you to finish. We must be off. Please do not tell me it is more important to bed that chit than to help me. Gabrielle's very life is at stake."

Responding to the tone of James' voice, Jared said, "Of course I will ride with you! It's just the frustration of incompletion," he grumbled. "I will be dressed in a moment."

Though James understood well enough how Jared must feel, the situation was still amusing. Laughing, he said to Jared, "If you dress quickly enough, you will be able to restore your own upset, by inflicting the same action upon Derek, for we go to his room next."

Unable to suppress his grin, Jared said, "I would be happy to accompany you."

In the end, Jared took too long and neither James nor Kevin was able to pull Derek from his companion. For he had chosen the mermaid fantasy and was deep in the water when they found him. He gave an exasperated sigh as he waded from the water, saying, "It's a damn good thing I had finished. It would have been impossible to walk away from a wanting women, had I not." Exchanging glances, Kevin and James just laughed.

Meanwhile, Stuart sat with Helena. "I was able to gather the necessary information from Henry." Stuart told Helena, in order to rescue Gabrielle, they would have to venture into the unknown. Even now plans were being made to prepare. He relayed all the information he had gathered, wanting to keep her fully abreast of the situation. They were to leave immediately. He did not believe his life, or anyone else's, were in great jeopardy. However, if for some reason, he did not come back, he wanted her to understand what to do.

He apologized for impregnating not just Polly, but Molly too. He grinned like a schoolboy at his folly, so he did not truly give the appearance of one who was repentant. He concluded that although the relationships had begun on a rocky footing, he had grown to love them both. He simply wanted Helena to know all his children would carry his name. Knowing marriage to both women impossible, he wanted to claim his children. He had been saving his coin a long time, making her promise to split it evenly between his two families. He wanted her promise to look after them all, as only she could.

"Stuart, I have complete faith in you," she said.

"Helena, accidents happen. I certainly plan to come back, this is merely a precaution."

"Stuart, they will always have a home here. You need not worry. I promise," she said as a single tear slid down her cheek.

"While in the city, I had to amuse myself for a short time. For when I arrived Henry was unavailable. I stopped by the saloon, for a drink. On my way back to the warehouse, I passed a small pawn shop." Here he reached inside his vest, taking out a small box. "I saw this in the window. It matches your eyes perfectly. It needs to be cleaned up a bit, for I suspect the band is silver. Yet the stone is perfect." He handed it to her. "Don't open it until after I've gone." His voice became scratchy. "If something were to happen to me in this escapade, I need you to know how special you are to me. You have given me a home, acceptance, a position, responsibility. You have made me feel happy and loved." Gathering her close, he said, "These are words that needed saying, for though we have felt them for some time, I wanted you to know my feelings. I have let you lean on me, as I have leaned on you. I want you always to remember me, if something happens," he said sadly.

"So you do believe this dangerous! You are trying to make light of this!"

Again he insisted, "I do not know the future. All of us will be careful. I have ever kept you informed of all things. Do not make more of this than necessary. All will be well." Stuart patted her arm.

She pushed him away and said, "You mean more to me than words will ever convey. Please do not talk of death."

"Fine," Stuart answered firmly. Changing the subject, he turned the tables on her. "Instead I will extract two promises. First that you will look for the men guilty of framing your family and second you will not turn away from love when it finds you."

"You ask ridiculous things!" she sputtered.

"You still do not sleep well at night. I know the nightmares and memories still bother you. In order to clear the cobwebs from your mind, you must clear your conscience."

She stared at him.

"It is not a job I would assign you. But one you have promised yourself to accomplish. Until you have, you will not rest."

"What about your second request? You know it is something I long ago gave up on. I can't possibly allow myself the indulgence of falling in love. I simply cannot trust any man enough. There would be chaos!"

"You learned to trust me! And there are others that you trust!" Stuart now sounded indigent.

"I love and trust few!" she said. "It is not the love between a man and woman, it is that of friends. Besides being slightly bitter, I am not stupid. Men only require a frequent bed and a warm meal. They don't want a commitment," replied Helena.

Stuart rolled his eyes in response. "You did not know me. You eventually learned to trust me."

"I trusted your judgment! Your cleverness always impresses me! However, when it comes to romance, you are as indecisive as the next man. Proof of your infidelity lies in the bellies of those two wenches you have impregnated."

Shock registered on Stuart's face. He was taken aback.

Instantly sorry, Helena covered her eyes with her hands, aware of her insult. "Oh, Stuart! I am so sorry! When you get me going, who knows what will come out?" She sighed. "I know in the beginning you were tricked. I also know you would have remained faithful. That in fact, to those two, you are. My temper simply got the best of me. I am so sorry." She hesitated, then continued, "It's just that there are just so few men comparable to you. Too many people depend on me. I must be strong. I will not become vulnerable! I will not be hurt!" she uttered.

"There are many good men...." Stuart began.

"I do not find the comfort you suggest I should. My past will not allow a man the closeness he would want. Besides, how many men would be able to remain faithful to me? Here, with hundreds of women, each more beautiful than the next? I would sooner remain an old maid than marry a faithless cur, causing me untold embarrassment and heartache!" She shuddered.

"You need not seek it, but it will eventually find you. Do not turn away from it! You need not remain alone. Find a way to make it work!" he demanded.

The fight had gone out of her. She looked up at him, gathering him close once more. "I promise to pray for you. I will miss you while you are gone. I also promise to work on both your requests, it is the best I can do."

"Promise?" he asked.

"I promise," she said. "Now you promise to do everything you can to make it back to me, your women and your children!" she demanded.

Laughing, he said, "That is one promise I can easily make!"

"Promise me!" she ordered.

"I promise!" he relinquished. "Truly, I do not believe we will be in any more danger than any other situation handled before. Now that I am to be a father, I've become a bit maudlin. Do not fret, I will be back before you know it!" Then, with another hug and a quick peck on the cheek, he vanished.

From the balcony, Helena stood watching the group ride out. Derek and Stuart, men she had depended on. James and Kevin, brave men, men her friends now loved. Men she had grown to like. Not having spent any time with Jared, he seemed to be on the quiet side and quite interesting. She smiled, his resemblance to James had not gone unnoticed, especially by the staff. The rest were all Kevin's men. Strong, independent soldiers, well used to a nomadic lifestyle. All physically sound, all in good spirits. What shape would they be in upon their return?

The group left a cloud of dust in their wake as the horses galloped off, hoping they were in time to rescue Gabrielle. Helena stood there until the last speck of dust had faded and the sun no longer provided even their shadows.

Taking a moment for herself, before returning to business, she opened the small box. There nestled upon the white velvet lining, sat a brilliant sapphire. Falling back and landing in the closest chair she said, astonished, "How can this be?"

Chapter 17

So far, Gabrielle had managed to save half a dozen assorted items, stashing them under her mattress. She wanted something on hand she could use to defend herself. Though she doubted the spoons and other miscellaneous items would save her life, they did make her feel better just knowing they were in her possession. Hester had become quite chatty, keeping Gabrielle company during her stay. Fortunately, as each day passed, Gabrielle regained her health. Unfortunately, it brought them one day closer to the evil Franklin's return.

Gabrielle begged Hester to escape with her. She promised her freedom. Hester did not buy that tale. She realized that a woman with a reputation would never be free. So Gabrielle promised her a position at a fabulous home, guarded day and night for her safety. Gabrielle went into great depth about how wonderful the girls were treated, how well they ate. The true happiness she could obtain. Yet when Hester demanded to know where, Gabrielle could not give her details. So rather than believe, Hester had come to the conclusion that Gabrielle would invent any tale to get out of there. She had become suspicious of Gabrielle and rarely let her out of her sight.

Hester had even gone to the trouble to getting another woman to stand guard over her while she retrieved the meals. Gabrielle was running out of time and running out of hope.

"Stop wiggling," shouted Hester.

"Why are you doing this? You have not cared about my appearance in all this time. Why now?" questioned Gabrielle.

Pulling the brush through her locks, for the final time, Hester began to arrange her hair. "Each day brings us closer to Franklin's arrival. You must look presentable."

Gabrielle remained silent. It was not Hester's fault. She had to repeat that over and over again, or she would become angry once more. Two days ago, her rage and frustration had gotten the best of her. Gabrielle had given up explaining, planning or begging. Finally she demanded her release. She had shouted, thrown things and lastly attacked Hester. Another girl had come rushing in to aid Hester after hearing the ruckus. Today was the first day she had been untied, so Gabrielle wanted to remain in control. Eventually she would find a way out, so she had to stay untied.

As she finished pinning up her hair, Hester reached for the face paints. Gabrielle rarely wore any cosmetics, but she remembered the time at Helena's that Kathleen had talked her into it. She had looked tempting, alluring and exotic, though she doubted Hester's ability to pull that off. Gabrielle only hoped to not look ridiculous. Hell, at this point, she didn't even care about that!

The hair and face finished, Hester looked towards wardrobe. She had accumulated several garments, from some of the other girls. As she laced Gabrielle into a corset, pulling the laces severely tight, Gabrielle could remain silent no longer. "Do I really have to wear this thing, when we don't even know which day he will be here? What if it is days?" Gabrielle whined.

"Then you will wear one for days!" answered Hester "I know you have not come to accept this as your home. Therefore, in order to avoid Franklin's wrath, I will have you ready. Whatever the hour of his arrival." She sighed. "You have been very selfish. You have only been concerned with your needs, your escape, your demands and your story. I have told you before, my very life depends on your cooperation."

Gabrielle appeared to give up, throwing her hands in the air. "All right! You win! I cannot have your unhappiness upon my conscience. I will play the devoted participant. I will give your boss the proper adulation. You will not be punished after my performance." Gabrielle smiled. "Hester, I am truly thankful for all you did to nurse me back to health. I can never thank you enough. However, know this. All I do, I do for you. Yet it will only be an act to win over his affection and then his trust. I will then escape! Don't you understand?" She calmed down and continued, "When I do, I want you to come with me!" At Hester's shaking head, Gabrielle said, "Just think about it?"

"I must say, you are the most talkative gal I have ever known. I think your name would be more appropriate if you were called 'Gabby'."

A knock on the door interrupted them. Hester went over to answer it. Gabrielle could not tell whom she was speaking with, but an argument started. Hester kept shouting no. She kept repeating that Franklin was not going to like it. Nothing seemed to sway the person at the door. Suddenly a large woman pushed her way through. "You have no choice!" she huffed. She seemed almost as round as she was tall. Her brown hair sprinkled with streaks of gray. When she talked, you noticed missing teeth. "I will explain to Franklin. Pointing to Gabrielle, she said, "I want her dressed and downstairs in five minutes. You want to come, fine. Neither of you is trained to cavort with customers so just stay on stage. Soon as the show is over, Edmund will escort you upstairs." Exiting, she said, "Don't make me come back up for you!" as the door slammed behind her.

"What was that all about?" asked Gabrielle.

As Hester finished tying off Gabrielle's corset and began pulling her dress overhead, she said, "Seems like you talk too much! Just like I said." She pulled the hooks closed as she continued, "Seems like when Sally was in here watching you, you told her you could play the piano. Hmm?"

Gabrielle tried to remember the mundane conversations with her jailer. Did she say anything about playing? She could not remember. "I may have mentioned it in passing, but what has that to do with–"

Hester interrupted, "Appears the band did not show up tonight. Either we provide music, or we have an uproar on our hands."

"They need music to sleep with men?" Gabrielle inquired.

"You are even more naïve than I was!" she muttered. "The gals go down and dance with the men first. Get them interested, you know? Later on, they bring all the fellows upstairs."

"I'm still in a quandary, what are we to do? Dance?" Gabrielle whispered.

"You are going to play the piano! I'll try to keep you covered. Franklin will be mighty displeased if some insistent fellow touches us before he's finished with us. 'Specially you, being a virgin and all," she muttered to Gabrielle as she tossed her a pair of shoes. "Put these on while I change." Moments later, Hester spun around, waiting for Gabrielle to hook up the back of her dress. Both were ready in moments. It wasn't until they were exiting that Gabrielle looked at her cleavage.

"I can't wear this in front of people!" she shouted. "They will drag me upstairs before I even sit down to play. Please!" she appealed to Hester. The garment was already so tight; there was no excess to pull up. Even the shoulders were skintight. Hester grabbed a shawl off the hook.

"This is the best we can do, now hurry!"

The last thing on her mind was her appearance, but Gabrielle convinced Hester she wanted a moment alone in front of the mirror. Her real reason for the pretense was to retrieve a fork she had stashed under her mattress. Though it would afford her little protection, it was all she had. Catching a glimpse of her reflection in the process she grimaced. She could only be thankful James would never see her like this. Her hair now sprinkled with powder appeared gray and piled atop her head in a botched attempt to give it style. Too many stray hairs had escaped and now stood out at attention. Her ghostly white face was covered with too much rouge and Hester had smeared a dark paste on her eyes to balance the color of her ruby red lips. Finishing with a heavy dose of perfume, Hester's ability as a lady's maid left little doubt when viewing the final product. Gabrielle thought she looked like a corpse but later decided the look would better protect her. In this getup she felt it was highly doubtful that anyone would be attracted, so she felt safe. She followed Hester down the corridor but as they descended the stairway, Gabrielle kept hoping for a glimpse of an exit. If she could find one, she would figure out a way to use it. However, as she descended her hopes were dashed, for between the darkness and the smoke, she couldn't see a foot in front of her. Still, she was downstairs, maybe she could think of something. Smiling as she followed Hester across the room, Gabrielle recalled her attire and proceeded with confidence. Had she only known the men in attendance rarely looked at the women's faces, all her misplaced confidence would have fled!!!

Gabrielle had no way of knowing the chaos that was about to unfold. The plan was working perfectly! The band had been a no-show, causing customers to become rowdier than usual. Seems a disgruntled group at the bar were partial to dancing with the gals. The men had insisted the establishment find some way to provide music.

James smiled. In reality the band was tied up and hidden in the stockade. Kevin's men now guarded both the front and back entrances. He and Stuart, Kevin, Jared and Derek were scattered at various positions throughout the room, easily blending into the crowd, yet ready to spring into action at a moment's notice.

Most of Franklin's thugs had been captured earlier with very little trouble. Surprise being their winning factor, they had effectively eliminated them. They were now at a critical part of the plan, unfortunately, the part they could no longer control or predict. Scattered inside were drunken, randy customers, many of them armed, accompanied by employees and high-strung unpredictable women.

Several of Kevin's men had immediately requested a tumble and were already upstairs with various women. With Gabrielle's whereabouts unknown, their strategic placement was necessary. Now they were at a crucial juncture.

The evening passed as usual. The smell of cheap gin mixed with the inferior perfume the girls wore created a heady aroma. The whiskey and conversation flowed rapidly, added to the thick smoke. Little lighting was provided and the corners of the room were actually black. The group at the bar had become louder and louder as they bragged about their adventures. Kevin knew they would be trouble. A large group of scantily dressed women came running down the steps and scattered into the thick crowd. Hoots and howls, followed by screeches and laughter, quickly permeated the air. Once the women had joined them the atmosphere immediately lightened.

The piano suddenly began to play, providing customers the opportunity to dance. Kevin's eyes eagerly surveyed the area. He nodded towards the front door to one of his men. His man catching the look grabbed a companion and swaggered towards the door. As they pretended to argue with each other, two henchmen at the front door went over to investigate. Moments later, they all disappeared outside. No one seemed to notice when after a while Kevin's two men strode back in, alone. They caused little attention as they sat back in their seats, drinking and blending into the crowd.

Jared had already approached the back steps. He was observing the large man standing at the bottom. The bald man stood, arms crossed, legs braced. Broad-shouldered and barrel-chested, Jared guessed his weight to be about eighteen or nineteen stone. Jared, at thirteen stone, would have a distinct disadvantage. He remained off to the side, quietly hidden, waiting for precisely the right moment.

Stuart and Derek would have their hands full when the time came. They had braced themselves at the bar, one on each side of the rowdy group. Standing there, drinking and participating in their conversation, even laughing as though part of their gang. The man next to Derek eyed him suspiciously at first, making Derek a bit nervous. Yet camaraderie began only after several drinks and a few bawdy songs were shared.

James was keeping a careful eye on all the customers around him, watching for a sign to see if any of them were on Franklin's payroll; who was armed, who was not. He was delighted, when the girls came downstairs, to see they had not made Gabrielle parade through the room with them. Hopefully he would not be separated from her much longer.

A slight movement on the left caught his eye. A small stage had been crudely constructed, running the length of the wall. Occasionally singers, dancers or storytellers took advantage of the space, though most often the band occupied that area. Though the stage was not elevated more than two feet, the chubby woman standing near the piano blocked his view of the piano player.

By the selection, the musician seemed quite accomplished. A clatter erupted from somewhere upon the stage. As the standing girl bent to retrieve the fallen item, James caught a glimpse of the piano player. His first surprise was to see it was a woman and not a man!

The pianist had done so well, he had taken for granted it was a man. He was hard-pressed to look past her homely face, now that he had seen her. However, as the tattered blue shawl about her shoulders fell to the floor, it revealed the low-scooped dress and ample charms now on display. Her arms appeared slim, her build slight and her hands petite.

Yet, the woman's face was grotesque. She had used white powder to cover her face, but rather than conceal, it seemed to amplify its flaws. The makeup was cracked giving the impression of large veins on her face. Her nose appeared large and swollen, her face, lumpy and blotchy. Not giving her more than a moment's glance he assumed the cosmetics were a poor covering for the pox.

Taking another look, James literally cringed at the sight of her. Her peppered hairstyle appeared misshapen, standing out in all directions. This gave her an even more frightening appearance. Though her body was inviting, James could not get past her face. His gaze returned to the chubby girl now hiding the piano player once again. The young blonde seemed innocent, not like the jaded women circling the floor. Deciding she was the singer, his interest returned to the main room.

As the evening progressed, Kevin and his men were successfully thinning out the crowd. The bartender was as sloshed as his customers, more and more girls had been escorted upstairs and the guards were now completely taken care of. James believed the time was right to approach the steps, attempting to sneak upstairs. Moving from one table to the next, James was now seated only one table away from the stage, the stairway in his view.

The rear door opened, a mean wind and gust of snow, accompanying the two men that entered. With a slam, the door closed and they continued inside. Reaching the landing, James could tell they stopped to chat with the bald man at the base of the stairs. A pillar blocked his vantage point, for although he had full view of the stairway, the men's faces remained obscure. He could not immediately identify the newcomers and remained vigilant. The music played, feet shuffled, loud conversations got louder, glasses clinked and women giggled. The two new customers, dressed in formal attire, seemed out of place. Little of what the men were saying could be heard. James continued to be an observer.

Jared stood in a darkened corner, still waiting for the opportunity to ascend the stairway. The two new customers were talking to the guard at the base of the stairs. With any luck, they would invite the man to join them, giving him the break necessary. He, too, continued to wait.

Gabrielle was playing all the songs she could remember. As she plodded along, tears ran down her face, causing streaks to line her face. She hadn't even noticed when the shawl slid from her shoulders. She was embarrassed and afraid. Silently tears pooled at the bottom of her face and chin, creating clumps in her makeup. The makeup had hardened and was not only itchy but also scary. The eyes that had been darkened to allure were now smudged, black and puffy.

Hester took a rag and blotted her face. "Gabby, stop crying, you are ruining your makeup."

Gabrielle looked up as though to say, 'you've got to be kidding,' but her face remained expressionless.

After the odd crash, Hester had reached down to pick up the item creating the noise. Holding out her hand for Gabrielle to see, Hester said, "Why would you bring tableware down with you, Gabby?"

Again Gabrielle remained impassive. How silly it all seemed now, trying to escape wielding a fork. She could not give an answer that would be acceptable to Hester, so she remained silent.

"Gladys will let you have a break soon. That will give me time to fix your makeup. Perhaps even time for a drink."

Gabrielle muttered, "I can have a rest? Why didn't you say something sooner? I would dearly love something to drink. I am so thirsty."

Hester couldn't see why Gabrielle had to wait to have a drink. She leaned over Gabrielle's shoulder, telling her she would be right back, and then headed over to the bar. By now, Gladys, who had been in command during Franklin's absence, had joined the three men at the base of the stairway. Then all four of them retreated to the rear of the building.

James was finally at the last table, closest to both the stage and the stairway. He was garnished a clear view with the pillar no longer in the way. James watched as Jared took the chance and quickly scrambled up the unguarded stairway, well aware that once Jared reached the top, he would immediately search for Gabrielle.

Gladys came running from the back of the building. Her arms waving in the air, she was shouting at the top of her lungs. Just as she reached the landing, one of the men caught up with her. Grabbing her from behind, he spun her around. A resounding crack rent the air as he slapped her, yet again.

"Where is my little virgin?" hollered Franklin.

Hester, on her journey for refreshments, reached the edge of the stage. As she descended the two short steps, she suddenly stopped in her tracks, as the scene unfolded in front of her. Hester didn't hear what Franklin was shouting, but she could see he was enraged. The veins on his neck stood out and his face became redder and redder. His right hand continued slapping Gladys as his left hand shook her by the collar. As the scuffle continued and Franklin moved closer to where she stood, Hester became alarmed. It did not appear as though Gladys had smoothed out the situation. Thinking only of shielding Gabrielle, Hester attempted to disappear by walking backwards up the steps. The slight movement caused Franklin to see her, turning in Hester's direction, easily discarding Gladys as he threw her to the ground. As Franklin approached Hester, the second man, directly behind Franklin, emerged. Hester's eyes remained glued on Franklin. Through the dim lights and heavy smoke, the man finally pushed his way into view.

Gabrielle, James and Derek all recognized the stranger in the same moment. The viscount! Spontaneously Gabrielle's hands dropped upon all the wrong keys, creating sour notes and unwanted attention. James immediately jumped from his seat, as Derek attempted to cross the crowded room. These three knew in an instant, if he was here, things had just gone from bad to worse.

Pulling the immobile Hester towards him, Franklin immediately began slapping her. Over and over again, he shouted about her lack of respect, her inability to follow orders and her slovenly appearance. Hester was screaming in return and trying with all her strength to push him away. She kicked and bit, to no avail.

Gabrielle ran towards the end of the stage, hoping to help Hester. Unfortunately two arms appeared out of nowhere, grabbing her. She looked up, into the evil, smug eyes of the viscount. He observed her speculatively. "Gabrielle?" Little recourse at hand, Gabrielle fainted.

James leapt into action. With a look of desperation upon his face he rushed to save the women. Kevin gave the signal and suddenly the bar became bedlam. The men in their group all reacted at once. In their attempt to free the women and capture anyone accosting them, the noise was deafening. Sounds of screams, groans and breakage spread throughout the room.

Ever the brave man, Franklin had turned to run as the riot broke out. Just as he reached the back door, it swung open, reverberating loudly as it hit the wall. Franklin's face ran smack into a giant Scottish fist. He fell to the ground in a heap. Realizing he had been successfully thwarted, Scott and his men jumped into the fray. As Scott and his men were pouring through the rear, Jake and another group ran in the front door. By now, James had reached the viscount. One of James' large hands was more than adequate to squeeze his neck. And James took immense pleasure watching the rising fear reflected in the viscount's eyes as he lifted him, still by one arm, from the ground. With a mere flick of his wrist, the viscount was flying across the room. James received great satisfaction when the viscount's body crashed against the wall. As the fight began to disapate, Jake located James, still bouncing Harrington's head against the wall, feet dangling, his limp body no longer putting up a struggle. Realizing James was beyond reason, Jake finally had to pull him off the viscount.

Jared was having trouble of his own, for he had come down the stairs after a futile search, only to run into the one person he had thus far successfully avoided. The bald man! Seeing Jared descend the stairway, he immediately attacked Jared. He was as strong as he appeared, causing Jared's face to connect with the floor time and again. Jared was finally able to get the better of him when the bald man stumbled over one of the bodies littering the floor. Spinning the man around, Jared's right hook connected and the man landed with a loud crash against the wall. Briefly the sound of fist on flesh was all that was heard. Moments later, it was all over. Heavy breathing from the last men standing was all that marred the perfect silence.

It wasn't until the men gathered together at the landing that they realized Stuart wasn't standing among them. Derek raced across the saloon, to the last place he had seen Stuart. Pulling two bodies off him, Derek successfully eased Stuart out from under the pile. Hearing Stuart's ragged breathing brought hope he was not too late. Blood seeped through Stuart's shirt. Ripping it open, Derek quickly located the injury. Thankfully, it looked like a knife wound, rather than that of a lead ball. Pulling off his own shirt, Derek used it to staunch the flow of blood. As he bellowed for assistance, a doctor was also sent for. James ran over and together they moved him to a bed upstairs.

No information would be gathered. The viscount was not talking, and during the scuffle, Franklin's head had fallen on a bootjack, bashing in his skull.

Gladys marched over to Franklin's immobile body, giving it a swift kick in the ribs, muttering something about making sure he was really dead. In her rage, she wanted to gouge out his eyeballs with her thumbs. She had been both mentally and physically abused for years. She had stood by and watched as he did the same to others. She just seemed to snap, pummeling his body with her fists. She was in frenzy. Jake, standing closest, tried to gently pull her back. When that didn't work, he simply yanked her away from the body. In her delirium she fought him. He slapped her, in an instant her hysteria calmed. Returning to reality, she seemed lucid, yet exhausted. So a woman named Dolly directed two girls to assist her upstairs. Once again peace descended upon the group.

In a private conversation of their very own, Kevin and Scott stood off to the side. Meanwhile, Jared happily greeted Jake with a slap on the back and a large bear hug. "What the devil are you doing here?" demanded Jared

"Not exactly the sound of gratitude, now is it?" Jake laughed in return.

"Don't get me wrong, I'm damn happy to see you, brother. I just can't believe it!"

"Are you forgetting James sent me north, to assist Scott? Remember he was spying on the viscount, so once he left we followed. I'm sure you have been as busy with your assignment as I was with mine." Jake didn't notice Jared's blush or silence following that comment. For although Jared had been busy, his assignment had led down the road to Helena's, but now was not the time to divulge that. Jared continued, "I had no idea you'd be here, until Scott recognized some of Kevin's men outside. Once the commotion started, we charged in, hoping to help."

"Yes, I remember. I simply can't believe the coincidence in your being here." They both embraced, then continued to stand there, grinning like fools.

At that moment, a shout came from Hester. She was now hovering around the woman still lying on the floor. Derek and James came downstairs, muttering something about Stuart having the constitution of an ox. Shaking Gabrielle, Hester tried again to waken her. With a loud groan, Gabrielle sat up. "Where am I?" stammered Gabrielle.

James reached the bottom step, immediately noticing two tantalizing bare legs amid the bunched up material gathered around her knees. He was easily aroused at the sight of the shapeliest legs he had ever seen. But just as quickly he felt guilty for being so affected by the uncovered, smooth, golden skin, for he had yet to rescue Gabrielle. Trying to stop his mind from wandering, he looked about.

James decided the gentlemanly thing to do was to assist the girl from the floor. Glancing once again in her direction, he noticed her face. Most of the makeup had rubbed off in the scuffle. Suddenly it became clear, the woman playing the piano earlier, the one currently lying on the floor, the woman in disguise, was his very own dear Gabrielle! James rushed across the floor, moving Hester out of the way and pulling Gabrielle into his arms in one swift motion. Cradling her in his embrace, he moved over to sit upon a lower step. In his attempt to soothe her, he caressed and kissed her continuously.

As Gabrielle regained consciousness, she was not opposed to the sensations invading her body. She smiled in response as she floated into reality. Her fluttering eyelashes gave James instant relief that she would be all right.

Gabrielle's eyes were not fluttering flirtatiously; she was simply trying to focus. When her vision returned, she suddenly bolted upright, springing out of his lap, landing loudly on the floor. Screeching in panic, she quickly jumped to a standing position and tried to escape.

Just as fast, James lunged for her, catching her close to him. Confused by her actions, he feared for her safety. What was her reasoning? He thought perhaps her modesty was of concern. After all, she was the center of attention with very little covering her. Perhaps Gabrielle was still under the influence of drugs or alcohol. Sadly, that possibility caused him to hold her even tighter.

Gabrielle continued to struggle. The tall stranger was holding her so tight she could barely breathe. In her fury, she began to pummel him with her fists.

Once she began hitting him, he was even more at a loss of what to think. James knew that even at full strength, Gabrielle would have little effect on him. In her already weakened condition, he barely felt the taps upon his chest; Gabrielle was diligently trying to continue. Thinking she would harm herself, James murmured words of tenderness and encouragement, hoping to calm her. Looking into her eyes, she seemed distant, cool, detached. The unkempt woman staring up at him appeared a stranger. Holding her at arm's length to observe her better, Gabrielle once again slipped from his grasp. Quickly she ran to hide behind the one person she recognized, Hester.

As Gabrielle flew across the room, the rest of the group became aware there was a problem. Everyone turned to look from James to Gabrielle, then back again. The commotion suddenly stopped, each was dumbfounded by the turn of events. Silent now, they stood gathered at the bottom of the stairs, all watching and waiting for a conclusion.

A large, red-haired giant stood closest to the stranger she had escaped from. Just as he made a move in Gabrielle's direction, the man near the steps said, "Kevin, wait."

"Kevin … hum … Kevin." That name sounded familiar. Gabrielle twirled the name around her tongue once again, "Kevin." Comfortable with both the sound of his name and the feelings associated with it, Gabrielle hesitantly moved closer to Kevin.

Kevin watched Gabrielle approach him and closed the gap in one smooth stride. Observing her look of turmoil, Kevin questioned, "Lass, is there na anything I can do? What is the problem?"

Gabrielle stood on tiptoe to whisper to Kevin, while she pointed at James, "That man was attacking me!" Her glistening, tear-filled eyes gazed back in Kevin's direction as she waited for him to do something.

Kevin looked from her forlorn expression over to James', then back again to Gabrielle. Kevin was clearly baffled by this predicament. Glancing once again at James' perplexed appearance, Kevin raised his eyebrows in question. In response to Kevin's questioning look, James shrugged his shoulders. He, too, was at a loss of what to do. Eventually the men would determine the cause of her unusual behavior and then figure out a way to solve the dilemma. Trying to be cautious, they remained silently standing there, ill at ease.

Jake had seen a shipmate act in the same odd manner once before. At the moment, he could not recall the name of the illness; only remembering the man had had a concussion. Jake believed in the fall, Gabrielle must have bumped her head. That was what was causing her disorientation and confusion. Talking in a soft, hushed tone, Jake slowly approached Gabrielle. "Gabrielle?"

When he received no response, Jake knew the problem was serious, for she didn't even recognize her own name. Slowly he continued forward, until he was standing directly in front of her. Jake said softly, "Do you know who you are? Do you know where you live?" He hoped to spark some recognition.

Gabrielle raised her eyes to look at him, and then shook her head no.

Across the room, Dolly shifted positions and with a huff demanded, "You gents could at least get us ladies a chair. I'm not used to standing this long, my damn legs are killing me." Then, as no one seemed inclined to respond to her needs, she hollered over to Gabrielle, "Gabby, you want a chair too, don't ya, hon?"

Gabrielle turned towards the vaguely familiar woman, smiling because she recognized the name. Thinking Gabrielle wanted to sit, the men scattered to provide chairs. Yet Gabrielle had smiled simply because the name seemed correct and at the same time she recognized Hester across the way.

Again, Jake softly asked Gabrielle. "Do you recognize anyone here? Do you know your name?"

Turning back to focus on the handsome man in front of her, she said, "I believe my name is Gabby and that he," pointing to Kevin, "is my customer."

Pandemonium broke out as James growled, his posture becoming completely rigid, his fists clenched. He made a move to get closer to Gabrielle, at the same time she spotted him and instinctively pressed closer to Kevin.

It seemed that she was having a problem with her memory, yet it was evident to James that if her memory eluded her, he was the only one here, she should recognize.

The doctor had finally finished with Stuart and descended the steps to head home. A short, skinny man whose suit-coat simply hung carelessly from his frame, he also possessed thinning gray hair and a warm smile. Scott's towering form stopped him at the bottom and pointed in Gabrielle's direction. "The lass has need of ya."

Jake stepped forward and talked under his breath to the doctor, before Derek said, "Another patient for you to see before you go."

As the doctor turned around, he motioned for Gabrielle to follow him back upstairs. Instead, Gabrielle held tighter to Kevin. This gave Kevin the indication that Gabrielle was about to argue or put up a struggle. As a means to an end, Kevin simply picked her up and carried her upstairs. Hester scurried behind them.

The doctor was eager to be off and head home. After a quick examination, he administered some laudanum in a glass of water. Hester protested, explaining that Gabrielle had been drugged with laudanum for several days previously. The doctor easily dismissed her concerns and while Hester was insisting he listen to her, Gabrielle gulped down the water. After pulling the covers over Gabrielle, the doctor gave a reassuring pat to Hester's shoulder, explaining, "You, be a good girl and watch over her, hum? The best thing for her is rest and when she awakens she will feel much better. That was quite a goose egg on the back of her head. There is no telling how long the recovery will take, an hour or a year. Who knows?" Gathering his instruments, he moved towards the door.

"You don't seem overly concerned," stated Hester.

"These things must run their course. If her memory never returns, she will create new ones. She is whole and healthy and must carry on. You will do her a great disservice if you dwell on what's missing opposed to what she has. There seem to be a great deal of people downstairs, worrying about her. Even if she never remembers anything, they will be here to help her." He smiled.

"I will be here too. Though we did not start out as friends, we became very close. I was instructed to teach her. Will she remember me, do you think?" said Hester.

"I cannot say what she will remember. You will have to talk to her when she awakens. Though I daresay she's had enough laudanum to keep her sleeping till morning."

With little more than a wave, he was out the door and down the stairs. His escape was quickly cut short though, as the group at the base of the steps crowded around him, all voicing their concerns. "Stop, stop, I cannot understand when you all speak at once. First let me explain, then if you have questions I will answer them." He paused before continuing, "The young lady upstairs has amnesia."

Jake's head bobbed up and down in agreement. "Amnesia, that's it," he muttered to himself.

The doctor continued, "I have given her a sedative and when she awakens she may be as good as new."

"Now that's good to hear!" said Derek.

The doctor glared at him, then tried to finish. "She may remember some things or she may remember nothing at all. It may stay like that for a day, a week or a year. On the bright side, most people gain their memories back completely, on the bad side, a select few never do."

James interrupted, "Are you saying Gabrielle may never regain her memory?"

"Yes, there is always that possibility, though it is very remote. More than likely she will begin to remember things in a few days, then the rest will gradually follow. Nevertheless, it is something you should be aware of," said the doctor.

"Can we tell her things about her past to speed her recovery?" inquired James.

"It is best to let the memories come back by themselves. Just try not to get her riled up. It may be difficult for her at first, for you will be virtual strangers. Her ideas may seem strange and out of character, for she no longer remembers how she would act. These things will come naturally and should not be forced. If she isn't causing injury to herself or anyone else, go along with her." Looking at the stunned and saddened expressions around him, he added. "Stop acting like the world has come to an end. The girl is healthy and will completely recover, physically. Though it would be wonderful for her to regain her memory, it's really only frosting on the cake." He sighed at their frustrated faces. "Look at it this way, now you have the opportunity to reintroduce yourselves. You will be able to rectify any mistakes and re-establish your friendships. Now, I am starving and am headed for home. I will be back tomorrow to check on both patients." With little ado, he disappeared.

"I'm sure everything will turn out fine, James," Jake said, slapping him on the back. "Let's head over to the bar and have a few."

"She keeps slipping from my grasp, somehow. I am nearly insane thinking she will not remember me or the times we have had together," he declared.

"If she does not remember, you will have to recreate those memories. The good thing is we have found her and she is safe." They headed over to the bar, still deep in conversation.

Scott muttered something about looking around the place and disappeared.

Derek, Jared and Kevin remained in place as James and Jake headed for a drink.

"You think she's going to remember us?" asked Derek.

"She won't remember me, for I've never met her." Jared added, "However, I will immediately rectify that problem, upon her waking." Here he sighed, "I can only hope for both their sakes we were not too late. For I know my brother, he will never accept her if she has been compromised. So, the real question is, did we make it before she was ruined?"

Kevin stared intently into each man's eyes for long minutes before answering, "We can only hope she has not been violated in some way. That itself would be reason enough to never again want to gain her memories. However, I think you underestimate the feelings James has for Gabrielle. He wants her beyond reason."

Derek smiled. His association with Helena and her girls had long ago changed his opinion of fallen women. It was a rare moment to share it with other men. "He will marry her then? No matter what?"

Kevin grinned. "James didn't want to. He denied it as long as possible. Yet, rather than lose her, he decided his requirements were a bit stringent. He has since re-thought the matter and will accept her unconditionally."

Jared muttered, "This does not sound like my brother. He has always demanded total loyalty and rejected such transgressions. Has James changed so much then?"

Kevin laughed. "He *changed* the moment he met her, he *realized* it upon almost losing her and he *admitted* it to himself just recently."

"How will James handle it if she can't remember him?" questioned Derek.

"If he is as smitten as you say, he will be crushed. For he has never given a woman his heart before," answered Jared.

Kevin grinned. "You lads worry for naught. If she does na remember him, he will bully and cajole his way back into her heart. He is a man possessed, he will na go down with out a fight." He slapped both men on the back and said, "Now let's get over to the bar, or they will drink all the good stuff!"

The customers had long ago disappeared. In his search of Franklin's office, Scott had found a small chest filled with silver coins along with several packets of five-pound notes. Scott took the time to disperse it evenly among the employees. Once the women realized they were no longer under Franklin's rule, they were ecstatic. Spontaneously each woman offered to service Kevin and Scott's men for free. At first Scott and Kevin had declined, reminding the girls that they were under no obligation. That if any of the men required there services they would pay accordingly.

Dolly, now in charge, pulled them off to the side. Telling them, that as men, they fought the battles and protected the weak. She suggested that these women, rarely treated with decency, wanted to feel a part of the liberation. Their only qualifications were pleasuring men. Dolly demanded they let their men enjoy themselves. Kevin and Scott both smiled at the outrage in her voice. Turning to the men, Scott announced, "The women here have offered each of you men an evening's entertainment. Any man who wants to participate, has my permission." As soon as the words were out of his mouth,

Kevin also nodded to his men. Their immediate response joined Scott's already cheering men.

As the evening progressed, the men in the bar and the men upstairs changed places, the line constantly moving. Turning to carry on about their business, Dolly said, "You gents did a good thing for your men. They'll be better for it in the morning. Now, if either of you would like to accompany me, I'll show you the proper way to treat a man." She smiled.

Though she was passably pretty, neither accepted. Scott replied, "My men will greatly appreciate the attention received tonight. They often lack even the simplest of comforts; we are often on the road. As for ourselves, we have business to attend to." Smoothly, he added, "Although both of us are disappointed to be unable to accept," causing her to smile. Moments later, they spotted her leading an inexperienced youth upstairs. They had been easily forgotten.

"You could have accepted, you know," chuckled Scott

"I am the married one. You could have though," was Kevin's retort.

"So marriage will keep you faithful? I had not taken you for the religious type," muttered Scott.

"Though I have not been married long, I have never been so captivated with a mere female. I have promised to be faithful and I will. It is that simple."

"I have not pondered marriage often, but your answer gives it a new light. My brother's wife and lemans cause him numerous headaches. Yet, he will not give up the variety. Yet you willingly decide to remain monogamous," murmured Scott.

"Someone will cross your path, making you change your mind. I thought you attracted to Helena?" questioned Kevin

"Yes, there is great attraction there. I will delight in having her."

"You sound sure of yourself," laughed Kevin

"I have never been denied by a women I desired. Though I admit she seems to be resistant. In observing her, I have found her weakness, however. She will come to me yet."

"You sound certain of her intentions. Are you sure I don't hear wedding bells?" Kevin asked.

Scott smirked. "It is lust you hear, not love, an itch that must be scratched. She tempts me, as she is so unusual. Most women cower and scurry, she is confident and demanding. That should be an arousing combination under the sheets."

Kevin insisted, "Pleasure yourself with her then before we leave. Maybe along the way we can find a nobleman's daughter to pledge your troth.

Someday even you will have to marry to obtain heirs."

Scott nodded his head in agreement. "Though I will never play the cuckold husband. Women cannot be trusted. When I finally give in and marry, I will pick someone on the shelf. Or a wench not gifted in beauty. In this manner she will be so grateful she will never betray me."

"Not a very romantic picture you are painting. If you do not intend to love a wife, what will bind you to her?" he asked.

"I will not marry for love and injure the feelings of either myself or my wife. She will be grateful and understand the arrangement. I will marry only to increase my fortune and beget heirs. My lust will be appeased when and where I see fit," he insisted.

"I may have gotten the wrong feeling, yet when you spoke of Helena before, I got the idea you were impressed with her. It did not seem like simple lust, but like you wished for something permanent."

Scott smiled. "Oh, I wished for something all right! Yet, permanence would not be possible. Are you forgetting her trade? She is beautiful and alluring to be sure, but marriage?"

Remembering James' first reaction to Kathleen, Kevin could not help himself. He laughed, for Scott too, was simply following suit. Thinking back, even he had been reluctant to fall in love with a woman of ill repute in the beginning. Yet love was like luck and landed in the most unlikely places. Grinning, Kevin slapped him on the back and said, "Let's just see what happens, shall we?" Heading over to the bar for a drink, Scott, a little bewildered by Kevin's attitude, followed suit.

Several times during the night, James checked on Gabrielle, only to find her still asleep. He wanted to be by her side when she awoke, but Hester was playing nurse and refused to let anyone stay. James would have demanded, but for Gabrielle's sake he chose not to cause a disturbance.

There was no way for Hester to know that any of the men requesting a visit had more rights than any of the others. She simply tried to protect Gabrielle as best she could by keeping all of them at bay and aiding Gabrielle herself. Each man that had come in had all but ignored Hester, concentrating only on Gabrielle's slightly bedraggled and sleeping form. Feeling tired, Hester had moved to her own bed. The last visitor was Kevin, and when he turned to leave, Hester made a request. "Could you please let Dolly know I'm up here with Gabrielle?"

"I believe she knows you are here. Is there a problem?" Kevin inquired.

"No, it's just that all the girls are supplying favors to the men in return for our freedom. I would be helping if Gabrielle had not needed me."

"You may go, if that is your wish. I will stay with Gabrielle," he offered.

Hester blanched, then responded hesitantly. "Gabby may awaken, she should be with someone she knows. I will stay."

"Gabrielle is comfortable with me. You may enjoy your evening, rest assured, she will be taken care of." Kevin turned away from Hester, moving to sit on the edge of Gabrielle's bed.

"Don't sit there!" Hester said in a harsh whisper. "Your huge frame will cause her to waken." She sighed, "If you insist I leave, you may have my bed." Pulling the covers down and moving to get up, she sighed forlornly once again.

This time Kevin picked up on the attitude he had missed earlier. "You do not sound very anxious to resume your activities."

Hester answered, "I have little experience and am not very good at this line of work. I have been told with practice I will become better." She shuddered.

Attuned to her bitterness, Kevin inquired, "You do not enjoy sleeping with men?"

"If sleeping is what they did, I guess I wouldn't mind so much. It's just that with all the moaning and grunting they do, sometimes they don't hear me telling them to stop...." Where had that admission come from? She immediately tried to retract her statement. "I mean," she gulped "it's not really so bad, I am getting better." Hester groaned. This conversation was going from bad to worse. "I mean I like living here and....."

Kevin had never met a woman that did not enjoy physical contact with men. He was full of disbelief. Yet hearing her complain, watching her turn red in embarrassment and then listening to her fears, created concern. At that point he interrupted to offer her solace. "When we depart you are welcome to come along and travel as Gabrielle's maid," he offered kindly.

James entered just as Kevin made the offer to Hester. Hester looked up from her wringing hands, just in time to see James' stricken expression. Though James would never deny aid to the young girl, he was upset that Kevin would offer to have this harlot in Gabrielle's proximity. So he added, "Gabrielle will not require a maid, however, we have plenty of other positions for you to choose from. For your support of Gabrielle we will do anything in our power to help you start fresh. However, surely you can understand why your nearness may be a reminder of unpleasant times for Gabrielle?"

Hester bobbed her head up and down. "I would not want to hurt her, she has only been kind to me. I will think on your invitation. For now though, you should both go. The doctor said she should sleep through the night, so you two should rest also. I will remain at my post." She smiled and added,

"Thank you for your generous offer, it is rare to meet such wonderful gentlemen." So saying, she pulled the covers back up and dismissed them. Amused, Kevin and James looked at each other, once more at Gabrielle, and then retreated.

After shutting the door and heading down the corridor, James said, "What the hell was that about? Why would you want the girl about Gabrielle?"

"I did not insist she accompany us. She told me she does not like being a whore and I offered her a simple solution. Once she is gone from here, she can do anything."

"I suppose so," James grunted. "She does not enjoy servicing men?"

"I guess not. Though for the life of me I can't think of a more enjoyable way to spend the evening. As she has been so helpful to Gabrielle, I could do nothing less than offer her freedom."

"You were right to do so," James grudgingly admitted. "Eventually I would have done the same. Funny that she talked so freely to you. I have been in that room dozens of times since our arrival, she never said a word."

"She believed Dolly might be looking for her. I was simply nearby when she wanted a message passed. She seemed anxious about it, so I inquired."

"We will let Gabrielle decide where to place her. If Gabrielle does not regain her memory, no matter how much it annoys me to have Hester about, I will have to suffer it for Gabrielle's sake. If her memory is restored, Gabrielle can decide what is best. In the end, we will just have to see what happens tomorrow." Completely in agreement, the two men joined the others.

Gabrielle woke late the next morning. Following a cup of hot tea and toast, she asked for a bath. However, after James saw the bathing chamber down the hall, her simple request turned into a major event. First he had the old bath water carted out, and then he demanded the room be scrubbed from top to bottom. Only after his third inspection did he allow the young lads to finally fill the tub with clean water. Oblivious to all the uproar down the corridor, Gabrielle sat up in bed, gaily chatting with Hester.

Later, Gabrielle had never felt better in her life. She relaxed in the hot water as Hester thoroughly washed her hair. "You have the most beautiful long, black hair, Gabby," said Hester.

"You do not have to play the lady's maid for me," insisted Gabrielle. "I can tend myself, I'm sure you have dozens of things to do today."

"Gabby, you will need my help dressing, so hush and let me finish."

Gabrielle didn't utter another sound as she lay back to soak. She relished the attention Hester showered upon her. So much so, Gabrielle even stood uncomplaining while Hester combed through her thick tresses. "I still can't believe what a mess your hair and makeup had become. The huge globs in your hair caused most of the tangles you are grimacing from and I will never get the stains from this garment," said Hester.

"Yes, I was truly a mess. I should have cleaned up last night, I hope no one saw."

Hester did not have the heart to tell her that everyone that knew Gabrielle had been up to check on her last night, so she kept silent. Unfamiliar with both hairstyles and being a lady's maid, Hester simply braided it. Though it made her appear even more young and innocent, the style was not unbecoming to Gabrielle. Hester had found suitable hose, pantaloons, shift and camisole for Gabrielle to wear. Unfortunately nothing in the entire building was appropriate for a lady.

The dress that covered the most leg revealed the greatest amount of cleavage. The garment concealing the entire chest displayed the most leg. No matter what Hester had Gabrielle put on, there was nothing decent about it. In the end, Hester decided to cover Gabrielle's legs and add a shawl to disguise the bosom. With Gabrielle's toilette complete, Hester left the room to return unused items.

Gazing into the mirror, Gabrielle smiled at her own reflection. Standing there, she felt no inclination to cover her exposed bosom. She was passably pretty and Gabrielle was content with what she saw. She felt carefree and happy, humming when she eventually emerged from the bathing chamber.

Upon opening the door, she immediately quieted as she spotted three men standing at the doorway of her bedroom. Remaining a short distance away, Gabrielle was able to observe them, concluding that they had to be related. The resemblance was so pronounced she even deduced they must be brothers. All of them had coal black hair, amber eyes and beautiful white teeth. Each also appeared both strong and handsome.

Now that the taller man was not trying to smother her, she could easily admire him. For although the larger man had frightened her last night, today his seductive smile and twinkling eyes easily made her heart race. She slowly walked towards them.

Their first glimpse of Gabrielle included visions of smeared makeup, greasy, unkempt hair, streaked foundation and hysteria. The calm and appealing vision floating in their direction couldn't possibly be the same slovenly woman from the previous night.

In unison both Jared and Jake began pushing and shoving each other to get to Gabrielle first. James settled the commotion by easily thrusting them both aside and reaching her first. "How are you feeling?" he immediately inquired. Without waiting for an answer, he quickly took off his jacket and eased it upon Gabrielle's shoulders.

"I feel wonderful," Gabrielle exclaimed. Then she began to remove the jacket, and as she did, James said, "If you remove the jacket, I will be forced to skewer someone for ogling you."

As though to prove a point he turned to look at his brothers. Neither brother appeared to have any common sense, for when James glared at them, neither turned away from admiring her form. Thinking Gabrielle may be embarrassed, he nudged them into compliance and then returned his gaze to Gabrielle. She stood there smiling, beautiful as ever, totally oblivious to the men's carnal thoughts. "Hester went to get a shawl, then I will return your jacket. Until then, I thank you. Again I must say, I feel wonderful."

"You do?" asked a concerned Jake

"Well enough to travel?" wondered Jared, who was quite ready to leave.

"I do." She nodded, answering both questions at once. Walking to the doorway, she said, "However, I don't believe my accommodations are large enough to accommodate all three of you." Standing closest to James, she said to the other men, "Would you two mind waiting outside?"

"I had thought to introduce you to my brothers, would you prefer to wait?" he questioned.

"I'm sorry, I did not mean to appear rude. Of course, introduce your brothers."

The first man introduced was called Jared, though only slightly shorter than James he was not quite as muscular. His face had a more defined structure, a finely chiseled line. He seemed quiet, yet his eyes were twinkling with mischief. His hair was neatly trimmed and his clothing seemed far tidier than the other two.

The second brother's name was Jake. He was closer to Jared's height, yet possessed James' more muscular build. His skin tone was darker than the other two, revealing a great deal of time spent outdoors. His smile revealed a dimple, which only added to his warmth.

Though they all seemed intelligent and confident, within moments she had witnessed distinct differences in their characters, just by their interaction with each other. Jared and James both defended Jake, so Gabrielle guessed him to be the youngest. Jake and Jared, in several instances, turned to James for advice and consent. Therefore Gabrielle guessed him to be the oldest, leaving Jared as the middle brother. Later she was proven correct.

Similar in height, build and temperament, it was easy to compare them. These men supported, trusted and respected one another. Yet for all their similarities, to her, their differences seemed obvious and pronounced. Jake appeared the most outgoing and Jared seemed very polished. Yet it was the one who hadn't bothered to introduce himself that continued to hold her interest. At first she had been slightly miffed by his oversight. Later, as he gently held her arm, coaxed a laugh from her and completely charmed her, she easily forgave him. Hearing one of the brothers call him James eliminated her need to ask it. Finally she pleaded with them to excuse her, as she sailed past all three men. After entering the room she turned and crooked her finger at James and said, "Aren't you coming in?" then smiled a radiant smile.

Turning to his brothers, he said, "She must need to talk to me alone. Please ready the horses, I would be as far from here as quickly as possible." Grinning he added, "Though I may be a few moments." He entered and shut the door. Both brothers turned and grinned at each other, shrugged their shoulders, then went to do as they were bid.

"You look very well, I can't even tell you were hurt," said James.

"And you, my lord, are a very handsome man as well," replied Gabrielle.

"I've told you before, no formal titles. James is the name I like to hear from your soft lips. Say it," he demanded.

"James," she said seductively.

He inhaled her scent and moved closer. Pulling her gently into his arms, she eagerly complied. His mouth hungry for a taste of her, fastened upon hers. It had been so long, too long. He could not get enough. He pulled her even closer, molding her easily in his embrace. She kissed him in return as though she had long craved him. Tearing his lips from her mouth to trail kisses upon her neck, he gently ran his hand over her bosom. Touching a nipple, she shuddered in response. He realized at that moment she had not put up a struggle of any kind. She was his for the taking. As he continued to hold and fondle her luscious body, he looked about the room. This dingy, dirty room was not the place he was going to first make love to Gabrielle. He needed to regain some control and composure. He tried to pull away, yet she had other ideas. He had to use both physical and mental strength to get her to stop. He liked the fact that she was no longer shy with him and wondered if they would make it back to Helena's before he took her. He sighed, pushing her away a final time. He was determined her first time would not be rushed. Taking a deep breath, he tried to come to grips with his emotions.

"Why are you pushing me away?" Gabrielle inquired.

"I would prefer to leave and have our time together in a more private and romantic place," he said.

"Where do you intend to take me? How long do you intend to be?"

"We will go back to Helena's."

"Helena's," she repeated. Yes, the name was familiar. A scattered vision of Helena's bolted through her subconscious. She nodded. "Yes, Helena's."

"How long until you can be ready to leave?" James inquired.

"Are we going to finish what we have started?" she asked mischievously.

"Not until we reach Helena's. Then I will love you the entire night through, if you are up to it," he responded.

"It's not me that has to be up to it!" laughed Gabrielle

That response was one expected of Kathleen, not the young, innocent Gabrielle he knew so well. Though she had lost some of her shyness, had her experiences caused her to become brazen? "Oh, I will be up to it," he answered cautiously, awaiting her response. Her arms reached up and held tight around his neck, as her mouth began to rain kisses upon his face. Without notice her kisses found his mouth and once again became deep and intoxicating. Reveling in the feeling once more, it became harder and harder to think straight. As he dragged her over to the small bed, he once again got hold of himself. His original intention to gauge her response and compare her to Kathleen became lost. Straightening, he said, "How long before you can be ready? As we are not finishing this until we get to Helena's."

"Then I am ready now," she smiled.

"Then let's go!" He grabbed her by the hand and practically dragged her from the room. The door reverberated on its hinges as it smacked against the wall upon their departure. Her feet barely hit the floor as they headed first down the corridor, then the stairs. Sparing no time for Gabrielle to glance about and recall events, he threw a cape about her shoulders and had her out the door in no time.

While James had had his hands full with Gabrielle, the others had been busy. His brothers, also eager to be off, had complied with his earlier request to ready their departure. It had not been easy to accomplish so much so quickly, just the fact that they had attested to both their fortitude and determination.

The first problem to arise had been Stuart's adamant refusal to ride in either a wagon or coach. Even after the doctor had reminded Stuart that riding horseback could tear open the wound Stuart would not change his mind. After using every argument they could think of, they pleaded. That, too, failed. Finally, their only option available, they appealed to his baser instincts. They used the women. Only after they blackmailed him into protecting the women also riding in the coach did Stuart finally relent to their badgering. So by the time Derek and several of Kevin's men returned from obtaining a coach, he was agreeable.

"I still can't believe you convinced him to give up his horse," said Derek.

"You'd believe it had you been here to go through it!" said an exasperated Jared. "He damn near wore us down. We had about run out of ideas when

Jake thought to appeal to his pride."

Jake smiled, "We all knew his injury would open just by getting on the damn horse. It was just a matter of out foxing him. When we told him he would be guarding the women, he accepted the responsibility. I nearly choked, he was so solemn. The reality is, they will be nursing him on the journey!"

"That was very clever. I was very worried about him. I have known him a long time and in all that time I had never seen him lowered by another. It was hard to admit, giant that he is, he is only human. I feared telling Helena he was no longer with us. Thankfully all is well," sighed Derek.

"We have yet to be thankful, for it is a long trip," sighed Jared.

"It will be over before you know it! Now let's get moving," Jake said as he slapped each of them on the back.

Having their discussion earlier, Kevin and Scott had already agreed that the viscount would disappear in a similar fashion to that of the sheriff. If Scott could get him to confess or divulge anything at all about Gabrielle's father, it would lighten their load considerably.

Scott and his men were long gone by sunrise, keeping everyone but Kevin in the dark. Not until the viscount had been dealt with would Scott and his men arrive at Helena's.

The travelers were completely ready by the time James and Gabrielle joined them. Previously James had thought to carry Gabrielle on his own horse, but after Kevin drew him aside, he agreed that she ride in the coach. It had been pure selfishness on his part to want her near anyway. After talking with Kevin he admitted it was not practical. Even Jared pointed out the discomfort for both Gabrielle and James. Yet at the moment, he didn't want to be sensible. He just wanted her near. With a curt nod he turned from the others and accompanied her to the coach. After a lingering caress, he shut the door and climbed upon his horse. Rather than ride in the front of the group, as was his usual want, James was content to join his brothers and several of Kevin's men and take up the rear.

Their route already planned, they hastily agreed on signals. A slight cool breeze would accompany them, adding discomfort for the women. Yet Kevin smiled, watching his breath as he exhaled, for the air felt good upon his skin. He and his men came from Scotland, where this temperature still wafting about meant summer.

Confident in command, comfortable in the saddle, and content with this chore, Kevin's horse edged forward. Kevin's distinguished form, easily spotted from the rest of the group, took the lead. With a sudden shout and a brief signal, they were off!

Deep in thought, they had traveled miles before James realized Scott and his men were not among their group. It was even longer before he found out why.

In the swaying, uncomfortable coach, the women were busy trying to make Stuart relax. He in turn, would offer them reassurance for their safety. Then a wheel would hit a large rut and each of the women would fly across the interior, only to slam into the other side. Stuart's large frame kept his body solidly in place. Yet even his size could not keep him safe. Between his shoulders being slammed against the wall and the women falling on him numerous times, his wound ripped open. It would have been quite comical to watch if he weren't in pain, Stuart decided.

After Stuart had dosed off, Hester whispered, "The doc didn't expect him to last this long." Explaining "He had put some laudanum in his drink earlier."

"It is possible Stuart would not allow himself to sleep, feeling responsible for our welfare. I suppose the medicine finally overpowered his determination. What happened to him, anyway?"

"He was hurt in a bar fight. A fight occurring during your rescue," Hester volunteered.

Gabrielle grimaced. "I suppose I am in debt to him too."

Hester smiled. "I guess you are, though I am sure you will find a way to repay him. Everyone was concerned for your welfare. I bet you didn't realize what a popular girl you are. Are you feeling well?"

"I really do feel fine, just a slight twinge now and again. Though that handsome James does not seem to want to give me time to heal. He has been all over me since this morning." She sighed. "I can hardly complain, for when I am with him I can think of little else."

"What do you remember from before your accident?" questioned Hester.

"My head starts to hurt when I try real hard to recall anything. The doctor said not to ask a lot of questions and let things gradually come back." Reaching out and grabbing Hester's hand, she squeezed it for reassurance. "I remember quite clearly that you are my friend. I also remember bits and pieces of this place called Helena's, that we go to." She paused. "I keep visioning a beautiful woman with red hair and startling green eyes. I believe she, too, is my good friend, though her name eludes me. I just know that we worked together there." Gabrielle hesitated. "My head begins to pain me, let's rest a bit. Stuart may need attention later on."

"I promised that Kevin fellow, that I would signal him if Stuart's injury should open. Though we've stopped the blood flow for now, should I signal Kevin?"

320

"We will wait until the wound bleeds again or Stuart awakens to ask. Otherwise I think it best to get as close to home as possible."

"If Stuart does not agree to stopping at the nearest inn, if his wound reopens, I am to plead fatigue. Then he will agree for my sake. It all has something to do with his pride and our lack of skill in healing."

Gabrielle giggled. "I suppose I will owe Kevin too." She pulled the blanket up and snuggled deeper within.

"By now, you probably owe half of England," exaggerated Hester.

Gabrielle pondered her problem. She could not accept how the debt of her freedom was weighing her down. Before she could go on with her life she needed to have a clean slate and be done. She could not remember if she had any assets, though she guessed not. Or she would not have been at Franklin's. Her head hurting, she closed her eyes to rest.

The journey was arduous. Every rut, bump and stone causing continuous discomfort. The carriage they had been able to obtain was a far cry from luxurious. The seats hard, the walls thin, the springs broken. Thank heaven for the small luxury of the brazier, or they would have all frozen.

Chapter 18

As they approached the castle, Kevin's men began to dismount and set up camp. They would remain on guard outside. The clip clop of the remaining horses and cumbersome carriage were still enough to cause a racket as they crossed the drawbridge. The group was guided towards the right upon entrance, into the formal courtyard reserved for guests. Though Kevin had sent a messenger on ahead, it was still a surprise to each of them to see a large group gathered on the steps upon their arrival.

Immediately upon dismount, stable hands quickly took charge of the horses. Unconcerned with the flurry of activities, James threw the reins to one young lad and headed directly over to Gabrielle. Arriving just as she was about to step out of the carriage, James quickly circled her waist with his hands. Using the ensuing havoc all around, he let his hands linger longer than proper, about her form.

Gabrielle's heart fluttered, simply by his nearness. The gesture of aiding her from the vehicle and the placement of his hands upon her had practically driven her over the edge. She was somehow sure she had never felt this way before. As he lowered her to the ground she stared into his eyes, which were fastened on her in return, his smile provocative, the gleam in his eye promising as he released her for a moment, then shifted, only to pull her once again close to his side. Standing at his side, she took a moment to gather her thoughts. Moments later she was ripped from his embrace by a whirlwind, spinning around only to see Kathleen. They both screamed at once, yet in the melee of so many visitors, no one noticed. The girls were now both jumping up and down, hugging each other. "I am so happy to see you! You have no idea how worried I have been!" shrieked Kathleen.

Gabrielle knew instinctively that this woman was important to her. Holding her, she felt strength and comfort.

Over her head Kathleen spotted Kevin, so she whispered, "Catch up with you later. Bye." Then she flew off in the opposite direction as she screamed, "Kevin!" and went running to him.

Trying to catch her breath, she stood for a moment. James, at her side once again, said, "Kathleen is rather unpredictable."

Gabrielle looked up at James. Kathleen, of course, how had she forgotten Kathleen's name?"

James was eager to get inside. He extended his arm to escort her and gain entrance to the castle. As they approached the steps, they reached Maude. She was embracing Gabrielle before she knew what was happening. Gabrielle did not recognize the older woman, but did not have the heart to say so. The old woman seemed so affectionate and friendly. Nor did she recognize the exquisite woman standing on her right, though Gabrielle realized they must all be her friends. She was determined to appear fine, so she smiled and hugged them all in return.

Helena became suspicious as Gabrielle continued to hug everyone, even the guards. Her eyebrows rose in question as she looked at James. He whispered, "She has been through very traumatic events, she is simply excited to be back." He appeared to watch her like a hawk and Helena wanted to believe him, so she let it go. They were just about to enter the castle when Molly and Polly both came running outside. Looking all over, they finally spotted Stuart being helped out of the coach. With shouts of glee one moment and groans of sympathy the next, they led the men helping Stuart to his room. In short order the bedlam from the courtyard faded and they were all shown to their rooms.

James had been leery of letting Gabrielle go, but the women were headed to the baths. So he joined the men and did the same. Helena had promised everyone a feast upon his or her arrival in the dining room.

The women were led to the baths above the kitchen. Kathleen was practically giddy upon their arrival. With the arrival of both her best friend and husband, she fairly glowed. Gabrielle, on the other hand, remained quiet and reserved. As the attendants helped them out of their clothes, little Serena made mention of that very fact. "Usually Gabrielle is the chatty one, and you," she pointed to Kathleen, "are the quiet one. Now your roles are reversed. You are going to give us all headaches, trying to keep things straight around here," she muttered.

Kathleen hadn't even noticed Gabrielle's silence until Serena mentioned it. "Gabrielle, whatever is the matter? Serena is right; usually you can't keep silent for five minutes. Do you feel all right?" Kathleen inquired.

Following a quick steam, each girl had been scraped of all dirt and sweat and sent to the next room to be scrubbed. As they each moved over towards the drains and the two attendants began to soap their bodies, Gabrielle responded, "I had a bit of confusion after my fall, but I am happy to say that except for an occasional headache I feel very good." She let out a long sigh, "Oh, you've no idea how glad I am to be back working here, as opposed to

The White Wolf!" she said.

Not exactly the answer Kathleen was looking for, though she was glad for Gabrielle's good health. Still, Gabrielle's answer seemed strange, and why hadn't she said a word about James? Hesitantly Kathleen responded, "Yes, I'm sure you are, but I thought you would be in a hurry to return to London."

"I was in London too?" questioned Gabrielle.

Realizing Gabrielle was having more difficulty with her memory than she seemed to let on, Kathleen slowly said, "Yes." Kathleen observed the perplexed look on Gabrielle's face. "You are certainly welcome here as long as you wish. Talk to Helena, there will certainly be no problem."

"I should hope not!" came the surprised reply. "I have always been a good worker. She should appreciate good help." Then Gabrielle casually lifted both arms into the air as the young girl had finished scraping away the dirt and had begun to rinse.

Kathleen's eyes popped out of her head, she really looked at Gabrielle this time. Standing there, completely nude and not the least embarrassed. Kathleen suddenly began to sense something was very wrong. "You don't seem very embarrassed. Have you become used to your body being on display?"

Gabrielle sighed, "It would be practically impossible to live here and have a shred of modesty. Why the sudden concern?"

"You just seem so comfortable, when you used to be so ill at ease."

"Kathleen, you are hardly one to talk. For though we are both standing here naked, it is you that reveal so much."

This caused Kathleen to laugh.

"Gabrielle, after your harsh journey, maybe you would prefer to have a massage before entering the pool. This will truly allow your body to relax," insisted Serena.

"I thought that followed the bath. Am I wrong?" asked Gabrielle.

"Though we will only use the oils and lotions after your baths, we have many techniques that will allow your battered body additional relief." Watching Gabrielle's hesitation, yet catching the yearning expression upon her face, Serena changed her tactic and simply patted the bench and said, "Come, lie up here."

Kathleen and Gabrielle each stretched out upon the benches for a massage. As the attendants pushed, pulled and massaged every sore muscle, their bodies melted like butter. "Later, after your baths, we will rub exotic scents deep into your skin. The softness and smell will be enchanting." Selena spoke softly.

As time wore on, talk lessened. A short time later Kathleen believed she had come up with the only possible reason Gabrielle no longer seemed shy. "Gabrielle?"

No response.

"Gabrielle?"

"Hum?"

"Gabrielle?"

"Gabby."

"I am not." Kathleen huffed.

"Am not what?" asked Gabrielle.

"Gabby!" responded Kathleen.

"Thanks, but you don't have to shout," said Gabrielle.

"What the heck are you talking about?" asked Kathleen.

"I wasn't talking about anything. You started all this."

Both remained silent. Finally Kathleen started again. "Gabrielle..."

"Why can't you remember my name? I like to be called Gabby."

Kathleen literally let her mouth fall open. "Gabby?" she said in exasperation.

"What?" answered Gabrielle.

Oh, this conversation was going no place fast. Moving past the weird name thing, Kathleen tried once again to find out the reason for Gabrielle's lack of modesty. "Have you allowed James to make love to you yet?"

Gabrielle sighed, "The way he hovers, I can't believe I have. Though my memories are foggy."

"Gabrielle, with a man like James, confusion or not, you would know if you slept with him!" Kathleen huffed indignantly.

"Now why are you feeling so put out?"

"I'm not put out, I'm perplexed. Are you or are you not still a virgin?" Just as she demanded the answer, Kathleen was sorry she asked, immediately covering her mouth with her hand. Remembering Gabrielle's recent imprisonment, anything could have happened. "Never mind, I'm sorry. I didn't mean that. Let's talk about something else."

"No, I want to talk about it. You know I have not been a virgin for a very long time. Hell, I wouldn't have worked here, now would I have?"

"Gabrielle ... ah ... err ... Gabby, what exactly do you do here?"

"How funny you should ask, when you were the one to teach me all I know," muttered Gabrielle.

As the attendants led them over to the small pool of water, they sat down upon the bench in the water. Kathleen took the opportunity to hold Gabrielle's hand and say, "If there is anything you need to tell me, I am here for you. I'm sure your abduction could not have been an easy thing to go through. I was not aware you had been physically hurt. I am here to confide in," consoled Kathleen.

"What are you talking about?" said Gabrielle.

"Gabby." The name sounded both unfamiliar and coarse, yet Kathleen continued. "If you are no longer a virgin, there must be questions you have. Concerns?"

"No, I have no concerns."

"What about James?"

"What about James?"

"Does he have concerns?"

"Why should he?" Searching Kathleen's troubled face, Gabrielle questioned, "Do you want him for yourself?"

"No! I don't want him for myself. He is yours!" was the indignant reply.

"My customer today, yours tomorrow, someone else's the next day. So?"

"Cus–customer?" Kathleen said, astonished.

"Yes, customer. Though he is quite a fine specimen. Perhaps he will want me for two nights."

"James?"

"Yes, James?"

"Gabby, are you saying you work here and James is your customer?"

"What have we been talking about?" muttered Gabrielle.

Kathleen suddenly realized what was wrong! Why Gabrielle was no longer a modest miss. The reason she wanted to be called Gabby. Why she tried to sound coarse and experienced, her attempt to imitate loose women.

Gabrielle believed she was one of Helena's girls! Kathleen needed to get out of there fast! She needed to get help. Who knew what would happen if Gabrielle insisted on going to work? "Gabby, I have to leave and take care of something." As Kathleen began to rise from the water, Gabrielle, too, followed suit. Kathleen gave her a playful shove, saying, "No, you stay here and relax. After your ordeal I don't want you to do anything but pamper yourself. When you finish here, take a nice long nap, and then I will meet you for dinner. Does that sound agreeable to you?"

Gabrielle couldn't think of anything she'd rather do, so she eagerly complied. "After my rest, I'm going to see to my hair and wardrobe. Helena said dinner would be in the private dining room about seven. If you don't catch me sooner, I will meet you there."

Kathleen nodded as she threw on a robe and darted out of the room.

Meanwhile the men had all gathered in the roman baths. After undressing them, the attendants brought them into the steam area. There they were left to lounge upon the benches, while the attendants retrieved their utensils. A short time later, when each man had begun to perspire the nubile young maidens returned. Each attendant began by scraping the sweat and dirt away with their strigils. The men were rinsed, followed by another scrubbing, then rinsed again. The beautiful attendants took the time to par the nails on both their hands and feet before leading them to the baths. Seated in the large pool of water, each man had a beautiful attendant hovering close by. Though neither James nor Kevin was seeking a bedmate, they did enjoy the lighthearted attention.

Jared, Jake and Derek however, were immersed in sexual gratification. Even so, when James and Kevin left the pool, the three younger men followed as James and Kevin headed to the benches. Now all of them were simply lounging about the area, Derek, Jake and Jared all seated upon separate couches, each now holding two voluptuous beauties, James and Kevin stretched out upon the benches being massaged with various scented oils. As the young, fair-haired beauty climbed upon the table, then up on the buttocks of James, she continued to rub sandalwood oil into his skin. From his sleeping position, with his head upon his forearms, James looked up at her boldness. Catching Kevin's raised eyebrow at the action, James returned his gaze with a shrug. Returning his head to the resting position he decided to enjoy the ministrations of the attendant.

Though his head was between the bosom of one girl and his hand busy with the other girl, Jake took a moment to inquire. "James, you think Gabrielle is going to be all right?"

James lifted his head to respond, "Gabrielle is going to be just fine. She appears slightly more amorous than before." He grinned, "Though I don't feel that is a bad thing." He paused. "Gabrielle even made it through the nightmare of her kidnapping without being raped. We can only thank God for that. Once the bump on her head fades, we will proceed with our plans."

Finishing up with the muscles in his shoulders, the small blonde slid down James' back as the men continued their conversation. Failure to entice James led her to insist the mousy brown-haired girl currently massaging Kevin trade places with her. As the men continued, the girl climbed upon Kevin's back. As James raised his eyebrow in question, this time Kevin simply shrugged.

"You are so lucky. Gabrielle is a wonderful woman," insisted Jared.

"I realize that. I also appreciate your saying so. She will be your sister-in-law. I would have us all get along," said James.

The men sat enjoying both the women and the solitude when suddenly the door opened, slamming against the wall. Racing into the baths was a beautiful, nearly naked woman, with a trail of thick red hair flying behind her. She grinned with amusement as Kevin's face turned red at being caught with a naked young girl upon his back. However, Kathleen had neither the time nor the inclination to play the jealous wife. For now, her priority was Gabrielle. Trying to locate these fellows, she had already been away from Gabrielle far longer than anticipated. Scurrying over to James, she stopped as she reached his side. Breathing heavy, she took a moment to catch her breath. "Ja … James. It's Gabrielle."

"What! What has happened?" answered a concerned James.

"Have you talked to Gabrielle? I mean really talked to her?" His face void of expression, Kathleen knew she must continue. Unable to find an easy way, she simply blurted out, "James, Gabrielle believes she is a prostitute."

Sitting up, James demanded, "What the hell did you say? What does that mean?"

"Just listen, will you! I don't have time to stand here and soothe your ruffled feathers. I have to get back to her side so she doesn't do anything foolish."

"What are you talking about? What would she do?" James was now even more confused than when Kathleen started.

"Her memory is in worse shape than you first thought. She thinks she was a whore at The White Wolf. She believes when she worked here at Helena's that she was one of the girls! Don't you understand? She thinks you're her customer."

"How the hell did she come to that conclusion?" he insisted.

"She said since she's known you, that you have been hovering about her. She believes it's because you want to bed her."

"Well, she's got that right," he muttered "How did she become so off track? How could I not notice? Are you sure about this?" he persisted.

"I'm damn sure! I have no idea why you didn't notice. At first even I did not know there was a problem. However, upon closer questioning she revealed her thoughts. Though of course, she has no idea there is a problem. She states things quite matter-of-factly. She will sleep with you one or two nights, someone else another. She even asked if I wanted to have you, for she thought you a magnificent specimen." Kathleen sighed. "Whatever shall we do?"

Deciding to take action quickly, James jumped off the table. "You go and stay as close to her as possible. Don't leave her side for a moment," he directed.

As he hit the floor, Kathleen tried to remain impassive, but James definitely was a great specimen. She tried to keep her eyes averted; yet the smile on her face clearly reflected the fact that she had not. After viewing James' manhood, Kathleen quickly headed over to Kevin before she said something improper to James. The young girl had long ago slid off his derriere, even so Kevin wondered if he would hear about it from Kathleen. Instead, she boldly looked him in the eye, letting him know she was not oblivious to what was going on. To his surprise she demanded no explanations and instead gave him a long, sensuous kiss. Then she gave him a quick slap to his buttocks and raced from the room laughing. As she hurried towards the doorway, her scanty robe flew behind her. Exposed were her huge bosom, firm buttocks and shapely legs. He smiled as he watched her exit. Then he noticed the others were also observing the fleeing vision. Loudly he cleared his throat so as to focus attention upon himself. A simple glare and shake of the head conveyed his meaning to the others. Heeding his warning, their eyes reverted to their own escorts. Though they all did stifle a laugh that Kevin turned out to be the jealous one.

Breaking the awkward silence, Kevin said, "Well, now you know the reason she is no jealous screaming shrew. A girl with a body like that has no the need." Then he continued, "You will forget what you ha seen and not speak of it again."

"She is a handful, I'll grant you that. Don't forget she also won't stay where she's put or do as she's told," muttered James.

"That was you she did no listen to, not me!" answered Kevin.

James' response was a look of disbelief.

"Well, we won't ha any boring evenings, that's for sure," muttered Kevin.

"I sure thought she was here to stop your fun, that time," shouted Jake.

The others all laughed in response, turning their attention once again to James.

Jared inquired, "Now what will you do?"

"I'm not sure, but I will come up with something," said James. With his robe now wrapped about him, he headed to the door recently vacated by Kathleen. "You fellows feel free to enjoy your bath and massage, who knows when you will have this opportunity again. I must make plans. I will meet you for dinner." Then he disappeared out the door.

Only the sounds of her footsteps slapping against the cold stone steps, echoed through the stairwell. Rushing from the Roman baths, she reached her room. Spending only moments to throw on a simple dress, she quickly headed back to Gabrielle. Returning down the same dimly lit stairway she came up she wondered how James would solve this dilemma. Then Kathleen's thoughts turned to her own husband. She laughed at the memory of finding little Juliet upon Kevin's form. Confident of Kevin's devotion, it was still reassuring for her to see his discomfort at being found in a compromising position. Even with nothing to be guilty of, his cheeks had fairly glowed with embarrassment. Upon her return to the baths, where Kathleen had left her, she was disappointed to find Gabrielle long gone.

Knowing Gabrielle had intended to do her hair and wardrobe before dinner, Kathleen headed to the costume area. No one had seen her. Kathleen was determined not to leave Gabrielle on her own, so she continued on her quest.

Heading over to see if Gabrielle was having her hair styled, once again Kathleen was disappointed. No one had seen Gabrielle or anyone fitting her description. No matter where she went, Kathleen ran into bad luck. Wardrobe, shoes, jewelry, none had seen the raven beauty. Kathleen failed to find Gabrielle. Running from room to room and floor to floor was getting her nowhere. Kathleen knew Gabrielle intended to meet for dinner and hoped for the best till then. With no alternative at hand, Kathleen headed back to attend her own toilette.

James was dressing in his formal attire, when the response to his request arrived. Eager to be off, James quickly grabbed his jacket and followed the servant to Helena's office.

Helena was already there, dressed in soft blue velvet. Though the beautiful amethyst gems about her neck caused one's eyes to stray to her cleavage, it was her beautiful well-rounded bosom that kept the attention focused there. After all, James was only human, as appreciative of a fine form as the next man.

Her eyes twinkled with mischief as she said, "How long would you like me to stand here?"

Shaken from his momentary bewitchment, he grinned, "Helena, you are as ravishing as ever. Thank you for meeting with me." He extended his arms to pull her closer.

Her reception of him was equally warm as she easily embraced him. Leading him into her office, she shut the door for privacy. Explaining Gabrielle's situation and his own solution, James and Helena became deeply immersed in discussion within moments.

A short time later a knock at the door interrupted their talk. As Gabrielle announced it was she, James jumped up to hide. Quickly moving off to the side, he concealed himself behind the thick drapes. Helena opened the door and her smile froze in place. Gabrielle was dressed in a most revealing outfit. In addition to her garish wardrobe, Gabrielle's face was thick with cosmetics. Though James had told Helena about the situation, it was entirely different to view Gabrielle so garbed. Leading Gabrielle inside, Helena motioned for her to take the seat so recently vacated by James. As Helena retraced her steps to her own seat, she viewed Gabrielle intently.

Wearing a vibrant red wig, the large curls covered most of Gabrielle's graceful heart-shaped face. Including a tight corset to her ensemble, it pushed her enchanting breasts upon display. The cream-colored blouse was worn off the shoulders, with the top two buttons undone. It was made of French gauze material and completely see-through. The skirt Gabrielle had chosen was a beautiful soft shade of green held up by a wide black belt with laces. The skirt was made with many folds, to easily float up while dancing. The cut of the fabric was longer on one side than the other, revealing a tantalizing bit of thigh.

As a businesswoman, Helena could market this woman and make a fortune. As a friend, Helena saw the dilemma firsthand. For this young woman was fascinating and more so for her innocence was tantalizing. Sitting down, she let Gabrielle begin.

"I wanted you to know I am feeling well and am ready to work," said Gabrielle.

"Gabrielle, I am glad you are well."

"Gabby," interrupted Gabrielle.

"Gabby?" questioned Helena.

"Yes, you must have forgotten. I prefer my nickname," was Gabrielle's response.

"Oh," a perplexed response.

"Before we get down to business. I would like to inquire as to my friend's whereabouts."

"I believe Kathleen is even now searching for you," smiled Helena.

"No, I mean Hester," replied Gabrielle.

"I spoke with her earlier and she seems inclined to stay. She has been sorely abused, so we will take her recovery slowly."

Gabrielle seemed confused by this answer. "Can I see her?"

"She has been given something to sleep, you will be able to spend time with her tomorrow."

This time Gabrielle answered, "Oh," and nothing more.

Returning to their earlier conversation, Helena began, "I am happy you are feeling better. However, wouldn't you, too, like to rest a bit?"

"No, nothing like getting right back on that horse," laughed Gabrielle.

She sounded nothing like herself, thought Helena.

"I'm ready to take on a customer as soon as you see fit," said Gabrielle.

James had been correct, Gabrielle believed herself to be a working girl.

How to correct all this? "Is tonight soon enough?" Helena tried to frighten her off.

"Tonight?" Gabrielle sounded surprised.

Maybe she would become shocked into her senses. "Yes, tonight. Why, is that bad?"

"No, it's just that tonight we have that dinner to celebrate everyone's safety, remember?" Thinking of one last interlude with James, she sighed, "I just didn't realize you would need me tonight."

Again Helena tried to get Gabrielle to forego the idea of sleeping with customers. "Gabrielle...." At the look on Gabrielle's face, Helena started again. "Gabby, there is no need for you to work tonight. There is no need for you to work ever. We could find something else for you to do. Or you could do nothing. Better yet, there are people in London that would care for you. I do not want you to feel your only recourse is to sleep with men. You have only to say no," Helena directed.

At first, remembering how James made her feel, Gabrielle was about to decline.

At Gabrielle's hesitation, Helena was hopeful. And as each moment passed, Helena started to believe Gabrielle had changed her mind.

Gabrielle believed she was in debt to all those around her. So, though Gabrielle hardly sounded excited, she finally answered Helena, "I am ready to work. We all do what we must." Then wistfully she added, "Though in truth I did enjoy the company of my earlier companion." Gabrielle added, "However, one must deal in reality. And I am determined to carry on." Shaking off both her case of desire for James and her melancholy attitude, she said, "What do you have in mind for me?"

Helena had hoped Gabrielle would give up this nonsense. Now she would have to agree to James' plan or Gabrielle would become ruined. Either way, if Gabrielle regained her memory, Helena was taking a huge risk with Gabrielle's feelings. With little hesitation Helena decided to go forward. "Your fantasy will take place this evening. I'm sorry you will miss the dinner; however, a customer has requested you. When you leave here, go up to wardrobe. This evening's list has been posted, they will give you your proper costume. From there you will receive direction to which fantasy room to report to." Helena tried once more. "For the last time, are you sure you don't want to change your mind? If you are determined to earn your keep, there are any number of other positions I can assign you."

Gabrielle nodded. "I am sure."

As Helena walked around the desk to give Gabrielle a hug, James could not stop himself from taking a peek around the curtain he still hid behind. Seeing Gabrielle dressed like that, he was dumbstruck. Though looking quite different than usual, she was as desirable as ever. The little bit of clothing and different-colored hair did nothing but tease his manhood. The sheer materials of the blouse put her round, perky breasts and erect nipples on display. She was dressed so alluring that if he didn't take this well in hand immediately, someone would attempt to ravish her. And he had been through too much to let her slip through his fingers again. If she didn't remember him, he would create new memories to bind them.

Shutting the door behind the exiting Gabrielle, Helena sighed. "You can come out," she said to James.

"Now you will co-operate?" he asked.

"Yes, I see no other way," she responded.

"Have someone send for me when all is ready. I must go talk to Kevin," James announced as he strode out the door.

After sending a servant to carry out her orders, Helena returned to her chair. Sitting behind the desk, staring out the window, she pondered. In fact, so absorbed in thought was she that Helena never heard the door, or the entrance of Kathleen. It wasn't until Kathleen shook her shoulder, that Helena returned to the present.

"You sent for me?" questioned Kathleen.

"Yes." Helena sighed. "I am well aware you no longer work here. Yet it has come to my attention that a fantasy in the making must have your presence."

"What you ask is impossible!" interrupted Kathleen. "It is not simply that I no longer work here, but that I am now married!" she screeched.

"I am aware of both. I would not put you in a position that would jeopardize your happiness. This is regarding Gabrielle. By the way, what is this Gabby business?"

"I spoke with Hester earlier. It is what she called Gabrielle. Apparently Gabrielle can remember recent events, yet is unable to recall old times without prodding. Though Hester said Gabrielle told her flashes of memories come up for a moment or two. Then without completion they fade again from Gabrielle's mind. I am worried."

"I am too. I have never encountered this illness called amnesia. I can only hope what we do is for the best. What is your opinion of Hester?"

"She has been exposed to sex and the business of it from an early age. She does not enjoy it and has experienced pain. I believe she will be an asset in your business, though she would rather be a servant."

"You are indeed observant. I, too, am of the opinion that while she can talk a good game and is not shy, she is indeed uncomfortable with the act of bedding a man. More than likely after she has had some rest I will have her work on setting up illusions. She gives the impression she wants to stay and would prefer not to work in the kitchens. She seems pleasant enough."

"You did not send for me to talk of Hester. What is going on?"

"Gabrielle will be working a fantasy tonight," she began.

Kathleen interrupted again, "You can't do that. She is not in her right mind."

"Do not treat me as a fool," Helena said, before Kathleen could carry on. "What I have in mind is for her sake. However, she would be quite upset if you were not there. Now have a seat and I will fill you in."

Gabrielle's first stop was the wig room, to return the wig she had picked out earlier. That she had spent nearly an hour trying on wigs till she found just what she had wanted didn't seem to matter to anyone.

Next she went back to the makeup room, where she had to endure their teasing. For the girl that had applied the cosmetics had complained that Gabrielle had demanded too much powder and rouge the first time around. But Gabrielle had insisted she wanted that look. So now that it had been rejected, Lynn was giving Gabrielle the good-natured ribbing she deserved. So Gabrielle's face was washed and scrubbed, then she even sat through a mud treatment. This time Gabrielle was not allowed to have her way in anything, for her new instructions included no makeup. That did not make sense to Gabrielle. How was she supposed to tantalize a customer and perform her job if she didn't add cosmetics to become attractive? Gabrielle argued and argued until Lynn finally relented and let her have a small amount of salve for her lips.

Having her hair styled had not been a picnic. After trying to stuff it under a wig this morning and facial ingredients falling into it this afternoon, it was now a tangled mess.

Sitting on the stool while Dorothy combed out her hair, Gabrielle began to fidget.

"Stop wiggling," said Dorothy.

"I can't help it, you're hurting me. Can't I just wear a wig?"

"My instructions for you said to leave the hair loose. Maybe your customer doesn't know how long and thick this stuff is," muttered Dorothy. "No matter, I just do what I'm told."

"Do I go to wardrobe next?" inquired Gabrielle

"Yes, then you can stop pestering me."

Discomforted by Dorothy's attitude, Gabrielle remained seated quietly until she was finished. Dorothy had tried to untangle her hair and become crabby.

Entering the costume area, Cecilia had Gabrielle up on a stool moments later. Without a word the silent woman had her measured and dressed. Gabrielle thought the lovely white dress beautiful beyond belief. No corset was needed, for the stays were sewn in. The strapless dress effectively held her chest in while allowing enough exposure to allure her customer. The bodice of her dress was made of silk brocade. The skirt had an overskirt of seed pearls, tied at the waist with a silk white sash. The long white gloves with twenty-eight pearl buttons added simple elegance. Matching white kid slippers peeked from beneath her gown to complete the ensemble. Cecilia smiled and waved her along, motioning her to the gem room.

Woman were scattered about the room, polishing and repairing the jewelry worn by everyone in the castle. Activity in the gem room came to a halt as Gabrielle entered. Nan took charge and found Gabrielle a strand of pearls with matching earbobs. The effect was both elegant and simple. The ensemble complete, Gabrielle was a vision. Nan personally led her down the corridor where Maude was waiting.

As she made her entrance, Maude quickly took stock. Gabrielle's long raven tresses had been left loose, they fell well below her hips. Her long-lashed dark brown eyes appeared large and luminous. Though petite and slender, her bosom was delightfully rounded and carried off the strapless gown perfectly. She stopped directly in front of Maude and waited.

"You look lovely, my dear," said Maude.

"Thank you. Everything feels so rich and sinful. Now I realize why I chose this lifestyle." Gabrielle smiled. "Can you tell me about my job this evening?"

It almost broke Maude's heart to carry on the charade. For Gabrielle appeared even more innocent than the day they had first met. Last time her naïveté had been from youth, this time it was due to her confused mind. She squared her shoulders, gathered her courage and bellowed out Gabrielle's assignment. "Your client has requested a wedding fantasy." Observing Gabrielle's skepticism, Maude continued. "I know you have never played a bride before, but you have only just returned and the client wanted you."

"Am I to understand a wedding fantasy rivals a true wedding?" Gabrielle questioned.

"Yes. You are to appear slightly confused and very naïve."

"I should be able to pull that off," chuckled Gabrielle. "For everything seems new to me."

Maude sensed Gabrielle's bewilderment and offered to let her off the hook. "If for any reason you do not feel up to it, you have only to say so and I will replace you."

"That really flatters my ego." Gabrielle laughed. "No, I am fine. Who am I to marry?"

"I'm not privy to the gent's name, but you will meet up with him soon enough. He probably won't use his real name anyway; after all it's just an illusion. I'm sure he is more interested with the wedding night and honeymoon than the actual ceremony. However, he requested an authentic wedding and that is what he will get."

Gabrielle's eyes grew even larger. "Is there anything special I should know?"

Maude not only saw the panic, she heard it in her voice. "Gabby," already instructed about Gabrielle's name preference, "Gabby, there is no need to worry. I understand the man you are to marry is a wonderful lover. He will treat you tenderly and your night will be everything you could hope for. After all, here everyone's fantasy comes true."

Gabrielle squared her shoulders and drummed up some confidence. "I am ready when you are."

"I do have a surprise for you though, I asked Kathleen to be your witness. That way if you are feeling even slightly nervous, you can ask her any questions you need," supplied Maude.

Gabrielle could not help herself and in her excitement pulled Maude into her embrace. "Thank you so much! It will be less frightening to have her near."

Then Maude led Gabrielle down to the small chapel.

Chapter 19

Scott and his men were in possession of the viscount and pretended to let him go, in order to follow him. Staying a safe distance behind him, the viscount finally caught a coach in Andover. From there they were able to ride their horses to continue the pace. He changed connivances in Winchester and continued past Petersfield. He slept in a barn outside of Pulborough when the weather had turned bad and stole a horse the next morning. Finally he led them directly to a large manor in Eastbourne. Scott and his men stood watch all day and then decided to use the darkness of night to their advantage. Once he and his men had gained control of the hall he immediately sent word to Kevin and James.

Kevin and Kathleen had just finished making love for the second time, when a rap at the door sounded. Appearing as disgruntled as he felt, Kevin went to answer the door. With his naked ass staring her in the face as he departed Kathleen had to stifle a giggle. Acknowledging that Kevin didn't have a modest bone in his body, she could only hope that whoever was at the door would not be too surprised. She giggled again as she lay back down to await his return.

Moments later rather than join her once again, he returned and began to dress.

"What has happened?" Kathleen questioned.

"I'm not sure, a messenger has arrived. He has been instructed to deliver the missive to only James or myself. I can only believe it's from Scott, for no one else knows our present location."

"Do you think this is good news?" Kathleen asked.

"I hesitate to guess." After pulling on his trousers and fastening his shirt, he also made quick work of his boots. "I will return as quickly as possible, though I'm not sure when that will be. Why don't you just do whatever you need to do to get ready for tonight? If worse comes to worse and I can't return quickly, at least I will see you there." Pulling her head forward, her neck in the palm of his hand, he presented her with a smoldering kiss good-bye. And though he hurried from the room on his errand, he was whistling as he went.

The message was indeed from Scott, so Kevin tracked down James directly after its reading. Secluded in the library, both men were in the midst of a private conversation with Derek and Jake.

The letter said:

The journey has progressed as expected. However, we did encounter one surprise, which I am sending back with my men. I would appreciate the assistance of my large red friend taking on the added burden of my men, until my return. My man will provide answers once he arrives. Until that time, please follow my requests.

It is imperative to send the friend with the vessel to the port where it is anchored. Include the youngest brother too, for both men and their experience will be needed on the second part of this journey.

I do not intend to commit any important information to paper and will give you a verbal accounting when we meet aboard ship.

The letter was not addressed, nor was it signed. Kevin sighed. Sitting with the other men in the large library, each man's expression was grim.

"Obviously, Derek is the one with the vessel and I am the youngest brother. What do you suppose he has in mind?" asked Jake.

"We will have to wait for his man to arrive to find that out. At least, James and I will. You and Derek must leave at first light and will find out the rest aboard ship," answered Kevin.

"We can't send them without knowing what is going on!" proclaimed an exasperated James. "At the very least you and I must accompany them," his last comment directed to Kevin.

"Scott would have asked for us all, had he needed all of us," Kevin concluded. "Scott is a seasoned warrior. He would have demanded us all if it had been necessary." He sighed. "Maybe there is something else he wants us to do. We will have to await his men."

Without warning, the door flew open! The loud sound of wood breaking against the wall was unmistakable. An angry, volatile Jared entered. "Why is it every time I am screwing some woman, you demand my presence?" he shouted.

"I had first sent for you because I believed we would all be leaving, posthaste." James smiled and then slapped him on the back to tease him. "Did I interrupt something?"

Suddenly the group of men surrounding the scene burst out in laughter.

"It is not funny!" Turning to the others, he said, "I'd like to see your reaction if it was you he kept interrupting!" he fumed. Marching over to the

338

array of alcohol across the room, he poured a cognac and made quick work of making it disappear. As the others continued to rib Jared, James reached his side.

"I must apologize, brother. We had only just received the letter from Scott. I assumed we were to be off immediately. You know I was not about to make a move without letting you in on everything. Now it appears you could have finished first, for only Derek and Jake will be leaving."

Jared smiled a wide grin all his own. "I'm not saying I didn't finish this time, I'm just saying it's getting to be damn inconvenient, this habit of yours!"

"Good, come then and read the message and give me your opinion."

Later that evening the three Armstrong men stood gathered together in the anteroom of the chapel. "I can't thank you enough for all you have done for me. I hope you understand under normal circumstances I would have had each of you stand as my witness. Yet with Gabrielle's frame of mind, I can't take the chance," said James.

"You don't have to worry about our feelings, brother. We are hardier than that," Jake said.

"Don't give it another thought. Though why would our presence cause her disturbance?" Jared inquired.

"It would not cause a disturbance, for she genuinely likes you. I am simply inclined to believe it may tip my hand. For though Gabrielle believes she is pretending to marry some man to provide a fantasy, in reality the marriage will be no sham. It will be as legal and binding as any other and after we consummate our marriage this evening, there will be no way to annul it." James paused. "I am just taking every precaution. I think perhaps your presence may give her reason to pause and reflect on the possibility of the validity of the marriage. I can't give her any reason to bolt."

"You don't feel the least bit the cad, for pulling the wool over her eyes in her condition?" Jake being the one to ask, but both brothers nodded in unison.

"No. I am in love with a woman that at this moment believes it is her duty to please men. Now while this seems both enticing and slightly amusing, it is disastrous. She has already broached Helena to put her to work. If you think I will take the chance of letting some other devil sample her wares, you can forget it. Though I agree what I am about to do is a bit shady, it is for her own good. I marry her so I can protect her."

Both brothers were now nodding in confirmation to his statement.

"Now do you see why standing next to my two brothers at the altar would alert her? It is my hope with Kevin and Kathleen up there, Gabrielle will believe it is just one large fantasy."

"I am certainly in your corner, brother. Though this is a sticky situation," sighed Jared.

"I, too, would do what you are about to do, if the woman I loved were at risk. But if and when she regains her memory, she may be very upset," announced Jake.

"I realize that. It is a chance I am willing to take. There is little alternative, and no time."

A brief knock at the door interrupted them. James allowed entrance and Kevin walked through the door. "Everything is ready. Should we begin?" said Kevin.

Hugging his brother, Jared said, "Good luck."

Jake gave him a hug, then a quick slap on the back. "We will stand and watch the wedding from the viewing chamber. For we could never miss our own brother's wedding."

Then both brothers departed in a rush of laughter.

Kevin spoke, "You nervous?"

"No. This is the most right thing I have ever done."

Kevin embraced his friend. "I have been there, my friend, am there still. Though it is rare for men in our position to marry for love, I believe we are better for it. Now let's go."

Having felt a bit nervous, Gabrielle was overcome with gratitude when Kathleen appeared and explained she was also included in this fantasy. The girls were in the anteroom on the other side of the chapel, anxiously waiting for the ceremony to begin. Walking over to the door, Kathleen opened it a crack. In feigned surprise, Kathleen squealed, "Oh my gosh! Wait till you see who requested this fake marriage." Hesitating a moment, she then continued. "Oh, even better for me, you should see who the best man is."

Darting over to the doorway, Gabrielle playfully shoved Kathleen out of the way to get a glimpse for herself. When she caught sight of James she smiled and muttered, "Oh, that devil!" Shutting the door and turning around to face Kathleen, she sighed, "I had been slightly put out when Helena had requested I work this evening. I was saddened by the fact that I wouldn't get to see him again." Gabrielle's eyes sparkled. "He must have felt the same."

Kathleen hugged her friend. "I'm so happy for you. This will be one fine fantasy."

Kathleen realized at once that even with her memory loss, Gabrielle missed and was attracted to James. Now Kathleen found she could breathe a bit easier about the whole sham. As the organ began to play, the women wordlessly wound their way to the back of the small chapel.

Meanwhile the viewing chamber was in utter chaos. Jared and Jake had thought to watch their brother marry from the quiet chamber above the chapel. However, the room was already thick with people and becoming more crowded by the moment. Maude and Helena were at the front, keeping two empty chairs for them. However, trying to get to them was a trial all its own. Over on the far side of the room lay Stuart, still recovering upon a chaise longue. Hovering nearby were two identical plump women with glossy black curls, bright rosy cheeks and classical dimples. Not only were they twins, but both pregnant as well. Jared and Jake exchanged looks of surprise upon viewing that sight. The room was filled with people whom Gabrielle had helped, worked with or befriended.

Derek stood in the corner, a blonde-haired pixie tightly molded to his body. He spotted Jake and Jared and moved across the room to join them, grinning as he dragged the woman clinging to his side along.

Each party seemed to reach Stuart's couch about the same moment. "Stuart, you old hound, glad to see you up and about," exclaimed Derek.

Jake held out his hand to Stuart and said, "I, too, am glad to see you are better." Smiling, he turned to the ladies and said, "Good evening, ladies."

Jared also extended his hand and said, "You're looking pretty well. You'll be joining us on another adventure before you know it!"

Both women glared at Jared in response to his casual remark. Stuart said, "Lads, these are my companions, Molly and Polly. I'm sure you are well aware by their appearance that they are sisters. It was only to save Gabrielle that I left here to begin with, for it will be some time before I leave again." He smiled. "You see, I'm about to become a father." There was a shout from Jake, then laughter all around. The men all gathered closer to congratulate him. All the back slapping and reveling seemed to take its toll as he slumped back into a reclining position. The women waved the visitors away, so the men finally made their way up to the front of the room. Reaching their chairs just as the music began, Helena held up her hand and suddenly the room became silent.

Though many candles were lit throughout the tiny chapel, the room appeared dim. James was slightly irritated at the level of noise coming from the viewing chamber as he stood silently at the altar. As he stood observing the crowd overhead, the music started. Suddenly all the commotion coming from the viewing chamber, which had earlier filled the room with loud echoes, became silent. At that moment, both James and Kevin turned their attention towards the back of the chapel. Each man had eyes for only his woman. Though Kevin was aware Gabrielle was standing behind Kathleen, it was only Kathleen that beguiled him. He watched her glide forward effortlessly, his breath caught in his throat at her beauty. Her ample bosom prominently on display for his enjoyment, her beautiful thick auburn hair had been left unbound, falling gently down her back. As she reached the front, he could not help but shower her with lewd grins as she stood there.

Though the short isle was only about twenty meters, it seemed so much longer. To James it felt like an eternity as he stood there waiting to make Gabrielle his wife. Oh, he acknowledged Kathleen as she came up the isle, but his eyes quickly passed her over, looking to Gabrielle.

She was more beautiful every time he laid eyes upon her. He had requested her hair not be styled, for this was the image burned in his memory. Her raven black tresses fell loosely down her back, reaching her waist. Gabrielle's face void of all superficial cosmetics remained radiant. The dress was white, setting off the deep bronze tone of her skin to perfection. The dress she wore put her bosom on display and he could barely tear his eyes away from the tempting treat. Finally he succeeded, only to gaze upon her lips, which would later be swollen from his kisses. She appeared shy, the blush of her cheeks, her hesitant steps an indication. Yet, the moment she reached the end of the isle and her eyes met his, her awkwardness disappeared. The smile he gave her as she put her hand into his warmed her to the depth of her soul. He was a calming influence and he felt her stop shaking the moment he held her. So the cleric began the ceremony.

It was over almost before it began. She had uttered a few simple responses along with her name and suddenly he had announced them man and wife. After the searing kiss James had given her, she walked around in a daze. A lad had appeared bearing several documents, which she diligently signed. Then Kathleen and Kevin had hugged and congratulated her. Before she knew what had happened, they had all disappeared.

She turned around and saw James standing close by. "Where did everyone go? And why so suddenly?" she questioned.

He didn't say a word, instead he moved closer. As his eyes met hers, her heart began to race. His strong arms wrapped around her and pulled her close. Gabrielle's cheeks were aflame as her lips parted. He had been denied too long to be tender; he ravaged her mouth, demanding surrender.

Yielding to him she moaned as she softened in his arms. He tightened his hold, pushing even further beyond any barriers or memory loss. Her left arm reached over his shoulder, her right arm around his waist. Instinctively she tried to press deeper into his embrace.

Her lips were as soft as he remembered, the taste of her, divine. He sensed her total surrender as she moaned once again, sagging against his large frame. Her feet were no longer touching the ground as he crushed her to him.

Finally he tore his lips away. Though his desire was evident, he wanted her first time to be somewhere other than the marble steps of a small chapel. As their lips parted, they both struggled to breathe. She looked up at him and blushed. He looked down upon her with smoldering preoccupation. In one swift motion he reached under her legs and carried her down the aisle. Her arms instantly reached around his neck for support and she eagerly held tight as they disappeared out the door.

Though the room had emptied, Helena had remained behind. She wanted to be sure things would be all right. Slowly the smile on her face grew. As the happy couple made their exit, she could breathe easy. She had done the right thing. She turned around and was surprised to see Jared and Jake still there.

"I assume you remained for the same reason as I?" she inquired.

"And that is?" replied Jared.

"To make sure that even in Gabrielle's impaired state, she was not taken advantage of," she said.

"Wouldn't now be to late, in any case?" questioned Jake.

"I like Gabrielle. Though I like James too, I was very uncomfortable pulling the wool over her eyes. I needed to be sure everything would be all right." She sighed.

"Jake is right. Even if there had been cause for worry, now that the ceremony is over, it would be too late," announced. Jared.

"Don't be too sure," muttered Helena

"What do you mean?" asked Jake

"Who do you think runs this place? Do you think I left no recourse? You forget yourselves in your arrogance, probably your brother has too."

With a look of cold steel, Jared stepped closer. "Madam, that is a real man of the cloth, is it not? This marriage is legal?" he demanded.

"Yes, yes. It is very legal. However, if I had not stayed to make certain of Gabrielle's happiness, certain documents may have disappeared. Or … another alternative would be to interfere with them consummating the marriage." With the looks on their faces she could no longer contain her laughter. "Fear not, gentlemen, she is happy. The documents are safe. They are legally wed. And in a short time I would assume also legally bed!" She laughed once again. "Now let's go celebrate."

"You have given us a hell of a scare, madam!" said Jared.

"Yes, I thought we could stop worrying once he got her to the altar. You have since pointed out several reasons why I have always thought women too devious," muttered Jake

"You really never had anything to fear," Jared said as he held the door for

Helena. "Though hardly required, James happens to be in love with her."

"Sometimes what we think is love turns out to simply be wanting what we can't have. I don't want Gabrielle's memory to come flooding back and accuse me of divided loyalties. I just had to be sure she would be safe."

Jake leaned in for a quick kiss on the cheek and whispered to Helena. "As she is now our sister-in-law, we can only thank you for your guarded interest."

Jared on the other hand took the low road and added, "We would also like those documents in our hands as quickly as possible. I don't want anything to happen." He caught her questioning gaze. "You understand, I trust?"

Holding out both her arms to the men, "Gentlemen, let us eat and drink and celebrate." As each man held an arm to escort her, they joined the revelry already started in the great hall.

James carried Gabrielle a fair distance before they passed through the doorway to the large circular stairway. Gabrielle was not familiar with this particular area, however, there were many places in the large castle she had not fully investigated. After starting up the stairs, she insisted he put her down and let her climb beside him. He paid little attention as he continued. It wasn't until they had reached the top that Gabrielle realized they must be in one of the towers. James quietly kicked the door open with his boot and they entered. The huge circular room was filled with lilies. The sweet, soft scent of the flowers combined with the candles scattered around the room created a romantic atmosphere. The alcove off to the left had a massage table and small tub. The sitting room they were presently in was decorated in soft creams and tans. A female servant came forward as they entered, motioning them over to the small alcove.

"My lord, I am to prepare your bride," the young girl stated.

James could feel Gabrielle's grip around his neck tighten. "She will join you in a moment." Walking over to the chaise longue, he set her down upon it. "Gabrielle, there is nothing to be frightened of. The girl is simply going to help you out of your gown and afterwards we will dine together."

Gabrielle's trembling chin shot up in defense. "I am not afraid. I must have done this many times. I am simply having trouble recollecting. You may go and see to your own preparations."

He tipped her chin up and kissed her once again. "It will not be long before I hold you once again." He then guided her into the alcove, where the servant awaited.

Though Gabrielle had explained that she did not have time for a massage, the servant had insisted it was all part of the fantasy. After lying upon the bench Gabrielle wondered why she had even argued, the fluid motion of her hands and the soft warm salve kneaded into the pores of her skin making her feel limp and relaxed. Gabrielle could not have known the wine she had been given, added to her lethargic effect, and the servant could not inform Gabrielle that herbs had been added to help with the pain she would later encounter. The young servant then helped Gabrielle into a beautiful silk nightgown. The soft texture seemed to cling like a second skin. The lavender material was backless, revealing the curve of her shapely buttocks. The v-shaped cleavage reached her navel. Thank goodness there was a matching nightrail to cover what the gown did not. After a second glass of wine, the servant guided her out to the sitting area, where both dinner and James already waited.

"I'm sorry, did I take too long?" she questioned

Giving her a smoldering look, he reassured her, "You look exquisite. I have only just arrived myself."

He had also gotten assistance undressing, though his massage did not relax him, quite the contrary, he was eager to begin. How he would make it through a long dinner, allowing her time to prepare herself, was beyond him. Yet he was determined to try, so as not to frighten her. Though if her kisses in the chapel were any indication, she would need little enticement. Seating her at the intimate table for two, with candles already lit, he poured the wine. They had been served salmon and though its taste was tender and delicious he was unaware. He barely knew what they talked of; all he could think of was undressing her.

The wine with dinner, added to the wine she had drunk earlier, was beginning to take effect. She was well aware of their exchange of pleasantries and the tasty dinner they had been served. Secretly she thought only about being held by him once again. Maybe it was the wine, but she no longer felt self-conscious or afraid.

Well aware that this was his fantasy, she wondered if she was supposed to make the first move. Sure that she had done this many times before, she was unable to recall just what needed to be done. Maybe if she took the first step, he would tell her what to do next....

She pushed her chair back away from the table. Moving to stand in front of him, she smiled at the surprised expression on his face. She gave what she believed to be a sultry smile. Without thought, she untied the ribbon holding the nightrail together. The next moment, she let it slide slowly to the floor.

He was mesmerized. James could not believe she had taken the initiative and started to disrobe in front of him. Standing before him, without guile, in complete splendor, she was seductive. The material clung to her body like a second skin. Held by two thin straps, the cleavage extended to her navel. His body reacted instinctively, instantly becoming hard. He couldn't help notice her nipples straining against the material of the gown. He stood and pulled her into his arms. As his arms reached around her, he realized there was no material in the back. He stepped back and took her arm and twirled her around. The view from every angle was breathtaking. Not wanting her newfound courage to abandon her, he once again pulled her close. As he molded her body to his, he ran a trail of delightful little kisses along her neck. She shuddered and sagged closer against him. He covered her mouth with a most sensual kiss. As the kiss deepened, he ran his hands up and down the length of her body. As his hands firmly gripped her buttocks and lifted her against him, heat traveled through her body. She instinctively began kissing him more fiercely, her hands pulling his lawn shirt from his pants to let her hands roam beneath. Running her hands sensually across the length of his back, her nails digging deep as she sighed. For several delicious moments he held her there. Desire heightened as their kisses became longer and the caresses firmer. Slowly he maneuvered her over to the large bed in the middle of the room. He put his hands upon hers and encouraged her to slide the shirt from his body. He stood as she explored his body and her effect upon him. His kisses became urgent and enflamed. He grazed her nipple as he cupped her breast in the palm of his hand. As he maneuvered his thumb back and forth, waves of delight ran through her. He was rock hard now as he slowly slid the gown down her body with his other hand. Gently falling to the floor, the gown pooled around her feet as he reached up and cupped her other breast. Gently rubbing each nipple, she gasped and arched against him. Their breathing became shallow and constricted. She leaned into him, her mouth upturned for yet another kiss. He kissed her even as he released the buttons of his breeches.

Gently laying her upon the bed, he was out of his drawers before she realized he had done anything. He leaned over her as she spread her palms upon his chest. He set out once again to make her forget everything and depend solely on instinct. His lips touched hers, this time in a teasing, lingering manner. He gazed upon her as she lay beneath him. Her bountiful breasts were high and firm, nipples now erect. The taut stomach, her petite frame, her curving hips. James sighed as he savored the moment. His manhood was hard and ready, yet he was wary of hurting her. So far this night, little had been said. Now he felt the need to reassure her. "Though I will try to be tender, you may feel slight discomfort. This is quite common, do not be afraid." He leaned down to kiss her once again. The fire was building. He wanted to be patient and gentle, but she was driving him wild. This time his mouth went to her breasts. He covered her nipple and began to suckle; as he did this Gabrielle's breath became ragged. The sensations he was creating caused her body to arch upwards. He guided his hand to her passage, thankfully she was already moist. Though he tried to go slowly finally he simply had to plunge deeply to get through her maidenhead. In that instant she tried to shove him away. He continued to hold her tight, whispering soft tender words into her ear, assuring her this was normal, that the pain would subside in only moments. As they lay there he was slowly pushing and stretching her. It no longer hurt so badly, yet she remained uncomfortable. So she continued to lie motionless. He began with little kisses upon her breasts, running a trail along her neck. Once again he grazed her lips with own, then he took command with a searing kiss. Her breath once again came in short gasps; he took advantage and began to press forward, moving with small, quick strokes. All the while he distracted her with brazen, heart melting kisses. Gabrielle's eyes were closed and as they lay entwined in each other's arms she felt irresistible. The feeling was not really unpleasant, though she couldn't quite see the big attraction. Moments later that all changed, she began to grow quite warm, her body responding to the rhythm he had created. Moving in motion with James, she found she liked the feeling, for suddenly she was overcome with sensations.

As he began to move harder and faster, Gabrielle was vanquished with emotion as she spiraled out of control and shouted "Ohhhh!"

James held her tight with a climax of his own, well satisfied by his endeavors. The entire time he had made love to his wife he had watched the miriad of emotions expressed upon her face. Initially starting from fear, changing to curiosity, going from disinterest to enthusiasm, then eagerness and finally bliss. He continued to hold her close.

Overwhelmed by her state of euphoria, she lay there quietly with a smile upon her face, content to revel in her pleasure. "By the look upon your face I believe you gained as much pleasure as I. We are well suited, I think," James said.

"You were right," she whispered. "It was uncomfortable at first, but then it was wonderful. Is it your size that makes it hurt before the enjoyment?" She believed herself a qualified courtesan, so he would have to be quickly search for an adequate answer. "I have heard it said that once you mate with your one true love, you never again experience pain or discomfort." She stared at him in disbelief. Then he smiled, "You will see the next time, for my fantasy is to last quite a while."

She sighed as she snuggled closer. She was quite content to have him for her fantasy.

One taste of her was not enough; he wanted to take her once again. Yet he dared not. She had been a virgin and would be tender for some time. He wanted her to be fully recovered when he took her again in the morning. Finally he had reached his goal. It had been an unusual struggle and a unique adventure. It was more than pure contentment upon his face as he held her tight and fell asleep. It was also pure exhaustion.

Though the party had lasted well past dawn, Stuart, Jared and Jake were already eating breakfast when Derek and Kevin joined them. Standing at the sideboard, Kevin filled his plate to overflowing before sitting at the table.

"Stuart, you're not eating?" asked Kevin.

"I was up early and ate with the girls before I joined you. I'm just having tea."

At his place near the end of the table, Jake, with a mouth full of food, quickly swallowed as he was too curious to let Stuart's situation pass without comment. "Sisters?" he asked.

Stuart had the grace to blush. "Though I will remind you that it is hardly any of your business, I am happy to cooperate with both your questions and your ribbing just this once. After this conversation, my life will never again be up for discussion, nor will I answer any questions. Do I make myself clear?" He looked them each squarely in the eye. Then he hesitated and with a beet red face sighed and said, "Yes, sisters."

"Good God, man, what were you thinking?" asked Jared.

Stuart laughed, "At first I was just thinking on a quick tumble." Then he sighed again. "Somehow Molly just got under me skin and stayed there. We were having a romping good time. She is in charge of the women; I'm in charge of the men. We often have the same problems and, as our conversations have pointed out, a lot of the same answers. We enjoy each other's company and no other has ever compared to her in bed."

"If you fell for Molly, how did her sister get into the act?" asked Jake.

"Seems for years Molly and Polly had been playing tricks on people by exchanging places. Molly had to oversee a particular fantasy one evening and asked Polly to fill in. Polly thought it was a hoot and was happy to oblige. Next thing you know, every time Molly couldn't make it, Polly stepped in. Somewhere along the line, Polly fell for me and one night her and Molly got into a huge catfight."

"Both women were fighting over you?" inquired Derek.

Stuart blushed again. "Don't want to brag or anything, but I do have my way with the ladies. I take the time to make sure they enjoy themselves, if ya know what I mean." He winked. "Seems the women folk are pretty appreciative of that."

Kevin laughed, "So you're in a castle where women fulfill men's fantasies and suddenly two women come across a fellow willing to take the time to please them. It's no wonder they were fighting over you. What did you do?"

"Well, first of all I want you men to know that I knew she had a sister working somewhere in the castle, but I swear on my mother's grave I knew nothing about them looking alike."

All the men laughed. "You want us to believe you were taken advantage of?" Derek said with a hoot.

"I must confess to that," Stuart muttered.

The men laughed again.

"So I walked into my apartment expecting to find Molly, naked in bed waiting for me. Instead I entered to find two identical-looking girls fussing and fuming. Then Molly tearfully explains the situation and admits that it is her fault because she asked Polly to entertain me to begin with. Polly jumps in and says she can't help it that she fell in love while doing her sister a favor. Then they turn to me and demand I pick between them!" He flushed and sighed. "Though I didn't tell them at the time that I had never known there was a substitute, I was bound and determined not to get in the middle again. So I told them they had played a dirty trick and I wasn't going to be a part of it. I told them I had feelings too and would not be used in this manner. I announced to them that I would take them both or neither, but never again would I be taken advantage of. Then I stormed out of the room."

"Wow," said Jake. "That takes balls! What the hell were those women thinking anyway?"

"Only of themselves, little brother, only of themselves," answered Jared.

"I take it you proceeded to get drunk, my friend?" questioned Kevin.

"I did indeed. At the time I thought it would make me feel better. Still I was sick of the thought of losing her, or them, I guess. For it had all been working rather well, up until that point. To find out I had been tricked was a great embarrassment, I had not been so foolish in love since I had been a green lad. Then I dragged myself back to my rooms and what do I find?"

Derek responds, "Obviously, since we have seen them both still with you, I take it they had compromised and decided to share you."

Stuart's smile lit up the room. "Upon opening my door, I found not one, but two naked women in my bed, now who would turn that down? They apologized for what they had put me through and begged for me to keep them both. So now my quiet little affair with one woman had blossomed into a threesome. I simply figured we would enjoy each other's company for a while and part ways when it was no longer enjoyable."

"I'm not sure any man could turn down two willing women in his bed every night," agreed Derek.

"I ask you, what would you have done?" Stuart questioned.

"I can't say I would be the one to throw two naked women from my bed," agreed Jared.

"I don't think any man would," said Jake.

With twinkling eyes, Stuart continued, "Well, it seems our make-up night turned out to be quite eventful. Not long after our unusual arrangement began, they both came to me claiming to be with child. Now suddenly our fun and games became a dilemma."

"Marriage is certainly out of the question, unless you pick between them," announced Jake. "Maybe the solution is to marry Molly, for she is the one you first picked."

"Why settle for one when he now has both?" asked Derek.

"Exactly," said Stuart. "It is very different living here as opposed to the outside world. Out there my children would be called bastards and treated with distain. Here the children are treated well, they will be loved by their parents and given an education." Stuart hesitated and then continued, "It is not what I would have chosen, but one must play the cards one is dealt."

"What a raw deal, the women here know about contraception. I think you were trapped, my friend," said Jared. "Maybe you should dump them both."

"Believe me, that occurred to me. Yet, I too am at fault. For though I possess condoms I am the first to admit I never use them. If I had, it would have prevented this fiasco."

"I agree with Jared, the women should have taken precautions, it is their business after all. For you to shoulder all the blame is absurd," said Kevin. "Yet with children on the way, it really matters not who is to blame, but where you go from here."

"I cannot give up either woman, for I have come to love them both. The worst part is that I still cannot tell them apart. If I am only with one of them I will never really know which one."

Now the men were rolling with laughter, with hoots and howls joined in.

"No wonder you want the package deal," smirked Jared.

"You will certainly have your hands full," laughed Kevin

"You don't dare complain about one to the other, for she may be the one you started with!" laughed Derek. Then the snickers began once more.

"You now see my plight. For though it is an amusing tale, one to poke fun at, or laugh over a mug of ale, it really is quite serious; they are very special to me. At this stage of my life I had given up the thought of having children, now to raise them I must keep them both. I am really appreciative of the fact that we live here, for though the rumors flew like fire at first, at least the women will not be ostracized."

"Sisters, both sleeping with the same man, both pregnant on the same night, both are continuing the arrangement. Now why would anyone think that unusual?" hooted Jake.

"Though it is a peculiar problem, I will not have my girls the butt of every joke." He stood to fill his cup again. "So now you know my funny story. Laugh and joke about it and get it out of your system. For though I cannot marry the pair of them, I demand the same respect as any other man with women in his care. I will treat each as I would a wife and expect my friends to do the same. Now this discussion is ended."

Jake could not resist. "Will you continue to sleep with them both?"

Stuart smiled. "If I must incur the ridicule, why would I deny myself the pleasure? I'm sure they will demand we continue to sleep three in a bed so I don't appear to favor the other in any manner." A smile from ear to ear, he continued, "I often am daunted by the task."

All the men laughed. After a refill of both food and drink, the subject turned to the matter at hand. "You sent the message?" inquired Kevin of Jared.

"Yes, the moment the nuptials were over. By tomorrow the Earl of Chatham should have received notice of his ward's wedding."

"Should we have waited?" asked Derek

"No, James gave direct orders not to send the messenger before the ceremony was complete, but to make damn sure we sent him directly afterward. He didn't want to take the chance of sending it before the ceremony and giving the guardian opportunity to ruin anything."

"He obviously didn't think anything would impede the bedding ceremony," laughed Derek.

"James would be insulted that you even hinted at that. There has never been a woman he has set his sights on that could resist him," said Jake. "The bedding is a foregone conclusion."

"He left instructions that he was not to be disturbed for any reason for five days," said Kevin.

"He will not be here to wish us well?" inquired Derek

"James and I said our farewells yesterday," said Jake. Looking at Derek, he continued, "You and I will be off as soon as we finish breakfast. Kevin and Jared will remain to be available once Scott's men arrive. Stuart will once again be able to concentrate on his duties." Jake smiled. "Though you will know what this is all about when the men come, it won't be until we meet Scott aboard Derek's ship that we will be apprised of the situation. Trust that we will be in touch as soon as possible."

"That was quite some party last night," muttered Jared.

They reminisced a bit about the exotic dancer at the dinner the night before, and then made plans. After their meal and discussion were concluded, Kevin, Stuart and Jared accompanied them to the door. As they mounted their steeds, Derek and Jake felt only the excitement of a new adventure wash over them. They said their farewells and departed. The three left standing on the steps scattered to various locations after Jake and Derek departed.

For several days Gabrielle and James had been holed up in their apartment, feeding each other, bathing each other and entertaining each other.

Kevin and Kathleen had basically been doing the same, however, Kevin took time during the day to run drills with his men in the courtyard. Kathleen enjoyed watching them.

Stuart's injury had healed and he continued to guard the castle and its inhabitants with diligence. Molly and Polly both worked at opposite ends of the castle, waddling around like ducks as their pregnancies increased.

Jared used the extended time of rest to pamper himself with various women in unique fantasies. He was confident there wasn't any woman in the castle he hadn't met. Just when he was sure of that, he met another. He also spent time in the stable, learning a few tricks for the treatment of difficult fillies and picking up a few cures for horse injuries.

Helena and Maude were having their afternoon meeting when the commotion in the courtyard started. A servant quickly alerted them of the arrival of Scott's men. Helena in turn sent a servant to find Kevin and have him deal with it. Rooms had already been assigned to the soldiers above the stables; she did not believe her presence was required. "Have you taken care of the water in the green room?" inquired Helena as she carried on with the business of running the castle.

"Yes, the rugs have all been hauled out to dry and the servants are mopping up the rest now," answered Maude. "Are we going with the duck for the count's masquerade party?"

"Yes, Has he arrived yet?" replied Helena

"No, I don't expect him until late today."

"Good, by that time all these men should be situated. Has Kevin said how long they will stay?"

"My understanding is that he will speak with the soldiers today and plan their departure. As soon as Gabrielle and James make their appearance this afternoon, we will be informed. You do think you made the right decision, don't you?" asked Maude

"About?"

"About Gabrielle."

"She was meant to be with James. I just am not certain about forcing her to marry."

"You can see she loves him just by looking at her. Everything will be fine," supported Maude.

"She is going to pitch a fit, when we suggest she leave with him. She thinks she works here. You should have seen her get up the night I agreed to let James marry her. She was determined to work a fantasy. "

"I remember. I also remember she would have slept with anyone; she truly believes she is one of our girls. I think you did right by her. James is her protection."

"Yes, I realize that or I never would have agreed to all this. I hope she becomes right in the head soon though."

"Have you checked on them?" asked Maude.

"Yes, several times." Then she laughed. "I know James insisted on the tower room because he did not want there to be a viewing chamber, where anyone could watch them. However, as you well know, there is a secret tunnel with a peep hole and I have ventured there to assure myself she is in good hands."

"And?" asked Maude

"And what?" returned Helena

"Is she in good hands?"

"He appears to be gentle and caring of her feelings. He is definitely a virile, handsome specimen and yes, I believe her to be in good hands."

Just as they were about to return to the day's plans, a knock at the door sounded.

Kevin quickly let himself in and hurried over to Helena. "We have a bit of a surprise to deal with. I could use your assistance."

Helena's eyebrows raised in inquiry.

"Gabrielle's father is here!" he said.

"What?" she sounded alarmed "He lives?"

"Apparently and demanding to see his daughter. James and Gabrielle will be available shortly, however can you smooth this over? I'm not even sure he knows where he is."

"You mean England?"

"I mean a place catering to men."

"Oh," she said. "I'm sure he has enjoyed the company of a woman, how awful would it be to tell him?"

"His daughter is here. How much do you want to tell him?" said Kevin.

"Fine." She turned to Maude. "Give him a tower room, far from everything. Then–"

Kevin interrupted, "He has been imprisoned for some time, I'm not at all sure he is up to the stairs."

"Very well, Maude, use one of the bed chambers on the first level. Keep him in the west wing and far removed from all activity. Suggest a bath. Give him a tour of the small bath and suggest a massage." Turning to Kevin, she said, "Let him believe he is in a hotel, however, I will not lie if I am asked. I will do my best to bend the truth, to help Gabrielle. But I don't believe a man alive will say no to a long bath and massage after what he has been through." Turning once again to Maude, she suggested a more mature woman like Claudia give him a massage. Turning back to Kevin, she said, "Maude will take care of everything. I will plan to have dinner with him, by then James and Gabrielle will be available. Maybe you and Kathleen should plan to join us?"

"Thank you for your assistance." Quickly he left the room, with Maude at his heels.

Later that evening, standing on the balcony, Helena quizzed Claudia. "How did everything go?"

"It was a very easy assignment. The gent was sincerely impressed with the thought of me wanting to pleasure him but turned me down. He said he was exhausted and suggested perhaps I would be available later this evening. Will I be?"

"I have no objection to his entertainment. Did he take you up on the massage?"

"He did indeed. Claimed he'd never had a better one. He was sleeping before I finished." She smiled. "I sort of just rousted him and led him into his room next door."

"He's still naked then?"

"Yes and sound asleep."

"Why don't you go to his room and wait for him to awaken? I want him thoroughly complacent when we begin our conversation later."

"Fine."

"If he asks you to dinner, please refuse. We have a lengthy discussion ahead of us. Tell him you will join him afterwards. You have done a good job. Have him awakened in two hours and guide him to my private dinning room."

Later that afternoon, James and Gabrielle made their way down from the tower. Gabrielle fairly glowed from happiness and James grinned like a Cheshire cat. Gabrielle wanted to talk to Kathleen and James was eager to hear if Kevin had heard from Scott's men. So they began their search for the other couple. They found them in the grand salon having a drink before dinner. The girls immediately gravitated to each other, hugging and giggling in greeting. They eagerly sat upon the divan and began to relate stories. James smiled as he crossed the room to where Kevin stood. Kevin was already pouring a drink for him, so by the time James reached him it was ready. With enthusiasm they grinned and slapped each other on the back. After a silent toast they quickly consumed their drinks, refilling them before walking even farther away from the women, where they began their long awaited conversation.

"It seem marriage agrees with you," Kevin said.

"I have never felt better," James agreed. "What of my brothers?"

"Jared has found a lass that interests him. Between her and the horses, he has been content."

"And Jake, he got off all right?"

"Yes, he and Derek will contact us when possible. They should meet up with Scott and Derek's ship by tomorrow. But I have talked with Daniel, Scott's man. So I can fill you in on what has been going on. Also, there is a little matter of a surprise for your wife."

Just then Gabrielle shrieked "Twins!" and the girls went into peals of laughter.

The men's attention had been averted towards them for a moment and Kevin snickered, "I will tell you what that was all about too, but before we talk about Stuart you need be apprised of what is going on."

Over on the chaise Gabrielle was feeling a bit overwhelmed. She had never even thought of children, what would she do if she were with child? Though Kathleen kept talking, Gabrielle heard little else.

After the men had finished their chat, they came over to escort the women to dinner. Kathleen took Kevin's arm and they were already to the doorway when they realized James and Gabrielle had not followed. They stood to wait as the other pair stood embroiled deep in conversation.

Though he hated the endearment, he used it, because in her confused state she preferred it. "Gabby?" She did not respond. Putting his hand beneath her chin he pulled it upwards, repeating "Gabby?"

"Yes?" she whispered.

"Has Kathleen said something to upset you?"

"Yes."

"Would you like me to talk to her about it?" James inquired.

"No."

"Is there something I should do?" he questioned.

"I'm not sure."

"Can you tell me about it?" he requested.

Though her chin quivered, she did not cry. She kept her eyes averted and whispered, "What if I get pregnant in your fantasy?" She sounded forlorn.

He smiled. James tipped her chin up even higher and his lips touched hers. As usual, the moment they did, she melted like butter. His teeth nipped at her lips and then his tongue teased them open, to delve inside. Moments later, passion getting the better of him, he decided to pull back. She was like putty in his hands, when he whispered, "Then you will have to give up your current occupation and marry me, for real. Become my wife, raise that child and live happily ever after."

"You would keep me and my child?" she asked.

"There is nothing I would not do for you, do you not feel it also?" insisted James.

He put his arm out and placed hers upon it, turning to escort her to dinner. Not hearing her retort.

"Then, I hope I am."

They all entered Helena's private dinning room only to find the guest of honor had not arrived. Gabrielle had only been told Helena had a dinner companion, so she was not aware of the identity of the visitor. No one wanted to shock her; they just wanted to see if she recognized him. The surprise turned sour as Helena announced to one and all that their guest had insisted on dinner in his room and would meet them for cocktails afterwards. Kevin raised his eyebrows over that statement. Helena merely shrugged. Kevin was well aware that Richard Cartwright had been more than a little anxious to find his daughter. Only one thing would stop a man from his duties and that was a woman. Considering their location, he was sure Helena had sent him a woman. Oh well, maybe that was for the best. Now they could have a friendly, relaxing dinner.

As expected, without any surprises dinner was calm and comfortable. Though Gabrielle did not remember all the people or places the rest of them reminisced about, the stories were interesting. When all of them got up to go into the study, Gabrielle excused herself.

On her way back, coming down the hall she ran into an older gentleman, entering the same room. He saw who it was and shouted with joy, "Thank heaven you are here! You look wonderful. You must come with me and get reacquainted." He reached out to hug her but she slipped away with the slipperiness of an eel.

Outraged that even here a man would be so bold she said, "Please, contain yourself!"

Curious at her lack of warmth and outraged by her insensitivity, he tried again, "You and I will spend the evening...."

She interrupted "I am not spending the evening with you. I am currently entertaining another gentleman. It would be to your advantage to seek out another. Now good evening." She turned and entered the double doors leading to the study. Just as she had reached the center of the room and was about to sit down, everyone within heard a loud shout at the same time.

"Gabrielle Josephine Cartwright!"

Suddenly Gabrielle spun around. After a glimpse of James, her eyes focused on the man standing in the center of the doorway. The room began to close in, she began to feel dizzy and whispered, "Father!" and then everything went black.

James caught her instantly and gently placed her on the settee. Her father pushed his way through the circle of her friends to get close enough to place something beneath her nose. Immediately her eyes flew open as she sputtered and coughed. "Father." She held out her arms.

Confused he embraced her, yet with uncertainty he eyed all those about them. "You'll find when dealing with women it helps to carry smelling salts," he explained.

They all laughed.

With blinding speed Gabrielle's memory came flooding back. She was still lightheaded, but less confused. Then everyone began to speak at once. James was excited and concerned that Gabrielle appeared to have gotten her memory back. He kept rubbing her back, asking how she felt. Helena said to Richard Cartwright that he should have a drink and sit down before they continued. Kathleen's only concern was Gabrielle. She kept pushing her father out of the way to hold her hand and attempt to soothe her. Kevin thought if anyone were to understand any of this it would be a miracle. He headed over to the bar and inquired if anyone else wanted one. Lord Cartwright must have heard over the entire medley for he answered affirmatively. Finally the chaos appeared to die down and everyone quieted.

Helena began as everyone chose a seat. First she made the introductions and then she began to explain. Richard Cartwright stared at her in amazement. She was a beautiful woman, but it was not her beauty that unsettled him but her similarity to another acquaintance. He fought the urge to question her until later and concentrated on her speech.

"Lord Cartwright, we have quite an amazing tale to tell. Please sit back and listen."

She began with finding Gabrielle in her home, informing him that his friend and sister had betrayed him and were about to force Gabrielle into marriage with the viscount. "She had run away and arrived here. She had done chores and taught children to earn her keep. It was during that time Gabrielle had been made aware that her home would be empty. So she had her friend Captain Anderson accompany Gabrielle to her father's home for his private papers. While she had easily obtained the information necessary to find her guardian during that visit, she had also heard harmful news. Her aunt and the viscount had hired someone to impersonate her and use her funds, allowing them to live the lifestyle they had been accustomed to. Now Gabrielle not only wanted to find her guardian for herself, she also sought revenge upon those she believed had done you harm. Returning to London, Gabrielle did indeed find her guardian, however, he too wanted her to marry someone she did not want to marry, so she ran away again. This time Sheriff Muden and his evil henchmen abducted her. James rescued her and brought her back to London. By this time Gabrielle and James had decided to wed and we believed the turmoil was over. However, while staying with the Earl of Chatham, she was kidnapped from her sleeping chamber and once again everyone was looking for Gabrielle. By this time it was not only Captain Anderson and James Armstrong trying to find her. Now his friends Kevin and Scott were involved along with his brothers Jared and Jake and not to mention her man Stuart. Time was running short and everyone was frantic to find her. She was now under the control of another evil man named Franklin. When help finally arrived and she was rescued, Gabrielle had something called amnesia. She was just recently returned here for recovery and she and James decided to marry. Now that you are back safe, that ends the tale."

James was amazed that their months and miles of adventure and anxiety could be summed up so neatly.

Kathleen was surprised that Helena had left half the adventures out, never including either herself or the trip to Scotland.

Kevin was impressed that she had told the truth and yet lied so cleverly.

Gabrielle was clearly dumbfounded.

Upset and confused, Richard Cartwright was determined to stay calm. Turning to Gabrielle, he said, "So you are really married?"

She began to blush as she tried to come up with an answer, "I ... a ... hum ... I ... a...." she sputtered. She looked to James and her face turned even redder, then her chin dropped to her chest.

James took pity upon her and answered, "Sir, we are indeed husband and wife."

Richard Cartwright sighed. "My earlier arrangements for the man I hand picked have been for naught, I see." Turning to James, he continued. "Though I wish circumstances were different and that I had been here, I welcome you to the family."

"Father, about the man you picked, I ah, I did not want to marry him," said Gabrielle

"Hugh is here? You have met him? How can that be?" asked a baffled Richard.

"Hugh?" said Gabrielle. "I thought you meant for me to marry William Pitt the Younger."

Bewildered by her comment, Richard Cartwright stared at his daughter as though she had two heads. "His father may have mentioned it a time or two, but I did not take him serious. He is too involved in politics, to ever devote enough attention to you."

Gabrielle sighed with relief, and then muttered "But my guardian told me...."

"My darling daughter," began Richard. "I am sorry you had to go through such turmoil. Although I suspect the earl had a hand in recent events. It truly was never my intent for you to marry his son."

Making a mental note to have a private discussion with the Earl of Chatham, James couldn't help but let out a shout of glee to have successfully thwarted his deceptive plans. Kathleen, Gabrielle and James, all exchanged glances. How close the earl had come to achieving his objective.

Richard turned to James again. "You will treat her well?"

"Without question, sir."

With her head hung down she could not believe James had lied to her father, just to save her reputation. She could not let him take the blame. She lifted her head to tell her father, just as James leaned down and gave her a big kiss instead.

"Sir perhaps you could explain what happened to you?" asked Kevin.

"First of all, I had no idea Penelope harbored such illusions, I assure you." He patted Gabrielle's hand. After refilling his drink, he began his own story.

Before he could start, Gabrielle noticed the ring on Helena's finger. She recognized it as the one from her father's hidden box. "Helena, how did you get that ring?"

Helena did not care for Gabrielle's tone. "This ring? Stuart gave me this ring." Remembering Stuart had found it in a pawnshop she asked "Why? What do you know of it?"

"It looks just like the ring I found at my father's the day we retrieved the information telling of my guardian. Kathleen and James looked and shook their head in agreement. So she said, "I believe it to be mine."

Suddenly a light dawned upon Richard Cartwright. Why the woman standing before him seemed so familiar. "Helena, is your family name Hollywell?" he questioned.

Now Helena felt like Gabrielle must have on numerous occasions. The room seemed to get smaller, the air harder to breathe; she collapsed upon the divan nearest her. Though she didn't faint, she felt damn close to it. Then she took deeper breaths to calm herself and seemed to fare better. Finally under control, she said, "It is not something I share.... How would you know that?"

Confirmation! Richard Cartwright smiled and moved closer to her. "My dear, I am well acquainted with your family." Turning to Gabrielle, he said, "Though you did indeed find the ring among my possessions, you are not the owner of the ring. In fact, the owner is wearing it."

Helena, more confused than ever, said, "Please explain this."

So Lord Cartwright began again, "Long ago, while serving in the military, I became fast friends with Lord Henry Hollywell. We were thick as thieves and each would have given our lives to protect the other. Though I stayed in the service much longer than he did, we remained in contact even when his term was up. He had gone home and was having the devil of a time with his devious brother. One brother was dependable, the other unreliable. One brother funloving and warm of heart, the other was mean-spirited and nasty. They looked similar in appearance, yet on the inside they were different as night and day. The heir and the spare, they were called. I remember his own people cringed at the thought of the younger brother ever inheriting for he was truly evil. He even raped a young woman, who became ripe with his child. Before long your father gave up trying both to befriend and guide his younger brother.

"Henry's father bought the younger brother, Herman, a position in the military and I didn't hear much about him for a long time. I even attended your parents' wedding." He smiled at Helena. "Your mother was the most beautiful debutante of the season. He scooped her up and married her before any of the other young bucks knew what had happened. Your mother received that beautiful sapphire from her mother on her wedding day. I believe I was told it was a tradition on your mother's family's side. Anyway, your father was taken with the ring and had an identical sapphire ring made to match in a man's style. They always wore their rings. Time passed and though I don't believe they had married for any reason but financial, they came to love each other. Finally your brother was born and there was such rejoicing." He turned and asked softly, "Do you remember your brother, my dear?"

Trying to regain her composure, Helena merely nodded yes.

"A short time later you arrived, making the family complete. Though I did not get to visit nearly often enough, we kept in touch. Your father was even my partner in several different investments. Soon I was married too with a child of my own, when I had heard about the kidnapping."

Everyone in the room held their breath.

"Seems young Hugh had been kidnapped and held for ransom. Your father always believed it was his brother Herman behind the scheme. Though the kidnapper returned the child when the amount was paid, your father was never unprepared again. We secretly had several alternative plans for any plot that would come up. I was a perfect accomplice. I did not have the same rank or title, I did not live nearby and I saw him rarely. It seemed that all our plans were for nothing for years went by and they lived happily. Then one day the three of them showed up on my doorstep.

Helena's eyes grew wide.

"You were ill and had been left behind in the safety of your grandmother's home. Your father explained how his brother had once again plotted to destroy him and his family. Only this time everyone believed them to be traitors to the crown. Both your parents gave me their matching rings, to hold. I gave them money and they were just about to leave when your parents reconsidered taking your brother. He would be safer with me, if nothing happened they would return for him. I was to keep him as long as it took. However, if anything happened to them, I was to use one of the plans to get him away safely." He sighed, "I'm sure you are aware of their deaths?"

Again, Helena could only nod.

"I was suspicious and later followed their trail. It appeared that their carriage overturned and looking below I saw their crushed bodies down below on the rocks. What had begun as a morning mist had developed into a heavy shower so I knew I could do nothing until the weather changed. But before leaving an idea occurred to me and I threw my cap upon the rocks below. I had hoped that if strangers discovered the bodies they would assume a third had already washed out to sea."

Now Helena jumped up "My brother was left with you? He is still alive?" she demanded.

"I'm sure this is quite a shock to you, but you must remember I was told to hide him at all cost. So I proceeded to follow the plans we had made. By the time I was assured your brother was safe I went to find you. Unfortunately by that time, your grandmother had died, her servants scattered. With the name Hollywell attached to treason I was sure you would change it, though I spent years trying to find you. As I had not heard of a death, I could only hope you had met a wonderful man and were married with children of your own. Are you married, my dear?"

Helena replied dully, "No."

So Richard continued. "I believe the viscount, Herman and Sheriff Muden were in cahoots. It must have been shortly after the viscount began seeing Penelope that my office had been ransacked and private papers stolen. Immediately I became suspicious. I could not trust this to anyone else and needed to get to Hugh. I never did get to him, though he has been trained to be suspicious. The viscount ordered my abduction and the sheriff carried it out. I remained in that rotting manor after that."

"Are you saying Helena's brother lives? That a reunion is possible?" inquired Kathleen.

"I do not believe it would be safe unless all three of them were dead. Though I know Herman was killed, that still leaves two more."

"Well, actually," Kevin began "I believe I heard it mentioned that the sheriff was no longer a problem either."

"He is dead?" questioned Richard.

"Yes," Kevin answered, looking directly at him. "It is also my belief that the viscount will have a nasty accident while on board Derek's ship. None of them will be around. Will it be safe for her to see her brother then?"

"Yes, for years I have been careful. I am positive they are the only ones with any knowledge of Hugh's true identity." Richard looked to Helena "Would you like that, my dear?"

Helena could barely comprehend all that had taken place. "So Derek, Jake and Scott are off trying to find my brother? He is coming here?"

"That is the plan," replied Kevin.

This is incredible. This is too ironic! What if Gabrielle had never landed on my doorstep? What if the sheriff and the viscount had tormented the situation for years? I cannot believe the odds that were against any of this happening."

"Maybe it was fate, for it did happen. I am thinking this is the best possible news!" insisted Kathleen.

"What has happened to all my father's investments? Where is his ring?" questioned Helena.

"I had control of all his investments until your brother came of age. At which time I turned over your portion also. He has a wonderful knack of turning a profit and your portion will be huge by now. I'm sure he will turn it over to you," Lord Cartwright added kindly.

"I do not need his money," she insisted. "I want to know why I wasn't aware of any of this. I would have looked for him years ago," she bellowed.

"I could not find you. Your parents' killers were still on the loose, was I supposed to advertise?" Richard questioned.

"You are right, Helena," Gabrielle interjected. "This is so ironic. If my aunt had never changed and forced the viscount upon me, I never would have fled. That we had some sort of connection is almost unfathomable."

"Really, you girls are not of equal rank. Gabrielle, you would have rarely attended the same social functions. It is ironic you met at all," Richard responded. "Now, let's decide what to do. For it will be nearly a year before they get back here."

"You realize when we leave here, my men along with Scott's men will have to stop at Cartwright manor and clean house? Don't you?" insisted Kevin.

I will accompany you. Gabrielle will want to spend time with her father and she will want to collect any personal belongings," James said.

"Clean house? Men don't clean house," said Gabrielle, clearly confused.

"Clean house as in get rid of the rats?" inquired Kathleen

Kevin, James, Jared and Richard all nodded in response.

"I suppose the best plan would be to all leave and meet back here next Christmas," suggested Jared.

"I am not sure this is the best place for a reunion of sorts," muttered James, wondering what his mother would say to coming here to meet Jake. And so far they had been able to pull the wool over Richard Cartwright's eyes about the hotel he was in. "With Kevin and Kathleen living in Scotland and Richard Cartwright living in Northumberland, Helena located outside of Bristol and Jared in London, it seems the most logical place for a reunion would be the one in the middle. Our castle in Scarborough is centrally located and will easily house us all. How is that?" James suggested. "When we receive word, we will send out messages to everyone."

Discussion began to break out all around, most were agreeable to his suggestion.

Helena said "The ring. What did you do with my father's ring?"

"Why, your brother wears it, my dear. It will help you recognize him, though you won't really need it. For as you have some of your mother's physical attributes, both of you better resemble your father. Though he is a fine specimen of a man now, your looks are so similar you will not have difficulty recognizing him." Richard smiled.

With everyone centering on the turmoil of Helena's family, Gabrielle took the opportunity to pull James aside. "You don't have to lie to save my reputation. I will tell my father we are not married," she whispered.

He tugged on her hair. "Will you also tell him we have slept together?"

"Yes, he should be told." She blushed.

"He will force us to marry, how will you feel?" he inquired.

"I will feel badly." At that James took offense, but then she continued, "I would never want you to feel you had to marry me, but I cannot say I would be upset."

Pulling her closer, he said, "After the last five days can't you do better than that?"

"You will become bigheaded if I tell you I don't want to live without you," she responded.

"So even if you were forced to marry me you would? What about if it was your choice?"

"If it were my choice, I could not think of a better wedding than our fantasy wedding already was, should we just repeat it?" she giggled.

"Honey, I was hoping you'd say something like that." Now that she had admitted she'd marry him anyway he could tell her the truth. "The truth is I did not lie to your father. Our fantasy wedding was as real as they come."

"You're kidding?" Just as he was about to pull her in to his embrace Richard Cartwright caused a commotion by shouting, "I believe a toast is in order." So they gathered together, family and friends, glasses in hand as Lord Cartwright began his toast. "To family and friends and the illusions they share!"

United in laughter they shouted, "Hear, hear!"

The End

Follow the men on their adventure to find
Helena's brother in the sequel:

Heir to Hollywell